DINOSAURS &
A DIRIGIBLE

Baen Books by David Drake

The RCN Series
With the Lightnings
Lt. Leary, Commanding
The Far Side of the Stars
The Way to Glory
Some Golden Harbor
When the Tide Rises
In the Stormy Red Sky
What Distant Deeps
The Road of Danger
The Sea Without a Shore

Hammer's Slammers
The Tank Lords
Caught in the Crossfire
The Butcher's Bill
The Sharp End
The Complete Hammer's Slammers, Vol. 1 (omnibus)
The Complete Hammer's Slammers, Vol. 2 (omnibus)
The Complete Hammer's Slammers, Vol. 3 (omnibus)

Independent Novels and Collections
All the Way to the Gallows
Cross the Stars
Foreign Legions, ed. by David Drake
Grimmer Than Hell
Into the Hinterlands (with John Lambshead)
Loose Cannon
Night & Demons
Northworld Trilogy
Patriots
Ranks of Bronze
The Reaches Trilogy
Redliners

Seas of Venus
Starliner
Dinosaurs & A Dirigible

The General Series
Warlord with S.M. Stirling (omnibus)
Conqueror with S.M. Stirling (omnibus)
The Chosen with S.M. Stirling
The Reformer with S.M. Stirling
The Tyrant with Eric Flint
Hope Reborn with S.M. Stirling (omnibus)
Hope Rearmed with S.M. Stirling (omnibus)
Hope Renewed with S.M. Stirling (omnibus)
The Heretic with Tony Daniel
The Savior with Tony Daniel

The Belisarius Series with Eric Flint
An Oblique Approach
In the Heart of Darkness
Belisarius I: Thunder Before Dawn (omnibus)
Destiny's Shield
Fortune's Stroke
Belisarius II: Storm at Noontide (omnibus)
The Tide of Victory
The Dance of Time
Belisarius III: The Flames of Sunset (omnibus)

Edited by David Drake
The World Turned Upside Down (with Jim Baen & Eric Flint)

To purchase these and all other Baen Book titles in e-book format, please go to www.baen.com.

DINOSAURS & A DIRIGIBLE

DAVID DRAKE

DINOSAURS & A DIRIGIBLE

A Baen Book

Baen Publishing Enterprises
P.O. Box 1403
Riverdale, NY 10471
www.baen.com

ISBN: 978-1-4767-3683-9

Cover art by Tom Kidd

First Baen printing, September 2014

Distributed by Simon & Schuster
1230 Avenue of the Americas
New York, NY 10020

Library of Congress Cataloging-in-Publication Data

Drake, David, 1945-
[Novels. Selections]
Dinosaurs & a dirigible / David Drake.
    pages cm
Dinsaurs and a dirigible
ISBN 978-1-4767-3683-9 (paperback)
I. Title. II. Title: Dinsaurs and a dirigible.
PS3554.R196A6 2014
813'.54--dc23
                                    2014019714

Printed in the United States of America

10 9 8 7 6 5 4 3 2 1

TABLE OF CONTENTS

DEDICATION:
To Ralph H. Eisaman, MD.

ACKNOWLEDGEMENTS:
Among the friends to whom I owe personal depts for help given me on *Dinosaurs & A Dirigable* are: Jim Baen, Bernadette Bosky; Jase Valentine; Karl Wagner, and my wife Jo, who is indeed a friend. They are not responsible for the mistakes, for the questions I didn't ask and the advice I didn't take, but bless them all for what they freely offered.

A LOOK INTO THE PAST

1

In the mid-'80s, I got a new editor at Tor and almost immediately handed in *Bridgehead* to her. A throwaway scene in the novel involves a distant world in which a family of creatures much like plant-eating dinosaurs are gamboling.

In good time I got back the manuscript. With it came a long editorial letter which, among other things, directed me to remove that scene. I don't have the letter any more because in the aftermath—which involved me getting the wonderful Harriet McDougal back as editor—Tom Doherty, Tor's publisher, suggested that I burn it. I haven't forgotten the editor's language after 30 years, though (and I'll probably be able to quote it on my deathbed): "Dinosaurs are reptiles, and reptiles do not nurture their young."

She was wrong about reptiles also (some of them *do* nurture their young), but the important point of this statement is that in 1985, an educated (if remarkably arrogant) person could believe that dinosaurs were reptiles and behaved like lizards, not mammals.

2

When Tor published three of the stories in the present collection in 1982 (as *Time Safari*), I wrote an afterword arguing forcefully for the

New Dinosaur which the stories describe: warm-blooded, quick-moving, intelligent creatures. *Dinosaurs and a Dirigible* doesn't include that afterword because there's no point in it. Nowadays *everybody* knows that dinosaurs were warm-blooded, quick-moving, intelligent creatures. They've watched *Jurassic Park* and any number of CGI dinosaur recreations on PBS and The Discovery Channel.

But I had another reason to drop the afterword: it embarrasses me. My (for a brief time) editor on *Bridgehead* isn't the only person in this story capable of behaving like an arrogant twit.

I'd been fascinated by dinosaurs all my life. When I was five, I read an article in *Junior Natural History Magazine* which told me that Brontosaurus couldn't walk on land because its joints were too weak to support its weight without water buoying up its body. I read the wonderful Sept 7, 1953, issue of *Life* with a Brontosaurus peering at me from the cover. I read Roy Chapman Andrews' account of finding a Protoceratops egg clutch over which a sandstorm had buried an Oviraptor, the dinosaur raiding the nest.

I even made a Triceratops out of clay in 1st grade art class. (It wasn't very good.)

Then in the late '70s, new information about dinosaurs reached the general public. Brontosaurs could walk on land just fine, and indeed they would have bobbed like corks in deep water. That head on the specimen from which the *Life* cover was painted was actually from a wholly different species found miles from the Brontosaurus. Worst of all, the Oviraptor was actually protecting its own eggs, not raiding the nest of another species.

Triceratops hadn't changed much. That was something.

Looking back to 1980, I realize that I was furious at the scientists who had lied to me when I was a kid. I wrote the afterword to *Time Safari* in that mindset. I was unfair, and more important I was wrong.

Nobody lied to me: very learned men were wrong. Perhaps some of them gave the impression of stating the revealed truth like priests, not scientists, but even those fellows were doing the best they could with the information available.

I was angry about a lot of things at the time, principally the Vietnam War (during which people in positions of power *were* definitely lying), and I was transferring that anger onto people who had simply made mistakes. I apologize.

3

Dinosaurs and a Dirigible contains four time travel stories centered on Henry Vickers, and one—*Travellers*—which is completely different. I sold the first Vickers story, *Time Safari*, to Jim Baen, for the Ace book/magazine *Destinies*.

That novella was intended as a one-off, but Jim almost immediately left Ace to join Tom Doherty's newly founded Tor Books. He called me and asked if I could do two more novellas in series with that one so that he could bring them out as a book. I wouldn't have needed much urging to do that even if I hadn't just quit lawyering to drive a city bus for $4.05/hour.

Before I go any farther, let me say that (fictional) animals are most certainly harmed in the making of these stories. The impetus for the original novella was Sprague deCamp's groundbreaking *A Gun for a Dinosaur*. I stole Sprague's concept of safaris going into the far past to hunt dinosaurs.

(For what it's worth, Sprague used the same situation in the story *Impractical Joke*, which came out at almost the same time as *A Gun for a Dinosaur*, but in a rival magazine. *Joke* involves interstellar exploration rather than time travel.)

For background I read many, many hunting memoirs. From them I gleaned a piece of information that becomes a common thread in both Sprague's story and mine, but which I arrived at independently: a safari guide's biggest problems come from the clients, not the wild animals.

After the film of *Jurassic Park* appeared, Tom Doherty asked me to do a new dinosaur story to replace *Calibration Run* from the original collection so that Tor could republish it under a new title (*Tyrannosaur*). (Tom has had better ideas, and I've agreed to better ideas.) I wrote *King Tyrant Lizard* for that use.

The four Vickers stories have never been bound together before the present collection.

4

Travellers is unique for me. I wrote it (like Time Safari) for Destinies. The story involves a dirigible crossing America from east to west during the Great 1896 Airship Flap. The Flap was real, in the sense that it was a real hoax by contemporary newspapers to raise circulation.

I use the British "ll" spelling of the title (my spell checker doesn't like it, nor have copyeditors over the years) for a reason. My first story (Denkirch) came out in an Arkham House anthology which Mr Derleth titled Travellers by Night. I've used double-L spellings ever since.

Nowadays you could call Travellers a proto-Steampunk story. I meant it as a love letter to rural America, however. At a time when the world in my head was a very harsh place, I wrote a story which was positive and looked forward to a world which was intrinsically good.

I'm proud of what I created, and I'm still more proud that I was able to do so under those circumstances.

5

Above I've discussed the genesis of these stories. That first collection (titled Time Safari like the initial novella) has a deeper importance to my career than any book except for my first, Hammer's Slammers. Tom and Jim were pleased with the way I had executed their directions, so (even before the collection came out as one of Tor's first books) Jim called to offer me a multibook contract. Within a few months I quit driving a bus and became a full-time freelance writer, as I remain to this day.

All because I was a kid who loved dinosaurs.

—**Dave Drake**
david-drake.com

KING TYRANT LIZARD

Henry Vickers sat motionless, watching the road and beyond it the forest where the tyrannosaur had escaped. Trucks hauling logging crews and their equipment snarled past him, raising a pall of reddish laterite dust: rain forest soil stripped of its cover, baked to a bad grade of limestone, and churned to grit by vehicles come to clear yet more land.

Vickers' eyes were slitted, and he'd tied a blue-checked bandanna over his nose and mouth. The three khaki-clad police were in their dwelling across the road, ignoring the heavy traffic.

A metal-roofed shelter shared duty as a waiting room for the small landing strip as well as being the customs post on the Malaysian side of the border with Indonesian territory. Bornean sunlight had warmed the air inside to blood temperature, but Vickers was used to heat.

He was used to waiting as well. A successful hunter was first of all patient, willing to accept the things he couldn't change and which made up most of his life. It seemed to Vickers that unchangeable things made up most of everybody's life, though a lot of people tried to pretend otherwise.

The other passengers on the ancient DeHavilland Buffalo that brought Vickers to the border were locals, returning from the bazaars of Kuching. Immediately after landing, they had dispersed with their purchases: incredible loads of plasticware, batteries, and the miscellaneous paraphernalia of civilization. One man walked a well-used step-through motorcycle into a trail through the jungle wall. Vickers couldn't imagine where the fellow would run the bike, assuming that it ran at all.

Because of the logging trucks, Vickers saw the shadow of the aircraft before he heard its engines. Winged blackness rippled over the sun-washed strip, paused, and shifted back abruptly. Vickers stepped out of the shelter, angling his head so that his hat brim shaded his eyes as he looked upward.

The plane was a shining tilt-rotor, transitioning from forward flight into a hover above the landing strip. The aluminum fuselage and stub wings bore a blue umbrella over stylized green trees, the logo of the Borneo Scheme.

Vickers had met Louise Mondadero, the Scheme's Field Director, fifteen years before when she was a senior ecologist working for the government of Kenya. They'd gotten along well enough to keep in touch, even after Louise took over the Borneo Scheme.

Her phone call two days before had been a surprise to Vickers, though. Almost as great a surprise as the call's contents.

When the twin nacelles locked into their vertical position, the tilt-rotor began to descend behind the wash of its props. Two of the Malaysian police got up from their hammocks to watch.

Vickers ducked into the shelter for his satchel and battered gun case, all the luggage he had brought with him from Nairobi. He started for the tilt-rotor as it touched down. To Vickers' surprise, the pilot shut off his turbines. Louise had emphasized that haste was essential, and Vickers was ready to go.

The pilot, a young man wearing a multi-pocket cotton shirt and shorts, flopped down the left cockpit-access door and jumped to the ground. Ignoring Vickers, he strode instead toward the busy roadway. The feathered props continued to spin twenty feet in the air, slowing only gradually.

Dr. Louise Mondadero got out from the other side of the cockpit. "Tom!" she called, her clear voice carrying over the truck noise and the dying moan of the turbines. "This isn't the time!"

Louise had cut her black hair short, and she looked noticeably

older than she had when Vickers last saw her five—six, dammit—
years before. As she trotted after "Tom," she clapped a straw hat on
her head. Sunlight made her sweat, though the dark olive complexion
from her Brazilian ancestry—roughly equal measures of
Mediterranean, African and Native American bloodlines—was
impervious to sunburn.

Vickers opened the tilt-rotor's side hatch and tossed his exiguous
gear inside. Six tube-and-fabric seats were folded against the
sidewalls. There was a wooden crate containing tools and ropes in
the cabin, but it looked more like litter than cargo.

"Henry, I'm terribly sorry," Louise called back over her shoulder.
"We'll be leaving in a moment."

Vickers gave her a neutral smile. He sauntered after her, paying
no attention to the implied order to wait. Ninety percent of a safari
guide's problems involved his clients rather than the wildlife. Vickers
figured that made him a lot more of an expert in whatever wild hair
had gotten up the pilot's ass than Louise herself was.

The pilot was already across the road, shouting at the customs
police and gesturing toward the vehicles crossing the border
unimpeded. Vickers didn't know a word of the standardized Malay
dialects spoken in Malaysia and Indonesia (much less the local tribal
languages), but it was easy enough to read what was going on.

The people on the ground had been paid off. By the time
complaint could be made at a level higher than the bribes had gone,
the damage would be done.

The police were blandly indifferent. The third Malaysian official
got up from his hammock and smiled at nothing, watching the one-
sided discussion out of the corners of his eyes.

As Vickers reached the near margin of the road, Louise
Mondadero put a restraining hand on the pilot's arm. He broke away
from her and stepped directly into the path of an oncoming flatbed.
The truck's engine was still lugging on the slight grade. The driver
managed to stop short of the human obstruction without fishtailing.

The pilot opened the cab door and shook his fist in the driver's
face. Following vehicles had to stop, creating a traffic jam in the
middle of nowhere.

David Drake

A white mini-pickup pulled out from the end of the line. It accelerated toward the blockage.

Vickers eyed the leading truck. The pilot had been saved from having to jump—or worse—by the fact this vehicle's cargo consisted of four turboprop engines and skeletonized alloy girders, a bulky load but not especially heavy. When joined, the girders would form the framework of a gigantic aerostat to float pallets of logs from the jungle more efficiently than tractors could drag them. The next truck in line carried the folded gas bags and the tanks of pressurized gas for inflation.

Vickers waited for the dust to settle—literally—before he joined the pilot and now Louise at the truck cab. The truck cast a gritty shroud forward when the driver braked his wheels. The cloud was reddish and opaque, more like a desert sandstorm than a human phenomenon.

Of course the moonscape to which logging operations reduced the land was inhuman as well . . .

Louise got the pilot down from the truck's running board by a combination of cajoling and her actual weight dragging on his wrist and shoulder. The name tag pinned over the pilot's left breast pocket read TOM O'NEILL. He was a short man in his mid-twenties, with black curly hair and a handsome face now distorted by an Irish temper.

Since the pilot was under control, Vickers turned to face the white pickup as it skidded to a stop. The driver and the two men in the open box were soldiers in dark green utility uniforms without markings of any kind. They carried Heckler & Koch submachine guns.

The passenger in the cab wore a dark business suit and an open-necked silk shirt. A pale blue handkerchief matching the shirt protruded from his breast pocket in a neat triangle. The man's hair was straight and black, and his dark Malay features would fit any age from Vickers' forty to sixty or older.

"Yes?" he said in English. "What is the trouble here, please?"

"Are you in charge here?" O'Neill demanded. He wasn't in the least cowed by the man facing him, which did nothing for Vickers' opinion of the pilot's common sense. The gunmen were cheap muscle, a type common in or out of uniform. The man in the suit was something else again, and a great deal more dangerous.

"I am Mr. Nikisastro," the man said. "I must ask you to leave my trucks alone, yes? Our permits are in order. If you—"

O'Neill bunched his right hand into a fist. A soldier lifted his submachine gun to strike with the extended butt. Another racked back the bolt of his weapon to charge it for firing.

Vickers grabbed the collar and shoulder of O'Neill's shirt with his left hand and jerked the pilot backward. Vickers was only a little above medium height and slim, but there was deceptive strength in his flat muscles. He pivoted so that he stood with his back to the logging official and guards, facing O'Neill, whose shoulder he still gripped.

"You Javan land-rapers have no business here!" O'Neill shouted. "All the forest here is controlled by the Borneo Scheme!"

"We are not in the forest," Nikisastro said. "And may I call to your attention the fact that your Borneo Scheme is not a government but rather a pact among several governments—of which mine is one. If you have a problem with our presence, your headquarters in New York should take it up with the proper officials in Jakarta—or with the government in Kuala Lumpur, since this is Malaysian territory."

"Tom," said Louise Mondadero, "we have business to attend to. Let's go. *Now.*"

O'Neill grimaced. He swatted at Vickers' hand. Vickers let go of the pilot and eased a half-step back.

O'Neill had to let off steam somehow, and he'd calmed down enough that he wasn't going to hit a man who might have him shot. Therefore he chose Vickers as a target, which was fine. That's what the guide was for, to take the anger of paying customers so that they wouldn't let it out on one another.

Vickers supposed he was going to be paid for this. It wasn't something he'd asked about when Louise called him in a panic across seventy degrees of longitude.

"You think we don't know what you're doing, but we do!" O'Neill said. "And we're going to stop you!"

The trucks of the last half of the column were now jammed bumper to bumper, all the way down the last switchback before the border crossing. Diesel engines rumbled and pinged in a background as loud as ocean surf. There must be forty vehicles in all, counting those which had passed earlier.

"Tom . . ." Louise said, but O'Neill was already on his way back to the tilt-rotor. Vickers and Mondadero followed the pilot.

One of the guards called a gibe in Malay. Nikisastro silenced his man with a command as sharp as a whiplash. The first of the stopped trucks clashed back into gear.

"Good to see you again, Louise," Vickers said in a neutral voice.

Louise stopped with her hand raised to lift herself into the aircraft's cockpit. She laughed, took off her hat, and wiped beaded sweat from her face with the woven brim. "Henry, I'm glad to see you, too. Things are in a hell of a mess, a *hell* of a mess, but I'm really glad to see you."

She banged the cockpit door closed and walked around to the cabin to join Vickers instead. O'Neill lit his right turbine. Warm air puffed from the downturned exhaust.

Louise clicked two adjacent seats out from the fuselage. Vickers strapped his satchel and gun case to the cargo net furled on the opposite side of the cabin. Louise looked over.

"That's all you brought?" she asked.

"All I need," Vickers agreed. "I was surprised that you were able to get me visas and permits so quickly. I had no trouble at all."

"That was the Scheme's New York staff," Louise said with a smile of pleasure. "Sometimes they make me crazy, but they're really very good."

O'Neill had both turbines spinning. He looked back into the cabin. "Are you . . ." he began. He saw the gun case. "That's your gun, is it, Vickers?" he said.

Vickers nodded. "Yep," he said. "I was telling Louise that I didn't have the problem I expected getting it through the various customs."

"Too bad," said O'Neill. "Well, maybe the baggage handlers will have broken it."

He turned back to the controls. The turbine whine increased to a throbbing howl. The tilt-rotor lifted straight up without the short run-out Vickers had expected. Vickers sighed. This wasn't a new problem either. There was always somebody on a photo safari who didn't understand how dangerous and unpredictable large animals could be. He, or more often she, objected to the rifle the guide carried just in case.

But it wasn't a problem Henry Vickers had expected in the present circumstances, when the beast being hunted was a tyrannosaur.

The tilt-rotor swung smoothly into transition mode. The wings and the engine nacelles on their tips pivoted so that the props pulled the aircraft forward through the air rather than up into it. O'Neill didn't have the sunniest personality of Vickers' acquaintance, but his handling of the controls was deft. Vickers could forgive a lot if somebody did his job well.

The tilt-rotor banked slightly to turn toward the standing forest. The highway formed one division of the Borneo Scheme, a ragged red pencil mark separating variegated two-hundred-foot treetops on one side from scrub and gullies on the other. The boundary was as obvious from the air as it would have been on a map.

The Scheme was an intergovernmental compact. Under its terms Malaysia, Brunei and Indonesia agreed to halt the destructive exploitation of much of the interior of Borneo in return for billions of dollars in development aid from the West. The money wasn't a significant factor in the agreement of tiny, oil-rich Brunei, but its sultan enthusiastically supported the creation of an internationally administered buffer between Brunei and his larger neighbors.

The forest canopy provided a deceptively even cap over broken terrain. When the protective cover was gone, heavy rainfalls ripped down the hillsides and clawed ravines through the soil.

On the other side of the highway, the Borneo Scheme administered medical and biological research funded by the West, though there was no attempt to bar the indigenous natives. Nomads continued to wander and hunt in the rain forest as they had done for tens of thousands of years, and after debate the more settled farming tribes had been permitted to remain as well. So-called slash-and-burn agriculture as the natives practiced it was a sophisticated long-fallow system of successional farming which didn't involve primary forest.

The logging convoy had halted within a mile of the international border. The leading trucks had started to unload their heavy equipment. Vehicles escaping from the traffic jam snorted down the road to join them. Louise stared at the encampment through the cabin window opposite until the aircraft leveled out and hid the scene.

Vickers pointed in the direction of the now-hidden laager. "What's going on?" he asked, raising his voice to be heard.

The tilt-rotor wasn't noisy compared to the Buffalo which flew Vickers from Kuching—but the Buffalo sounded like the interior of a metal garbage can rolling down a rocky hillside. The tilt-rotor's engines were inherently quiet, and in forward flight the props' thrumming no longer reflected from the ground, but to save weight the cabin walls weren't soundproofed.

Louise grimaced. "Indonesian politics," she said. "It's the Javan Empire, really. This doesn't have anything to do with us if it's what I think it is. But we're going to be in the middle of it anyway."

She turned to look out the window behind her, using the expanse of forest canopy to settle her mind. Vickers looked also, though from curiosity and to be companionable rather than because of any pleasure the sight gave him. The forest's variety surprised him. There were a dozen identifiable shades of green, as well as patches of orange, red, and even violet. He didn't know whether the latter were trees in bloom or simply flushes of new leaves which lacked the chlorophyll of mature growth.

"Logging will start," Louise said in the flat voice of a radiologist pointing out a cancerous mass to other physicians. "The Indonesians will move troops in under a claim of protecting the Borneo Scheme. Then their troops will take over the entire island before anyone can stop them."

She shrugged and wiped her eyes with the back of a hand. Vickers pointedly avoided looking directly at her. "What they really want is Brunei for the oil, of course, but they'll take the rest as well. Eventually I suppose they'll take the whole South Pacific."

"But that logging operation is Indonesian, isn't it?" Vickers said in puzzlement. "That was what—"

"Yes, clever, isn't it?" Louise said bitterly. "If Malaysia does manage to react quickly enough to stop the logging, Indonesia will invade to protect its citizens from foreign brutality. Otherwise, Indonesia will invade as a guarantor of the Borneo Scheme. If it's the latter case, there's at least a chance that Jakarta will leave the Scheme in place after it's absorbed the island. Less whatever Nikisastro has managed to strip, of course."

"I—" Vickers said. Gray haze spread across the forest immediately below: cloud, not smoke. They were crossing a hidden valley deep enough to trap water vapor even this late in the morning. The sight threw Vickers' thoughts temporarily out of the course they had been following.

"What do the Indonesians have to do with your tyrannosaurus escaping?" he resumed. The cloud below gave him an uneasy feeling even though it was not the mark of destruction he had first thought.

"Nothing," Louise said. "Except that bad luck never comes alone."

She gave a brittle, hacking laugh. "If it comes in threes, I can't imagine *what* else is going to happen. Maybe an asteroid will hit Borneo."

The aircraft banked to port and began to circle. Vickers couldn't see a landing strip below, but glinting metal drew his eyes. Chromed fittings fastened a network of solar collectors to the treetops. A road, visible as a linear pattern beneath the upper canopy, crossed through the same vicinity. Nearby was a circular clearing no more than a hundred feet in diameter. O'Neill pivoted the rotors upward into hover mode again.

"Louise . . ." Vickers said as the tilt-rotor began its vertical descent. "We'll get your tyrannosaurus, no problem. And for the rest, it'll work out all right. Nowadays the world will never stand for the sort of flat-out invasion you're worried about."

The aircraft settled past masses of leaves tufting out from branch tips. The cabin interior darkened because foliage cut off much of the light. The landing site was minimal even for the tilt-rotor. Vickers understood the desire to preserve the habitat being studied, but it seemed to him that the Scheme had carried the principle rather too far.

Louise glared at Vickers. "Won't stand for it, Henry?" she

repeated. "The world stood for it when Javans massacred two hundred *thousand* ethnic Chinese, didn't they? They stood for it when Javans machine-gunned unarmed civilians in Dili who were mourning victims of a previous army massacre. They stood it when Javans invaded West Irian and the Moluccas and killed any of the natives who protested. Oh, the world will stand for this too, never doubt!"

They touched down so lightly that Vickers scarcely felt the landing-gear struts compress. Over the dying whine of the turbines, Vickers heard a brassy *bong-bong-bong*. He couldn't tell whether the signal was animate or mechanical.

"But I'll worry about Nikisastro later," Louise added, more mildly. "First we absolutely *must* recapture the tyrannosaur."

It was hot and muggy and the air didn't move. Louise lifted the satchel before Vickers could stop her. He followed her out of the aircraft with the rifle case.

O'Neill looked at Vickers with a grim smile. "Nice tan you've got," the younger man said ironically. "You'll lose it quick enough here, though. The rain forest is like nothing you've ever seen."

A house forty feet by twenty stood at one side of the clearing. It was of local construction, pole-framed with platform floors and a roof of leaf thatching. There were no walls. Very similar to those in the hinterlands of El Salvador . . .

"I've seen rain forest," Vickers said softly. "It was a long time ago, but I've seen it. I just didn't like it very much." Didn't like the things he'd done there, rather, but the environment and the actions were bound together in Vickers' memory. He wouldn't let it make a difference.

Louise was already inside, opening one of the large chests there. Natives—two men, three women, and a pair of ambulatory children plus a babe in the arms of its mother—appeared from the forest, chattering cheerfully. Vickers heard pigs squealing nearby and smelled the sharp pungency of hog feces.

Louise and the pilot both began to talk with the natives. Vickers walked into the house and set his rifle case down on the table of poles lashed across the railings in one corner of the structure.

The road Vickers had deduced from the air passed through the landing strip. At the margin of the forest near the point they joined stood a small metal shed and a four-hundred-gallon tank marked DIESEL FUEL ONLY, with a further legend below in Malay script. The cap was secured by a heavy padlock.

Louise and O'Neill separated from the natives and returned to the shelter. "None of this would have happened if we hadn't gotten involved in animal experimentation," the pilot said.

"That wasn't our option, Tom," Louise replied as she took a series of electronic devices from the chest she'd opened: satellite phone, fax, and notebook computer. "And besides, the treatment of AIDS would justify a greater compromise with my principles than what is in fact required."

Louise plugged each piece of equipment into a power strip on the end of an orange extension cord. Such low-draw devices couldn't justify the extensive solar array Vickers had seen in the canopy. He wondered what else the station used electricity for.

"So we're whores and now we're just haggling over price, is that it?" O'Neill gibed.

Louise gave her subordinate a level glance. "Tom," she said, "I have some messages to answer. While I'm doing that, would you please show Henry the compound and explain the situation to him."

The words formed a question which was absent from the flat tone. The implicit rebuke made O'Neill's face squinch in something between a frown and a grimace. "Sure," he muttered. "Come on, Vickers."

Vickers put his hat on, then took it off and tossed it onto the rifle case before he followed the younger man. Humidity and the enveloping green dimness made him nervous as a caged cat.

"Look," he said, "this really *is* a tyrannosaurus we're going after? And you found it in the forest?"

"No, no," O'Neill said. "Or rather, yes, it's a tyrannosaur, but it doesn't come from here. Its natural habitat would be veldt or pine forest, nothing like this jungle."

They were following a path from the rear of the shelter. The undergrowth had been cut back within the past few days, but fresh shoots already stretched in from either side. Vickers couldn't imagine how anything managed to germinate. There was scarcely more light than there would be in a cave.

"That's one of the reasons it's so cruel to keep the beast here," O'Neill said. "They did it just for secrecy. There was already a construction road here to Site IV, but the only westerners present were whoever came on the weekly run for the specimens the Punans—the forest nomads—had collected. Louise and I now split the runs between us, so nobody else in the Scheme knows anything about it. In the field, that is. Some of them do in New York, of course. It was New York's idea."

Vickers set his feet with care to avoid tripping on exposed roots or sliding despite the cleats on his ankle boots. The forest floor was damp, and the thin layer of loam slipped easily over the substratum of clay.

It occurred to him that Louise had picked O'Neill of all her subordinates to share the secret of the tyrannosaurus. And he was a *very* good pilot.

The leaves of the undergrowth tickled Vickers' limbs. Narrow-crowned trees stabbed sixty to a hundred feet up into the twilight, while above them stretched a nearly-solid blanket of green, the main canopy. It was almost like being under water.

Vickers wished he'd brought the Garand instead of leaving it cased in the shelter. The rifle would be of only psychological purpose at this stage in the proceedings, but he could use a security blanket.

"Here's the pen," O'Neill said. "Don't come any closer than you are until I shut off the field."

They'd arrived at a double gate in a twelve-foot chain-link fence. A second, similar fence stood sixty feet inside the first. The intervening space had been cleared of undergrowth, but the trunks of forest giants rose unaffected by the construction. The canopy remained unbroken, perfect camouflage against aerial surveillance.

"How big is the fenced area?" Vickers asked.

"About an acre," O'Neill replied. He unfastened the padlock which held the gate's crossbar, a six-inch I-beam, in place and put his weight against the bar.

"Don't," he repeated as Vickers instinctively stepped forward to help. "The outer fence is protected by a low-frequency generator that'll knock you out unless you're wearing a cancelling device." He patted a case the size of a cigarette pack clipped to the right epaulet loop of his shirt. Vickers had taken it for a communicator of some sort.

O'Neill left the gate open as he walked to a switchbox on the inner gatepost. The scale of the project suddenly struck Vickers. Two thousand feet of fencing—minimum—plus the heavy beams required to support it, trucked into the middle of the jungle and erected. Then the fifty-foot-long lizard had to be brought in the same way . . .

And just where had that lizard come from to begin with?

O'Neill threw the main switch on the side of the box. "All right," he said. "You can come in now. Not that there's anything to see. The gates were open the night the tyrannosaur escaped, although the low-frequency generator was operating and the inner fence was properly electrified."

He looked at Vickers in cold challenge. "The Javans let him out. That's the only possible explanation. They did it to sabotage the Scheme."

A tunnel of half-inch steel sheeting penetrated the inner fence beside the gateway. The tunnel was sharply conical, only a foot in diameter on the near end but widely flared inside the compound.

O'Neill noticed Vickers' questioning glance. He rang his knuckles on the tunnel wall. "For feeding the tyrannosaur," he explained. "That is, for drawing the beast into position with hog carcasses so that the bottle which collects pituitary hormone can be changed."

O'Neill thrust his clenched fist through a hole in the side of the tunnel near the small end. "Could be changed, that is."

"Where . . ." Vickers asked carefully, "did the tyrannosaurus come from?"

"That's a secret," O'Neill said. He opened the inner gate, similar to the outer one. "From me, at least."

"I've heard," said Vickers, "that the Israelis have a time-travel project."

"The fellow in charge of the team trucking in the tyrannosaur was named Stern," O'Neill said. "Not that that means anything. The Scheme's General Secretary is a Hirschfeld, after all, and he comes from Montreal."

Vickers knelt to look at tracks in the gateway. "I don't suppose it matters," he said.

Which was a lie. If this involved something that the Israelis considered top secret, then . . . Louise Mondadero might be at risk of losing more than her job.

A male Punan stepped out of the forest. "Appeared" would have been a better description, because Vickers saw no movement, just a squat, dark man wearing blue Adidas running shorts and a sheathed bush knife on a belt of rattan fiber.

The native smiled at Vickers, but he waited to speak until O'Neill noticed his presence. The two talked in a quick exchange.

"This is Pa Teng," O'Neill explained to Vickers. "He'll track the tyrannosaur for us. He's a great hunter."

"Ask him what these are," Vickers said, pointing at the marks in front of which he squatted.

"What?" said O'Neill. "The tyrannosaur's tracks, of course."

"Not them," Vickers said drily. The tyrannosaur's huge clawed feet gouged deeply into the dense soil at each ten-foot stride. There was no mistaking them. The marks that interested Vickers were faint and slender, pressed against the clay when it was wet and remaining as vague hints now that the surface had dried. They appeared to be the tracks of something four-toed and too delicate for a human with a foot so long.

"We looked at those," O'Neill said dismissively. "Louise says they're the outlines of leaves driven against the soil by rain. Otherwise maybe the Javans or their agents disguised their prints when they opened the cage."

Pa Teng squatted beside Vickers. He probed delicately at one of the markings with a leaf stem, then spoke in his own language.

Vickers raised an eyebrow in query toward O'Neill. The pilot frowned and said, "He says they're from a monitor lizard. I suppose that's possible. I've seen monitors more than six feet long in the forest."

Vickers rose to his feet. "You didn't have your tracker look at the site when you found the tyrannosaurus was missing?" he said. Though he kept his tone neutral, the question itself was an obvious judgment.

O'Neill flushed. "We had things on our mind other than scrapings that didn't appear to have anything to do with the problem. That still don't have anything to do with the problem. A monitor lizard sniffed around the site when the gates were open."

O'Neill spoke to the Punan, then strode past Vickers toward the trail to the site building. Pa Teng followed him. "I have equipment to prepare," O'Neill called over his shoulder.

The unsurfaced road by which the construction material had arrived was being allowed to grow over again. It was noticeable only by lack of the middle-height trees between the undergrowth and the overarching canopy.

Vickers fell into step behind the other men. "I heard what Louise said about AIDS," he said mildly, as though he hadn't noticed O'Neill's anger. "I'm not clear what a dinosaur has to do with it, though."

"It shouldn't have anything to do with it," O'Neill replied. The jungle softened his voice, smothered it, even though he was only ten feet ahead of Vickers on the trail and generally visible. "Animal experimentation is wrong, and the end *doesn't* justify the means. But the short answer is that pituitary hormone from adult reptiles has been found to have a degree of reversing effect on the decline in the human immune system."

"I see," said Vickers. He wondered if that was linked to the fact reptiles continue to grow all their lives, unlike mammals where growth basically stops at sexual maturity. Given the cost of this site, the effect had to be more than a wild theory. "But you can remove the hormone from *living* animals?"

"Oh, there you are," Louise called from the open-sided building. "I was just about to check the floaters, but you're better at that, Tom."

She was holding two bolt-action weapons. Vickers recognized them after a moment's reflection as capture guns: smoothbores which fired hypodermics loaded with anesthetic. The barrel tubes were startlingly thick, giving the weapons an awkward look. A tyrannosaur weighed as much or more than a bull elephant, so the dose of drug to bring it down would have to be correspondingly large.

"I'll get them out," O'Neill said. "I checked them before we picked up Mr. Vickers, of course."

He looked at Vickers. "If the reptile is big enough, a pituitary probe can be inserted and left in place without sacrificing the animal, but the quantities of hormone available are extremely small even from large crocodiles. If you can accept the principle that man has the divine right to do anything he pleases with *lower*—"

The sneer in O'Neill's voice was vivid.

"—forms of life, then the tyrannosaur was a very successful subject. Until it escaped, at least."

O'Neill stalked off toward the metal shed while Vickers re-entered the building. Pa Teng lay down in a rattan hammock strung nearby.

"He's upset about the escape," Louise said quietly, nodding in the direction of O'Neill's back. "I discovered it, but he'd made last week's run. He thinks he must have failed to lock the compound properly. That's nonsense, of course. The inner gate is never unlocked."

Vickers opened his case and removed the four twenty-round magazines from their nests of foam. They were intended for use in a Browning automatic rifle. Vickers' Garand had been modified to accept them in place of the normal eight-round internal magazine, greatly increasing his firepower.

"That cage is a pretty expensive construction," he said without looking toward Louise, "and I don't even want to guess what bringing a dinosaur here—to this time—would have cost."

"Nothing else appearing," Louise said deliberately as she removed and stacked packets from the open chests. "Sub-Saharan Africa will lose ninety-five percent of its population in the next twenty years. Not from AIDS directly, but because AIDS will have destroyed the social structure of the countries affected. Starvation killed more Peruvian natives after the Spanish conquest than measles and smallpox did directly. The diseases broke down the infrastructure which maintained the irrigation system necessary for agriculture."

The rifle case held one hundred rounds of .30-06 ammunition, nose-down in the foam. Vickers began thumbing cartridges one at a time into a magazine. The rounds were hand-loaded from match brass, but the tips of the bullets themselves were painted black: They were military armor-piercing ball.

Vickers was willing to sacrifice some long-range accuracy for steel-cored bullets which he was *sure* would punch through the braincase of a charging cape buffalo, so long as the shooter was steady and knew where to aim.

At Dr. Mondadero's request, the New York office of the Borneo Scheme had faxed four-view drawings of a tyrannosaur's skull to Vickers before he left Nairobi. It gave him something to study on the long flight.

"It occurs to me that many governments would consider a working time machine to be a military secret," Vickers said as he began loading the second magazine.

"It is also true that the diplomatic leverage which a cure for AIDS would provide might look more important to a politically isolated country than the opportunity to make their enemies' grandfathers vanish," Louise replied in an equally oblique fashion. "Especially as I gather attempts to arrange the latter had been entirely unsuccessful. The time apparatus apparently works only in the far past."

O'Neill drifted out of the shed in a floater, a cylindrical device with a static repulsion system. When the pilot was clear of the shed's metal roof, he deployed the solar cells which recharged the zinc-air batteries in the floor of the floater. The floaters generated identical electrical charges in the unit and in the volume of air directly beneath, causing the device and its contents to float so long as the charges were maintained. The problem was . . .

"We're going to use those?" Vickers said. "Look, Louise, I'd sooner hike. Those things are *way* too unstable to fly outside a closed hangar. I've seen it tried."

"We've been using them for three years here in the field," Louise said crisply. "The air beneath the canopy *is* almost as still as that within a closed room. Now, I'll admit we have to get higher than that to recharge the batteries, but Tom and I both have a great deal of experience. And Tom could fly a brick if you gave it a power plant."

Vickers sucked his lower lip in as he finished loading the fourth magazine. He split the twenty loose rounds remaining between the breast pockets of his shirt. He was carrying a ridiculously large quantity of ammunition, but he'd never gotten in difficulties from having too many cartridges.

"You're in charge," he said. His lack of enthusiasm was obvious in the thin tone.

O'Neill brought a second floater out of the shed. The little craft could only hold two adults and a small amount of stores. Vickers wondered how long the operation would take. Perhaps they would be able to live off the land.

"That's not . . ." Louise said, her eyes on the Garand as Vickers lifted it from its nest. "That is, that's a .30-06, isn't it? I thought for this you'd bring something much heavier. An elephant gun. Ah—if cost . . ."

Vickers chuckled. "I'm not too poor to buy the tools I need, Louise," he said. "This is choice. A lot of my friends think it's a pretty screwy choice, but it hasn't let me down yet. It'll do its job on the tyrannosaurus if I do mine."

"I . . ." Louise said. "I asked you to come because I trust you, Henry. To—back us up, and to keep your mouth shut afterwards, if that's an option. So I won't second guess you."

Vickers laughed with real humor. Their positions of a moment before had been reversed. "Thank you, Louise, and I'll ride in the floaters like a good boy."

He hefted the Garand and locked a magazine home in the well before he continued. "Look, knockdown power, all that stuff, is a myth. To stop an animal, you've got to destroy major blood vessels or the central nervous system. With this—" He patted the Garand's full wooden stock. "—I can get deep enough to be sure of doing that."

The weapon was older than he was. It balanced well in his arms, and its ten-pound weight made it more comfortable to shoot than a lighter rifle would have been. While the recoil of a .30-06 wasn't in the same league as that of the most powerful magnum cartridges, neither was it anything to sneeze at if repeated shots were necessary.

O'Neill rejoined them. The floaters waited in the sunlight of the clearing with their solar receptors deployed to top off the battery charge. The pilot looked at Vickers and the rifle with a hatred so fierce that his eyes glazed.

"You know . . ." O'Neill said. His voice was under control, his whole personality was under control—but that control was as tensely dynamic as that of the mainspring of a cocked pistol. "We shouldn't be doing any of this. The tyrannosaur escaped to freedom. We're being given a chance to let Nature go her own way."

"Are you ready to go?" Louise asked. She hefted a pair of small knapsacks on one arm and held a capture gun in the other hand.

"Yes," O'Neill said, nodding. "Yes, of course." Then he added, "I mean it, Louise!"

"There's nothing natural about a tyrannosaur in Borneo, Tom," Louise said coldly. "The animal will starve if we don't find it soon."

Vickers opened his small satchel and judged the contents against the flimsy floaters. He took out two pairs of boot socks, put them in a cargo pocket of his trousers, and closed the satchel again. The weight of his rifle and ammunition was as much as he wanted to add to the load.

"Starvation *is* natural, dammit!" O'Neill snapped. "*Death* is natural; it's being kept in a cage by humans that isn't natural. For that matter, there's millions of pigs in the forest. I'm not so sure that the beast is going to starve."

"There are pigs, and there are Punan and Kayan tribesfolk as well," Louise said. "In addition to which, there is the responsibility which we—you and I—accepted. Do you have a problem with that, Tom?"

O'Neill shook his handsome head. "No," he said in a tired voice. "No, of course not. I'm sorry, Louise. My gear is already loaded."

He turned and walked toward the floaters. "This is hard for him," Louise murmured to Vickers as they followed the younger man at a distance of ten strides. "But he'll be all right."

Vickers hadn't seen Pa Teng get up from the hammock, but now the Punan reappeared from the jungle wearing a broad smile and carrying a homemade shotgun. The gun barrel was a length of water pipe, and the lock mechanism appeared to involve a band of inner tube rubber driving a nail sharpened to form the firing pin. A pouch of knotted rattan cord held four green plastic twelve-gauge shotgun shells.

"I'd understood only traditional weapons were permit-led within the Scheme's boundaries," Vickers said quietly. "Blowguns and spears, that is."

"If you ask the staff in New York, they'll agree with you," Louise replied. "Here on the ground, it's necessary to make allowances. Even Tom agrees with that. We're paying Pa Teng with shotgun shells."

The base of each floater was a thick disk of gray plastic. Above it, plastic tubes formed a cage forty inches high to safeguard the passengers and to provide cargo attachment points. Several knapsacks were already strapped onto the frames.

The control yoke was on a column at one edge of the disk. The four square yards of solar collectors spread from an eight-foot staff on the opposite edge.

O'Neill and Pa Teng began to talk in Punan. Both men made quick hand gestures. O'Neill's obvious fluency was another point in the man's favor, but the exchange brought a tangential thought to the surface of Vickers' mind.

"Pa Teng lives here at the site?" he asked, looking toward Louise.

"His family is here," she replied. "They tend the pigs that we need for the tyrannosaur. Pa Teng himself spends much of his time in the forest."

"Ask him if he or his family saw any strangers around the time the beast got out," Vickers said.

O'Neill looked up from his conversation. "They didn't," he said. "Of course we asked."

Louise spoke in Punan; Pa Teng replied at some length. She looked back to Vickers. "He says, 'No one but the ghosts,'" she said, frowning.

O'Neill asked the Punan a further question. This time Pa Teng's reply was shorter and coupled with a shrug that would certainly have meant indifference in a Westerner.

"Ghosts are ghosts," Louise translated for Vickers. She still frowned. "He didn't say anything about that before."

"He hasn't said anything now," O'Neill said. "Not that makes sense."

Pa Teng sauntered off toward the edge of the clearing. "He's going to go on foot," O'Neill explained. "He says he'll ride later if he gets tired."

"Could he track from the air?" Vickers asked.

Louise shrugged. "We can stay just above the ground," she said. "The floaters are faster than walking, and obstructions—"

"There are ravines and steep slopes all through the area," O'Neill said. "Don't be misled by the canopy."

"Yes," Louise agreed. "Not that the terrain affects Pa Teng the way it would us."

She indicated the floaters with her chin. "Tom," she said, "I'll take Henry and we'll stay low. You go high so that you'll have a full charge when we have to trade off."

She looked at Vickers. "Do you agree with that, Henry?" she asked.

"I need to be where I can get a shot quickly," Vickers said, focusing on Louise to avoid eye contact with O'Neill. "If necessary. That means on the deck in this cover."

"Let's go before we lose Pa Teng entirely," O'Neill said as he got into the farther floater.

The younger man was making an obvious effort to avoid having a problem. As Louise said, it was hard for him.

Because it was obvious even to Vickers that if the terrain was as described, the capture guns were merely for show. There was no way in hell that they were going to get a five-ton dinosaur back to the compound alive.

As O'Neill took off, Louise waved Vickers aboard the remaining floater. Vickers slung the Garand so that he could grip the railing with both hands. He was as tense as if he were facing a firing squad.

Louise giggled as she swung the gate in the protective railing closed behind her. "You're going to be sore all over if you stand so stiff, Henry," she said. "Relax."

She lifted the floater smoothly, setting the solar panels to fold while in motion. Directional control was by a principle similar to that of directing a plate spinning on a stick: By adjusting the angle at which the two charges repelled one another, Louise could move the floater in any direction she desired.

The virtually frictionless motion made Vickers' stomach turn. They were only a few feet in the air and travelling at less than ten miles an hour. Despite that, he felt as if he were in free fall and about to hit the ground hard enough to splash.

They drifted through the forest wall. Louise lifted them so that they overflew most of the undergrowth, but leaves brushed the floater's base. The roots of an air plant twitched Vickers' hat. He grabbed the rifle's charging handle before he associated the contact with its cause. He tried to relax. He had to keep control of his nerves. The jungle was creeping into his soul.

Vickers took off his bush hat, then deliberately spun it over the side of the floater. The neck cord tangled in the saw-edged leaves of a clump of bamboo.

Louise looked at him. "I won't be needing that here," he said.

"You might when we're above the canopy charging the batteries," she said. "But I don't suppose it matters very much."

She throttled back on the yoke. Vickers saw Pa Teng just ahead of them, walking easily despite the treacherous footing.

The tyrannosaur had slipped through the undergrowth without damaging the foliage in any way that Vickers could see at this height and distance in time. The beast's footprints were another matter. The clawed feet tore the thin soil like power shovels, scattering the brown leaf mold and leaving scars in the red clay beneath.

Tracking the dinosaur from the floaters would be easy, especially since the beast was travelling in a straight line and ignoring the contours of the land. That surprised Vickers. The large mammals he had hunted almost invariably chose the path with the gentlest gradient. Perhaps he was making the mistake of measuring a predator against the herbivores which were the only land mammals approaching it in size.

Louise turned on the six-inch audiovisual link attached to the railing beside her controls. After a burst of snow, the screen projected a wobbly close-range image of the canopy in full color.

"Is it working at your end, Tom?" Louise called.

"Yes, yes, I've got the display," O'Neill replied. "There's some updraft turbulence here, but that should steady before we have to change places."

His voice was thin but clear and static-free. For the sake of ruggedness, the links were military specification units. That meant they hopped frequencies to avoid detection also, which Vickers supposed did no harm.

"I trust I'll be able to handle it," Louise said drily. "I have for three years, after all."

She raised the floater slightly to clear the upthrust roots of a fallen giant. The gap in the canopy already had been closed by half a dozen lesser trees, racing up the column of sunlight for a chance to succeed to mastery of the location.

Louise was as expert as she had promised. Vickers was becoming used to the greasy feel of the floater's progress. He now could twist his body normally to look around without fearing that he was going to flip them over like a tossed coin.

Despite that, Vickers couldn't relax. The jungle enclosed him, pressing down from all sides. It wasn't a matter of visibility either. While the floater drifted at mid-height, Vickers could see much farther than was normal in the East African plains to which he was accustomed. There grasses grew ten, even twelve feet tall, forming an opaque curtain. But you could see the sky. The rain forest was a box— a box of enormous volume, but an enclosure nonetheless.

Besides, it was very similar to the shadowed, windless jungle in which a younger Henry Vickers had hunted men. At the time, the events in which he took part hadn't been a problem. The memories of them were something else again.

The floater drifted beneath a tree whose limbs were covered with bromeliads. Spiky, red-tipped leaves sprang out in clumps wherever seeds had found lodging in crevices of the bark. Dried fronds hung down from the tufts like the hair of a drowned woman.

Vickers swore very softly. He concentrated his attention on Pa Teng who sauntered along below.

The tyrannosaur had collapsed the steep wall of a ravine in

mounting it. Roots and flecks of glittering mica marked the fallen clay. The Punan hunter climbed the bank to the side of the beast's path. He would have sunk ankle deep where the soil was turned.

A tank couldn't have driven a straighter track through the jungle. The tyrannosaur skirted large trees, but nothing else affected its course.

A tree of medium height shot its leaves out in circular fans a yard across, trembling on twigs which sprang from the top of the trunk. Louise eased the floater lower and to the right to avoid brushing the foliage. Pa Teng was briefly invisible. Vickers heard him hoot with surprise.

Vickers unslung the Garand and chambered a round with a clang of steel on steel. His eyes flicked through a 180-degree panorama. Everything around him was focused in his mind.

Louise tilted the floater directly through a wall of saplings bordering a trail unseen until that moment. A sounder of long-skulled Malay hogs had been walking down the trail in single file when the tyrannosaur burst among them.

Judging from the separate splotches of blood, the carnivore had scooped at least three of the four-hundred-pound mammals into its jaws and bolted them before the rest of the sounder fled. The dinosaur's foot had ripped a gap in the far side of the trail where the beast pursued a hog trying to escape.

Flies buzzed over the blood and fragments of flesh which had dribbled from the tyrannosaur's jaws. The sound of the insects was louder than the torpid hiss of the floater's propulsion mechanism.

"Son of a bitch," Vickers muttered.

Louise set the floater down where the dinosaur's track widened the trail. The stench of meat rotting in this heat and humidity was as foul as gases belched from the bottom of a swamp.

Pa Teng stared at the carnage, gabbling in amazement. He held his shotgun out of the way. Now that the tigers and stunted rhinos had been hunted to extinction, no creature natural to the forest threatened an adult human. It didn't occur to the Punan that he might need a weapon for defense.

Not that a load of buckshot from a wire-wrapped water pipe would have been much use for the purpose.

O'Neill dropped from the canopy with a crackle of foliage to land beside them. "I told you it would be able to find food in the forest," he said with satisfaction.

"I'm wondering just how it did that," Vickers said. "The trail we followed is as straight as a compass course. To dinner."

Pa Teng had vanished into the forest. He called something to the Westerners, his voice directionless because of the baffling vegetation. Louise lifted her floater and followed the tyrannosaur's obvious track. Vickers raised his rifle to his shoulder. He kept the muzzle high to prevent the front sight from snagging on branches.

Twenty feet from the trail, a depression in the loam and undergrowth showed where the tyrannosaur had settled for the night. Blood spattered the ground; the head of a pig sat upright on the stump of its neck. The carnivore had caught its prey from behind this time. The serrated teeth sawed off the head when the jaws closed. Flies clustered on the eyes and blackened the hog's open mouth.

O'Neill settled alongside again. "I wonder how fast he's travelling," he said. His voice was artificially calm.

"We'd best be getting on," Louise said, a reply to the surface level of O'Neill's question. "Tom, I need to recharge my batteries. Henry, would you mind changing to the other floater? Or . . ."

"I don't have any problem with riding with Mr. O'Neill," Vickers said. He stepped out of Louise's vehicle and unlatched the guardrail of the other. He paused to make eye contact with O'Neill before he got aboard. "Unless he'd rather otherwise?"

"No, no," the younger man said. "It's my job."

He didn't sound enthusiastic, but he seemed to mean what he said.

Louise spoke to Pa Teng. The Punan hesitated a moment, then disappeared along the tyrannosaur's track again.

O'Neill lifted the floater. The little aircraft moved as smoothly as if it were on rails.

"One thing I want clear with you, Vickers," O'Neill said. He looked at his passenger without affecting the floater's steady ride.

Palmetto fronds wavered in the breeze of their passage. "You're not going to shoot from my vehicle. Do you understand?"

"I'll do the job Dr. Mondadero hired me to do," Vickers said. He watched Pa Teng as an excuse to avoid eye contact with O'Neill. "I'm not—" He turned toward the pilot after all. "Look, O'Neill, I'm not here to collect a new trophy. Louise has been a friend for fifteen years. She called because she was in a bind. I'd have come if what she needed was somebody to clean her cesspool, okay?"

O'Neill transferred his attention to his flying. "The only way to protect the rain forest," he muttered, "seems to be to make compromises. But that's like sawing off your leg to prevent gangrene spreading. What you've got left isn't what it should be anymore."

Vickers nodded. That was more nearly a direct apology than he'd expected from the younger man.

"Do you know how the tyrannosaurus was caught in the first place?" Vickers asked, out of curiosity and to keep the conversation going in a neutral path.

The floater dipped to avoid the blooms of orchids hanging as much as ten feet below the branch on which the roots were anchored. A delicate scent perfumed the still air. Dangling like this, the flowers weren't hidden among the foliage of the parent tree and other epiphytes.

O'Neill indicated the barrel of the capture gun clipped vertically to the rail beside him. "With these," he said. "With the actual rifles, very possibly. The people who delivered the tyrannosaur trained Louise and me to use them in case there was a problem. The concern was that a tree might fall across the fences, both of them, in a storm. Not likely, but possible."

"That's good," Vickers said. "I wasn't sure there'd been a field test. How long does the drug take to work?"

O'Neill frowned. "Don't be in a hurry to shoot," he snapped in a return to his earlier tone. "They say up to thirty minutes, though it depends on where the dart hits. And a double dose is lethal, so I won't be shooting more than once."

Assuming you hit it, boy, Vickers thought. *Which I don't assume. And that still leaves the question of how you think we're going to carry our friend home.*

Aloud he said, "Don't worry about me being trigger-happy. Remember, I'm paid for showing my clients a good time. Shooting the wildlife myself doesn't put dollars in my pocket."

Pa Teng suddenly knelt beside a log covered with orange shelf fungus. He took a shotgun shell from his macramé pouch and slipped it into the weapon. O'Neill brought the floater to a hover ten feet above and slightly to the side of the Punan.

Vickers couldn't see or hear anything but the normal forest noise. He still carried the Garand charged. His index finger clicked forward the safety lever at the front of the trigger guard, readying the weapon to fire.

A pig stepped through the undergrowth on the other side of the fallen log. It raised its long snout in the air and snorted. Pa Teng pulled back on the rubber-band firing mechanism.

O'Neill shouted and thrust his control yoke forward. The floater dived toward the hog, spooking it sideways. Pa Teng released the striker. The shotgun boomed. A cloud of smoke, remarkably dense and white because of the saturated humidity, enveloped both hunter and prey.

The smoke cleared. The hog lay on its back, its legs thrashing. Pa Teng ran to his victim and cut its throat with his bush knife, an impressive tool whose clip-pointed blade was ground from a leaf of truck spring. O'Neill landed the floater and shouted to the Punan.

Vickers got out of the vehicle. He didn't notice the slight vibration of the floater's suspension until his feet were on solid ground again. "What's the problem?" he demanded. "We're not close enough to alert the tyrannosaur."

O'Neill turned. "There was no need to shoot anything. We've got food along, plenty of food!"

Louise landed beside the others. "It's time we set up camp for the night anyway," she said. "It was only a pig, Tom. Pa Teng wouldn't understand not shooting a pig that offered itself."

The Punan paid no attention to the argument. He wiped the blade of his knife with a leaf, then dug dry punk from the heart of the fallen log. A few more swipes of the bush knife provided saplings for kindling.

Vickers released the Garand's magazine, tucked it under his belt, and pulled back carefully on the rifle's charging handle to extract the round from the chamber. He caught the cartridge as the ejector started to kick it free of the weapon.

The bolt closed on the empty chamber. Vickers slipped the extracted round into the magazine, which he replaced in turn in the receiver well.

The only way to be absolutely sure that weapon was safe was to carry it with an empty chamber. If the Garand dropped on its buttplate—and who knew what could happen in the field?—there was a fair chance that the bullet would punch through Vickers himself the long way.

Vickers was weary almost beyond words. He had been either moving or waiting on hard seats for two and a half days, ever since getting Louise's panicked call. Despite that, he methodically made his rifle safe, because that was how he was.

There were better marksmen than Henry Vickers—a few. There were better trackers, and many, many guides who formed better rapport with their clients.

Vickers was steady. He'd made mistakes, but he'd never made the same mistake twice. He knew he looked silly sometimes, but he followed procedures nonetheless. He'd stayed alive, and so had every other person for whom Vickers took responsibility.

He'd wondered what technique the Punan would use to ignite the punk. Vickers had heard that some forms of bamboo had enough silica in the stems to strike sparks from a flint chip.

Pa Teng took a disposable butane lighter from a belt pouch and applied it to his fireset. A smoky flame sprang up immediately.

Louise and O'Neill hung condensing cloths from nearby saplings before they unpacked other materials from the knapsacks. The cloths, one-meter squares of thick fabric, absorbed water vapor and wicked it into the clear plastic collecting bottle hanging from the center of each piece. In the forest's saturated atmosphere, the bottles began to fill at once.

"Anything I can do?" Vickers asked. Insects crawled into the corners of his mouth. He ignored them, merely blinking to brush away the mites that settled in his eyes. He wasn't wearing insect repellent. Not only did the long-chain molecules alert wildlife more quickly than a human's normal scent, they degraded Vickers' own sense of smell.

Besides, repellents didn't work very well. Better to accept the bites and prickles as a cost of doing the business he chose to do.

"Just relax, Henry," Louise said. She and O'Neill looked gray with fatigue also. They probably hadn't gotten much sleep since the tyrannosaur escaped either.

Pa Teng had a haunch of the pig on a spit over his smoky fire. The bristles singed off with a stench worse than that of carrion. While his meat cooked, the Punan lopped bamboo for a shelter. His movements were casual but assured.

Vickers squatted down with his back to a tree, leaning the rifle against the trunk beside him. He closed his eyes to prevent gnats from crawling into them.

He didn't realize he'd gone to sleep until he heard Tom O'Neill's voice saying softly, "Should we wake him?"

"No need," Vickers murmured. Tropic sunset had fallen like a knife-switch darkening the sky.

It was raining. He heard the patter of drops infinitely multiplied, spattering from leaf to leaf to lower leaf. Nothing seemed to reach the forest floor except a haze scarcely noticeable in the saturated humidity.

Pa Teng had finished the shelter. It had a floor of saplings and, for a roof, a slanting frame of poles covered with a triple layer of broad leaves. Smoke from the fire filled the covered wedge. The gray cloud might inhibit mosquitoes, but the cure struck Vickers as little better than the problem.

"We have stew," Louise said, indicating a container at the edge of the fire. "Freeze-dried and reconstituted, of course."

Strips of pork quivered on a dozen slight wands over the fire, drying in the smoke. Vickers wasn't sure whether the meat could be said to be cooking in the normal sense of the word.

He got up. His legs were stiff, but he'd expected that and paused before he took a step.

"Ah . . ." Louise added. "Tom and I are vegetarians . . ."

"The stew has all the proteins required for healthy life," O'Neill said. His tone was sharper at the beginning of the statement than it was by the time he'd completed it.

"Sounds good," Vickers said. "But if you don't mind, I'll have some of Pa Teng's meat, too. Seeing that it's already dead."

The Punan lay at the far end of the shelter. He was curled up and asleep, his head pillowed on his right arm.

"Of course not," Louise said as she ladled up a mug of stew for Vickers. "We've eaten. I wanted to let you rest."

Before he took the stew, Vickers removed the Garand's magazine. He checked the rifle's bore against firelight refleeting from the bolt face. The others watched him in surprise.

He set the rifle down in the shelter. "A thirty-caliber hole seems pretty small," Vickers said, "but there are wasps that think it's just the best place in the world to build a mud nest. I've seen what happens if a gun's fired that way, and I don't care to have it happen to me."

The stew was good and the pork remarkably good, though Vickers couldn't imagine why. The meat was unsalted, seasoned only by the tang of the smoke. He supposed he was glad to be back in the field on a real hunt.

"Do you suppose . . ." he said carefully. "The people with the time machine, the Israelis, let's say. Do you suppose they might need an experienced hunter on their project?"

O'Neill had been staring pensively at the fire. He turned and in a voice of cold anger said, "You and your sort destroyed the wildlife of East Africa. Now you want to go back in time and denude the past too!"

"Tom," Louise said, leaning forward so that her head and torso blocked the men's view of one another.

"No, it's all right," Vickers said. He frowned with the effort of choosing the right words, choosing them for himself rather than out of concern for what O'Neill might think.

Louise leaned back on her arms again.

"What I'd like," Vickers continued, "is to do the only work that

I'm really good at. And you're right, there isn't a future for that in Africa, for a lot of reasons."

"When we're done with this business, I'll talk to some people, Henry," Louise said. Her mouth bent in a wry smile. "Of course, the way this turns out may determine whether they'll be willing to talk to me."

Borneo Scheme stores provided Mylar air mattresses that folded to the size of a cigarette pack but smoothed the irregularities of the shelter's sapling floor. The conditions weren't uncomfortable for someone used to being outdoors, but Vickers slept badly nonetheless now that the nap had taken the edge off his fatigue.

He wasn't used to the humid atmosphere or the sounds of the rain forest. Branches creaking, the rain continuing to patter down from the canopy after the clouds had passed. Birds, frogs, monkeys and deep booming notes which Vickers guessed might be forest nomads like Pa Teng communicating by striking hollow logs to create the low-frequency sounds that carried farthest through the night.

Vickers dreamed. Three humanoid figures stared at him from a rosy glow. Their faces were triangular, and they had no clothing, body hair, or external genitalia. "What do you want?" the dreaming Vickers called.

"What?" said O'Neill. It was dawn. Clear light ignited the ground fog. The fire had gone out.

The alien figures had vanished. Everything else was as it had been a moment before in Vickers' waking dream.

"I think we can follow the tyrannosaurus from the floaters," Vickers said. "Especially if it keeps running a straight course. And I think we'd better, because it's travelling as fast as we can—Pa Teng can—on foot."

O'Neill looked up from his breakfast coffee. "It's trying to get as far away as possible from the cage we held it in."

Louise frowned. "There's nothing familiar to it here," she said. "It's not running *away,* it's trying to find the sort of habitat from which it was taken."

"Look, it doesn't matter what it's doing," Vickers said. "All that matters is that we catch up with it. Will Pa Teng ride in the floaters? Because if he won't, I'm pretty sure I can follow the trail this thing leaves."

The Punan was gorging on chunks of pig. He'd eaten pounds of meat the previous night and was well on the way to equaling his performance for breakfast. Vickers was reminded of the way lions bolted significant fractions of their body weight whenever meat was available. Natural patterns of behavior weren't necessarily attractive.

"Yes," said Louise. "Yes, he's ridden with us for amusement before."

O'Neill nodded agreement. "I wouldn't take him above the canopy, though," he said. "Forest people are uncomfortable in direct sunlight—even the occasional jungle clearing. If Pa Teng reacted badly, he could overbalance the floater."

He spoke to Pa Teng. The nomad replied with hog grease dripping down his chin as he continued to chew a fist-sized chunk of meat. He didn't seem perturbed or even terribly interested in what O'Neill was telling him.

Louise stood up. "I'll take the high shift first," she said. "And Henry's right, the tyrannosaur isn't wasting any time. So we'd better not either."

The four of them moved together to the floaters. Pa Teng paused to stretch his arms. He let out a belch of happy repletion.

The canopy unrolled beneath Vickers with the varied sameness of a piece of carpeting. Individually each treetop differed from its neighbors. In the larger sense, the pattern was a single, seamless whole.

He kept his eyes lowered, on the jungle. They were heading east; the glare of the rising tropic Sun was punishing if he glanced up. He shouldn't have made the gesture with his hat.

Vickers switched off the link between the floaters. "Could O'Neill have let the tyrannosaurus out?" he asked bluntly.

"Yes," Louise said, "but he wouldn't have. There is no possibility that he would have."

"A lightning bolt didn't neatly unlock the gates, Louise," Vickers pressed. "Even if it had, it wouldn't have slid the crossbars open.

Somebody let the beast out, and I don't believe your native staff could have managed the electronic locks even if they had the desire."

A monkey leaped between treetops just below the floater. The beast's arms were spread wide, its tail canted slightly. It caught a branch and vanished as suddenly as it had appeared. The monkey was the first forest mammal Vickers had seen in the forest since the hog that Pa Teng shot.

"I know how it looks," Louise said. "Tom or me. I don't buy his notion of Indonesian saboteurs any more than you do. But I'd as soon believe that *I* let the tyrannosaur out—and I didn't."

She looked at Vickers. The floater quivered, reminding Vickers that it was balanced on a ball of static electricity. The bobble made him nervous, though he didn't comment.

"He's an honorable man, Henry," Louise said. "He might have resigned because of his opposition to animal research. I can even *imagine* that he might have freed the tyrannosaur. But if he did, he would have told me immediately what he'd done. He wouldn't have just left the cage empty for me to find."

Vickers didn't reply. Part of him wanted to sneer at the woman for denying on the basis of gut instinct what *had* to be true. The trouble was, Vickers trusted Louise's instincts also.

"I . . ." he said toward the forest roof. A tree in brilliant red flower trembled with glittering motion. Sunlight was being reflected from the wings of nectar-drinking birds and insects which spread pollen as their payment. To give himself a moment to frame his next words, Vickers turned the television link on again. "Louise," he said, "have you ever seen . . . men, I guess you'd call them, with faces like—" He sketched a triangle in the air with both hands, up from the chin and then across the flat top.

The floater wobbled violently. Louise refocused her attention on her flying. "Where did you see them?" she demanded in a tight voice.

"In a dream last night," Vickers said. "This morning. What do you know about them?"

He stared at the tip of the woman's right ear, poking out through her short hair. Her refusal to meet his eyes came from more than concern over controlling the floater.

"I've been dreaming about them, too," she said. "For three nights. Since I came to Site IV and found the tyrannosaur missing."

"Vickers?" O'Neill's voice demanded through the module's speaker. The sound shocked Vickers. The Scheme personnel were so used to operating alone that this was the first time they'd communicated through the link since they checked it. "Do you mean faces like wedges, very sharp chins?"

"That's right," Vickers said. "I—don't think they're human. If they're real."

"If we've all three been dreaming about them, they're real *something,*" O'Neill said with a logic Vickers couldn't challenge. "Their skin seems to be scaly." He paused, then added, "I don't see how this could have anything to do with the Javans, though."

"Nor do I," Louise said. Her voice held a touch of the mocking humor Vickers had heard before when O'Neill said something *young.* O'Neill was smart and able, but he had a tendency to get focused on the answer. Experience would cure the problem, assuming he lived long enough.

The camera on the floater O'Neill piloted had been brushing through the pale, broad leaves of new growth. The shoots would die in a week or two unless chance brought down one of the giants shading them. The tyrannosaur's clawed feet had punched as neatly as stencil-cutters into the loam.

Louise spoke in Punan. The transmitted image bobbed and swayed violently. O'Neill shouted in Punan also. The image steadied; Pa Teng spoke, his voice jaggedly animated.

"I'm sorry, Tom," Louise said. "I should have realized that he'd jump if my voice addressed him out of the air."

She glanced at Vickers with a faint grin. "He says those are the ghosts. That doesn't frighten him. The surprise of my voice did."

Vickers nodded, showing that he heard, though God knew he didn't understand. Anything.

After a moment's thought, he charged the Garand again. Sometimes a fraction of a second could be more important than an increased risk of accident.

* * *

After two hours of maneuvering through the forest at a rapid pace, O'Neill called Louise down. Vickers traded places with a nonchalant Pa Teng beside a steep-banked stream. The water six feet below was so clear that Vickers thought the gully was dry until he noticed the refraction of ripples downstream of each leaf and branch, standing waves in a fluid medium.

The tyrannosaur had crossed the stream at an angle, tearing a ramp in the bank. Such exhibitions of strength were becoming familiar by repetition. O'Neill stepped off the floater to loosen up with a few toe-touching exercises.

"It's still moving in a straight line," he observed.

"It's moving in a different straight line," Vickers said.

The Scheme officials looked at him in question. Vickers raised the lensatic compass from his side pocket, then let it drop back. A lanyard attached the instrument to a D-ring on his shirt. "From the cage to where it slept the first night," he said, "the tyrannosaurus traveled an 83-degree vector, close enough. Since then it's been moving at one-oh-two. Just as straight. Is there anything on this line?"

"Rain forest," O'Neill said with a puzzled shrug. "There's nothing else within fifty miles of here in *any* direction."

Vickers looked upward. The treetops fitted like jigsaw pieces, irregular but never overlapping. Ragged lines of white sky separated each giant from its neighbors.

"We'd best move on," he said as he climbed aboard O'Neill's floater.

O'Neill rose through the canopy in a gentle corkscrew. When he was clear of the branches, he unfurled the solar array. Now that the Sun was high, the opaque panels shaded the men in the floater. A glance at the charging indicator showed Vickers that O'Neill had run his batteries uncomfortably close to the end of their power.

O'Neill followed Vickers' eyes. "I thought we'd make better time with me on the deck," he said quietly. His words were unlikely to be intelligible through the link's microphone. "I thought of suggesting that Louise and I change instead of you and Pa Teng. But she'd have been insulted."

Vickers looked at the younger man with new appreciation.

O'Neill certainly was the better pilot. Under his control, the floater was as steady above the canopy as it had been in the still atmosphere of the forest.

The solar array was stiff when deployed. It acted as an airfoil, catching and multiplying the breezes that twitched across the high treetops. Since the fulcrum on which the floater balanced was beneath the floor, the wind's torque acted through a long lever. Perhaps Louise had never been in danger of losing control of the floater, but Vickers' heart had jumped several times when he thought she was.

"What do you think about the . . ." Vickers said, watching the forest. "The dreams."

O'Neill glanced at him. "I don't have enough data to think anything," he said. He didn't sound hostile so much as extremely careful.

After a few moments of steady flight, Vickers said, "Seems funny that dinosaurs were around for longer than mammals and still didn't develop intelligence, isn't it?"

"Fish have been around longer yet," O'Neill said sharply. "Humans happen to have what we call intelligence, so we put a premium on it. Nature doesn't. Besides, what's so intelligent about stripping and poisoning our planet to the point that it may not be able to support *any* kind of life in the foreseeable future?"

"I was just wondering if the Israelis were sure about everything they brought back in their time machine," Vickers said. Beneath him, light glinted from a branch covered with bromeliads. The upturned leaves trapped water in hundreds of tiny pools, spangling the normal patterns of green on green.

The flight fell into a rhythm. There was nothing to say, and only the same things to see. Vickers slipped into a familiar reverie, a gray background from which anything abnormal would spring out in brilliant light.

Shouts in Punan and a cry of inarticulate despair snarled through the link's speaker. The TV image whipped violently as the lower floater swayed.

"Take us down!" Vickers shouted. He slipped the Garand's

charging handle back slightly to check the glint of brass indicating he'd already chambered a round.

O'Neill threw a lever on his control column. The solar array above the men began to fold by creaking stages.

"Forget that!" Vickers said. "Strip 'em off if you have to! If you don't get us down fast, I'll take her down myself!"

Pa Teng was hooting, a meaningless, repetitive pulse. Louise shouted to the Punan, raising her voice to be heard over his wail of grief. There was an edge of fear in her tone.

Louise's floater landed, but Vickers still couldn't make any sense out of the chaotic image her link camera sent. Broken poles and branches had been tossed in all directions. Some of them were tied to one another.

O'Neill dropped toward the forest floor as ordered. He used his body weight as well as the control yoke to hook the little vehicle around branches. Because the solar panels were still in the process of folding, their area and aspect changed continuously. For an instant, Vickers thought the floater had overbalanced; then, as O'Neill had planned, the braking effect of the part-furled array caught them and pulled the floater upright.

The smell of death and rotting flesh lay like fog over a low ridge. There had been four shelters in the nomads' camp, each basically similar to the one Pa Teng built in a few minutes the night before.

Mats woven from bark fiber had softened the pole floors. The cloth was shredded now. The tyrannosaur's jaws had torn a yard-long ellipsis through the center of one mat. The edges of the gap were bloody. Blood had sprayed twenty feet high on tree trunks. A ring of feasting flies emphasized each spatter with glittering chitin.

The tyrannosaur's claws had scuffled through the fire at the open end of one shelter, scattering it. Debris and new growth on the forest floor were too damp to burn, but the hot coals had shriveled a wedge of ferns.

There had probably been twenty or so Punans in the camp. Because they were asleep when disaster struck, they'd been unable to flee instantly the way the sounder of hogs had done when it met the tyrannosaur.

Raggedly severed limbs lay all about the encampment. A child's head and torso were face-down near where O'Neill landed the floater. The dinosaur had swallowed everything below the victim's waist.

Pa Teng knelt, clinging to the guard rails of Louise's floater. His face was turned upward. He keened like a distant siren, never stopping to breathe. Louise hugged the Punan and murmured in his ear. Her face was twisted with anguish.

Responsibility which we accepted, she had said to O'Neill, meaning the tyrannosaur. In Louise's mind, this carnage was her responsibility too.

Vickers stepped off the platform, the Garand cradled in his hands. He scanned the trees, some of them six feet in diameter. You could hide a regiment of tyrannosaurs in this jungle, each monster poised to lunge out behind a jaw full of serrated teeth.

In a fraction of a second, Henry Vickers could spin and point his rifle in any direction. In a fraction of a second, his eye could place the Garand's sight picture on a spot between the gun muzzle and the big reptile's brain. In a fraction of a second, his right index finger would squeeze the trigger off its sear and send a steel-cored bullet punching through flesh, bone, and soft nerve tissue.

There was no target. The slaughter around Vickers was hours old. The killer had passed on.

A voice called timidly from nearby.

"Don't shoot!" O'Neill cried in English. He sprang toward Vickers, his arms spread while his eyes searched for the person who had spoken. It was next to impossible to tell the direction of a sound in the forest.

Vickers raised the Garand's muzzle straight up to indicate that he understood. Louise stood and called out in Punan.

Pa Teng ceased wailing, though he continued to grip the floater. O'Neill spoke to him in a low voice.

Louise walked toward one of the collapsed shelters. The palm-leaf thatching shivered; a young woman wriggled out. The roofline had been undisturbed until she appeared. She'd lain where disaster covered her, afraid to move until she heard human voices.

Louise opened her arms. After a moment's hesitation, the nomad woman embraced her educated sister.

Pa Teng clambered out of the floater. He and the Punan woman began to talk in quick, bubbling bursts. Vickers wasn't sure that either was listening to the other or to the occasional questions that Louise or O'Neill added to the mix.

Vickers scanned the forest, moving his head and body slowly while his eyes flicked across the shadowed landscape. He was giving his peripheral vision full opportunity to identify a threat while there was still time to do something about it.

O'Neill turned and said, "According to the woman, ghosts brought the monster to them. They came in a ball of light, driving the monster before them."

"They've been feeding it once a day," Vickers said. He continued to watch their surroundings, though O'Neill's information implied that the tyrannosaur had passed on. "I wonder what it's getting for dinner tonight. Men again or pigs?"

Then he said, "I'd like to get moving soonest."

A shrill electronic note quivered from one of the floaters. The jungle's noises were so many and varied that, for a moment, Vickers thought the sound was natural. He whirled to see if a forest creature was warning of the tyrannosaur's approach.

Louise stepped away from the Punans. She exchanged a glance with O'Neill.

"You were going to tell them not to contact you unless the world was about to end," O'Neill said.

"Yes," Louise agreed. "That's what I told them."

She stepped to the floater she'd piloted and threw a switch on the side of the link module. "Mondadero here," she said in a flat voice.

"Dr. Mondadero?" the link's speaker had a high-pitched male voice. "This is Carlsbad in New York. We've just processed EarthSat images and there's *logging* going on within the Scheme borders. Logging! This is large-scale, absolutely blatant! You must act at once at your end while we protest to the Malaysian UN delegation. I've sent the images and Global Positioning Coordinates to the field database in Kuching for you."

"Yes, I understand, Dr. Carlsbad," Louise said. She was leaning over the guardrail to put her mouth closer to the module's pickup. She looked unutterably weary. "I'll get on that as soon as possible."

"As soon as *possible!*" the voice at the other end of the satellite communicator repeated. "Doctor, did you hear what I said? A logging—"

"I'm quite busy now, Dr. Carlsbad," Louise interrupted. "Good day."

She broke the connection, then opened the link's side panel and pulled the fuse. For a moment she stared at the silent module with her fist clenched; then she flung the fuse into the jungle.

"Louise," Tom O'Neill said, "we've got to stop the logging before it becomes an international event. It's Nikisastro, I'm sure."

Louise straightened. "Yes," she said. She opened the gate of her floater. "Just as soon as we've dealt with the tyrannosaur. Let's go."

"*No,* Louise!" O'Neill said. His voice was tight and desperate but not loud. "The logging is more important. The logging is the whole Borneo Scheme. We've got to deal with it first."

"Can you look around you and say that, Tom?" Louise shouted. "Look at them! Look at them!"

In an excess of revulsion that was close to insanity, Louise thrust her foot against the child's partial corpse beside her, raising a cloud of flies. Their wings thrummed a bass note.

"Louise, I see," O'Neill said softly. "But this is more important. This is the whole world's future here."

"O'Neill," Vickers said, "take the floater that's partly discharged and do whatever's possible. Louise, you and I'll chase the tyrannosaurus in the other one. If it laid up for the night, then it can't be very far ahead now. We'll catch it soon."

He looked at the Punans, Pa Teng and the female survivor. They sat alongside one another on a pole which had been part of a shelter's floor frame. They were chanting together, their voices low.

"I'll be able to track the beast," Vickers said. "I doubt Pa Teng would come along now even if we needed him."

"Yes," Louise said crisply. "Yes, all right. Let's get going."

She got aboard the floater her subordinate had been piloting. The little craft started to lift as Vickers jumped aboard.

"We have two hours," Louise said tightly. "After that, we'll have to recharge for at least another hour before I'll want to trust the batteries again."

"Two hours should do it," Vickers said. He didn't have any real idea; he was speaking to calm a friend who'd just taken a series of emotional jolts. "If it continues this business of driving a straight line, we can probably shoot a compass course in the canopy if we have to."

A casing of vines wrapped a tree so thoroughly that no sign of the support structure within was visible. A yellow-striped lizard watched from a gnarled loop. It flicked its forked tongue toward Vickers as the floater passed.

What are you hunting, little fellow? Vickers mused.

The carnage in the Punan camp had unexpectedly relaxed him. They would catch up with the tyrannosaur, and when they did, Henry Vickers would kill the beast. There was no longer a need to wait for the Scheme officials to use their capture guns, to argue, to lapse into despair, and—as the beast started to regain consciousness—for Louise finally to tell Vickers to finish off the logy animal.

Vickers' position had ceased to be that of friend to Louise Mondadero and employee of the Borneo Scheme. He was a human being, and the tyrannosaur had proved that it was too dangerous to live in a world with humans.

"I heard what you were saying to Tom," Louise said, her eyes on her flying. "That you think the ghosts come from the past. They couldn't. They would have left remains, just as the dinosaurs themselves did. Especially if they were . . . intelligent."

"I don't know where they came from," Vickers said. "I don't even know if they exist."

A wave of small birds swept up from the rain forest floor, disturbed by the floater's hissing passage. There were scores, *hundreds* of individuals, and at least a dozen species. Their calls were cheerful cacophony as they brushed and banked about the mechanical intruder in their domain.

"They could be from the future, though," Louise said in a cold, harsh tone that Vickers didn't like to hear from his friend. "From the time after we've wiped ourselves and most other life off the planet."

The tyrannosaur had laid up near its kill during the night, crushing a thirty-foot circle of undergrowth. When the beast got up, its tracks resumed their straight line through the forest.

Vickers checked his compass surreptitiously. He wasn't sure how Louise would react to what he was doing. Ninety-five degrees was as close as he could make it. There was, he now realized, a Global Positioning Satellite receiver in the link module which could give him a vector accurate to a few centimeters in a kilometer.

Vickers hoped O'Neill wouldn't get lost, because Louise had disabled the other module completely. Well, she had a lot of things on her mind. Vickers had only one: centering his front blade in the ring of the rear sight, with the beast's skull a snarling blur in the distance beyond them.

"People have been talking about the end of the world for as long as there've been people, Louise," Vickers said. He was calm because he knew exactly what he was to do. "We're still here."

"Sure, Henry," she said savagely. "Every year the air and water are poisoned a little bit worse, every year the land is stripped a little barer, every year there's tens of millions more people to speed up the decline. And everything's fine. Just the way you're fine when you fall out of a window—until you hit the ground!"

Tracking was even less difficult than Vickers had expected. The tyrannosaur's strides were as regular as a heartbeat, each of ten feet or so through the undergrowth. They were a little closer on uphills, and they strung into long gouges on downslopes: the beast's heels dug in, and sometimes there was the mark of a dewclaw.

The floater swept beneath a branch from which hung scores of football-shaped nests woven from plant fibers. Nesting birds with slim, curved beaks cried raucously at the humans' sudden appearance.

A wasp stung Vickers on the forehead. Another settled on his right wrist. He slapped the second one and was stung on the back of the neck. Wasps shared the tree with the birds; they swarmed to defend it, though fortunately they didn't pursue the human intruders far.

Louise swung the floater around a tree. Orange flowers sprang directly from the trunk. A stray sunbeam touched a bloom and lighted it into a torch flame.

The angry splotch of a wasp sting glowed on Louise's right cheekbone. "They're evil, Henry," she said.

He glanced at her. "The ghosts, you mean?" he said.

"They're not ghosts, they're aliens," Louise said. "Alien to us, at least. Maybe you're right about them, them being from another time."

Vickers shrugged. "I don't know where they're from," he repeated. "If they're real—"

In his gut, he didn't believe the slender, scaled figures existed. Intellectually he knew that the evidence suggested the—ghosts, whatever—had to be real, but the emotional core of Vickers' mind refused to accept that.

"—then they're sure not human. Doesn't make them evil, though."

"The Punan camp," Louise said grimly. The vine-covered branch of a fallen tree *whanged* the side of the floater. She had mistaken the obstruction for the whippy weakness of a sapling. They were traveling recklessly fast.

"They needed food for the tyrannosaurus," Vickers said. His voice was wooden in its lack of affect. "They're not human, so pigs and men are all the same. It's only evil if men do it to other men."

There had been other villages like that one, half a world and half a lifetime away. Vickers hadn't forgotten those villages either.

"It's all *right* with you, Henry?" Louise shouted. "It's all right? What's the matter with you?"

"I said they weren't evil, Louise," Vickers replied softly. "It's not all right, no. But there's only three of them and—"

His face changed. His mind was so completely in the past that he forgot to keep his expression neutral.

"—I've got a hundred rounds. That should be plenty."

The terrain was rising. Louise twitched the floater abruptly upward. She had almost plowed into the ground while transfixed by a glimpse into the soul of a man she thought she knew.

They flew on. By this time, they could anticipate the twists to one side or the other when major obstructions diverted the dinosaur's course. The track swung back, as surely as a pendulum.

"Do you suppose they're taking it to their ship?" Louise murmured. "Or machine. I don't even know what the Israelis' apparatus looks like."

Vickers shook his head. The question didn't touch his area of present focus, so he barely heard the words.

They were getting close. A smell that at first Vickers couldn't identify made the hair on the back of his neck lift. A combination of snake smell and carrion . . . Although the tyrannosaur appeared to be an active hunter rather than a scavenger, flesh caught between its teeth would rot. There were no tick birds here in the forest to clean the beast's jaws like those of crocodiles on a mudbank.

Vickers began to hear a rasping quiver whenever the floater topped a ridge. At first he thought it was the sound of a distant storm, but it was too constant for that. "Louise?" he said. "Do you hear that noise?"

She looked at him. "Yes," she said, "but I don't know what it is. It isn't the tyrannosaur."

The tyrannosaur had brushed a tree, pulling aside the shrouding vines. The bark beneath was rough. Scales the size of Vickers' thumbnail glittered against it. Most were dark, but one was a bright yellowish green.

"We're getting very low on power," Louise said.

The charge indicator was in the red zone. Vickers grimaced. "We're nearly up with him," he said. "Hold on for as long as you can."

The terrain climbed. When the floater crested the ridge, the sound hit them redoubled. Superimposed on the rumble of diesel engines was the high scream of a chainsaw. They were nearing the logging operation.

Louise's face set. Neither she nor Vickers spoke.

A hump in the ground ahead might once have been a fallen tree. Insects and microbes had reduced it to a mauve pile, covered now by broad-leafed ferns. The tyrannosaur had ripped through the obstruction without swerving. Torn fronds quivered at the edges of where the punky wood had fallen in to fill the gap.

Louise pulled back on her control yoke. The floater lifted a foot, then staggered and dropped like a man falling down stairs.

"We've got to get into the sun—" she shouted as the floater crashed through ferns in an explosion of brown spores "—light!"

They came out the other side of the fern thicket. Louise fought her controls. The floater balanced but would not rise. The charge indicator pulsed red, and a warning buzzer sounded.

"We don't—" Louise said, and the tyrannosaur thirty feet away cocked its head toward them. Its belly scales were cream-colored, while its back was slate gray with vertical green stripes. The beast disappeared through a screen of elephant ear plants.

Vickers stepped off of the floater without thinking at the conscious level. He'd gotten the Garand only halfway to his shoulder before the sudden target vanished. He ran after the tyrannosaur, holding the butt of the heavy weapon in the crook of his right arm so that he had a hand free to grab supports.

Surface roots, hard and slippery, spread a net across the ground. Vickers stumbled. He caught himself on one of a trio of arrow-straight stems springing from a common base. Spines or an insect stabbed his palm, but the pain didn't register for the moment. He continued to jog along the dinosaur's track.

Behind him, Louise spiked skyward in the lightened floater. Vickers hoped it wouldn't lose power before she could deploy the solar array, but that was out of his hands.

The ground climbed. The slope was no more than one in five, but Vickers' legs were weak for lack of use in the past several days. He didn't let himself think of failing. He would catch and finish his quarry if he had to crawl on his belly to do so.

The noise of snorting engines hit Vickers like the first rush of a storm. He shouldered through a stand of saplings. Sword-shaped leaves sprouted directly from their trunks. Sunlight dazzled him.

He was at the edge of a wide logging road. Diesel exhaust mingled with the sharp smells of turned earth and freshly cut vegetation. To his left, a four-wheeled grapple skidder with a 'dozer blade in front and a hydraulic grab on the other end rolled thunderously down the middle of the road at a walking pace. The grab held the butt end of the hundred-and-fifty-foot tree the tractor was dragging toward the aerostat tethered at the edge of the forest a quarter of a mile away.

The tyrannosaur was a hundred yards down the road to the right, among half a dozen Indonesian sawyers. Most of the men were running. A pair of bare legs protruded from the beast's jaws. The tyrannosaur's skull flexed like that of a snake swallowing. Peristaltic motion of the throat muscles dragged the victim the rest of the way down.

Vickers clicked his safety lever forward. He dropped into a sitting position for steadier aim. That was a mistake. After Vickers' days in the rain forest, the logging road looked like bare wasteland, but the trash of branches and bulldozed saplings formed a muzzle-high screen between Vickers and his target.

He staggered to his feet again. He was breathing hard from his run, and his skin was slick with sweat.

A sawyer turned with his chainsaw raised. The cutting bar was nearly as long as the man wielding it was tall. White exhaust spurted as the Indonesian revved the saw's two-stroke engine. The hooked teeth glinted in the sunlight that filled the clearing.

The tyrannosaur paused. Vickers aimed, breathed deeply, and began to let his breath out slowly as his finger took up the trigger's slack. The muzzle had been describing a three-inch circle in the air. Now it steadied.

The torque and weight of the big saw pulled the bar down despite the Indonesian's desperate efforts to keep it between him and the tyrannosaur. The beast's huge head darted forward like that of a robin taking a worm. Vickers slacked his trigger instinctively lest he hit the man instead of the tyrannosaur.

The sawyer screamed and tried to fling the saw like an awkward medicine ball. The tyrannosaur's jaws clopped shut in a spray of blood, severing the man's torso at diaphragm level.

The grapple skidder blocked any further chance of a shot, though Vickers caught glimpses of the chaos across the road. Men screamed as they ran, but human voices were lost in the continuing roar of logging machinery. A bulldozer with a high land-clearing blade and a roof of heavy screen sat empty and idling. The space between its treads would have been excellent protection, but none of the panicked loggers thought to hide there.

Nikisastro's pickup turned into the fresh-cut road and accelerated. Ruts sent the vehicle bounding high on its suspension. The two guards in back clung to the sides for dear life.

The tyrannosaur ignored the remaining sawyers. It strode off on a course converging with that of the grapple skidder. The beast's movements were deceptively swift. Because of its size, what appeared to be a deliberate walking pace accelerated the tyrannosaur from a halt to about fifteen miles per hour in a single stride.

Vickers ran into the road to get around the log bouncing behind the skidder. The tree's top had been roughly trimmed, but some branches remained. One of them broke, springing toward Vickers and making him duck.

The tyrannosaur's head bobbed back and forth with each stride, like that of a bird hunting in short grass. The beast stepped close to the grapple skidder. The driver's mouth opened in a silent scream. He jumped out the far side of his cab.

The tractor's huge rear wheel ground over him and rolled up briefly red. The driverless equipment rumbled on until it left the cleared roadway. It climbed partway up the bole of a giant tree and stalled there.

A floater with its solar array spread swooped down on the tyrannosaur. Louise was piloting left-handed. She held the capture gun in her right, supporting the fore-end on the floater's guardrail.

The beast turned at the motion and darted its huge head in the direction of the floater. The muzzle of the capture gun recoiled up and to the right as Louise fired. She slid the control yoke in the opposite direction, curving past the tyrannosaur's gape. Slamming jaws shredded a corner of the solar array, but inertia carried the craft free.

Vickers gulped air to clear fatigue poisons from his blood. He didn't dare shoot for fear of hitting a human being. There were men and pieces of abandoned logging equipment everywhere.

The white truck skidded to a halt two hundred yards from where Vickers stood. The driver and Nikisastro got out of the cab, the former waving a submachine gun. The two guards in back had been clinging with both hands to keep from being flung out of the truck box. They straightened and unslung their weapons.

A man wearing a yellow hard hat stepped from the forest behind where the grapple skidder had crashed. He obviously had no idea what had been going on. He was only twenty feet from the tyrannosaur when he and the beast saw each other.

The man turned and ran, losing his helmet to a low branch. The tyrannosaur followed with the shocking acceleration of a terrier jumping a rat. The long, rigid tail flicked side to side, parallel to the ground, balancing the huge body as the beast vanished into the forest.

Louise's floater pogoed twenty feet in the air in the middle of the logging road. She was trying to load the capture gun one-handed without losing control of her little vehicle.

Nikisastro pointed to Louise and shouted. His three guards raised their submachine guns.

Vickers' surroundings shrank to the dimensions of his sight picture. Everything else was a gray blur which had no present meaning. His breath steadied; his arms were as firm as a sandbag rest. The top of the front blade in the center of the rear circle, the sight's protective horns flaring to either side. The driver's throat above the post because the Garand was sighted for one hundred yards and Vickers had to allow for bullet drop at the doubled range.

He didn't feel the sear's crisp release. *A puff of white from the muzzle, the steel buttplate recoiling* hard *against his shoulder, and the empty brass sailing a high arc to the right dripping its own faint trail of smoke.*

Vickers let the recoil help him turn, bringing the sights down on the first of the gunmen in the back of the pickup. His squeeze started as the front post steadied and continued through the fraction of a second after powder gases blew their miniature white curtain from the muzzle again.

Recoil, the third target with his submachine gun already shouldered. The second Javan toppling backward out of the truck box at the periphery of Vickers' circle of vision. *Squeeze* and the submachine gun flying apart in a spray of sparks. The gun's shredded magazine flung cartridges in all directions as the armor-piercing bullet wobbled on and through the gunman's chest.

The muzzle blast of Vickers' high-velocity cartridges was terrific, but he heard only the third *wham!* as he started to relax and the world softened again into color. The driver fired a long burst into Louise's floater.

Vickers hadn't missed. His bullet had stabbed in and out of the Javan's upper chest, severing one of the pulmonary arteries on its passage. There was a hole in the windshield of the truck behind the man, and a mist of blood coated the glass.

Despite that, the bullet had no shock effect because the fellow had been pumped with adrenaline when it hit him. The armor-piercing projectile hadn't struck a major bone or the spinal column, and the volume of oxygenated blood already in the brain was sufficient to sustain consciousness for a full minute. The Javan carried through the action he had started, unaware that he was already dead on his feet.

The batteries in the base of the floater ruptured in a yellowish haze. Louise dropped the capture gun and grabbed the control yoke vainly with both hands. The floater dropped with a sickening lurch.

The solar array spilled air. It tilted like an ownerless umbrella cartwheeling down the street. Louise tried to cling to the guardrail. The floater flipped upside down and plunged to the ground. Knapsacks flung their contents across the stripped dirt.

The Garand steadied in Vickers' hands. This time the front post was on the driver's forehead. The bullet, striking three inches below the point of aim, blew out the back of the man's skull in a spray of blood and fresh, cream-colored brains.

Nikisastro saw Vickers for the first time. He opened his mouth to shout, but he must have known that would be useless. He ran toward the cover of the trees.

That too was useless. A running enemy was still an easy target at two hundred yards.

Henry Vickers was no longer a civilian: the jungle had won its struggle for his mind. Mercy was as alien to him as it was to the rifle in his expert hands.

The tyrannosaur burst from the forest wall, its jaws gaping toward Nikisastro. Vickers squeezed, aiming again for the man's head because failure had taught him not to trust the effect of AP rounds on a human torso.

The Javan's skull blew apart. The bullet acted as a piston that converted soft nerve tissue into hydraulic working fluid. Nikisastro's limbs flew wide in a spastic convulsion.

Vickers raised his sights to the tyrannosaur. He visualized the point that would take his steel projectile through the reptile's brain as their fellows had penetrated human targets.

A rosy curtain swelled to hide the dinosaur. *Three slender figures . . .* Vickers' trigger finger continued to take up slack.

Vickers was no longer in Borneo or in any part of the world he had known. *A wind as hot as that from a furnace door shocked him. There was no Sun, only a sky that filtered light to a sullen red.*

His eyes blurred, stung by astringents in the air. The breeze bit his exposed skin. Dust blowing from the surrounding wasteland was the only visible motion. His lungs burned, and he knew that when he breathed he would die.

Vickers turned. His mouth was clamped shut and his eyes brimmed with cleansing tears. There was nothing alive in the hundred-foot radius his vision could penetrate through the acid atmosphere, but a colossal statue had fallen facedown onto the ground behind him. The metal from which the figure was cast had suffered only pitting and tarnish, but the stone base was crumbled to gravel.

The statue was of a humanoid figure, unclothed and sexless. Its three-fingered left hand had been raised in greeting. When the statue fell, the arm broke at the elbow; it lay beside the rest of the body.

The statue's triangular face had a supernal stillness, divorced from every human emotion. Drifts of dust piled in the lee of the metal figure, but the wind had scoured patches of ground clean as well. The surface beneath was artificial. It must have been mirror-smooth until ages of acid grit had worked on it.

The atmosphere crushed down on Vickers like the roof of a collapsing tunnel, suffused with glowing death—

He stood in the logging road again. His skin burned, and his eyes streamed with tears. Tawny dust clung to the coat of oil protecting the Garand's bolt and receiver. Vickers sucked in a deep breath and blew it out again, clearing his nose and lips of the poisonous reek which had immersed them.

The three alien figures hung between Vickers and the tyrannosaur. The light that bathed them was the sky of the dead world from which Henry Vickers had just returned.

Vickers lowered his rifle. He blinked furiously to clear his eyes, though he could see well enough through his tears to shoot had he wanted to.

The tyrannosaur was staggering drunkenly from the dose of anesthetic that Louise had fired into its throat. The hypodermic dart must have entered a major blood vessel to work so quickly.

Vickers walked toward the crashed floater at a deliberate pace. He was afraid that if he tried to move faster, he would fall and perhaps be unable to rise. He didn't see any members of the logging crew, though the engines of abandoned equipment still thumped at idle.

Fifty yards from Vickers, the tyrannosaur dipped its great head to Nikisastro's corpse. The beast's three-clawed forelimbs were too short to grip prey so small; they scrabbled in the air as the jaws worked the victim down unaided.

Louise crawled from beneath the flimsy wreckage of the floater. She had a pressure cut on her forehead, but the solar panels and the pole supporting them had cushioned the shock of the crash.

"Tom's in the back of the pickup," she called.

Vickers knelt to help her. "Were you hit?" he demanded. "I—it was my fault, I didn't put him down and there's no *excuse.*"

"No, no," she said. She pulled her right leg free of the crumpled guardrail. Her limbs flexed normally. The only blood Vickers could see was on her forehead. "I'm fine, but untie Tom!"

The tyrannosaur's legs splayed. The beast skidded prone on the sharp keel of its breastbone. Because of the birdlike delicacy of the creature's movements, the way the ground shook at the impact of the five-ton body was a subconscious surprise to Vickers.

The tyrannosaur flopped onto its left side. Its tail thrashed stiffly, thumping the russet soil twice before subsiding into random muscle twitches. The hormone-collecting bottle gleamed at the base of the great skull.

Glancing over his shoulder to be sure that Louise really was all right—she was getting to her feet—Vickers stepped to the back of the pickup. His eyes had cleared, but his stomach lurched violently in reaction to events of the past hour.

Vickers deliberately looked at the driver. The head shot had flung the man against the cab of the pickup, from which he had caromed forward onto his face. The bullet and the pressure wave it sent through the dead man's brain had blown a fist-sized cavity from the back of his skull.

If you can do it, you can look at what you've done. If you don't like what you see, you can stop doing that sort of thing in the future.

For twenty years, Henry Vickers had been able to avoid killing human beings. God willing, he could go at least another twenty years before he *chose* to do it again. It's always a choice.

Tom O'Neill lay in the box of the white truck, trussed like a chicken with a piece of his own shirt stuffed in his mouth to gag him. A good thing Louise had seen O'Neill from the air; otherwise he might have lain in the truck till the Sun cooked him.

Vickers pulled the gag out before cutting the wrist and ankle ropes with his folding knife. Blood from the guards, already blackening as it dried, dappled O'Neill. The Javans had hurtled off the other side of the truck box.

"Vickers, they killed Louise!" O'Neill blurted between gasping breaths. "The bastards shot her, *shot* her!"

"Don't squirm or I'll cut you," Vickers said. "Louise is all right. Maybe a bit shaken."

"She's . . ." O'Neill said on a rising note of question. "Oh, thank God." Then he added, "Vickers? I saw them right here in broad daylight. They're not ghosts or dreams, they're *real.*"

"I saw them too," Vickers said. He cut the last cord. "They don't mean any harm. I guess in their terms, what happened in the forest was just the cost of doing business. There isn't always time for mercy."

Nikisastro's henchmen had pulled the nylon rope almost tourniquet tight. Though, from their standpoint, O'Neill was probably lucky they hadn't shot him out of hand when he landed in the middle of the operation to harangue them.

Vickers looked around at the strip of road through what had been virgin forest. For the first time, he *saw* the devastation logging caused. Louise was walking cautiously toward the pickup.

"Maybe they are ghosts," Vickers said softly. "Wherever it is they come from sure as hell isn't worth having. I think they're trying to keep other places from going the same way."

O'Neill pulled himself into a sitting position, using his elbows because his hands wouldn't grip properly. He clenched and opened his fists, working life back into his fingers. "Louise," he said, "what do we do now?"

"Now," Vickers interrupted, "we use a bulldozer and log chains to drag your tyrannosaurus into a cargo sling. Louise says you can fly anything, O'Neill. Can you fly that blimp over there?"

"The aerostat?" O'Neill said, following the direction of Vickers' nod. He interlaced his fingers and bent them outward against the opposite hands. The rope marks stood out red and raw, but the blood supply hadn't been cut off long enough to do nerve damage. "Yeah, I can do that. So we fly the tyrannosaur back to the compound?"

O'Neill stood up in the truck box. He swayed slightly but kept his balance.

"That's right," Vickers agreed. "Louise, let's get going. I've driven a Cat, but it'll take more than one set of hands with the log chain."

"Are you sure they're going to let us borrow their aerostat, Henry?" Louise asked as she fell into step alongside Vickers, headed toward the idling bulldozer.

"Oh, I don't think that'll be a problem," Vickers said, his tone as thin as a knife edge. He stripped the partial magazine from his Garand and replaced it with a full one. He carried the weapon in his hands instead of reslinging it.

"The other thing I want you to do . . ." he added, his voice human again, "is to dump the last hour of data from your floater's link to the world media. There's no way to cover up about the tyrannosaur now, so don't even try. When everybody's evening news is full of a dinosaur in the middle of Borneo, there'll be so many

Western reporters around here that your Javan friends won't *dare* play games."

Vickers set one foot on the bulldozer's bogey coupler, paused, and swung himself up into the cab. He'd be fine so long as he didn't overdraw on his slight remaining reserves of strength.

Behind him, Louise sucked in her breath with a sharp hiss. "Henry," she said. *"Henry."*

He turned, the rifle's butt rising smoothly toward his shoulder; then he relaxed. The three slender humanoids hung in ruddy light above the comatose tyrannosaur. Their slim-boned left arms lifted together.

"It's all right, Louise," Vickers said. "They're just waving goodbye."

CALIBRATION RUN

The sabertooth sprang from cover just as Vickers bent to pick up the partridge he had shot. Holgar Nilson had been dynamiting rock samples a hundred yards away. He shouted as he leveled his Mauser. The blond Nilson would have had an easy shot—except that Vickers' own body blocked the Mauser's line of fire.

The thud of the cat's paws crossing to leap again warned Vickers an instant in advance of Nilson's cry. The sandy-haired guide was holding his shotgun at the balance, not ready to fire—and not that birdshot would have affected the 500-pound killer.

The cat swung down its lower jaw, locking out of the way everything extraneous to stabbing with its six-inch upper canines, as it made its third and final leap. Its bared palate was white as bone.

Vickers flung himself backwards, trying desperately to raise the shotgun. The sabertooth's hide was mottled brown on black, its belly cream. As it sprang, its forelegs splayed and the ten black claws shot out of the pads. Every tense muscle of the cat's body quivered in the air. Its weight slammed Vickers' torso against the stony ground while the blast of Nilson's rifle rumbled about them.

The cat's eyes were a hand's breadth from Vickers' face as they glazed and the life went out of them. A shudder arched the creature's back, rocking the serrated fangs downward. Vickers screamed but the points were not piercing his chest, only compressing it, and the thrust itself was a dying reflex. Blood had been spurting from the cat's throat where the Brenneke bullet had entered. Now the nostrils drooled blood as well and the cat's muscles went limp.

Holgar Nilson ran to the linked bodies, cursing in Norwegian. Vickers could not breathe. The carcass sagged over him like a bag of rice, pinning him so tightly that he could not move his index finger enough to put the shotgun on safe. The weapon was pressing against his right leg. It would blow his foot off if it fired now. Nilson tugged at the sabertooth ineffectively, his panic little less than that of his partner trapped under the cat. The big Norwegian was waving his Mauser one-handed while his eyes scanned the brush in quick arcs. "There was another one," he gasped, "the male. But it ran off when I fired."

"Here, let me help," said Linda Weil, dropping the first-aid kit to seize one of the sabertooth's fangs. The curved inner edges of the teeth could shear flesh with all the cat's brutal strength behind them, but they did not approximate real knife blades. In any case, the fangs were the only handholds available on the slack carcass. Weil was a short, broad-hipped woman. She twisted, using the thrust of her legs against the passive weight of the sabertooth. The great brown-and-black body slumped away fluidly; its haunches still covered Vickers' calves. Nilson stopped groping blindly and looked down. He gripped a clawed foot and rotated the cat's hindquarters away from his partner.

Vickers was sucking deep breaths. His face and tunic front were covered with blood. He put the shotgun on safe and cocked an arm behind him to help him rise.

"No, no," said the dark-haired woman, touching the guide's shoulder with a restraining hand. "Just wait—"

Vickers lurched upright into a sitting position. "I'm all right," he wheezed. Then, "It was my fault. It was all my fault."

"The buckle," said Nilson. "Look at your pack buckle." The Norwegian's composure was returning. His left index finger touched one strap of the pack Vickers had been wearing to hold small specimens. The steel buckle was warped like foil against its padding where it had blocked the thrust of the sabertooth's fang. The brushing contact of Nilson's finger caused pain to stab Vickers.

"Damn," muttered the older guide as Linda Weil helped him off with the empty pack and unbuttoned his tunic. The blood that sprayed Vickers was the cat's, but he knew from the pain that he might well have a cracked rib of his own. The female paleontologist's fingers were cool and expert. She had been chosen as an on-site investigator for the Time Intrusion Project as much for her three years of medical school as for her excellent series of digs in the Sinai with a University of Chicago team.

A square mark larger than the buckle's edges was stamped in white above Vickers' left nipple. "I don't hear anything grating," Weil said. "We'll strap it. Maybe when we get back to Tel Aviv they'll want to drain the hematoma."

"It was waiting for me like I was a goddamn antelope," Vickers said. He was a stocky man of thirty-five who usually looked as calm as a fireplug. Now he rubbed the back of his hand over the sockets of his pale eyes, smearing the splotches of tacky blood. "Holgar," he said, "I wasn't ready. I wouldn't have had a snowball's chance in hell except for you."

"Holgar, we'll want the skull and limbs of this macheirodont when you have a chance," said Linda Weil, pointing toward the sabertooth as she stood. She looked back at Vickers before she continued, "And frankly, I think that if anyone's error can be said to have led to this—problem, near disaster—it was mine. Both of you are used to animals that've had hundreds of thousands of years to learn to fear man. That's not the case here. As you said, Henry, we're just meat on the hoof so far as the bigger carnivores here are concerned. *I'm* the one who should have realized that."

Vickers sighed and stood up carefully. He walked over to the spur-legged partridge, ten feet away where he had dropped it when the cat struck. Raising the heavy bird, he gestured with it to Weil. "It's a francolin like the one we got in the snare two days ago," he said. "I thought I'd roast it for dinner instead of keeping it for a specimen."

The dark-haired paleontologist nodded back. "After I get you bandaged," she agreed. "I think we could all do with a meal and a chance to relax."

* * *

Hyenas had already begun to call in the sullen dusk. Time spent in the African bush gave the ugly, rhythmic laughter a homely sound to the pair of guides, but Linda Weil shuddered with distaste.

Holgar Nilson laughed. He patted the paleontologist on the thigh with a greasy hand. "They are only predators like ourselves," he said. "Perhaps we should invite them to join us for dinner one night, yes? We have so much in common."

Weil switched the francolin drumstick to her left hand and squeezed Nilson against her thigh with her right. "I don't question their right to exist," the woman said. "It's just that I don't like them." She frowned, scientist again. "We could use a specimen, though. There's a good enough series of hyena fossils known Topside that fresh examples ought to be more datable than most of what we've gathered."

"You know," said Vickers, speaking in a conscious effort to break out of the shell of depression that surrounded him, "I've never quite understood what use the specimens we bring back were going to be. For dating, that is. I mean, taking radiation levels from the igneous rocks should give them the time within a few thousand years. And if I understand the Zeiss—" he gestured with his thumb— "its photographs ought to be down to the minute when they're compared to computer models of star and planet positions."

The 200mm reflector bolted to the intrusion vehicle was lost in the darkness, as was the normal purr of the motor drive that rotated it by microns along the plane of the ecliptic. As Vickers gestured, the mechanism gave one of its rare clicks, signaling the end of an exposure as the telescope reset itself to lock on another portion of sky. The click might have been that of a grenade arming for the level of response it drew from Holgar Nilson, though the younger guide kept the edges of his anger sheathed in bluff camaraderie. "Come, come," he said, "machines fail. Anyway, the sky could have been overcast for months, for years, for all they knew Topside. And for the rock dating to work, they must compare the samples we bring back with samples from the same rock a million years in the future. How are they to be sure of that, hey? When they only *think* so far we are inserted into the same place, with latitude and longitude changing as the continents move."

Vickers nodded, realizing why his partner reacted so defensively. "Sure," he said, "and the more cross-checks, the better. And I suppose the astronomical data is going to be easier to correlate if they've got a fair notion of where to start."

"Besides," said Linda Weil harshly, "I don't think anyone quite realized how useless anything I came back with would be for the intended purpose. Oh, it'll have use—we've enormously expanded human knowledge of Pliocene life-forms, but as you say, Henry, for dating—"

She paused, looking out over the twilit hills. They had been fortunate in that their intrusion vehicle, an angular block of plates and girders, had been inserted onto high ground. During daylight they had a good view over the brush and acacias, the short grass and the beasts that lived there. Now the shadows of the trees and outcrops had merged with the greater shadow of the horizon, and the landscape was melding into a velvet blur. "The whole problem," Weil said toward the darkness, "is that we've got an embarrassment of riches. Before—when I was Topside—a femur was as much as you were likely to get to identify an animal, and a complete skull was a treasure. We decided what the prehistoric biomass looked like by reconstructing a few fragments here, a few fragments there . . ." She chuckled ruefully and looked back at her male companions. "And here we are, in the middle of thousands and thousands of animals, somewhere in the past I've been studying for years . . . and I'm nowhere near being able to accurately place the time into which we've been inserted, the way I've been hired to do—because I can't swear that a single species is one that we 'know' from fossils. I feel as if I've spent my working life throwing darts at a map and convincing myself that I've travelled to the places the darts hit."

"Well, you've travelled here, for certain," said the blond man, "and I at least am glad of it." He raised his hand to Weil's shoulder and tried to guide the woman closer to him for a kiss.

"Holgar . . ." the woman objected in a low voice, leaning free of the big hand's pressure.

"I'll get a couple hyenas tomorrow," Vickers said morosely. The fire he stared at glinted from his face where grease from the bird smeared him. "Unless I screw up again, at least. Christ, Holgar, maybe I'd have been better off if you were a second slower with your shot. Hunting's about the one thing I'd decided I could handle. If I'm no good for that either, then I may as well be a cat's dinner." Unwatched, the shorter guide's hands turned and turned again the section of francolin ribs from which he had gnawed only half the flesh.

Nilson looked disconcerted. He lowered his hand from the paleontologist's back and resumed attacking his meal. Absently, Vickers wished that one of the three of them had had the skill to make gravy to go with the mashed potatoes, which were freeze-dried and reconstituted.

"Ah, Henry," said Linda Weil, "I think that's just shock talking. You aren't incompetent because of one mistake—it's the mistakes that make us human. The planning for this, this expedition, was mostly yours; and everything's gone very well. Except that all I can really say about the time we're at is that we're a great deal farther back than the round million years they intended to send us."

"You see, Henry," Nilson said, "what you need is a wife." The Norwegian gestured with the fork he had just cleared of its load of canned peas. "You have no calm center to your life. Wherever I go, I know that my Mary is there in Pretoria, my children are growing— Oskar, Olaf, and little Kristin . . . do you see? That is what you need."

Vickers looked at the bigger man. Nilson had jarred him out of his depression as Linda Weil had been unable to do with her encouragement. The paleontologist's complexion was dark, but it was no trick of the firelight that led Vickers to see a blush on her face. She looked down at her hands. "Maybe I've been looking in the wrong places," Vickers said dryly. "Your wife is British, if I remember?"

Nilson nodded vigorously as he chewed another mouthful of peas.

"Both of mine were Americans," the older guide said. "Maybe that's where I went wrong." He turned his face toward the night. His profile was as sharp and thin as a half-worn knife. "The sporting goods store I tried to manage was in Duluth," he continued, "and the ranch was in Rhodesia. But I could hunt, that I could do. Well." He looked at Weil again. In a normal voice he added, "Well, I still can. I'll get you a hyena in the morning."

"Actually," said Weil, visibly glad of the change of subject, "what concerns me more is that something's raiding our box traps. Several of those to the west had the lids sprung when I checked them this morning. The rest were empty. Probably *was* a hyena; I don't think a mongoose would be strong enough. But apart from being interested in whatever's doing it, I'd like to have the damage stopped."

"We could lay a sensor from the intrusion alarm under one of the traps," Holgar said. His enthusiasm rang a little false. It was a reaction to the embarrassment he finally had realized that his earlier comment had caused. "Sleep close with the shotgun."

"I've got a three-bead night sight on the Garand," Vickers said, the problem reflecting his mind away from the depression that had been smothering him. "I can sandbag the gun and the spotlight a hundred yards away. That ought to be far enough we won't disturb whatever it is." He frowned and turned to Linda Weil. "Thing is, I can't make sure of something at night unless I give it a head shot or use soft points that'll blow the body apart if it's small. What's your preference?"

The paleontologist waved the question away. "Save the skull if you can," she said. "But—we've just seen how dangerous the predators here—now, that is—can be. Are you going to disconnect the warning system around us?"

"Just move one pick-up," Nilson said with a laugh. His left fingertips caressed Weil's cheek playfully. "Otherwise you might get a closer and sooner view of a hyena than you expected, no? And what a waste that would be."

Vickers noticed that his hands were still trembling. Just as well the administrators Topside hadn't permitted any liquor among the supplies, he thought. Though usually it wouldn't have mattered to him one way or the other. "It's all right," he said aloud. "I probably won't be sleeping much tonight anyway. Holgar, let's rig something now while there's still enough daylight to work with."

They were forced to finish moving and resetting the nearest of the traps by lamplight after all. When the door mechanism was cocked and the trigger baited with nuts and fruit, Vickers made his own preparations. His rifle was an Ml Garand, modified by a Marine armorer to accept twenty-round BAR magazines. He rested it on a sand-filled pair of his own trousers, its sights aligned on a point just above the center of the trap. The variable-aperture spotlight was set for a pencil beam and also aimed at the trap. The light should freeze the trap robber long enough for Vickers to put a soft-nosed .30-'06 bullet through its chest.

Around two AM the alarm rang. It was a hyrax which had blundered into the trap in search of the nuts. The Hyracoidea had been driven to holes and the night by the more efficient grazing animals who followed their family's Oligocene peak. The little creature in the trap wiggled its whiskers against the electric glare. Vickers switched off the spotlight, hoping the live bait would bring the robber shortly. But to his own surprise, he managed to fall asleep and it was dawn rather than the intrusion alarm that awakened him the second time.

Vickers' neck was stiff and his feet were cold. A sheen of dew overlay his nylon parka and the fluorocarbon finish of his rifle's metal surfaces. The fire was dead. Hot coffee was the only reason to kindle another fire: the Sun would be comfortably warm in an hour, a hammer in three. But hot coffee was a good enough reason, God knew, and a fire would be the second priority.

The flap of the tent which Linda Weil shared with Nilson opened while Vickers was still wiping the Garand with an oily rag. It was a habit ingrained in the hunter before steel could be protected by space-age polymers. Caring for the rifle which kept him alive was still useful as a ritual even if it were no longer a practical necessity.

"No luck?" asked Weil as she pulled on her jacket in the open air.

"Well, there's a hyrax," Vickers replied. "I guess that's to the good. I was about to put on a pot of—"

The intrusion alarm pinged. The hunter looked by training at the display panel, even though most of the sensor locations encircling the camp were in plain sight in the daytime. The light indicating the trap sensor was pulsing. When Vickers flicked his eyes downhill toward the trap, the paleontologist's breath had already drawn in.

The guide rolled silently into a prone position, laying his rifle back across the makeshift sandbag. He looked over but not through the Garand's sights, and his index finger was not on the trigger. Weil was too unfamiliar with guns to appreciate the niceties which differentiate preparations from imminent slaughter. She snatched at Vickers' shoulder and hissed, "Don't shoot!"

The guide half-turned and touched Weil's lips with the fingertips of his left hand. "Are they chimps?" he mouthed, exaggerated lip movements making up for the near soundlessness of his question. "They don't look quite right."

"They're not chimps," Weil replied as quietly. "My God, they're not."

The tent passed Holgar Nilson with a muted rustle and no other sign. When the intrusion alarm rang, the Norwegian had wasted no time on dressing. Neither of the others looked around. They had set the trap where neither trees nor outcropping rocks interfered with the vantage, and where most of the mesh box itself was clear of the grass. The blade tips brushed the calves of the three beasts around the trap now. They were hairy enough for chimpanzees, and they were only slightly taller than chimps standing on their hind legs; but these creatures stood as a matter of course, and they walked erect instead of knuckling about on their long forearms like apes.

Vickers uncapped his binoculars and focused them. The slight breeze was from the trap toward the humans up the slope. The beasts did not seem to be aware they were being watched. Their attention was directed toward the trap and its contents.

The hyrax was squealing in high-pitched terror now. The top of the trap was hinged and pegged closed so that it could be baited and emptied without reaching through the heavily sprung endgate. The traps that had been raided the day before had simply been torn apart. This one—

The tallest of the—hominids, it didn't mean human, the word was already in all their minds—the tallest of the hominids was a trifle under five feet. His scalp was marked by a streak of blond, almost white, fur that set him apart from his solidly dark companions. He was fumbling at the latch. Without speaking, Vickers handed the binoculars to Linda Weil.

"My God," she whispered. "He's learned to open it."

The hyrax leaped as the lid swung up, but the hominid on that side was too quick. A hand caught the little beast in mid-air and snatched it upward. The hominid's teeth were long and startlingly white against the black lips. They snapped on the hyrax's neck, ending the squeals with a click.

The other black-furred hominid growled audibly and tried to grab the hyrax. The white-flashed leader in the middle struck him with an open hand. As the follower sprang back yelping, the leader turned on the one holding the hyrax. Instead of trying to seize the prey directly as the lesser hominid had done, the leader spread his arms wide and burst into angry chattering. His chest was fully expanded and he gained several inches of height by rising onto the balls of his feet.

The smaller hominid's face was toward the watchers. They saw his teeth bare as he snarled back, but the defiance was momentary and itself accompanied by a cringing away from the leader. He dropped the hyrax as if he had forgotten it, turning sideways as he did so. As if there were something in the empty air, the follower began to snap and chitter while the leader picked up the hyrax. The mime continued until the white-flashed hominid gave a satisfied grunt and began stalking off northward, away from the human camp. The other hominids followed, a few yards to either side of the leader and perhaps a pace behind. The posture of all three was slightly stooped, but they walked without any suggestion of bow-leggedness and their forelimbs did not touch the ground. The leader held the hyrax by its neck. Not even the binoculars could detail the position of the hominid's thumb to the paleontologist.

"That's amazing," said Holgar Nilson. He had dressed while watching the scene around the trap. Now he was lacing his boots. "They didn't simply devour it."

"Not so surprising," Linda Weil said, the binoculars still at her eyes. "After all, there were more traps in the direction they came from. They're probably full." She lowered the glasses. "We've got to follow them."

"Look at the way they quarreled over the coney," Nilson protested. "They're hungry. And it's not natural for hungry animals not to eat a fresh kill."

Vickers eyed the Sun and shrugged off his parka. If they were going to be moving, he could get along without the insulation for the present so as not to have to carry the warm bulk later in the day. "All right," he said, "they seem to be foraging as they go. It shouldn't be too hard to keep up, even without a vehicle."

"They should have sent a Land Rover with us," complained the Norwegian guide as he stood, slinging his Mauser. "We are bound to make some changes in the environment, are we not? So how can they worry that a Land Rover would be more of a risk to the—to Topside?"

"Well, we'll manage for now," Vickers said, stuffing a water bottle and several packets of dehydrated rations into his knapsack. Despite the bandage, it felt as though his chest was being ripped apart when he raised his arm to don the pack. He kept his face still, but beads of sweat glittered suddenly at the edge of his sandy hair. "I think it's as well that we all go together," Vickers added after a moment to catch his breath. "There's nothing here that animals can hurt and we can't replace, and I'm not sure what we may be getting into."

The three hominids were out of sight beyond one of the hills before their pursuers left camp. Both men carried their rifles. The paleontologist had refused the auto-loading shotgun, saying that she didn't know how to use it so it would only be in her way. Weil and the younger guide began pressing ahead at a near run through the rust and green grass. Vickers was more nervously aware than the others of the indigenous predators lurking in these wilds. Aloud he said, "Don't be impatient. They're not moving fast, and if we blunder into them over a rise, we'll spook them sure." Nilson nodded. Linda Weil grimaced, but she too moderated her pace when the guides hung back.

At the looted trap, the paleontologist herself paused. Vickers glanced around for sign, but the ground was too firm to show anything that could be called a footprint. Dark smudges on the otherwise dew-glittering grass led off in the direction the hominids had taken, but that track would stand less than an hour of the Sun's growing weight.

Weil turned from the trap. "What's this?" she demanded, pointing. "Did you bring this here when you set the trap?"

Nilson frowned. "It's just a piece of branch," he said.

"Holgar, there's no tree within fifty yards," said Vickers quietly. To the paleontologist he added, "It was pretty dark when we set up the trap. I probably wouldn't have noticed it anyway. But I didn't see any of the—others—carrying it either. For now, it's just three feet of acacia branch, broken at both ends."

Weil nodded curtly. She uncapped her neck-slung camera and took several exposures of the trap and the branch lying beside it. She did not touch either object. "Let's go," she said and began striding along the dim trail again at almost the pace she had set at the start.

When they crested the next rise, even Vickers felt a momentary concern that they might have lost their quarry. Then he caught the flash of sun on blond fur a quarter-mile away and pointed. They watched through their binoculars as two, then all three hominids moved about the trunk of a large tree.

"They're trying to dig something out of a hole at the root of the tree," Vickers said, "and I'll swear they're using a stick to do it." Then he added, "Of course, a chimpanzee might do the same thing."

"Linda," said Holgar Nilson, "what are these creatures?" He rubbed his forehead with the back of the hand holding his binoculars. His right thumb tensioned the sling of his rifle.

Linda Weil at first gave no sign that she had heard the question. The blond guide's eyes remained fixed on her. At last she lowered her glasses and said, "I suppose that depends on when we are. If we're as far back as preliminary indications suggest we are, those are ramapithecines. Primates ancestral to a number of other primate lines, including our own." She would not meet Nilson's stare.

"They're men, aren't they?" the younger guide demanded.

" 'Men' isn't a technical term!" snapped the paleontologist, raising her chin. "If you mean, 'They belong to the genus Homo,' I'd have to say no, I don't believe they do. Not yet. But we don't have any data." She spun to glare at Vickers. "Do you see?" she went on. "What a, what a laughingstock I'll be if I go back from my first time intrusion and say, 'Well, I've found the earliest men for you, here's a smudgy picture from a mile away'? They drove Dubois into *seclusion* for finding Java Man without an engraved pedigree!"

Vickers shrugged. "Well," he said, "it isn't anything that we need to jump the gun about."

Licking their fingers—the leader still carried the hyrax—the hominids wandered away from the trees again. Weil snapped several photographs, but her camera had only a lens selected for close-ups of animals too large to carry back whole.

The landscape itself was beyond any camera, and the profusion of life awakening with the dawn was incredible. Vickers had been raised on stories of the great days of African hunting, but not even Africa before the advent of nitro powders and jacketed bullets could equal the animate mass that now covered what someday would be Israel. Standing belly-deep in the grass they cropped were several species of hipparion, three-toed horses whose heads looked big for their stocky bodies. The smallest of them bore black-and-white stripes horizontally on their haunches. When the stripes caught sunlight at the correct angle, the beasts stood out as candid blazes. The horses were clumped in bodies of twenty to forty, each body separated from the others by a few hundred yards. These agglomerations could not be called herds in the normal sense, for they mixed hipparions of distinctly different sizes and coloration.

Indeed, antelopes of many varieties were blended promiscuously among the hipparions as well. Vickers had vaguely expected to see bovids with multiple, fanciful horns during the intrusion. Linda Weil had disabused him with a snort. She followed the snort with a brief disquisition on the Eurasian Cenozoic and the ways it could be expected to differ from the North American habitat which the popularizers were fonder of describing.

Oryx had proven to be the most common genus of antelope in the immediate area, though the region was better-watered than those Topside which the curved-horned antelopes frequented. There were other unexpected antelopes also. On the first day of the intrusion, Nilson had shot a tragelaphine which seemed to Vickers to differ from the rare inyala of Mozambique only in its habits: the lyre-horned buck had stared at the rifle in bland indifference instead of flashing away as if stung.

The hominids were moving on; the human trio followed. Weil

was leading as before but Holgar Nilson had begun to hang back. Vickers glanced at the younger man but did not speak. In the near distance, a buffalo bellowed. The guides had scouted the reed-choked bottom a mile away, beyond another range of undulations, but they had not actively hunted it yet. Earlier, the dark-haired paleontologist had commented that a sampling of bovine skulls and horn-cores might be helpful in calibrating their intrusion. Vickers nodded toward the sound. "On our way back," he suggested, "if it's late enough that the buffs have come back out of the reeds after their siesta, we might try to nail you some specimens."

"For God's sake, let's not worry about that now!" snapped Weil. She stumbled on a lump of exposed quartz which her eyes, focused on the meandering hominids, had missed. Vickers had guided tourist hunters for too many years to think that he had to respond.

The clumps of grazing animals seemed to drift aside as the hominids straggled past, but the relative movement was no more evidently hostile than that of pedestrians on a crowded street. Still, when one of the hominids passed within a few yards of a group resting under a tree, up started a 400-pound antelope of a genus with which Vickers was not familiar. After a hundred yards, the antelope turned and lowered its short, thick-based horns before finally subsiding beneath another tree. A jackal might have aroused the same reaction.

The hominids had skewed their course twice and were now headed distinctly southward, though they still gave no evidence of purpose. "Reached the end of their range and going back," Holgar Nilson said. He spoke in a tone of professional appraisal, normal under the circumstances, and not the edged breathiness with which he had earlier questioned the paleontologist. "Do we still follow them?"

Linda Weil nodded, subdued herself by embarrassment over her outbursts at the two guides. "Yes, but I want to see what they were doing at the base of this tree first," she said, nodding toward the acacia ten yards away. She unlimbered her camera in anticipation.

Vickers stopped her by touching her elbow. "I think we can guess," he said quietly, "and I think we'd better guess from here. Those bees look pretty peeved."

"Ah," Weil agreed. The dots flashing metallically as they circled in and out of the shade crystallized in her mind into a score or more of yellow-bodied insects. Fresh dirt of a pale reddish tinge had been turned between a pair of surface roots. The stick that had done the digging was still in the hole. Up and down it crawled more of the angry bees. "Surely they aren't immune to bee stings, are they?" the woman asked.

Vickers shrugged, wincing at the pressure in his chest. "I'm not immune to thorn scratches," he said. "But if I'm after an animal in heavy brush, that's part of the cost of doing business."

The hominids were almost out of sight again. "We'd best keep going," said the paleontologist, acting as she spoke.

While they walked uphill again, Vickers swigged water and handed his bottle around. The water was already hot from the sun on his dun knapsack, and the halogens with which it had been cleared gave it an unpleasant tang. Neither of Vickers' companions bothered to comment on the fact.

"This is where we got the horses two days ago," Nilson said, gesturing toward the low ridge they were approaching.

Vickers thought back. "Right," he said. "We got here due west from the bottom of the trap line. We've just closed the circuit in the other direction, is all."

They heard the growling even before they crested the rise. Nilson unslung his Mauser. Vickers touched Linda Weil to halt her. He knelt to charge his Garand, using the slope of the ground to deflect the sound of the bolt slapping the breech as it chambered the first round of twenty. The paleontologist's face was as tense as those of the guides. "All right," Vickers whispered, "but we'll keep low."

In a swale a quarter mile from their present vantage point, Vickers had dropped a male hipparion. It was large for its genus; a good 400 pounds had remained to the carcass after the hunters had removed the head and two legs for identification. Hyenas are carnivores no less active than the cats with which they share their ranges, but virtually no carnivore will refuse what carrion comes its way. A pack of hyenas had found the dead horse. They were still there, wrangling over scraps of flesh and the uncracked bones, as the hominids approached the kill.

The snarls that the intrusion team heard were the warning with which the hyenas greeted the newcomers.

"We've got to help them," said Nilson.

Vickers glanced at the junior guide out of the corner of his eye. He was shocked to see that Nilson was watching over his electronic sight instead of through his binoculars. "Hey, put that down!" Vickers said. "Christ, shooting now'd screw up everything."

"They'll be killed!" the Norwegian retorted, as if that were an answer.

"They know what they're doing a whole lot better than we do," Vickers said, and at least on that the men could agree.

There were six of the shaggy carnivores. Two of them paced between the remains of the hipparion and the hominids who gingerly approached it. "I'd have thought they'd be denned up this time of day," Vickers muttered. "When you don't know the animal, its habits don't surprise you . . . But those'd pass for spotted hyenas Topside without a word. Damned big ones, too. They ought to act like the hyenas we know."

At the distance and through the foreshortening of the binoculars, it was impossible to tell for certain how near the hominids had come to the kill. The foremost of the brindled hyenas was surely no more than twenty feet from the hominid leader. The carnivore turned face-on and growled, showing teeth that splintered bones and a neck swollen with muscles like a lion's. Holgar Nilson gasped. His hand sought again the pistol grip of his slung rifle.

The white-flashed hominid jabbered shrilly. He squatted down. The hyrax was still clutched in his left hand, but with his right he began to sling handfuls of dirt and pebbles at the hyena. To either side, the other hominids were also chattering and leaping stiff-legged. One hominid held a rock in each hand and was clashing them together at the top of each jump.

The pelted hyena only snarled back. Its nearest companion retreated a few paces to the scattered carcass, its brushy tail lifted as if to make up for the weakness of the sloping hindquarters. The other four members of the pack were lying on their bellies in a loose arc behind the hipparion. One of them got to its feet nervously.

The empty-handed hominid suddenly darted toward the carcass. He almost touched the ribs, streaked white and dark red with the flesh still articulating them. The nearest hyena leaped up snapping. Its jaw thumped the air as if a book had been slammed. The hominid jumped sideways with a shriek to avoid the teeth, then cut to the other side as the foremost hyena rushed him from behind. Sprinting, the hominid retreated to his starting position with the snarling hyena behind him.

The hominid doubled in back of his leader, still squealing. The carnivore skidded to a halt. The white-flashed leader had dropped the hyrax at last. He hunched with his head thrown forward and his arms spread like a Sumo wrestler's. Each hand was bunched around a heavy stone, held in a power grip between the palm and the four fingers. Unnoticed by the watching humans, the leader had prepared for this moment. The angle hid the hominid's bared teeth from the watchers, but his hissing snarl carried back to them on the breeze.

Only the one hyena had followed through on its rush; now it faced the three hominids alone. Snarling again to show teeth as large as the first joint of a man's thumb, the carnivore backed away. The white-furred hominid hurled a rock that thumped the hyena in the ribs. The beast snapped and snarled, but it would neither attack nor leave its position between the carcass and the hominids. Its powerful shoulders remained turned toward its opponents while its hind legs sidled back and forth nervously, displaying first one spotted flank and then the other to the watching humans. Making as much noise as a flock of starlings, the hominids also retreated. At a safe distance from the hipparion carcass and its protectors, they turned and resumed their leisurely meander southward. The hominid with the pair of stones continued to strike them together occasionally, though without the earlier savage insistence. Chips spilled from the dense quartz glinted like sparks in the air.

Holgar Nilson let out his breath slowly. Linda Weil lowered her binoculars and said, "Holgar, what's gotten into you? I *know* why *I'm* so tense."

The Norwegian scowled. Vickers glanced at him and then raised his glasses again. He did not know how personal the conversation was about to become. "I—" said the blond man. Then, "Hyenas are terrible killers. I've seen what they can do to children and even to a grown man who'd broken his leg in the bush."

"Well, we're here as observers, aren't we?" said the paleontologist. "I don't understand."

Nilson turned away from her gaze and did not reply. The woman shrugged. "We need to be moving on," she said. Her face, like that of the younger guide, was troubled.

The hyenas had disappeared back into shallow burrows they had dug around the site of the kill. The humans skirted them at a distance, knowing that another outburst might call the hominids back from the rise over which they had disappeared. "Sort of a shame not to bag one now when we know where they are," Vickers said regretfully as he glanced toward the hipparion. The ribs stood up like a beacon. "I'd expected to be stuck with a night shot . . . and nobody's as good in the dark, I don't care what his equipment is." Neither of the others made any response.

No unusual noise gave warning as the intrusion team neared the next crest, but Holgar Nilson halted them with a raised hand anyway. "They turned their direction to go where they knew carrion was, the horse carcass," he said. The senior guide nodded, pleased to hear his partner use his flawless sense of direction. "But if they are making a large circle, so to speak, and they have been looting our traps west of the camp, then we must be close to where they started."

Nilson's logic was good; all three made the obvious response. Both men tautened their rifle and binocular straps and got down on their hands and knees. Since the grass was thick and over a foot high, there was no need to go into a true low crawl with their weapons laid across crooked elbows. The paleontologist looked dubious, but she followed suit. Her camera finally had to be tucked into the waistband of her trousers. The ground, prickly with grass spikes and flakes of stone, slowed their progress more than did concern over security.

The hominid camp was in a clump of acacias less than 200 yards down the next slope.

"Oh, the Lord have mercy," whispered Nilson in Norwegian as his eyes adjusted to the pool of shade on which he focused his binoculars. It was hard to tell how many of the hominids were present; anything from a dozen to twenty was possible. Clumps of grass, shadows, and the emerald globes of young acacias interfered with visibility. The three hominids which the intrusion team had been following were standing. The white-flashed leader himself was the center of a clamoring mass of females and infants. Vickers noted that although many hands were stretched out toward the leader and the prey he carried, neither was actually touched by the suppliants.

Much of the confusion died down after a few minutes. The small hominids made way or were elbowed aside by additional males. Their external genitalia were obvious, though the flat dugs of the females were hidden by their fur. Most of the males were empty-handed, but one of them was dragging forward what could only be the femur of a sivatherium. The bone was too massive even for the molars of the great hyenas; in time it would have been gnawed away by rodents, but nothing of a size to matter would have disputed its possession with the hominids. Vickers frowned, trying to imagine what the latter with the relatively small jaws expected to do with a bone which was beyond the range of hyenas and the big cats.

But the troop's first order of business was the hyrax. It provided a demonstration that the jaws and limbs of the hominids were by no means despicable themselves. The leader gripped the little animal with his teeth and systematically plucked it apart with his hands. One of the males reached in for a piece. The leader cuffed him away and dropped the hyrax long enough to jabber a stream of obvious abuse at the usurper. With something approaching ceremony, the leader then handed the fleshy hind legs to two males. Despite the confusion, Vickers was sure that at least one of them had been a companion of the leader during the morning's circuit.

Dignity satisfied, the white-flashed hominid continued parceling out the hyrax. The leader's motions were precise; each twist or slash of nails that still resembled claws stripped away another fragment. As each hominid received a portion, he or she—a foreleg had gone early to a dun-furred nursing mother—stepped back out of the ruck. There was some squabbling as members of the troop bolted their allotments, but Vickers did not notice anyone's share actually hijacked.

"Nineteen with him," Linda Weil counted aloud as the leader stood alone in the widened circle of his juniors. Every member of the troop—Vickers found he had an uneasy tendency to think 'tribe'—every member of the troop had been given a portion of the hyrax. The leader held only the head and a bloody tendril of hide still clinging to it. With a croak of triumph the leader bent and picked up the lump of quartz he had carried since the encounter with the hyenas. He rotated the hyrax head awkwardly with his thumb, then brought his two hands together with a resounding *smack.* Dropping the stone again, the leader began to slurp the brains greedily.

"Goddamn it, you know they're men," Holgar Nilson whispered hoarsely.

"It's nothing more than sea otters do," the paleontologist replied, but she kept the glasses to her eyes and would not face her lover.

Vickers looked from the one to the other, Weil tense, Nilson angry. "I don't think otters share out meat like that," Vickers said. "I don't think I've ever seen animals share out meat that well. Maybe wolves do." He paused before adding, "That doesn't mean they're not animals."

The hyrax was a memory, though a memory that had provided each hominid with a good four ounces of flesh in addition to whatever protein individuals might have scavenged for themselves during the morning. Now the females were bringing out the results of their own gathering: roots and probably locust pods, though it was hard to be sure through the binoculars. Females appeared to be approaching males one on one, though the distinguishing marks of most hominids were too subtle for immediate certainty. The dun-colored mother and an adolescent female whose pelt was a similar shade stood to either side of the leader, cooing and attempting to groom his fur as they offered tubers of some kind.

But the males had not completed their own program as yet. The leader barked something which must have been more in the line of permission than a command. Two of the males responded almost before the syllable was complete, squatting down and chopping furiously with rocks gripped in either fist.

"I can't see them!" Linda Weil said.

Vickers looked at her. Grass blurred all but the heads and flailing arms of the squatting hominids. The *crack!* of stone on bone denser than teak ricocheted up to the watchers. "Ah, they're breaking up the giraffe thigh with rocks," the guide said.

"I know that!" snapped the paleontologist. "Of course they are! And I can't see it!"

Long flakes of bone were spitting upward, catching stray darts of sunlight that made them momentary jewels. The remaining hominids surrounded the activity in a chattering circle, the nuts and tubers forgotten. Occasionally one of the onlookers might snatch at a splinter of bone which would quickly be cast aside again after a perfunctory mumbling.

Linda Weil stood up, holding her camera.

The motion drew the eyes of one hominid. His chirp focused every head in the troop. It was the minuscule whirr of the camera that set off the explosion, however. The hominids fanned forward like a rifle platoon, the half-dozen adult males serried out in front while the young and females filled the interstices a pace or two behind. Even at a distance, their racket was considerable. Each throat was snarling out a single, repetitive syllable as loudly as the lungs beneath could drive it. Some of the females threw handfuls of dirt. It pelted the backs of the males, only the wind-blown dust carrying any considerable distance toward the humans.

The males were not throwing anything. For a further icy instant, Vickers studied their hands through the binoculars. Then he dropped the glasses onto their strap and unslung his Garand. One or both fists of each male hominid bulged with a block of stone. The whole troop was beginning to advance.

"Holgar," Vickers said without taking his eyes off the hominids, "you and Miss Weil strike for camp right now. I'm going to follow just as quick as it's safe. *Right now!*"

Both Nilson and the paleontologist turned to speak, so it was the senior guide alone who saw the rush of the sabertooth from the instant it burst from cover. Dirt flew as the cat's paws hit, its legs doubling under as its spine flexed to fire it along on another leap. In motion, the sabertooth's mottled body looked so large that it was incredible that it could have sheltered behind the small acacia from which it had sprung. Even more amazing was the fact that it had reached the acacia, for the grass to a considerable distance in every direction seemed sparse and featureless.

Despite their noise and apparent concentration, the hominids saw the sabertooth almost as quickly as Vickers did. They had reacted to the humans as if to a territorial challenge; the response evoked by the big cat was one of blind panic. The orchestrated threats dissolved into patternless shrieking. The individual hominids, even the leader, blasted away like shot from a cylinder bore.

The sabertooth was only a leap from its victim, the dun mother. Nothing the troop could have done at that point would have made the least difference.

Nilson's Mauser was fitted with an electronic-bead sight, awesomely fast for a shooter trained in its use. The rifle was up and on and as suddenly wrestled away as Linda Weil lunged at it. "No!" the paleontologist shouted, "No! *Don't—*"

The dun hominid knew she had been chosen. She plucked off the infant which clung to her with all the strength of its tiny arms. The nearest member of the troop was the adolescent female, possibly an older daughter. To her, poised between love and terror ten feet away, the mother hurled her infant. Then, at the last possible moment, the mother cut against the grain of the charge with an agility that could scarcely have been bettered.

It was not enough. The machairodont twisted. It was unable to flesh its teeth as it intended, but its splayed forepaws commanded a swath six feet broad. The right paw smacked the hominid in the middle of the chest. Four of the five claws hooked solidly and spun the light hominid into the path along which the killer's momentum carried it. The jaws crunched closed. One of the long canines stabbed through a shoulder blade to bulge the dimple at the base of the victim's throat.

The surviving hominids had regrouped and were scampering away westward like wind-scud. Vickers retrieved his binoculars. The adolescent had already passed her burden onto an adult female without an infant of her own. The males were bringing up the rear of the troop, but the looks they cast over their shoulders as they retreated were more anxious than threatening. The leader still carried the block of quartz he had found near the hyenas. All the rest had dropped their weapons in the panic. The leader continued to call out, his voice a harsh lash driving the troop. Behind them, the sabertooth had begun to feast noisily.

"If you'd've shot," Linda Weil was shouting, "it'd be the last time they'd let us get within a mile of them! They're *smart,* I tell you. Smart enough to connect a noise we make with things falling dead!"

The big Norwegian had wrenched away his rifle too late to shoot to any purpose. He stood with the Mauser waist high, half-shielded by his body as if he expected the paleontologist to snatch at the weapon again. "It's all right for *you* to frighten them!" the guide shouted back. "When I want to save their lives, what then? You scream, you prevent me! Look at that—" he waved toward the blood-splashed grass beneath the acacias, the muzzle of his rifle quivering as he released the fore-end to gesture. "That could be the end of our race down there!"

After a quick glance at his companions, Vickers had resumed giving his attention to the scene focused in his glasses. Neither of the humans appeared to be immediately dangerous, and the big cat certainly was. It was ripping its prey apart by mouthfuls, pulling against stiff forelegs which pinned the small carcass to the ground. The hominid's bones affected the killer no more than a sardine's bones affect a hungry human. The cat was obviously aware of the humans watching it, but for the moment it had food and did not feel threatened.

"We aren't here to save animals," Weil said, pitching her voice normally in contrast to the shouts she had exchanged with Nilson a few moments before. "We're here to observe them. Those, ah, primates reacted to me as they would to another troop of primates— display, threats—warnings, that's all. They'll continue to let me come close enough to observe. But if you'd shot, from then on they'd have reacted to us the way they did to the machairodont—and I damned well doubt any of us can stalk the way that cat did!"

Holgar Nilson's face was red beneath his hat brim. He turned and spat, knocking dust from the heads of brazen oat-grass. "Observe?" he said. "Meddle! You're going to meddle us all out of existence!"

"It's already been a pretty long day, as early as we started," Vickers suggested with what was for him unusual diplomacy. "I think we've seen about all we're going to see today . . . and if we're going to discuss it, I'd rather it was after a meal and coffee. A lot of coffee."

Vickers led his sullen companions back past the looted trapline. He was not sure whether either of the others noticed that three of the traps were still set, even though the tops of all of them had been unlatched. Since the bait was still there, it meant that the hominids had opened the traps purely for fun.

"All right," said Holgar Nilson. "I'll tell you just what's bothering me." The blond man's concern had not affected his appetite. He gestured with the remnants of his hipparion chop, an experiment which the others were willing to call a failure. "You play games with me with words, but these *are* men we've found. What I am saying is, what if these are the only ones? What if we do something that gets them all killed? Like we did this morning, drawing their attention to something that shouldn't be in this, in this time at all so that they don't see the tiger waiting to kill them!"

Weil raised her hands in frustration. "I couldn't guess within a million years what time we've been inserted into, Holgar," she said. "You know that. The chances of us being landed on exactly the right time and place to find the absolutely earliest individuals who could be called human—that's absurd! Now, I'm not saying the troop we've observed isn't typical of the earliest, well . . . men."

Vickers swallowed the bite of coarse, musky hipparion flesh he had been chewing for some time. "That's fine, what you say about likelihood," he said quietly. "But I suppose there had to be a first some time. It's an open secret, in the Project at least, that the reason some of the brass Topside is so excited about time intrusion is the chance that it *will* turn out to be possible to change the past."

"You're both still looking for the missing link!" the paleontologist said with more acid than she had intended to show. "There isn't any such thing, isn't, wasn't, whatever. There were at least three primate stocks we know about that could have and would have become Homo sapiens in time. One of them did—and both the others, Australopithecus and Homo habilis, so called, were thought to have been direct ancestors during your lifetime and mine. They could have been, they were that close; and if it weren't for competition from our own stock, one or the other of them would certainly have evolved into a higher hominid that you couldn't tell from your next-door neighbor."

The younger guide's face was still as a death mask. "That's all very well," he said, "but would they *be* my next-door neighbor? Would they *be* my wife, my children? Will there be my farm in the Transvaal as I left it if we upset the—the past that all that grows from? This cosmic viewpoint is very scientific, no doubt, but *I* at least am human!"

Linda Weil swallowed with difficulty though her mouth held nothing but saliva. "I—" she said. Then, "Holgar, don't let's talk about this now. I can see you're upset and I . . . I'm upset also. This is . . . this is a very big opportunity for me. I shiver when I think how big an opportunity it is."

Nilson looked at her silently, then tossed the rib bone toward the coals. Ash spurted and the rib spun off into the grass beyond. "I'm going to shoot a hyena," the guide said, wiping grease from his hands on the grass. He gripped his Mauser and stood. They had been eating as they always did, beneath a nylon fly. Sunlight now bisected the tall man diagonally. "Or perhaps you want as many as possible carnivores left alive, now, to kill men?"

Weil's forehead scrunched up, but she would not call to the Norwegian as he walked away. Vickers said, "Look, Holgar, hang on a moment and I'll—"

Nilson's head spun around. "No, thank you!" he said. "I will take no risks—we are both aware of how dangerous the land is now, are we not? But I will do this thing alone, thank you."

Vickers shrugged. Technically the younger man was his subordinate, but they were several million years from any further chain of command. Vickers' own bad experience the day before did not make Nilson's proposal unreasonable. Only the situation was unreasonable, and that wasn't something Vickers could help the Norwegian with. "All right," he said, "but call in every half-hour on the radio."

The blond man nodded but did not turn around again as he stalked off.

Linda Weil cursed in a dull voice. She looked at the forkful of meat she was holding and put it down again. "Vickers," she said, then paused to clear her throat. "Ah, Henry, I'll need a specimen of these primates before we go back."

The guide met her eyes while continuing to chew. "Tell you the truth," he said, "I don't know that I'm ready to shoot anything quite that, ah, anthropoid, without a good reason. What do you need a specimen for?"

"Oh, of course killing one was out of the question," the paleontologist said. Vickers continued to look at her, blinking but not speaking. Touching her tongue to her lips, Weil went on, "The specimens would be for the same purpose as the others that we've gathered, dating . . . We're probably dealing with an advanced ramapithecus. I think that's the safest assumption. But a careful examination of dentition and cranial capacity, plus the knee and pelvic joints in particular, could . . . well, it's—possible—that the primates we've observed could really belong in the genus homo after all. If we knew that, we'd know as much about when we are as those macheirodont specimens, for instance, can tell us. Among other things."

Vickers' face softened in a tired grin. "So in terms of the task I've been sent to aid you in," he said, "you're justified in ordering me to help gather primate specimens. You can burn me with the administration Topside if I start—having qualms the way Holgar seems to be."

The woman scowled and looked away. "I'm not threatening you," she said. "You're not the sort who needs to be threatened to get him to do his job—are you? I'm just pointing out that it *is* your job; that yes, I *am* the one who has final say over what specimens are to be collected. That's why they sent a paleontologist."

"All right," said Vickers, "but if you had a notion of retrieving that sabertooth's kill, you can forget it." He stood up and walked to the edge of the fly, where he could observe the tiny dots that were vultures a thousand feet above the plain.

"Umm?"

"Our friend treated it just like a cat with a field mouse," the guide explained. "Ate the whole head while I watched it. Its mate would likely have done the same thing with me—if it hadn't been for Holgar." He paused. "You might find the knee joints. I wouldn't count on anything much higher up."

"Oh," the paleontologist said, her careful eyes on the guide's back. "Well, to tell the truth, that wasn't really what I had in mind anyway." After a moment, Vickers turned around. Weil continued, "There's nothing we need to know that can't be learned as well or better from X-rays of a living specimen. Without hurting it a bit. All we have to do is carry one back Topside."

"Jesus," said the guide in disbelief. "Jesus Christ." He spread his hands, then closed them and looked away from the dark-haired woman. "Did it ever occur to you," he said, speaking toward the heat-shimmer above the fire, "that Holgar could be right? That we mess up this, this *present,* and when we get back Topside there's nothing there?" He jerked his head back to look at Weil. "Or that what is there is as different from us as baboons are from chimps? Does that bother you?"

"It doesn't bother me," Linda Weil said calmly, "because it's absurd. I'm bothered by the realistic problems of completing my task. That's all."

Vickers smiled again. "That's really all?" he asked, letting his eyes brush Nilson's empty camp stool.

The woman blushed, a dark rush of blood to a face already as tan as Vickers'. "That's neither here nor there!" she said. "Now, how can we capture a specimen?"

"Oh, there's ways," the guide said. He put his hands in his hip pockets and turned away once more. For a moment he whistled snatches of "Blue Water Line" through his teeth. "Yeah, there's ways," he continued, "although it'll be a lot easier if we can get Holgar to cooperate."

"He'll cooperate," Linda Weil said grimly. "I'm going back with my specimen. His choice is whether it comes aboard in a cage or gets packed in sealant like the rest."

"I got two," Nilson said, thumbing toward the bloody tangle on the collapsible sled he was drawing. "A male and a female, I wanted. But when I dressed them out, both were pregnant, so I just left the other with the offal."

Vickers glanced at what was left of the hyena. For specimen purposes and the need to pack it in alone on the titanium sled, Nilson had used a heavy-bladed knife to strip the beast to head, spine, and limbs. The ribs, hide, and the whole abdominal cavity had been abandoned at the kill site as useless; and for that matter, this was about the first use Vickers had heard of for any part of a dead hyena. "Just about impossible to sex a hyena, even after you open them up," he agreed. "I know people to this day who'll swear they're hermaphroditic, that if you shut two males in a cage for a week, one'll change so they can screw." Vickers' eyes, but not the Norwegian's, flickered toward the intrusion vehicle where Linda Weil occupied herself with a microfiche catalog of the Pliocene specimens known Topside.

"Well," said Nilson. He dropped the tow line and walked toward the frame-supported drum which stored their water. It was pumped through a plastic line from the stream a thousand feet east of them. The spigot could be adjusted to dribble sun-heated water in an adequate shower. The younger guide leaned his rifle against the trestle set there for the purpose, out of the splash but in easy reach if occasion demanded it. Vickers nodded in approval. The Mauser chambered powerful 9.3-by-64mm cartridges. Needlessly big for hyena, perhaps . . . but both the hunters were of the school that used what worked for them; and if their tastes were radically different, then they were alike in their scorn for purists who could not hunt without a battery of a dozen guns.

"Ah, Holgar," the senior guide said, knowing that he had to be the one to broach the subject but increasingly uncomfortable with his role, "I think we have to talk about this hominid business."

"I don't want to talk about it," Nilson said, unzipping his filthy trousers and hanging them on the trestle.

"Well, I don't know that I do either," said Vickers, "but I guess that isn't an option." He picked up the sprayer he had filled when Nilson approached the camp. It was Vickers' task to seal the specimen since his partner had done the even messier job of dressing it out. More important, the work gave Vickers something to do with his hands. The stripped carcass was already black with flies, but the sealant would suffocate those it did not drive away. Vickers began to pump. Raising his voice to compensate for distance and the spatter of water, he continued, "While you were getting the hyena, we rigged a net trap down by our water supply. There's a grove of locust trees there, and when we knew what to look for we found plenty of sign that the hominids were gathering pods. Maybe the troop we saw, maybe another one. It's hard to guess what their ranges are."

"We ought to leave them strictly alone," the younger man said distinctly. "We ought to get out of here at once, go back on the intrusion vehicle before we do irreparable harm. If we haven't already done irreparable harm." He twisted off the spigot and stepped barefoot away from the muddy patch under the tank.

Vickers set down the sprayer but did not immediately turn the specimen over to cover the other side. "Yeah," he said. "Well. Look, Holgar, we're not going to hurt anything, we're going to capture one ape to study." The sandy-haired man did not at the moment mention Weil's intention of carrying the specimen back Topside. "You know goddamn well yourself from baboons that we could take a lot more than that on a one-shot basis and you wouldn't be able to tell the difference in five years' time."

Nilson was toweling himself off without speaking. Vickers noticed that Linda Weil, a hundred feet away, was no longer even pretending not to be watching the men from the platform. Sucking on his lips in frustration, Vickers went on, "I cut a section off the end of the drive net we used for small animals. We've got it sprung between a pair of trees and it's command-released so there's no chance of it being tripped by a pig or going off when the hominid we want's in a position to maybe get hurt. But that means that one of us has to be watching it in the morning when the foragers are out."

The younger guide left his bloody, sweat-stained clothes hanging and padded back toward the tent and his footlocker. "Holgar," Vickers said, trying to control the tremor in his voice. His skin prickled on the inside with the dry anger he had not felt since his second wife left him. "I'm talking to you. Don't walk away like that."

The Norwegian turned at the tent flap, rolled up during the day. "You haven't said a thing that touches me, you know," he said. "Not a damned thing."

"The *hell* it doesn't touch you!" the older man shouted back. "Somebody's got to watch the trap, and somebody's got to squire Linda around tomorrow. She wants to poke through their old camp and see if she can locate the new one . . . And that's her *business!* Now, you can do whichever you want, but if you think you're going to pretend you're nowhere around—look, buddy, I wouldn't have to be a lot madder than I am before I'll put a soft-nose through the chest of one of the goddamned animals and get a specimen that way. We've got jobs to do, and sulking like a little kid who didn't get the bike he wanted for Christmas doesn't cut it!"

The bigger man slung his towel to the ground between them as if it were a gage of battle. "That slut up there," he shouted, "she has everything to gain from meddling, does she not? And you—I know you, I've watched you—you have nothing to lose, that's your trouble. But what about me and all the people like me? When we get back Topside, will it be all right for us if everything is the same—except the people all have purple skins and tails?"

"Holgar, you've heard the options," Vickers said in a voice as hard as a gunlock.

"All right, I'll mind the trap!" Nilson stormed. "You didn't really think I'd go off with her, did you?" Still nude, the Norwegian snatched up his sleeping bag in one hand and his foot locker in the other, dragging them out of the tent. "And may God have mercy on your souls!"

"Yeah," said Vickers tiredly. "We all need a little mercy." He walked away from the half-prepared hyena, scanning the horizon. He wished he saw something there that he had an excuse to kill.

* * *

"Will the machairodont still be at the camp site?" Linda Weil whispered in the near darkness.

"Possibly," Vickers said, more concerned with his footing than he was with the question. Early morning had seemed a likely time to observe hominids revisiting their former camp, so the guide and paleontologist had set out as soon as there was enough light to shoot by. "Frankly, I'm a lot more worried that it may be somewhere between here and there."

"Oh," Weil said. Then, "Oh—*that's* what you meant when you said we couldn't leave before you could see to shoot."

The guide looked over his shoulder. "Good lord, yes," he said in amazement. "You didn't think I was planning to shoot one of *them*, did you?"

There was more skylight now than there had been only minutes before. The paleontologist stepped around Vickers and a thorny shrub without pausing. "I don't interfere with the hunting decisions you and Holgar make, you know," she said. "The animals I've worked with all my life are bones that can't hurt you unless you drop them on your foot. Or you let them lead you to an assumption that makes your colleagues say you're a fool—that can hurt too."

"I'd better lead," said Vickers after a glance behind that assured him that the Sun was still below the horizon.

There were several minutes marked by the whispering of grass against leather and the occasional clack of stones slipping under a boot sole. At last the guide said, "That hominid can't have gone more than eighty pounds on the hoof, so to speak. Dressed out, maybe half that . . . and that's counting a lot that that sabertooth eats and you and I wouldn't. Now, I've seen lions gorge forty pounds in a sitting, and they were a lot smaller than our friend. Still, it was a good five days before a lion that full even thinks of moving on . . . All things considered, and assuming that the sabertooth kept eating the way it started yesterday while we watched it, I'd expect to find the fellow snoozing under the trees where it made the kill."

"Oh," said the paleontologist. "Ah, do you think—I'd still rather call them primates—do you think they'll come back even if the machairodont is gone?"

Vickers laughed. "And do I think there's life on Saturn? Look, how would I know?" By using common sense, the right half of his brain told him. It was always easier to plead ignorance, though . . .

"All right," the guide said slowly, "there was nothing permanent about that camp. The troop probably roams the area pretty widely. And they dropped everything when they took off, but everything wasn't—anything, really. We saw some of them carrying rocks, but they were as like as not to drop them. And the roots and such they'd gathered, that wasn't anything they were storing, just a day's supply and as easy to replace as recover. So no, I don't think they'll come back."

Vickers missed Weil's muttered response, but it might have been a curse. "You mean," she said more distinctly, "that the chances are we won't be able to get near the campsite because the cat's still there, and even if the cat's gone, there won't be any real chance of seeing living hominids there again."

"Well, don't worry about the sabertooth," Vickers said, smiling at the term "hominid" which the other had let slip. "I—" his expression sobered. "Look," he went on, "I blew it bad the other day and let that cat almost get me. That doesn't mean I can't nail one if it's sleeping in a place you want to look over."

Weil nodded, though the guide in front of her could not see the gesture. "How is your chest?" she asked.

Vickers shrugged. "It hurts," he said. "That's good. It reminds me how stupid I can be."

They were in sight of their goal now, though the paleontologist did not yet recognize the clump of acacias from this angle. The anvil tops of the trees, forty feet in the air, were already a saturated green in the first light of the Sun. Vickers touched Weil's shoulder and knelt down. The dark-haired woman crouched and studied the scene. At last she recognized the swell of the hill to the right from which they had watched the camp and the kill the day before. "All right," she whispered to the guide. "What do we do now?"

"We wait," said Vickers, uncapping his binoculars, "until I've got a clean shot at that sabertooth or I'm awfully damn sure it's nowhere around." With the lenses just above the thorny shrub between him and the acacias, Vickers studied the blurring gray-on-gray beneath the trees.

Vickers could feel movements all around them. A trio of squabbling finches fluttered into the bush inches away from his face, then scurried back again without having taken any obvious interest in the humans. The grass moved, sometimes in sympathy with a puff of wind, often without. The landscape was becoming perceptibly brighter, its colors returning as pastel hints of the richness they would have in an hour.

Over a ridge a half-mile south of the humans ambled a family of sivatheres. As they walked, the beasts browsed high among the thorny acacias. The sivatheres were somewhat shorter than the largest of the true giraffes with which Vickers was familiar, but that difference was purely a matter of neck length. The sivatheres were higher at the shoulder and were greatly more massive in build than giraffes Topside. Males and females alike were crowned with a cluster of four skin-covered horns, blunt as chair legs. "You know," whispered the guide as he stared at the graceful, fearless creatures, "I ought to be able to get one of those for you if this doesn't pan out . . ." The stocky man had done his share of trophy-hunting in the past, and the old excitement was back in a rush as he watched the huge animals move.

"Quite unnecessary," retorted Linda Weil. "I've compared their ossicones to those of known species, and there's no correlation. These are a new species and that's no help at all in the question of dating."

Vickers lowered his binoculars. He was conscious of the mechanism that had caused him to suggest the sivatheres as a target. Despite that embarrassment, however, he said, "But it's the pattern of the teeth, not the horns, that's really diagnostic, isn't it? What you mean is, you're more interested in the hominids than you are in doing your job." The woman looked away, then met his eyes silently. "Look," the guide continued, "I tore a strip off Holgar because he wasn't doing his job. But if you're going to pull the same crap yourself in your own way—well, we may as well go back Topside right now."

The guide had not raised his voice, but the iron in it jolted the woman as effectively as a shout could have. She touched Vickers' wrist in a pleading, not sexual fashion. "Henry, this may not be exactly what they sent us here to find," she said, "but I'm certain in my own mind that even the people in the engineering section will be able to see how desperately important it is. A chance through time intrusion to actually *see* which theories of human nature are true, whether our ancestors were as violent as Chakma baboons or as friendly as Capuchin monkeys. This might be a chance to understand for the first time the roots of the political situation that makes the— men in Tel Aviv so anxious to refine time intrusion into a, well, a weapon."

Vickers shook his head. He felt more frustration than disagreement, however. "The men *and women* in Tel Aviv," he corrected. "Well, understanding the roots of their problem is fine, but I suspect that they'd trade it for a way to get a nuke into Berlin around '32." He sighed. "But this isn't getting our job done, is it?" Vickers turned his binoculars onto the acacia grove again.

For a moment, Vickers was in doubt about the dark shape at the base of one of the trees. It could have been a root gnarling blackly about a boulder bared by ages of wind and rain. Then the shape rolled over and there could be no doubt at all that the sabertooth had slept where it killed. Vickers let the binoculars hang gently on their strap and lifted his Garand.

Weil's breath sucked in. It was that, rather than her fingers clamping on his biceps, that caused Vickers to slack the finger pressure that would an instant later have sent a 150-grain bullet cracking downrange. The guide's seated body held the rigid angle of which the rifle was a part, but his eyes slanted left to where the woman was pointing. "I'll be damned," Vickers mouthed. He lowered the butt of his weapon.

The sabertooth lay 200 yards in front of them, a clout shot at a stationary target. But a hominid was quartering toward the acacias from the left, already as close to the trees as he was to the watching humans. The hominid was sauntering with neither haste nor concern, a procedure which seemed both insane and wildly improbable for any creature his size when alone in this habitat. Vickers had the glasses up again. From the hominid's build, from the way his arms hung as he walked . . . from the whorled grain of his fur that counterfeited two shades in a pelt of uniform gray . . . the guide was sure that this hominid was the one that had made the unsuccessful snatch at the carcass in the midst of the hyenas. That hominid had been present when the sabertooth struck—and therefore he could not conceivably be walking toward those murderous jaws in perfect nonchalance.

Weil's camera was whirring. Vickers suspected that she would learn more through her binoculars than through the view finder, but there are people to whom no event is real unless it is frozen. No doubt many of them worked with bones. The hominid was only fifty yards from the sprawling cat. He stopped, scratched his armpit, and began calling out in a sharp voice. He was facing the end-most tree in the grove as if someone were hiding in its branches. Nothing larger than a squirrel could have been concealed among the thorns and sparse foliage.

The sabertooth's wakefulness was indicated not by its movements but by the sudden cessation of all the tiny changes of position a sleeping animal makes. The great head froze; the eyes were apparently closed but might have been watching the hominid through slitted lids. The cat could not have been truly hungry after the meal of the previous day, but neither had the dun female provided so much meat that another kill was inconceivable. The cat grew as still and tense as the mainspring of a cocked revolver.

Vickers made a decision. He started to raise the rifle again. Linda Weil shook her head violently. "No!" she whispered. "It—it's their world. But if none of the other primates are in sight, ah, afterward, kill the machairodont before it has time to damage the specimen."

The guide turned his head back toward the grove with a set expression. He held the Garand an inch short of firing position despite his anger. But they were just animals . . .

The cat charged.

Considered dispassionately, the initial leap was a thing of beauty. The torso which had seemed to be as solid as a boulder was suddenly a blur of fluid motion. Vickers could now understand how he had been so thoroughly surprised by this killer's mate; but the recollection chilled him anew.

The hominid himself was not in the least surprised. That was evident from the way he sprinted away from the cat at almost the instant that the carnivore first moved. There was no way that the hominid could match the sabertooth's acceleration, however. When the forepaws touched the ground the first time, they had covered half the distance separating killer from prey, and when the paws touched the second time—

It was as if the sabertooth had stepped into a mine field, and the mines were alive. Vickers had counted six adult males in the hominid troop. The cat's leap after the first had carried it into the midst of the other five. Sparse as the grass and brush had seemed, it had served to cloak the ambush not only from the humans but also from the sabertooth. Murderously intent on its running prey, the cat's upper canines were bared and its claws were unsheathed to sweep its victim in. A pair of hominids leaped from either side like the jaws of a trap closing. If their own fangs were poor weapons in comparison to those of the 600-pound carnivore, then the blocks of stone they carried in their fists were impressive weapons by any standard. They smashed like sledge hammers, driven by the strength of the long arms.

Whatever might have come of the tumbling kaleidoscope, it should have involved the death of the hominid acting as bait. The cat's paws were spread, certain to catch and rend even if reflex did not also flesh the long fangs an instant later. The bait, the Judas goat, made one last jump that would not have carried him free had not the white-flashed leader risen behind the sabertooth and seized the cat's rigid tail.

The hominid's mass could no more have stopped the flying cat directly than it could have stopped a moving car; but 120 pounds applied to a steering wheel can assuredly affect a car's direction. The cat's hindquarters swung outward with the impact. Mindless as a servo-mechanism, the same instinct that would have spun the cat upright in a fall reacted to counter the torque. The claws twisted away from their target. The sabertooth landed on the ground harmlessly, and the thud of its weight was overlaid by the sharper sound of stones mauling its ribs and skull.

The cat had charged silently. Now it screeched on a rising note and slashed to either side. Hominids sprang away. This was not the blind panic of the previous day. Rather, they were retracting themselves as a rifle's bolt retracts to chamber another round. The leader still gripped the base of the cat's tail, snarling with a fury the more chilling for the fact it was not mindless. When the sabertooth tried to flex double to reach its slender tormentor, the hominid that had acted as bait smashed a rock against the base of the cat's skull.

The sabertooth would have run then, but its left hip joint was only shards of bone. Escape was no longer an option. The cat tried to leap and failed in a flurry of limbs. Hominids piled onto the flailing body. One of the attackers was flung high in the air, slashes on its chest filling with blood even as the creature spun. That was probably the last conscious action the carnivore took. All that Vickers could see for the next several minutes was a montage of stone-tipped arms rising and falling with a mechanical certainty. They made a sound on impact like that of mattocks digging a grave in frozen soil.

"God," whispered the hunter.

Vickers had seen baboons kill a leopard, and he knew of well-enough attested instances of dholes, the red hunting dogs of India, killing tigers that had tried to drive them off their prey. The calculated precision of what he had just watched impressed Vickers in a way that the use of stones as weapons had not, however.

"Oh, I've died and gone to heaven," breathed the paleontologist. "This is incredible. It's just incredible."

Vickers shivered. He peered through his binoculars but kept a firm grip on the rifle with his right hand. He was checking, not wholly consciously, to make sure he could account for all six males of the troop. He had sometimes felt a similar discomfort in baboon country, though never so intense. "I don't think," he said carefully, "that we'd better track, ah, these further today. They're apt to act, ah, unpredictably. Used to be I thought if worst came to worst and they rushed us, one shot'd stop them. Right now, I don't know that would be a good idea."

Weil looked at the guide's thin profile, measuring his mind with her eyes. "All right," she said at last, "we'll go back for now instead of seeing where they"—she nodded—"head. We'll see what Holgar has found. But it all depends on Holgar."

"I hope to God you're right," muttered Vickers as he began the task of backing away without arousing the hominids' attention. They were hooting cheerfully around the machairodont, surely dead by now. The furry arms still rose and fell.

The closest human-sized cover was 200 yards from the locust trees but that was close enough. Nilson had to admit that his senior had done a masterful job of arranging the trap. The section of netting lay flat. Each pair of corner ropes was slanted across the net to a bent branch on the other side. When the trigger peg was pulled out to release the branches, the net would be snatched upward and rolled shut simultaneously—while still under enough unreleased tension to prevent anything within from escaping unaided. The release line itself led to a patch of brush on a rocky outcrop. It would become unbearably hot by ten in the morning, but by then the hominids should have visited the grove if they were coming at all.

Nilson desperately hoped that the troop had completely evacuated the region in the aftermath of the sabertooth's attack.

The Norwegian morosely fingered the handle of doweling around which Vickers had clamped the release line. Anyone else would have used nylon cord for the line; Vickers had disconnected the braided steel cable from the winch to use instead. The nylon could easily have taken the strain, but it would have stretched considerably over the distance when Nilson pulled on it. That could be enough warning to send the hominids scurrying away before the trap released. The steel would require only a single sharp jerk with enough muscle in it to overcome the line's dead weight.

Nilson studied the watercourse through his binoculars, for want of anything better to do at the moment. A half-squadron of hipparions dashed up to the bank, paused, and dashed away again without actually touching the water. The nervous horses were ignored by the score or so of antelopes already drinking. From their size and markings they appeared to be impalas; but if so, the species was different enough from those Topside for the females as well as the males to bear horns. There was no sign of hominids.

The younger guide had considered failing to spring the trap or deliberately botching the operation—perhaps managing to frighten them away permanently without capturing one. But even though this was Holgar Nilson's first expedition with Vickers as his partner, he knew already what result such sabotage would bring. If Vickers found the trap had been released at the wrong time, or that it had not been released when there was sign in the grove that hominids had been present . . . well, the senior guide was accurate out to 500 meters with his Garand. There was not the slightest chance that he would not shoot a hominid if he thought Nilson had tried to call his bluff.

The half-light had become true dawn. Even the gray of the bush pig's hide was a color rather than a shade. The sow watched as her piglets drank and stamped at the edge of the water, light glinting on the spikes of her tusks.

Something was moving in the grove.

Even before he shifted his glasses, Nilson knew that the hominids had arrived as he had feared they would. There were three of them, all females. Two were fully adult, each carrying a nursing infant. The third was shorter and slighter, the adolescent who had received the infant from the tiger's victim. Now she was holding a large leaf or a swatch of hide. Fascinated, Nilson forgot for a moment why he was stationed there, forgot also his fear and anger at the situation.

The adult hominids were gathering locust pods from the ground. When each had a handful, she dropped it onto the makeshift platter which the adolescent carried.

Nilson swore under his breath. An incipient basket was a more frightening concept to him than was an incipient axe. They were men, they were ancestors of him and of all the billions of other humans living Topside, who *had* been living Topside before the intrusion team started meddling . . .

One of the adults moved off to the left, hunched over and momentarily hidden by bushes. The other adult chittered happily. Ignoring the thorns, she began to climb the trunk of one of the trees that armed the trap.

The trap. The adolescent was holding her bundle in one hand and with the other hand was plucking curiously at the nylon meshes on which she stood. Nilson touched the release handle. He did not pull it. Then he had a vision of the hominid as she would look through the sights of Henry Vickers' rifle, the front blade bisecting her chest and the whole head and torso framed by the ring of the rear aperture. Nilson jerked the line.

The whittled peg flipped from its socket and the two anchor lines slashed against the sky. Their twang and the victim's shriek of alarm were simultaneous as the net looped crosswise in the air. It hung between the branches, humming like a fly ambushed and held by a jumping spider.

The two adult hominids and their infant burdens disappeared screaming like children near a lightning strike. The Norwegian hunter could not be sure that the one who had been climbing had not been flung from her perch and killed when the trap sprung. There was no time to worry about that now. Snatching up his Mauser and the sled, Nilson began running through the grass toward the grove. Antelope exploded from the water. Hipparions joined the rout with less grace but a certain heavy-footed majesty.

Nilson pounded into the grove, panting as much from nerves as from the 200 yards he had run. The net was pulled tight enough to bulge the meshes around the captive, though not so tight that it choked off the hominid's helpless bleats. Locust pods spilled from a horsehide apron were scattered on the ground beneath the trap.

"Sweet Jesus," the guide muttered. "Oh, my children, my Mary."

Vickers had planned a safe method of completing the capture single-handedly as well. It proved as effective in practice as the trap itself had. The hominid hung six feet in the air, only eye height for the Norwegian. He flung a second square of netting over the taut roll. Then, through the edges hanging low enough to avoid the captive's teeth and claws, he wove a cord back and forth in a loose running seam. When Nilson had reached the hominid's feet, he pulled the cord and tightened the outer net over the inner one like cross-wrapped sheets. As soon as he tied off the lace, the guide had a bundle which the captive within could not escape even after the tension of the branches was released. Holding the head end of the bundle with his left hand, Nilson cut the anchor cords one at a time, dampening the backlash and ultimately supporting the hominid's weight with his own unaided strength. She mewed and twisted within the layers of net, baring her teeth but unable to sink them into the Norwegian's arm.

Nilson found it easier to think of the creature as a beast now than it had been when he watched her moving freely at a distance. She was small, and small without the softness of a human child of the same size. Her jaw was prominent, her forehead receding, and her nose little more than the bare nostrils of a chimpanzee. Most of all, the covering of coarse brown fur robbed the captive of her humanity.

And the fur was as specious an indicator as the rest of them, which the guide knew full well. The hominid had no more hair than Nilson did himself. Only the fact that the body hairs of later-evolved hominids were short and transparent by comparison to those of the captive permitted Nilson to pretend the captive was inhuman. That did not matter. The fact that Nilson *could* pretend to be dealing with a beast and not an ancestor was the only thing that allowed him to do what circumstances forced him to do.

The big man set his captive down gently. With practiced speed, he extended the titanium frame of the sled and locked its members into place. He picked up the hominid again, lifting her off the ground one-handed instead of dragging her as a smaller and weaker man would have had to do. The sled had integral tie-downs with which he fastened his burden securely despite her squirming. It would be to no one's benefit for her to break halfway loose and injure herself. The best Nilson could hope for now was that Weil would examine the hominid briefly and release her. Unharmed, the creature could go on about whatever business she would have accomplished had the time intrusion not occurred.

The guide settled his slung rifle and began trudging toward camp at a pace that would not upset the sled on the irregular ground. As a matter of course, he glanced around frequently to be sure that he was not being stalked by a predator. He paid no particular attention to the brush surrounding the locust grove, however.

Nilson would have had to look very carefully indeed to see the glint of bright eyes hidden there. The eyes followed him and the captive hominid step by step toward his camp.

* * *

"I'll put a kettle of water on and do the dishes," Henry Vickers said. "No need for you two to worry about it."

The firelight brought out attractive bronze highlights in Linda Weil's dark hair. It softened the lines of her face as well. "Oh, I don't think that will be necessary," she said with a comfortable smile. "We can carry them Topside dirty and let somebody there worry about them."

Both men turned and stared silently at the beaming paleontologist. The hominid whimpered outside the circle of firelight. She was in a cage, the largest one available but still meant for considerably smaller specimens. Weil ignored the sound. She turned to Holgar Nilson who stared glumly at his hands. "Holgar," she said, "you did a great job today. I know how much you hated doing it, but you did it splendidly, professionally, anyway. Because of that, we're able to return Topside first thing tomorrow and not—not interfere with the creatures living here any further."

Nilson looked up slowly. His face was as doubtful as that of a political prisoner who has just been informed that the revolution has made him president. "Do you mean," he asked carefully, "that you're already done examining, ah, it?" A quirk of his head indicated the cage at which Nilson had refused to look ever since he had transferred his captive to it.

The paleontologist gave a brief headshake, a tightening around her eyes showing that she was aware of what was about to happen. "No," she said, "we'll carry the specimen back with us Topside. The sort of testing necessary will take years."

"No," said the Norwegian flatly. Then he cried, "God in heaven, *no!* Are you mad? Henry"—turning to the senior guide who would not look at him, stretching out both hands to Vickers as if he were the last hope of a drowning man—"you cannot permit her to do this, will you?"

"Look, one cull from a troop," muttered Vickers to his hands. "Not even breeding age . . ."

Nilson's eyes were red with rage and the firelight. "I—" he began, but the alarm pinged and cut off even his fury.

Both men focused on the panel, their hands snatching up their rifles. Linda Weil was trying to place the source of the sound. The indicator for Sensor Five, northeast of the camp, was pulsing. From the dial, the intruder was of small to medium size: an impala, say— or a hyena.

The guides exchanged glances. The Norwegian shifted his rifle to a one-hand hold, its butt socketed on his hip. He picked up the spotlight. Vickers leveled the Garand, leaning into it with all the slack in the trigger taken up. He nodded. Nilson flicked on the light and slashed its narrow beam across the arc the sensor reported. Nearby bushes flashed white as the spot touched them; further out, only shadows pivoted about the beam. According to the sensor, the intruder was still there, 150 meters out in the night. It did not raise its eyes to give a pair of red aiming points when the light touched them.

"Turn it out," Vickers whispered across the breech of his rifle.

After-effects of the fierce white beam shrank the firelit circle to a glow that scarcely cast the men's shadows toward the bush. The sensor needle quivered as the intruder moved. Vickers fired into the night.

The crack of the .30-'06 made Weil scream in surprise. The muzzle flash was a red ball, momentary but as intense as a bath in acid. Chips of jacket metal spun burning into the night like tiny signal rockets. The sensor jolted, then slipped back to rest position as the intruder bounded back into darkness.

"What was it?" Linda Weil demanded. Her palms were clamped to her ears as if to squeeze the ringing from the drums.

"I don't care so long as it's gone," Vickers said, slowly lowering the Garand. "I've seen a man after a hyena dragged him out of his tent by the face."

"The world might be better off if we *were* killed here," said Holgar Nilson bitterly.

Vickers looked at the younger man. He did not speak. Nilson spat on the fire. "I am very tired now," he said. "I will sleep." He nodded toward the intrusion vehicle, its supporting beams sunk to knee-height in the ground. The metal glowed with a soft sheen of oil where rust had not already crept. "There. I wish you both comfort."

The blond man's footsteps could be heard on the steel even after his form had blurred into the night. "I shouldn't care, should I?" said the woman, speaking toward the fire but loudly enough for Vickers to hear her.

Vickers walked to the water tank and began filling the eight-liter cauldron. The stream rang from the galvanized metal until the water buffered itself. "I don't know," the guide said. "If somebody thinks he's accomplishing anything by sleeping on steel planking, I guess that's his business." He set the pot directly on the coals, twisting it a little to form a safe seat.

"After all, I was only recreation anyway, wasn't I?" the dark-haired woman resumed. "What was a twenty-seven-year-old man going to want with a woman five years older when he got back to a place with some choice? Even if he didn't already have a family!"

"Look, that's out of my field," said the guide. He had already switched magazines in the Garand. Now he checked his pockets to see if they held a loose round to replace the one he had just fired into the night.

"Well, he can *have* his damned security!" Weil said. "*I've* got success that he couldn't comprehend if he had to. Do you realize—" her index finger prodded the air toward Vickers—"just how big this is? By bringing back this specimen, I've just become the most important researcher into human prehistory in this century!"

The guide's expression did not change. Linda Weil pulled back with a slight start. "Well, we all have in a way," she amended in a more guarded voice. "I mean, I couldn't have done this here without you and, and Holgar, of course. But the . . . well, it's my *field*, of course."

Vickers laid the Garand carefully across the stool on which he had been sitting. He tested the dishwater with the tip of a thumb. "You know," he said, "I've got some problems about carrying her" —he gestured toward the dull whimpering—"back with us, too. Look, you've got your camera, and they aren't expecting us back Topside for three more days anyhow. Why don't we stay here, you do your tests and whatever, and then—" Vickers spread his hand with a flare toward the hills, completing the thought.

The look that flashed across the paleontologist's face was as wild as the laughter bubbling from the throat of a hyena. Weil had control of herself again as quickly. "Do you really want to keep her three days in a cage she can't stand up in, Henry?" the woman asked. "And you *know* that we couldn't accomplish anything here, even with a reasonable length of time—which that isn't. Quite aside from the fact that they'd all suspect I'd made the story up myself. A few photos for evidence!"

"Holgar and I are here as witnesses," Vickers said. He lifted the cauldron's wire handle with a stick.

"Marvelous! And where did you do *your* postgraduate work?" Weil snapped. She softened at once, continuing, "Henry, I know my colleagues. They'll doubt, and they *ought* to doubt. It's better than another Piltdown Man. Oh, there'll be another expedition, and it may possibly be as incredibly fortunate as we've been—but then it'll be their names on the finds, not mine. And it's not fair!"

Water sloshed as Vickers shifted the pot. A gush of steam and flying ashes licked his boots. "I don't think she's human," he said quietly, "but if she is, I don't think we've got any business holding her. Not here, not Topside. You know they'd never be able to find this, this slot in time close enough to put her back in it once she leaves."

"Henry, for God's sake," the dark-haired woman pleaded, "we're not talking about some kind of torture. Good grief, what do you think her life span's going to be if we leave her? Five years? Three? Before she winds up in a sabertooth's belly!"

Vickers gave the woman an odd look. "I think both the sabertooths in this range," he said, "have eaten their last hominid."

"All right, a hyena then!" the paleontologist said. "Or until she goes into anaphylactic shock from a bee sting. The point is not just that when we go Topside, everything here will be dead for five million years. The point is that the specimen will live a much longer life in comfort that she'll appreciate just as much as you do. And she'll advance our knowledge of ourselves and our beginnings more than Darwin did."

"Yeah," said the guide. He slid the trio of aluminum plates into the water. "I like modern comforts so much that I spend all the time I can in the bush." He stirred the dishes morosely with the tableware before he dropped that in as well. "Okay, I've been wrong before. God knows, I've generally been wrong."

Five distant hyenas broke out in giggling triumph. No doubt they had just killed, Vickers thought. He spat in the direction of the sounds.

Holgar Nilson swore in Norwegian. He had been doing a last-minute check of his ammunition as they all stood on the sun-struck platform of the intrusion vehicle. As rudimentary as their camp had been, it had taken four hours of solid work to strike it and restack the gear and specimens on the steel. "We can't go yet," Nilson said. "I can't find one of my cartridge cases—we can't leave it out there."

Vickers had already unlocked the vehicle's control panel. Now he took his hand from the big knife switch, but his voice was sour as he said, "Look, Holgar, have you forgotten to count the one up the spout?"

"No, no, it's not that," the big man insisted. "Of course, I don't have a shell in the chamber for returning to Tel Aviv." Nilson held a twenty-round ammunition box in his left hand. Twelve spaces were filled with empty brass; four still held live rounds, their cases bright where they showed above the Styrofoam liner. Only three of the remaining four spaces could be accounted for by the rounds in the Mauser's magazine. "Leaving the brass here—what will it do to the future?"

"Oh, for Chrissake," Vickers said. "Look, we're leaving the lead of every shot we've fired here, aren't we? And this isn't the first team that's been sent back, either."

Linda Weil stood beside the wire mesh cage. The hominid hunched within, scratching at the dusty floor, did not look up. She had not eaten anything since her capture, despite offers of locust pods and what must have been to her an incredible quantity of antelope haunch. The paleontologist looked up from her specimen and said, "Yes, and after all, we've been evacuating wastes, breathing, sweating ourselves. I think it's wise at this point to clean up as much as we can, but I don't think we need be concerned over details."

"When I want your opinion, slut, I'll ask for it!" Nilson shouted.

Earlier that morning the younger guide had ignored Weil's occasional, always conciliatory, comments. Now his face was red and the tendons stood out in his neck. The woman's face distorted as if she had been struck.

"Damn it all anyway," said Vickers. "We're about five minutes away from never having to see each other again if we don't want to. Let's drop it, shall we?"

The other guide took a deep breath and nodded.

Vickers reached for the control switch again. Actually, he wouldn't have minded going on further intrusions with Nilson if the big man could get over his fear of possible future consequences. Nilson was hard-working, a crack shot . . . and besides, he had already saved Vickers' life once.

"Oh, hell," Vickers said. He dropped his hand from the switch. "We forgot to pick up those goddamn rock samples in the confusion. Hell. I'll get them."

Nilson held out a hand to stop the senior guide. "No, let me," he said. Giving Vickers a sardonic smile, he inserted another fat cartridge into the chamber of his rifle. He had to hold down the top round in the magazine so that the bolt would not pick it up and try to ram it into the already-loaded chamber. "After all," he continued as the action snicked closed, "it was I who forgot them. And besides, I don't care to stay with the—remaining personnel."

"Do you think I care?" Linda Weil shrieked. The blond man ignored her, his boots clanking down the two steps to the gritty soil. Far to the west a storm was flashing over a rocky table, but here around the intrusion vehicle not a breath stirred. The grass was scarred by signs of human use: the blackened fire pit and the circle cleared around it; the trampled mud, now cracking, beneath the shower frame; the notches in the ground left by the sled's sharp runners. A hundred yards away was the outcrop shattered by Nilson's dynamite a moment before his shot saved Vickers' life. Like the other damage they had done to the land, this too was transitory. It only speeded up the process that frost and rain would have accomplished anyway over the next five million years.

Nothing in the landscape moved except Holgar Nilson, striding purposefully toward the broken rock.

"Something isn't right," Vickers muttered. His eyes narrowed but they saw nothing to justify what he felt. Reflexively, he charged his Garand. The bolt rang like an alarm as it stripped a round into the chamber.

"What's the matter?" Linda Weil demanded.

"Stay here," Vickers said. *"Holgar!"*

The Norwegian turned and waved. He had almost reached the outcrop. He continued walking.

Vickers swung over the stairs, his left hand locking to the rail while his right controlled the weapon. "Holgar!" he shouted again. "Stop! There's something—"

When the younger guide paused a second time, the hominids sprang from ambush.

Vickers set his feet and dropped the fore-end of the Garand into his waiting left palm. Nilson's eyes widened, but the leveled rifle was a warning more certain than a shout. He was already swinging the Mauser to his shoulder as he spun to face his attackers. The six male hominids were strung in a line abreast, ready to cut him off whichever way he dodged. Their hands held stones. In the center of the rushing line, the blond-flashed leader was only twenty feet from Holgar.

The big Norwegian dropped his rifle and turned. "Don't shoot them!" he screamed to Vickers. "You'll wipe—"

Nilson crumpled, limp all over. The hominid standing over him raised his stone for another blow, white fur and white quartz and bright blood spattering both. Vickers fired three times, so swiftly that the last shot was still echoing before the brass of the first had spun into the bronze-red grass. He aimed for their heads because there was no time for anything but certainty and nothing but a head shot is instantly certain. Fresh brains are not gray but pinkish-white, and the air was pink as the three nearest hominids collapsed over the body of Holgar Nilson.

The survivors were dashing away with the gracefulness of deer, their torsos hunched slightly forward. Vickers pounded like a fencepost running. He carried the Garand across his chest with its safety still off. After a long moment watching, Linda Weil picked up the medical kit and clambered down the steps to follow the men.

At the tangle of bodies, Vickers slung aside one hominid still arching reflexively in death. Beneath him the leader was as rigid as the block of quartz still locked in his right hand. Neither the entrance nor the exit wound of the bullet had damaged the white fur. Vickers rolled that carcass away as well.

Holgar Nilson was still breathing.

The crown and brim of Nilson's hat had been cut by the force of the blow, and the back of the Norwegian's head was a sticky mass of blood and short blond hair. But the skull beneath seemed whole when Vickers probed it, and the injured man's breathing was strong if irregular.

"Why did you kill them if you cared so much?" Linda Weil demanded as she knelt panting in the bloody grass. "He told you not to shoot, didn't he? *He* didn't want it."

The guide shifted to give Weil more room. He did not speak as she soaked a compress from her canteen and held it to the gash. His index finger crooked up to put his rifle on safe, but his eyes had resumed their search of nearby cover.

The dark-haired woman stripped a length of tape from the dispenser and laid it across both scalp and compress. "Do you want to know why?" she said. "You killed them because you hoped he was right. You hoped that you wouldn't be a failure when we got back to the future because there wouldn't *be* a human future any more. With all your talk, you still tried to wipe man off the planet when you got an excuse." Her fingers expertly crossed the initial length of tape with two more.

"Take his feet," Vickers said. "The quicker we get him Topside, the quicker he gets to a hospital."

"I'm sure he wouldn't want to be touched anymore," said the paleontologist as she stood. "Not by a slut like me." She closed the medical kit. "Besides," she added, professionally rotating the head of the hominid leader to look at it, "I have my own duties. I'm going to carry this one back."

Vickers looked at the woman without anger, without apparent

emotion of any sort. Holgar Nilson outweighed him by fifty pounds, but when Vickers straightened with his partner locked in a packstrap carry, the motion was smooth and perfectly controlled. The stocky man reached down with his free hand and gripped the sling of Nilson's Mauser. He began walking the hundred yards back to the intrusion vehicle. His steps were short but regular, and his eyes kept searching the bush for danger.

There was no couch but the steel floor of the intrusion vehicle on which Nilson had slept the past two nights. Vickers laid his partner down as gently as he could, using a sleeping bag as a pillow beneath the side-turned head. Only then did the guide let himself relax, dragging great shuddering gasps of air into his lungs. His Garand leaned against him, held by the upper-sling swivel. He wondered whether his arms were strong enough even to level the weapon if danger should threaten.

Linda Weil had given up her attempt to carry the dead specimen. She was now dragging it by the arms, her back to the intrusion vehicle. Vickers started to go back to help her, then he looked down at Nilson. He eased back on his heels.

The hominid had begun sobbing.

Enough of the fatigue poisons had cleared from Vickers' muscles that he was willing to move again. He knelt beside the specimen. Her long, furry hands covered her eyes and muzzle. A tear dripped through the interstices between her fingers and splashed on the floor. Vickers' eyes followed the drop to the starburst it made in the dust. He was still heavy with fatigue. The tear had fallen beside one of the patterns the hominid had scratched in the dust with her fingertip. The guide stared dully at the marks. The abstract design suddenly shifted into a pair of stick figures. Once his mind had assimilated the pattern as a mother and child, Vickers could not believe that he had not seen it before.

"Jesus," the guide prayed.

Long fingers could reach the latch of the cage through the mesh, so Nilson had wired it shut in lieu of a padlock. Vickers leaned his rifle against a stack of labeled cartons and began to untwist the wire with both hands.

"Vickers!" cried the paleontologist. "What are you doing?"

The latch clicked open. Vickers dropped the door of the cage.

"Omigod!" the paleontologist shrieked, letting her burden fall so that she could run the last twenty yards to the vehicle.

The hominid looked from the opening to Vickers through the mesh. Her eyes were brown and shining with more than tears. She leaped instead of crawling through the opening and hit the platform running. She broke stride when she straightened—the cage had been only a meter high—but her leap from the intrusion vehicle landed her ten feet out in the grass. Linda Weil made a despairing clutch at the little creature, but the hominid was yards away before the paleontologist's arms closed. The adolescent ran in the direction the adults had taken after the ambush, and she ran with the same loping grace.

Linda Weil stumbled forward until she caught herself on the edge of the intrusion vehicle. The sounds she was making were not words, nor were they obviously human. Vickers stepped down and touched her shoulder. "You've still got your specimens," he said quietly. "I'll help you load them."

The woman raised her head, dripping tears and mucus and despair. "You did that because you hate me, didn't you?" she asked in a choking voice.

Vickers' face was very still. "No," he said. "I did it because I don't hate anybody. Anybody human."

From the bush came the sound of joyful voices. The words themselves were not intelligible to humans born five million years in the future.

TIME SAFARI

The tyrannosaur's bellow made everyone jump except Vickers, the guide. The beast's nostrils flared, sucking in the odor of the light helicopter and the humans aboard it. It stalked forward.

"The largest land predator that ever lived," whispered one of the clients.

"A lot of people think that," said Vickers in what most of the rest thought was agreement.

There was nothing in the graceful advance of the tyrannosaur to suggest its ten-ton mass, until its tail side-swiped a flower-trunked cycad. The tree was six inches thick at the point of impact, and it sheared at that point without time to bend.

"Oh dear," the female photographer said. Her brother's grip on the chair arms was giving him leverage to push its cushion against the steel backplate.

The tyrannosaur's strides shifted the weight of its deep torso, counterbalanced by the swinging of its neck and tail. At each end of the head's arcs, the beast's eyes glared alternately at its prey. Except for the size, the watchers could have been observing a grackle on the lawn, but it was a grackle seen from a june bug's perspective.

"Goddamn, he won't hold still!" snarled Salmes, the old-money client, the know-it-all. Vickers smiled. The tyrannosaur chose that moment to pause and bellow again. It was now a dozen feet from the helicopter, a single claw-tipped stride. If the blasting sound left one able, it was an ideal time to admire the beauty of the beast's four-foot head. Its teeth were irregular in length and placement, providing in sum a pair of yellowish, four-inch-deep saws. They fit together too loosely to shear; but with the power of the tyrannosaur's jaw muscles driving them, they could tear the flesh from any creature on Earth— in any age.

The beast's tongue was like a crocodile's, attached for its full length to the floor of its mouth. Deep blue with purple veins, it had a floral appearance. The tongue was without sensory purpose and existed only to help by rhythmic flexions to ram chunks of meat down the predator's throat. The beast's head scales were the size of little fingernails, somewhat finer than those of the torso. Their coloration was consistent—a base of green nearing black, blurred by rosettes of a much lighter, yellowish hue. Against that background, the tyrannosaur's eyes stood out like needlepoints dripping blood.

"They don't always give you that pause," Vickers said aloud. "Sometimes they come—"

The tyrannosaur lunged forward. Its lower jaw, half-opened during its bugling challenge, dropped to full gape. Someone shouted. The action blurred as the hologram dissolved a foot or two from the arc of clients.

Vickers thumbed up the molding lights. He walked to the front of the conference room, holding the remote control with which the hotel had provided him. The six clients viewed him with varied expressions. The brother and sister photographers, dentists named McPherson, whispered in obvious delight. They were best able to appreciate the quality of the hologram and to judge their own ability to duplicate it. Any fear they had felt during the presentation was buried in their technical enthusiasm afterward.

The two individual gunners were a general contractor named Mears and Brewer, a meat-packing magnate. Brewer was a short man whose full moustache and balding head made him a caricature of a Victorian industrialist. He loosened his collar and massaged his flushed throat with his thumb and index finger. Mears, built like an All-Pro linebacker after twenty years of retirement, was frowning. He still gripped the chair arms in a way that threatened the plastic. Those were normal reactions to one of Vickers' pre-hunt presentations. It meant the clients had learned the necessity of care in a way no words or still photos could have taught them. Conversely, that familiarity made them less likely to freeze when they faced the real thing.

The presentations unfortunately did not have any useful effect on people like the Salmes. Or at least on Jonathan Salmes, blond and big but with the look of a movie star, not a football player. Money and leisure could not make Salmes younger, but they made him look considerably less than his real age of forty years. His face was now set in its habitual pattern of affected boredom. As not infrequently happens, the affectation created its own reality and robbed Salmes of whatever pleasure three generations of oil money might otherwise have brought him.

Adrienne Salmes was as blond and as perfectly preserved as her husband, but she had absorbed the presentation with obvious interest. Time safaris were the property of wealth alone, and she had all the trapping of that wealth. Re-emitted light made her dress—and its wearer—the magnet of all eyes in a dim room, and her silver lamé wristlet responded to voice commands with a digital display. That sort of money could buy beauty like Adrienne Salmes'; but it could not buy the inbred assurance with which she wore that beauty. She forestalled any tendency the guide might have had to think that her personality stopped with the skin by asking, "Mr. Vickers, would you have waited to see if the tyrannosaurus would stop, or would you have shot while it was still at some distance from the helicopter?"

"Umm?" said Vickers in surprise. "Oh, wait, I suppose. If he doesn't stop, there's still time for a shot; and your guide, whether that's me or Dieter, will be backing you. That's a good question." He cleared his throat. "And that brings up an important point," he went on. "We don't shoot large carnivores on foot. Mostly, the shooting platform—the helicopter—won't be dropping as low as it was for the pictures, either. For these holos I was sitting beside the photographer, sweating blood the whole time that nothing would go wrong. If the bird had stuttered or the pilot hadn't timed it just right, I'd have had just about enough time to try for a brain shot. Anywhere else and we'd have been in that fellow's gut faster'n you could swallow a sardine." He smiled. It made him look less like a bank clerk, more like a bank robber. "Three sardines," he corrected himself.

"If you used a man-sized rifle, you'd have been a damned sight better off," offered Jonathan Salmes. He had one ankle crossed on the other knee, and his chair reclined at a 45-degree angle.

Vickers looked at the client. They were about of an age, though the guide was several inches shorter and not as heavily built. "Yes, well," he said. "That's a thing I need to talk about. Rifles." He ran a hand through his light brown hair.

"Yeah, I couldn't figure that either," said Mears. "I mean, I read the stuff you sent, about big bores not being important." The contractor frowned. "I don't figure that. I mean, God almighty, as big as one of those mothers is, I wouldn't feel overgunned with a one-oh-five howitzer . . . and I sure don't think my .458 Magnum's any too big."

"Right, right," Vickers said, nodding his head. His discomfort at facing a group of humans was obvious. "A .458's fine if you can handle it—and I'm sure you can. I'm sure any of you can," he added, raising his eyes and sweeping the group again. "What I said, what I meant, was that size isn't important; penetration and bullet placement are what's important. The .458 penetrates fine—with solids—I hope to God all of you know to bring solids, not soft-nosed bullets. If you're not comfortable with that much recoil, though, you're liable to flinch. And that means you'll miss, even at the ranges we shoot dinos at. A wounded dino running around, anywhere up to a hundred tons of him, and that's when things get messy. You and everybody around are better off with you holding a gun that doesn't make you flinch."

"That's all balls, you know," Salmes remarked conversationally. He glanced around at the other clients. "If you're man enough, I'll tell you what to carry." He looked at Vickers, apparently expecting an attempt to silence him. The guide eyed him with a somewhat bemused expression. "A .500 Salmes, that's what," the big client asserted loudly. "It was designed for me specially by Marquart and Wells, gun and bullets both. It uses shortened fifty-caliber machine gun cases, loaded to give twelve-thousand-foot-pounds of energy. That's enough to knock a tyrannosaurus right flat on his ass. It's the only gun that you'll be safe with on a hunt like this." He nodded toward Vickers to put a period to his statement.

"Yes, well," Vickers repeated. His expression shifted, hardening. He suddenly wore the visage that an animal might have glimpsed over the sights of his rifle. "Does anybody else feel that they need a— a *gun* like that to bring down anything they'll see on this safari?"

No one nodded to the question when it was put that way. Adrienne Salmes smiled. She was a tall woman, as tall as Vickers himself was.

"Okay, then," the guide said. "I guess I can skip the lesson to basic physics. Mr. Salmes, if you can handle your rifle, that's all that matters to me. If you can't handle it, you've still got time to get something useful instead. Now—"

"Now wait a goddamned minute!" Salmes said, his foot thumping to the floor. His face had flushed under its even tan. "Just what do you mean by that crack? You're going to teach *me* physics?"

"I don't think Mr. Vickers—" began Miss McPherson.

"I want an explanation!" Salmes demanded.

"All right, no problem," said Vickers. He rubbed his forehead and winced in concentration. "What you're talking about," he said to the floor, "is kinetic energy. That's a function of the square of the velocity. Well and good, but it won't knock anything down. What knocks things down is momentum, that's weight times velocity, not velocity squared. Anything that the bullet knocks down, the butt of the rifle would knock down by recoiling—which is why I encourage clients to carry something they can handle." He raised his eyes and pinned Salmes with them. "I've never yet had a client who weighed twelve thousand pounds, Mr. Salmes. And so I'm always tempted to tell people who talk about 'knock-down power' that they're full to the eyes."

Mrs. Salmes giggled. The other clients did not, but all the faces save Salmes' own bore more-than-hinted smiles. Vickers suspected that the handsome blond man had gotten on everyone else's nerves in the bar before the guide had opened the conference suite.

Salmes purpled to the point of an explosion. The guide glanced down again and raised his hand before saying, "Look, all other things being equal, I'd sooner hit a dino—or a man—with a big bullet than a little one. But if you put the bullet in the brain or the heart, it really doesn't matter much how big it is. And especially with a dino, if you put the bullet anywhere else, it's not going to do much good at all."

"Look," said Brewer, hunching forward and spreading his hands palms down, "I don't flinch, and I got a .378 Weatherby that's got penetration up the ass. But—" he turned his hands over and over again as he looked at them—"I'm not Annie Oakley, you know. If I have to hit a brain the size of a walnut with a four-foot skull around it—well, I may as well take a camera myself instead of the gun. I'll have *something* to show people that way."

Salmes snorted—which could have gotten him one of Brewer's big, capable fists in the face, Vickers thought. "That's another good question," the guide said. "Very good. Well. Brain shots are great if you know where to put them. I attached charts of a lot of the common dinos with the material I sent out, look them over and decide if you want to try.

"Thing is," he continued, "taking the top off a dino's heart'll drop it in a couple hundred yards. They don't charge when they're heart-shot, they just run till they fall. And we shoot from up close, as close as ten yards. They don't take any notice of you, the big ones, you could touch them if you wanted. You just need enough distance to be able to pick your shot. You see"—he gestured toward Brewer with both index fingers—"you won't have any problem hitting a heart the size of a bushel basket from thirty feet away. Brains—well, skin hunters have been killing crocs with brain shots for a century. Crocodile brains are just as small as a tyrannosaur's, and the skulls are just as big. Back where we're going, there were some that were a damn sight bigger than tyrannosaurs. But don't feel you have to. And anyway, it'd spoil your trophy if you brain-shot some of the small-headed kind."

Brewer cleared his throat. "Hey," he said, "I'd like to go back to something you said before. About using the helicopter."

"Right, the shooting platform," Vickers agreed.

"Look," said the meat packer, "I mean . . . well, that's sort of like shooting wolves from a plane, isn't it? I mean, not, well, Christ . . . not sporting, is it?"

Vickers shrugged. "I won't argue with you," he said, "and you don't have to use the platform if you don't want to. But it's the only way you can be allowed to shoot the big carnosaurs. I'm sorry, that's just how it is." He leaned forward and spoke more intensely, popping the fingers of his left hand against his right palm. "It's as sporting as shooting tigers from elephant back, I guess, or shooting lions over a butchered cow. The head looks just as big over your mantle. And there's no sport at all for me to tell my bosses how one of my clients was eaten. They aren't bad, the big dinos, people aren't in their scale so they'll pretty much ignore you. Wound one and it's kitty bar the door. These aren't plant eaters, primed to run if there's trouble. These are carnivores we're talking about, animals that spend most of their waking lives killing or looking for something to kill. They *will* connect the noise of a shot with the pain, and they *will* go after whoever made the noise."

The guide paused and drew back. More calmly he concluded, "So carnosaurs you'll hunt from the platform. Or not at all."

"Well, what happens if they come to us?" Salmes demanded with recovered belligerence. "Right up to the camp, say? You can't keep us from shooting then."

"I guess this is a good time to discuss arrangements for the camp," Vickers said, approaching the question indirectly. "There's four of us staff with the safari, two guides—that's me and Dieter Jost—and two pilots. One pilot, one guide, and one client—one of you—go up in the platform every day. You'll each have two chances to bag a big carnosaur. They're territorial and not too thick on the ground, but there's almost certain to be at least one tyrannosaur and a pack of gorgosaurs in practical range. The other guide takes out the rest of the clients on foot, well, on motorized wagons you could say, ponies we call them. And the pilot who isn't flying the platform doubles as camp guard. He's got a heavy machine gun"—the guide smiled—"a Russian .51 cal. Courtesy of your hosts for the tour, the Israeli government. It'll stop dinos and light tanks without a bit of bother."

Vickers' face lost its crinkling of humor. "If there's any shooting to be done from the camp," he continued, "that's what does it. Unless Dieter or me specifically tells you otherwise. We're not going to have the intrusion vehicle trampled by a herd of dinos that somebody spooked right into it. If something happens to the intrusion vehicle, we don't go home." Vickers smiled again. "That might be okay with me, but I don't think any of the rest of you want to have to explain to the others how you stuck them in the Cretaceous."

"That would be a paradox, wouldn't it, Mr. Vickers?" Miss McPherson said. "That is, uh, human beings living in the Cretaceous? So it couldn't happen. Not that I'd want any chances taken with the vehicle, of course."

Vickers shrugged with genuine disinterest. "Ma'am, if you want to talk about paradox, you need Dr. Galil and his team. So far as I understand it, though, if there's not a change in the future, then there's no paradox; and if there *is* a change, then there's no paradox either because the change—well, the change is reality then."

Mr. McPherson leaned forward with a frown. "Well, surely two bodies—the same body—can't exist simultaneously," he insisted. If he and his sister had been bored with the discussion of firearms, then they had recovered their interest with mention of the mechanics of time transport.

"Sure they can," the guide said with the asperity of someone who had been asked the same question too often. He waved his hand back and forth as if erasing the thought from a chalkboard. "They do. Every person, every gun or can of food, contains at least some atoms that were around in the Cretaceous—or the Pre-Cambrian, for that matter. It doesn't matter to the atoms whether they call themselves Henry Vickers or the third redwood from the big rock . . ." He paused. "There's just one rule that I've heard for true from people who know," he continued at last. "If you travel into the future, you travel as energy. And you don't come back at all."

Mears paled and looked at the ceiling. People got squeamish about the damnedest things, thought Vickers. Being converted into energy . . . or being eaten . . . or being drowned in dark water lighted only by the dying radiance of your mind—but he broke away from that thought, a little sweat on his forehead with the strain of it. He continued aloud, "There's no danger for us, heading back into the far past. But the intrusion vehicle can't be calibrated closer than 5,000 years plus or minus so far. The research side"—he had almost said 'the military side,' knowing the two were synonymous; knowing also that the Israeli government disapproved intensely of statements to that effect—"was trying for the recent past"—1948, but that was another thing you didn't admit you knew—"and they put a man into the future instead. After Dr. Galil had worked out the math, they moved the lab and cleared a quarter-mile section of Tel Aviv around the old site. They figure the poor bastard will show up sometime in the next few thousand years . . . and nobody better be sharing the area when he does."

Vickers frowned at himself. "Well, that's probably more than the government wants me to say about the technical side," he said. "And anyway, I'm not the one to ask. Let's get back to the business itself—which I do know something about."

"You've said that this presentation and the written material are all yours," Adrienne Salmes said with a wave of her hand. "I'd like to know why."

Vickers blinked at the unexpected question. He looked from Mrs. Salmes to the other clients, all of them but her husband staring back at him with interest. The guide laughed. "I like my job," he said. "A century ago, I'd have been hiking through Africa with a Mauser, selling ivory every year or so when I came in from the bush." He rubbed his left cheekbone where a disk of shiny skin remained from a boil of twenty years before. "That sort of life was gone before I was born," he went on. "What I have is the closest thing there is to it now."

Adrienne Salmes was nodding. Mr. McPherson put his own puzzled frown into words and said, "I don't see what that has to do with, well, you holding these sessions, though."

"It's like this," Vickers said, watching his fingers tent and flatten against each other. "They pay me, the government does, a very good salary that I personally don't have much use for." Jonathan Salmes snorted, but the guide ignored him. "I use it to make my job easier," he went on, "by sending the clients all the data I've found useful in the five years I've been traveling back to the Cretaceous . . . and elsewhere, but mostly the Cretaceous. Because if people go back with only what they hear in the advertising or from folks who need to make a buck or a name with their stories, they'll have problems when they see the real thing. Which means problems for me. So a month before each safari, I rent a suite in New York or Frankfurt or wherever the hell seems reasonable, and I offer to give a presentation to the clients. Nobody has to come, but most people do." He scanned the group. "All of you did, for instance. It makes life easier for me."

He cleared his throat. "Well, in another way, we're here to make life easier for you," he went on. "I've brought along holos of the standard game animals you'll be seeing." He dimmed the lights and stepped toward the back of the room. "First the sauropods, the big long-necks. The most impressive things you'll see in the Cretaceous, but a disappointing trophy because of the small heads . . ."

"All right, ladies and gentlemen." said Dieter Jost. Vickers always left the junior guide responsible for the social chores when both of them were present. "Please line up here along the wall until Doctor Galil directs us onto the vehicle."

The members of Cretaceous Safari 87 backed against the hangar wall, their weapons or cameras in their hands. The guides and the two pilots, Washman and Brady, watched the clients rather than the crew preparing the intrusion vehicle. You could never tell what sort of mistake a tensed-up layman would make with a loaded weapon in his or her hands.

In case the clients were not laymen at all, there were four guards seated in a balcony-height alcove in the opposite wall. They wore civilian clothes, but the submachine guns they carried were just as military as their ID cards. The Israelis were, of all people, alert to the chance that a commando raid would be aimed at an intrusion vehicle and its technical staff. For that reason, the installation was in an urban setting from which there could be no quick escape; and its corridors and rooms, including the gaping hanger itself, were better guarded than the Defense Ministry had been during the most recent shooting war.

Dr. Galil and his staff were only occasionally visible to the group on the floor of the hangar. The intrusion vehicle rested on four braced girders twenty feet high. On its underside, a cylindrical probe was repeatedly blurring and reappearing. The technicians received data from the probe on instruments plugged into various sockets on the vehicle. Eighty million years in the past, the cylinder was sampling its surroundings on a score of wavelengths. When necessary, Dr. Galil himself changed control settings. Despite that care, there was no certainty of the surface over which the travelers would appear—or how far or under it they would appear. The long legs gave the intrusion vehicle a margin that might otherwise have been achieved by a longer drop than anything aboard would have survived.

"Well, this is it, hey?" said Jonathan Salmes, speaking to Don Washman. To do so, Salmes had to talk through his wife, who ignored him in turn. "A chance to hunt the most dangerous damned creatures ever to walk the Earth!" Salmes' hands, evenly tanned like every other inch of exposed skin on him, tightened still further on the beautiful bolt-action rifle he carried.

Washman's smile went no further than Adrienne Salmes. The pilot was a big man also. The 40mm grenade launcher he held looked like a sawed-off shotgun with him for scale. "Gee, Mr. Salmes," he said in false surprise. "People our age all had a chance to learn the most dangerous game on Earth popped out of a spider hole with an AK-47 in its hands. All the *men* did, at least."

Vickers scowled. "Don," he said. But Washman was a pilot, not a PR man. Besides, Salmes had coming anything of the sort he got.

Adrienne Salmes turned to Washman and laughed.

A heavyset man climbed down from the intrusion vehicle and strolled across the concrete floor toward the waiting group. Like the guards, he wore an ordinary business suit. He kept his hands in his pants pockets. "Good evening, ladies and sirs," he said in accented English. "I am Mr. Stern; you might say, the company manager. I trust the preparations for your tour have been satisfactory?" He eyed Dieter, then Vickers, his face wearing only a bland smile.

"All present and accounted for," said Dieter in German. At his side, Mears nodded enthusiastically.

"By God," said Jonathan Salmes with recovered vigor. "I just want this gizmo to pop out right in front of a tyrannosaurus rex. Then I'll pop *him*, and I'll double your fees for a bonus!"

Don Washman smirked, but Vickers' scowl was for better reason than that. "Ah, Mr. Salmes," the guide said, "I believe Mr. Brewer drew first shot of the insertion. Fire discipline is something we *do* have to insist on."

"Naw, that's okay," said Brewer unexpectedly. He looked sheepishly at Vickers, then looked away. "We made an agreement on that," he added. "I don't mind paying for something I want; but I don't mind selling something I don't need, either, you see?"

"In any case," said Stern, "even the genius of Dr. Galil cannot guarantee to place you in front of a suitable dinosaur. I must admit to some apprehension, in fact, that someday we will land an intrusion vehicle in mid-ocean." He gestured both elbows outward, like wings flapping. "Ah, this is a magnificent machine, but not, I fear, very precise." He smiled.

"Not precise enough to . . . put a battalion of paratroops in the courtyard of the Temple in 70 AD, you mean?" suggested Adrienne Salmes with a trace of a smile herself.

Vickers' gut sucked in. Stern's first glance was to check the position of the guards. The slightly seedy good fellowship he had projected was gone. "Ah, you Americans," Stern said in a voice that was itself a warning. "Always making jokes about the impossible. But you must understand that in a small and threatened country like ours, there are some jokes one does not make." His smile now had no humor. Adrienne Salmes returned it with a wintry one of her own. If anyone had believed her question was chance rather than a deliberate goad, the smile disabused them.

Atop the intrusion vehicle, an indicator began buzzing in a continuous rhythm. It was not a loud sound. The high ceiling of the hangar drank it almost completely. The staff personnel looked up sharply. Stern nodded again to Vickers and began to walk toward a ground-level exit. He was whistling under his breath. After a moment, a pudgy man stepped to the edge of the vehicle and looked down. He had a white moustache and a fringe of hair as crinkled as rock wool. "I believe we are ready, gentlemen," he said.

Dieter nodded. "We're on the way, then, Dr. Galil," he replied to the older man. Turning back to the safari group, he went on, "Stay in line, please. Hold the handrail with one hand as you mount the steps, and do be very careful to keep your weapons vertical. Accidents happen, you know." Dieter gave a brief nod of emphasis and lead the way. The flight of metal steps stretched in a steep diagonal between two of the vehicle's legs. Vickers brought up the rear of the line, unhurried but feeling the tingle at the base of the neck which always preceded time travel with him. It amused Vickers to find himself trying to look past the two men directly in front of him to watch Adrienne Salmes as she mounted the stairs. The woman wore a baggy suit like the rest of them, rip-stopped Kelprin, which would shed water and still breathe with 80-percent efficiency. On her, the mottled coveralls had an interest which time safari clients, male or female, could rarely bring to such garments.

The floor of the intrusion vehicle was perforated steel from which much of the anti-slip coating had been worn. Where the metal was bare, it had a delicate patina of rust. In the center of the twenty-foot square, the safari's gear was neatly piled. The largest single item was the 500-gallon bladder of kerosene, fuel both for the turbine of the shooting platform and the diesel engines of the ponies. There was some dehydrated food, though the bulk of the group's diet would be the meat they shot. Vickers had warned the clients that anyone who could not stomach the idea of eating dinosaur should bring his own alternative. It was the idea that caused some people problems—the meat itself was fine. Each client was allowed a half-cubic meter chest for personal possessions. Ultimately they would either be abandoned in the Cretaceous or count against the owners' volume for trophies.

The intrusion vehicle was surrounded by a waist-high railing, hinged to flop down out of the way during loading and unloading. The space between the rail and the gear in the center was the passenger area. This open walkway was a comfortable four feet wide at the moment. On return, with the vehicle packed with trophies, there would be only standing room. Ceratopsian skulls, easily the most impressive of the High Cretaceous trophies, could run eight feet long with a height and width in proportion.

On insertion, it was quite conceivable that the vehicle would indeed appear in the midst of a pack of gorgosaurs. That was not something the staff talked about; but the care they took positioning themselves and the other gunners before insertion was not mere form. "Mr. McPherson," Dieter said, "Mr. Mears, if you will kindly come around with me to Side 3—that's across from the stairs here. Do not please touch the red control panel as you pass it."

"Ah, can't Charles and I stay together?" Mary McPherson asked. Both of the dentists carried motion cameras with the lenses set at the 50mm minimum separation. A wider spread could improve hologram quality; but it might prove impossibly awkward under the conditions obtaining just after insertion.

"For the moment," Vickers said, "I'd like you on Side 1 with me, Miss McPherson. That puts two guns on each side; and it's just during insertion."

Boots clanking on the metal stairs, the safari group mounted the vehicle. Four members of Dr. Galil's team had climbed down already. They stood in a row beside the steps like a guard of honor in lab smocks. Galil himself waited beside the vertical control panel at the head of the stairs. The red panel was the only portion of the vehicle which looked more in keeping with a laboratory than a mineshaft. Even so, its armored casing was a far cry from the festooned breadboards that typically marked experimental machinery.

Not that anyone suggested to the clients that the machinery was as surely experimental as a 1940 radar set.

Dr. Galil shook hands with each member of the group, staff and clients alike. Vickers shifted his modified Garand rifle into the crook of his left arm and took the scientist's hand. "Henry, I pray you God speed and a safe return," Galil said in English. His grip was firm.

"God's for afterwards, Shlomo," the guide said. "You'll bring us back, you and your boys. That's what I have faith in."

Dr. Galil squeezed Vickers' hand again. He walked quickly down the steps. The hangar lights dimmed as the big room emptied of everything but the intrusion vehicle and its cargo. Vickers took a deep breath and unlocked the T-handled switch in the center of the control panel. He glanced to either side. Miss McPherson was to his left, Mrs. Salmes to his right.

Adrienne Salmes smiled back. "Did you put me with you because you think you can't trust a woman's shooting?" she asked.

Vickers cleared his throat. "No," he lied. More loudly, he added,

"We are about to make our insertion. Everyone please grip the rail with your free hand. Don't let your rifles or cameras project more than two feet beyond the railing, though." He threw the switch. A blue light on the hangar ceiling began to pulse slowly, one beat per second. Vickers' belly drew in again. At the tenth pulse, the light and the hangar disappeared together. There was an instant of sensory blurring. Some compared the sensation of time travel to falling, others to immersion in vacuum. To Vickers, it was always a blast of heat. Then the heat was real and the Sun glared down through a haze thick enough to shift the orb far into the red. The intrusion vehicle lurched in a walloping spray. Ooze and reeds sloshed sideways to replace those scalloped out of the slough and transported to the hangar in Tel Aviv. The vehicle settled almost to the full depth of its legs.

"Christ on a crutch!" snarled Don Washman, hidden from Vickers by the piled gear. "Tell us it's a grassy clearing and drop us in a pissing swamp! Next time it'll be a kelp bed!" In a different voice he added, "Target."

All of Vickers' muscles had frozen when he thought they were about to drown. They were safe after all, though, and he turned to see the first dinosaur of the safari.

It was a duckbill—though the head looked more like that of a sheep than a duck. Jaw muscles and nasal passages filled the hollows of the snout which early restorations had left bare. The dinosaur had been dashing through the low pines fringing the slough when the crash and slap of the insertion caused it to rear up and attempt to stop. Reeds and water sprayed in a miniature echo of the commotion the vehicle itself had made.

The firm soil of the shore was only ten feet from the vehicle, roughly parallel to Side 4. The duckbill halted, almost in front of Washman and Jonathan Salmes. Scrabbling for traction in muck covered by two feet of water, the beast tried to reverse direction. The pilot leveled his grenade launcher but did not fire. Vickers stepped to the corner where he could see the target. It lacked the crests that made many similar species excellent trophies, but it was still two tons at point-blank range and the first dino the clients had seen in the flesh. "Go ahead," he said to Salmes. "It's yours."

The duckbill lunged back toward the shore, swinging the splayed toes of its right foot onto solid ground. Salmes' rifle slammed. It had an integral muzzle brake to help reduce recoil by redirecting muzzle gases sideways. The muzzle blast was redirected as well, a palpable shock in the thick air. The duckbill lurched, skidding nose-first through a tree. Its long hind legs bunched under it while the stubby forelegs braced to help the beast rise. If it could get to the well-beaten trail by which it had approached the slough, it would disappear.

"Good, good," said Vickers. His voice was tinny in his own ears because of the muzzle blast. "Now finish it with another one at the base of the tail." Fired from such short range, Salmes' bullet could be expected to range through the duckbill's body.

It was certain to rip enough blood vessels to let the beast's life out quickly, and it might also break the spine.

The second shot did not come. The duckbill regained its feet. There was a rusty splotch of blood against the brown-patterned hide of its left shoulder. Vickers risked a look away from the shore to see what was the matter with Salmes. The client had a glazed expression on his face. His big rifle was raised, but its butt did not appear to be solidly resting on his shoulder. Don Washman wore a disgusted look. Beyond both gunners, Mr. McPherson knelt and shot holo tape of the beast leaping back toward the trees.

"Shoot, for Chrissake!" Vickers shouted.

Salmes' rifle boomed again. A triple jet of smoke flashed from the bore and muzzle brake. Salmes cried out as the stock hit him. The bullet missed even the fringe of ten-foot pine trees. The duckbill disappeared into them.

Vickers carefully did not look at Salmes—or at Adrienne Salmes, standing immediately behind the guide with her rifle ready to shoot if directed. She had snickered after her husband's second shot. "First, we'll find a dry campsite and move the gear," Vickers started to say.

The forest edge exploded as the duckbill burst back through it in the midst of a pack of dromaeosaurs.

In the first flaring confusion, there seemed to be a score of the smaller carnivores. In fact, there were only five—but that was quite enough. One had the duckbill by the throat and was wrapping forelegs around the herbivore's torso to keep from being shaken loose. The rest of the pack circled the central pair with the avidity of participants in a gang rape. Though the carnivores were bipedal, they bore a talon on each hind foot that was a sickle in size and lethality. Kicking from one leg, the hooting dromaeosaurs slashed through the duckbill's belly hide. Soft, pink coils of intestine spilled out into the water.

One of the half-ton carnivores cocked its head at the group on the intrusion vehicle. The men on Side 4 were already spattered with the duckbill's blood. "Take 'em," Vickers said. He punched a steel-cored bullet through the nearest dromaeosaur's skull, just behind its eyes.

Washman and Adrienne Salmes fired while Vickers' cartridge case was still in the air. The pilot's grenade launcher chugged rather than banged, but the explosion of its projectile against the chest of a carnivore was loud even to ears numbed by the muzzle blasts of Salmes' rifle. The grenade was a caseless shaped charge which could be used point-blank without endangering the firer with fragments. Even so, the concussion from less than twenty feet rocked everyone on the near side of the vehicle. There was a red flash and a mist of pureed dinosaur. A foreleg, torn off at the shoulder, sailed straight into the air. Two of the dromaeosaurs bolted away from the blast, disappearing among the trees in flat arcs and sprays of dirt and pine straw.

Vickers' target had fallen where it stood. All four limbs jerked like those of a pithed frog. The dromaeosaur Adrienne Salmes had shot dropped momentarily, then sprang to its feet again. The tall woman worked the bolt of her rifle smoothly without taking the butt from her shoulder. The grenade explosion did not appear to have disconcerted her. The guide, poised to finish the beast, hesitated. Adrienne shot again and the dino's limbs splayed. Its dark green hide showed clearly the red and white rosette between the shoulders where the second bullet had broken its spine.

Dieter Jost leaned past Mr. McPherson and put a uranium penetrator through the brain of the duckbill, ending its pain. All four of the downed dinosaurs continued to twitch.

"Jesus," said Don Washman quietly as he closed the breech on a grenade cartridge.

Although he had only fired once, Henry Vickers replaced the 20-round magazine of his Garand with a fresh one from his belt pouch. "Mr. McPherson," he said, "I hope you got good pictures, because I swear that's the most excitement I've had in a long time in this business."

Dieter had moved back to watch the slough with Steve Brady. Most of the clients crowded to Side 4 to get a better view of the Cretaceous and its denizens. Adrienne Salmes had not moved from where she stood beside Vickers. She thumbed a second cartridge into the magazine of her rifle and closed the breech. "Still doubt I can shoot?" she asked with a smile.

"Heart and spine," the guide said. "No, I guess you can back me up any day of the week. I tell you, dromaeosaurs aren't as impressive as some of the larger carnivores, but they're just as dangerous." He looked more carefully at her rifle, a Schultz and Larsen with no ornamentation but the superb craftsmanship that had gone into its production. "Say, nice," Vickers said. "In .358 Norma?"

The blonde woman smiled with pleasure. "It's the same rifle I've used for everything from white-tails to elephant," she said. "I'd planned to bring something bigger, but after what you said, I had five hundred bullets cast from bronze and loaded at the factory for me. Johnnie—" she glanced at her husband, now loudly describing how he had shot the duckbill to the other clients. "Well," Adrienne continued quietly, "I'm the hunter in the household, not him. I told him he was crazy to have a cannon like that built, but he listens to me as badly as he listens to everyone else."

"That may be a problem," Vickers muttered. More loudly, he said, "All right, I think it's time to start setting up camp on top of this ridge. Around now, it's asking for trouble to be any closer than a hundred yards to the water, especially with this much meat nearby. After Steve and I get the ponies assembled, we'll need everybody's help to load them. Until then, just try not to get in the way."

Sometimes working with his hands helped Vickers solve problems caused by the human side of his safaris. It did not seem to do so on this occasion. Of course, a client who was both arrogant and gun-shy was a particularly nasty problem.

But Vickers was irritated to realize that it also bothered him that Don Washman and Mrs. Salmes seemed to be getting along very well together.

The campfire that evening provided an aura of human existence more important than the light of its banked coals. The clients had gone to sleep—or at least to their tents. That the Salmes at least were not asleep was evident from the sound of an argument. The double walls of the tents cut sound penetration considerably, but there were limits. Steve Brady shoved another log on the fire and said, "Damn, but I swear that chainsaw gets heavier every time I use it. Do you suppose the Israelis designed them to be air-dropped without parachutes?"

"You want a high horsepower-to-weight ratio, you don't use a diesel," agreed Dieter Jost with a shrug. "If you want a common fuel supply for everything and need diesel efficiency for the ponies, though—well, you get a heavy chainsaw."

"Can't imagine why she ever married him," Don Washman said. "Beef like that's a dime a dozen. Why, you know he didn't even have balls enough to chamber a third round? He's scared to death of that gun, scared almost to touch it now."

"Yeah," agreed Vickers, working a patch into the slot of his cleaning rod, "but the question's what to do about it. I don't have any good answers, God knows."

"Do?" Washman repeated. "Well, hell, leave him, of course. She's got money of her own—"

Brady broke into snorting laughter. Dieter grimaced and said, "Don, I do not think it is any business of ours how our clients live. The Salmeses are adults and can no doubt solve their own problems." He pursed his lips. The fire threw the shadow of his bushy moustache misshapenly against his cheeks. "As for our problem, Henry, why don't we offer him the use of the camp gun? The .375? I think Mr. Salmes' difficulty is in precisely the same category as the more usual forms of mechanical breakdown or guns falling into the river."

"Fine with me if you can talk him into it," Vickers said dubiously, "but I wouldn't say Salmes is the sort to take a well-meant suggestion." He nodded toward the tent. The couple within seemed to be shouting simultaneously. "Or any other kind of suggestion," he added.

"Things would sure be simpler if they didn't allow booze on safaris," Brady said.

"Things would be simpler for us if our employers paid us to sleep all day and drink schnapps," said Dieter Jost. He tugged a lock of hair absently. "That does not comport well with economic realities, however. And so long as each of our clients has paid fifty thousand American dollars for the privilege of spending two weeks in the Cretaceous, it is unrealistic to assume that the staff will be treated as anything but the hired help. If drunken clients make the job more difficult, then that is simply one of the discomforts of the job. Like loading gear in the heat, or tracking down an animal that a client has wounded. It is easier for our employers, Mr. Stern and those above him, to hire new staff members than it would be to impose their underlings' view on persons of the sort who take time safaris."

"Moshe Cohn was head guide when I made my first insertion," said Vickers aloud. His cleaning rod rested on his lap beside the Garand, but he had not run it through the bore yet. "He told a client—a Texan, it was a US safari that time too—that he'd be better off to slack up a little on his drinking while he was in the field. The client was generally too stiff to see a dino, much less shoot one." The guide's forefinger tapped the breech of his rifle as he recalled the scene. "He said to Moshe, 'Jew-boy, you sound just like my third wife. One more word and I'll whip you with my belt, just like I did her.' Moshe broke his hand on the Texan's jaw. When we got back, the government—the Israeli, but very pragmatic, government—fired Moshe and denied him compensation for his hand. Ten days in the field with broken bones, remember." Vickers paused, then went on, "That taught me the rules. So far, I've been willing to live by them."

Don Washman laughed. "Right, when you hit a client, use your gunstock," he said and opened another beer.

Technically, Steve Brady had the first watch, even though all four staff members were up. The alarm panel was facing Steve when it beeped, therefore. "Jesus!" the stubby, long-haired pilot blurted when he saw the magnitude of the signal fluorescing on the display. "Down the trail—must be a herd of something!"

Don Washman upset his fresh beer as he ran to the spade grips of the heavy machine gun. It was in the center of the camp, on ground slightly higher than its immediate surroundings but by no means high enough to give the weapon an unbroken field of fire. The staff had sawed clear a campsite along the game trail leading down to the intrusion vehicle two hundred yards away. Assuming that animals were most likely to enter the area by the trail, Dieter had sited the tents on the other side of the gun. The next day they could assemble the six-foot-high tower for the gun, but time had been too short to finish that the first night.

While the other staff members crouched over weapons, Vickers darted to the three occupied tents. The sensor loop that encircled the camp 100 yards out could pick up very delicate impacts and relay them to the display screen. This signal, however, was already shaking the ground. Miss McPherson poked her head out of the tent she shared with her brother. "What—" the dentist began.

The file of huge ceratopsians rumbled into sight on their way to the water to drink. They were torosaurs or a species equally large. In the dim glow of the fire, they looked more like machines than anything alive. Their beaks and the tips of their triple horns had a black glint like raku ware, and they averaged twice the size of elephants.

The tent that Mears and Brewer shared shuddered as both clients tried to force their way through the opening simultaneously. Vickers lifted the muzzles of their rifles skyward as he had been waiting to do. "No shooting now," he cried over the thunder of the dinosaurs. "In the morning we'll follow them up."

Adrienne Salmes slipped out of her tent before Vickers could reach over and take her rifle. It was pointed safely upward anyway. Despite the hour-long argument she had been engaged in, the blonde woman looked calm and alert. She looked breathtakingly beautiful as well—and wore only her rifle. "If you can wait a moment for my firepower," she said to Vickers without embarrassment, "I'll throw some clothes on." The guide nodded.

The bony frills at the back of the ceratopsians' skulls extended their heads to well over the height of a man. Less for protection than for muscle attachment, the frills locked the beasts' heads firmly to their shoulders. The bulging jaw muscles that they anchored enabled the ceratopsians to literally shear hardwood the thickness of a man's thigh. The last thing a safari needed was a herd of such monsters being stampeded through the camp. A beast wounded by a shot ill-aimed in the darkness could lead to just that result.

Mears and Brewer were staring at the rapid procession in wonder. The left eye of each torosaur glinted in the firelight. "Mother o' God, what a trophy!" Brewer said.

"Best in the world," Vickers agreed. "You'll go back with one, never fear." He looked at the McPhersons to his other side. The dentists were clutching their holo cameras, which were almost useless under the light conditions. "And you'll get your fill, too," Vickers said. "The trip isn't cheap, but I've never yet guided a client who didn't think he'd gotten more than he bargained for." Though a drunken SOB like Jonathan Salmes might spoil that record, he added silently.

Adrienne Salmes re-emerged from her tent, wearing her coveralls and boots. Mears and Brewer had been so focused on the herd of torosaurs that the guide doubted the men had noticed her previous display. She was carrying a sleeping bag in addition to her rifle. Vickers raised an eyebrow. Adrienne nodded back at the tent. "Screaming beauty seems to have passed out," she said, "but I'm damned if I'll stay in the tent with him. Going on about his shoulder, for God's sake, and expecting sympathy from *me*. Is it all right if I doss down in the open?"

The ceratopsians were sporting in the water, making as much noise as the Waikiki surf. Vickers smiled. "They could eat tree trunks and drink mud," he said, as if he had not heard the client's question. "And I still meet people who think mammals are better adapted for survival than dinos were." He turned to Adrienne Salmes. "It's all right, so long as you stay out of the gun's way," he said, "but you'll wash away if it rains. And we're bound to get at least one real gully washer while we're here."

"Hell, there's an easy answer to that," said Don Washman. He had strolled over to the tents when it became clear no predators had followed the torosaurs. "One of us is on watch all night, right? So there's always a slot open in the staff tents. Let noble hunter there sleep by himself, Hank. And she shoots well enough to be a pro, so let her stay dry with us too." He gave his engaging smile.

The other clients were listening with interest. "Maybe if Mr. McPherson wants to trade—" Vickers began in a neutral voice.

Adrienne Salmes hushed him with a grimace. "I'm a big girl now, Mr. Vickers," she snapped, "and I think I'm paying enough to make my own decisions. Don, if you'll show me the tent, I'll resume getting the sleep I've been assured I'll need in the morning."

Washman beamed. "Let's see," he said. "Steve's got watch at the moment, so I suppose you're my tentmate till I go on at four in the morning."

They walked toward the tent. Dieter, standing near the fire with his rifle cradled, looked from them to Vickers. Vickers shrugged. He was thinking about Moshe Cohn again.

"Platform to Mobile One," crackled the speaker of the unit clipped to Vickers' epaulet. Vickers threw the last of the clamps that locked the two ponies into a single, articulated vehicle. "Go ahead, Dieter," he said.

"Henry, the torosaurs must have run all night after they left the water," the other guide announced through the heavy static. "They're a good fifteen klicks west of camp. But there's a sauropod burn just three klicks south and close to the river. Do you want me to drop a marker?"

Vickers frowned. "Yeah, go ahead," he decided. He glanced at but did not really see the four clients, festooned with gear, who awaited his order to board the ponies. "Any sign of carnosaurs?"

"Negative," Dieter replied, "but we're still looking. I spotted what looked like a fresh kill when we were tracking the torosaurs. If we don't get any action here, I'll carry Miss McPherson back to that and see what we can stir up."

"Good hunting, Dieter," Vickers said. "We'll go take a look at your sauropods. Mobile One out." Again his eyes touched the clients.

He appeared startled to see them intent on him. "All right," he said, "if you'll all board the lead pony. The other's along for trophies—sauropods this time, we'll get you the ceratopsians another day. Just pull down the jump seats."

The guide seated himself behind the tiller bar and clipped his rifle into its brackets. His clients stepped over the pony's low sides. The vehicle was the shape of an aluminum casket, scaled up by a half. A small diesel engine rode over the rear axle. Though the engine was heavily muffled, the valves sang trills which blended with the natural sounds of the landscape. Awnings were pleated into trays at either end of the vehicle, but for today the trees would be sunscreen enough.

Don Washman waved. He had strung a tarp from four trees at the edge of the clearing. In that shade he was pinning together the steel framework of the gun tower. The alarm and his grenade launcher sat beside him.

"Take care," Vickers called.

"You take care," the pilot responded with a broad grin. "Maybe I can lose the yo-yo and then we're all better off." He jerked his head toward the tent which still held Jonathan Salmes. Dieter had tried to arouse Salmes for breakfast. Because Vickers was sawing at the time, no one but Dieter himself heard what the client shouted. Dieter, who had served in at least three armies and was used to being cursed at, had backed out of the tent with a white face. Vickers had shut down the saw, but the other guide had shaken his head. "Best to let him sleep, I think," he said.

Remembering the night before, Vickers wished that it was Brady and not Washman who had the guard that day. Oh, well. "Hold on," he said aloud. He put the pony into gear.

Just west of the crest on which they had set up camp, the height and separation of the trees increased markedly. Small pines and cycads were replaced by conifers that shot over one hundred feet in the air. Everything east of the ridgeline was in the floodplain, where the river drowned tree roots with a regularity that limited survival to the smaller, faster-growing varieties. The thick-barked monsters through which Vickers now guided the ponies were centuries old already. Barring lightning or tornado, they would not change appreciably over further centuries. They were the food of the great sauropods.

The forest was open enough to permit the pony to run at over 15mph, close to its top speed with the load. The saplings and pale, broad-leafed ferns which competed for the dim light were easily brushed aside. Animal life was sparse, but as the pony skirted a fallen log, a turkey-sized coelurosaur sprang up with a large beetle in its jaws. Mears' .458 boomed. There was an echo-chamber effect from the log which boosted the muzzle blast to a near equal for that of the Salmes' .500. Everyone on the pony jumped—Vickers more than the rest because he had not seen the client level his rifle. The dinosaur darted away, giving a flick of its gray-feathered tail as it disappeared around a trunk.

"Ah, don't shoot without warning," the guide said, loudly but without looking around. "It's too easy to wound something that you should have had backup for. Besides, we should be pretty close to the sauropods—and they make much better targets."

Even as Vickers spoke, the forest ahead of them brightened. The upper branches still remained, but all the limbs had been stripped below the level of sixty feet. One tree had been pushed over. It had fallen to a 45-degree angle before being caught and supported by the branches of neighboring giants. The matted needles were strewn with fresh blankets of sauropod droppings. They had a green, faintly Christmassy scent. Vickers stopped the vehicle and turned to his clients. "We're getting very close," he said, "and there'll be plenty of shooting for everybody in just a moment. But there's also a chance of a pack of carnosaurs nearby for the same reason that we are. Keep your eyes open as we approach—and for God's sake don't shoot until I've said to." His eyes scanned the forest again and returned to Adrienne Salmes. A momentary remembrance of her the night before, a nude Artemis with rifle instead of bow, made him smile. "Mrs. Salmes," he said, "would you watch behind us, please? Carnivores are likely to strike up a burn as we did . . . and I can't watch behind us myself."

Adrienne grinned. "Why, Mr. Vickers, I think you've just apologized for doubting I could shoot," she said. She turned and faced back over the towed pony, left arm through the sling of her rifle in order to brace the weapon firmly when she shot.

Vickers eased forward the hand throttle. They were past the marker beacon Dieter had dropped from the shooting platform. The responder tab on the guide's wrist had pulsed from green to red and was now lapsing back into fire-orange; he cut it off absently. The sounds of the dinosaurs were audible to him now: the rumble of their huge intestines; the slow crackle of branches being stripped of their needles, cones, and bark by the sauropods' teeth; and occasional cooing calls which the clients, if they heard them over the ringing of the diesel, probably mistook for those of unseen forest birds.

The others did not see the sauropods even when Vickers cut the motor off. They were titanosaurs or a similar species, only middling huge for their suborder. Vickers pointed. Mears, Brewer, and McPherson followed the line of the guide's arm, frowning. "It's all right now, Mrs. Salmes," Vickers said softly. "The dinos will warn us if predators get near." Adrienne Salmes faced around as well.

"Oh, Jesus Christ," someone whispered as he realized what Vickers was pointing out. It was incredible, even to the guide, how completely a score or more of thirty-ton animals could blend into an open forest. In part, it may have been that human minds were not used to interpreting as animals objects which weighed as much as loaded semis. Once recognized, the vast expanses of russet and black hide were as obvious as inkblot pictures which someone else has described.

Silently and without direction, McPherson stepped from the pony and spread the lenses of his camera. Vickers nodded to the others. "They won't pay attention to a normal voice," he said—in a quieter than normal voice. "Try to avoid sudden movements, though. They may think it's a warning signal of some kind." He cleared his throat. "I want each of you to mark a target—"

"That one!" whispered Mears urgently, a boy in a toy store afraid his aunt will renege on her promise of a gift unless he acts at once. The big contractor was pointing at the nearest of the sauropods, a moderate-sized female only thirty feet away.

"Fine, but wait," the guide said firmly. "I'll position each of you.

When I call 'fire,' go ahead—but only then. They won't attack anything our size, but they might step on one of us if they were startled at the wrong time. That big, they don't have to be hostile to be dangerous."

The nearby female, which had been browsing on limbs twenty feet high, suddenly stepped closer to a tree and reared up on her hind legs. She anchored herself to the trunk with her forefeet, each armed with a single long claw. It shredded bark as it gripped. With the grace and power of a derrick, the titanosaur's head swung to a high branch, closed, and dragged along it for several yards. It left only bare wood behind.

With his left hand, Vickers aimed a pen-sized laser pointer. A red dot sprang out on the chest of the oblivious titanosaur. "There's your aiming point," the guide said. "If she settles back down before I give the signal, just hit her at the top of the shoulder."

Mears nodded, his eyes intent on the dinosaur.

Vickers moved Brewer five yards away, with a broadside shot at a large male. McPherson stood beside him, using a panhead still camera on the six sauropods visible within a stone's throw. The dentist's hands were trembling with excitement.

Vickers took Adrienne Salmes slightly to the side, to within twenty yards of another male. He chose the location with an eye on the rest of the herd. Sauropods had a tendency to bolt straight ahead if aroused.

"Why does this one have bright red markings behind its eyes?" Adrienne asked.

"First time I ever saw it," the guide said with a shrug. "Maybe some professor can tell you when you get back with the head." He did not bother to gesture with the laser. "Ready?" he asked.

She nodded and aimed.

"Fire!"

The three gunners volleyed raggedly. The thick tree trunks acted as baffles, blurring the sharpness of the reports. The gunfire had the same feeling of muffled desecration as farts echoing in a cathedral. The red-flashed titanosaur began striding forward. Adrienne Salmes worked her bolt and fired again. A wounded animal gave a warning call, so loud and low-pitched that the humans' bowels trembled. Mrs. Salmes fired again. The titanosaur was a flickering picture in a magic lantern formed by open patches between six-foot tree boles. The huntress began to run after her disappearing prey.

Vickers grabbed her shoulder, halting her with an ease that belied his slender build. She turned on him in fury. "I won't let a wounded animal go!" she screamed.

"It won't go far," Vickers said. He released her. "We'll follow as soon as it's safe." He gestured, taking in the bellowing, mountainous forms padding in all directions among the even larger trees. "They'll circle in a moment. Then it'll be safe for things our size to move," he said.

Russet motion ceased, though the tidal bellowing of over a dozen sauropods continued. Mears was still firing in the near distance. Brewer had lowered his rifle and was rubbing his shoulder with his left hand. "Let's get everybody together," the guide suggested, "and go finish off some trophies."

Brewer's expression was awed as they approached. "It really did fall," he said. "It was so big, I couldn't believe . . . But I shot it where you said and it just ran into the tree." He waved. "And I kept shooting and it fell."

The haunches of the titanosaur were twice the height of a man, even with the beast belly-down in the loam. McPherson pointed at the great scars in the earth beneath the sauropod's tail. "It kept trying to move," he said in amazement. "Even though there was a tree in the way. It was kicking away, trying to get a purchase, and I thought the *tree* was going to go over. But it did. The dinosaur. And I have a tape of all of it!"

Mears, closest to the bellowing giants, was just as enthusiastic. "Like a shooting gallery!" he said. "But the tin ducks're the size of houses. God Almighty! I only brought one box of ammo with me. I shot off every last slug! God Almighty!"

The titanosaurs had quieted somewhat, but they were still making an odd series of sounds. The noises ranged from bird calls as before to something like the venting of high-pressure steam. Vickers nodded and began walking toward the sounds. He had caught Adrienne

Salmes' scowl of distaste at the contractor's recital. If the guide agreed, it was still not his business to say so.

The herd was larger than Vickers had estimated. Forty of the sauropods were in a circle facing outwards around a forest giant, which was so much bigger than its neighbors that it had cleared a considerable area. Several of the beasts were rearing up. They flailed the air with clawed forefeet and emitted the penetrating steam-jet hiss that seemed so incongruous from a living being. Mears raised his rifle with a convulsed look on his face before he remembered that he had no ammunition left.

McPherson was already rolling tape. "Have you reloaded?" the guide asked, looking from Salmes to Brewer. The blonde woman nodded curtly while the meat packer fumbled in the side pocket of his coveralls.

"I don't see the one I hit," Adrienne Salmes said. Her face was tight.

"Don't worry," the guide said quietly. "It's down, it couldn't have made it this far the way you hit it. It's the ones that weren't heart-shot that we're dealing with now."

"That's not my responsibility," she snapped.

"It's no duty you owe to me," Vickers agreed, "or to anything human."

Brewer snicked his bolt home. Vickers' laser touched the center of the chest of a roaring titanosaur. Orange pulmonary blood splashed its tiny head like a shroud. "On the word, Mr. Brewer," he said, "if you would."

Adrienne said, "All right." She did not look at Vickers.

Across the circle, eighty yards away, a large male was trying to lick its belly. Its long neck strained, but it was not flexible enough to reach the wound. The laser pointer touched below the left eye. "There?" the guide asked.

Adrienne nodded and braced herself, legs splayed. Her arms, sling, and upper body made a web of interlocking triangles.

The guide swung his own weapon onto the third of the wounded animals. "All right," he said.

Adrienne's Schultz and Larsen cracked; the light went out of the gut-shot sauropod's eye. Undirected, the rest of the great living machine began slowly to collapse where it stood. Brewer was firing, oblivious of his bruised shoulder in the excitement. Vickers put three rounds into the base of his own target's throat. Its head and neck were weaving too randomly to trust a shot at them.

Either the muzzle blasts or the sight of three more of their number sagging to the ground routed the herd. Their necks swung around like compass needles to iron. With near simultaneity, all the surviving titanosaurs drifted away from the guns. Their tails were held high off the ground.

Adrienne Salmes lowered her rifle.

"God Almighty, let me use that!" Mears begged, reaching out for the weapon. "I'll pay you—"

"Touch me and I'll shove this up your bum, you bloody butcher!" the blonde woman snarled.

The contractor's fist balled. He caught himself, however, even before he realized that the muzzle of the .358 had tilted in line with his throat.

"The river isn't that far away," said Vickers, pointing in the direction the sauropods had run. "We'll follow in the pony—it's a sight worth seeing. And taping," he added.

The undergrowth slowed the hunters after they recrossed the ridgeline, but the titanosaurs were still clearly evident. Their heads and even hips rocked above the lower vegetation that sloped toward the river. The herd, despite its size and numbers, had done surprisingly little damage to its rush to the water. The pony repeatedly had to swing aside from three-inch saplings which had sprung back when the last of the titanosaurs had passed.

But the beasts themselves were slowed by the very mechanics of their size. Their twelve-foot strides were ponderously slow even under the goad of panic. The tensile strength of the sauropods' thigh bones simply was not equal to the acceleration of the beasts' mass to more than what would be a fast walk in a man. The hunters reached a rocky spur over the mudflats fringing the water just as the leading titanosaurs splashed into the stream 150 yards away. The far bank of the river was lost in haze. The sauropods continued to advance without reference to the change in medium. Where a moment before they had been belly-deep in reeds, now they were belly-deep in brown water that was calm except for the wake of their passage. When the water grew deeper, the procession sank slowly. The beasts farthest away, in mid-stream over a quarter-mile out, were floating necks and tails while the forefeet propelled them by kicking down into the bottom muck.

"Don't they hide underwater and snorkel through their necks?" Brewer asked. Then he yipped in surprise as his hand touched the barrel of his Weatherby. The metal was hot enough to burn from strings of rapid fire and the Cretaceous sunlight.

Vickers nodded. He had heard the question often before. "Submarines breathe through tubes because the tubes are steel and the water pressure doesn't crush them," he explained. "Sauropods don't have armored gullets, and their lungs aren't diesel engines inside a steel pressure hull. Physics again. Besides, they float—the only way they could sink would be to grab a rock."

As Vickers spoke, the last titanosaur in the line sank.

"Well, I'll be damned!" the guide blurted.

The sauropod surfaced again a moment later. It blew water from its lungs as it gave the distress cry that had followed the shooting earlier.

The mild current of the river had bent the line of titanosaurs into a slight curve. The leaders were already disappearing into the haze. None of the other beasts even bothered to look back to see the cause of the bellowing. No doubt they already knew.

The stricken titanosaur sank again. It rolled partly onto its left side as it went under the surface this time. It was still bellowing, wreathing its head in a golden spray as it disappeared.

"I think," said Adrienne Salmes dryly, "that this time the rock grabbed the dinosaur."

Vickers grunted in reply. He was focusing his binoculars on the struggle.

Instead of rising vertically, the sauropod rolled completely over sideways. Clinging to the herbivore's left foreleg as it broke surface was something black and huge and as foul as a tumor. The linked beasts submerged again in an explosion of spray. Vickers lowered the binoculars, shivering. They were not common, even less commonly seen. Great and terrible as they were, they were also widely hated. For them to sun themselves on mudbanks as their descendants did would have been to court death by the horns and claws of land animals equally large. But in their own element, in the still, murky waters, they were lords without peer.

"Christ Almighty," Mears said, "was that a whale?"

"A crocodile," the guide replied, staring at the roiling water. "Enough like what you'd find in the Nile or the Congo that you couldn't tell the difference by a picture. Except for the size." He paused, then continued, "The science staff will be glad to hear about this. They always wondered if they preyed on the big sauropods, too. It seems that they preyed on *any* goddamn thing in the water."

"I'd swear it was bigger than the tyrannosaurus you showed us," Adrienne Salmes observed, lowering her own binoculars.

Vickers shrugged. "As long, at least. Probably heavier. I looked at a skull, a fossil in London . . . I don't know how I'd get one back as a trophy . . . It was six feet long, which was impressive; and three feet wide, which was incredible, a carnivore with jaws three feet *wide*. Tyrannosaurs don't compare, no. Maybe whales do, Mr. Mears, but nothing else I know of."

There were no longer any titanosaurs visible. The herd had curved off downstream, past the intrusion vehicle and the hunting camp. They were lost against the haze and the distant shoreline by now. The water still stirred where the last of them had gone down, but by now the struggles must have been the thrashings of the sauropod's autonomic nervous system. The teeth of the crocodile were six inches long; but they were meant only to hold, not to kill. The water killed, drowning a thirty-ton sauropod as implacably as it would any lesser creature anchored to the bottom by the crocodile's weight.

"We'd best take our trophies," Vickers said at last. No one in the world knew his fear of drowning, no one but himself. "The smell'll bring a pack of gorgosaurs soon, maybe even a tyrannosaur. I don't want that now, not with us on the ground."

The guide rubbed his forehead with the back of his left hand, setting his bush hat back in place carefully. "The ponies convert to boats," he said, patting the aluminum side. "The tread blocks can be rotated so they work like little paddle wheels." He paused as he swung the tiller bar into a tight circle. "I guess you see why we don't use them for boats in the Cretaceous," he added at last. "And why we didn't keep our camp down on the intrusion vehicle."

Vickers was even quieter than his wont for the rest of the morning.

The shooting platform had returned before the ponies did, the second of them dripping with blood from the titanosaur heads. Two heads had Mears' tags on them, though the contractor had finished none of the beasts he had wounded. The best head among those he had sprayed would have been the one the guide had directed Adrienne Salmes to kill—with a bullet through the skull that destroyed all trophy value.

There were no game laws in the Cretaceous, but the line between hunters and butchers was the same as in every other age.

The McPhersons greeted each other with mutual enthusiasm. Their conversation was technical and as unintelligible to non-photographers as the conversation of any other specialists. Jonathan Salmes was sitting on a camp stool, surly but alert. He did not greet the returning party, but he watched the unloading of the trophies with undisguised interest. The right side of his face was puffy.

"We've found a tyrannosaur," Dieter called as he and the pilots joined Vickers. That was good news, but there was obvious tension among the other members of the staff. Brady carried a spray gun loaded with antiseptic sealer. A thorough coating would prevent decay for almost a month, ample time to get the heads to proper taxidermists.

When Dieter was sure that all the clients were out of earshot, he said in a low voice, "Don has something to tell you, Henry."

"Eh?" prompted Vickers. He set one of the sauropod heads on the spraying frame instead of looking at the pilot.

"I had to clobber Salmes," Washman said, lifting out the red-flashed trophy. "He was off his head—I'm not sure he even remembers. There was a mixed herd of duckbills came down the trail.

He came haring out of his tent with that gun of his. He didn't shoot, though, he started chasing them down the trail." The pilot straightened and shrugged. Steve Brady began pumping the spray gun. The pungent mist drifted downwind beyond the gaping heads. "I grabbed him. I mean, who knows what might be following a duckbill? When he swung that rifle at me, I had to knock him out for his own good. Like a drowning man." Washman shrugged again. "His gun wasn't even loaded, you know?"

"Don, run the ponies down to the water and mop them out, will you?" Vickers said. The pilot jumped onto the leading vehicle and spun them off down the trail. The two guides walked a little to the side, their rifles slung, while Brady finished sealing the trophies. "It's going to have to be reported, you know," Vickers said. "Whether Salmes does or not."

"You or I might have done the same thing," Dieter replied.

"I'm not denying that," the senior guide snapped. "But it has to be reported."

The two men stood in silence, looking out at a forest filled with sounds that were subtly wrong. At last Dieter said, "Salmes goes up in the platform with you and Don tomorrow, doesn't he?"

Vickers agreed noncommittally.

"Maybe you ought to go with Steve instead," Dieter suggested. He looked at Vickers. "Just for the day, you know."

"Washman just flies us," Vickers said with a shake of his head. "I'm the one that's in contact with the client. And Don's as good as pilots come."

"That he is," the other guide agreed, "that he is. But he is not a piece of furniture. You are treating him as a piece of furniture."

Vickers clapped his companion on the shoulder. "Come on," he said, "Salmes'll be fine when he gets his tyrannosaur. What we ought to be worrying about is three more for the others. If Salmes goes home with a big boy and the rest have to settle for less—well, it says no guarantees in the contracts, but you know the kind of complaints the company gets. That's the kind of problem we're paid to deal with. If they wanted shrinks instead of guides, they'd have hired somebody else."

Dieter laughed half-heartedly. "Let us see what we can arrange for lunch," he said. "At the moment, I am more interested in sauropod steak than I am in the carnivores that we compete with."

"Damn, the beacon cut out again!" Washman snarled. There was no need of an intercom system; the shooting platform operated with only an intake whine which was no impediment to normal speech. The silence was both a boon to coordination and a help in not alarming the prey. It did, however, mean that the client was necessarily aware of any technical glitches. When the client was Jonathan Salmes—"Goddamn, you're not going to put *me* on that way!" the big man blazed. He had his color back and with it all his previous temper. Not that the bruise over his right cheekbone would have helped. "One of the others paid you to save the big one for them, didn't they?" he demanded. "By God, I'll bet it was my wife! And I'll bet it wasn't money either, the—"

"Take us up to a thousand feet," Vickers said sharply. "We'll locate the kill visually if the marker isn't working. Eighty tons of sauropod shouldn't be hard to spot."

"Hang on, there it's on again," said the pilot. The shooting platform veered slightly as he corrected their course. Vickers and Salmes stood clutching the rail of the suspended lower deck which served as landing gear as well. Don Washman was seated above them at the controls, with the fuel tank balancing his mass behind. The air intake and exhaust extended far beyond the turbine itself to permit the baffling required for silent running. The shooting platform was as fragile as a dragonfly; and it was, in its way, just as efficient a predator.

By good luck, the tyrannosaur had made its kill on the edge of a large area of brush rather than high forest. The platform's concentric-shaft rotors kept blade length short. Still, though it was possible to maneuver beneath the forest canopy, it was a dangerous and nerve-wracking business to do so. Washman circled the kill at 200 feet, high enough that he did not need to allow for trees beneath him. Though the primary airflow from the rotors was downward, the odor of tens of tons of meat dead in the sun still reached the men above. The guide tried to ignore it with his usual partial success. Salmes only wrinkled his nose and said, "Whew, what a pong." Then, "Where is it? The tyrannosaurus?"

That the big killer was still nearby was obvious from the types of scavengers on the sauropod. Several varieties of the smaller coelurosaurs scrambled over the corpse like harbor rats on a drowned man. None of the species weighed more than a few hundred pounds. A considerable flock of pterosaurs joined and squabbled with the coelurosaurs, wings tented and toothless beaks stabbing out like shears. There were none of the large carnivores around the kill—and that implied that something was keeping them away.

"Want me to go down close to wake him up?" Washman asked.

The guide licked his lips. "I guess you'll have to," he said. There was always a chance that a pterodactyl would be sucked into the turbine when you hovered over a kill. The thought of dropping into a big carnosaur's lap that way kept some guides awake at night. Vickers looked at his client and added, "Mr. Salmes, we're just going to bring the tyrannosaur out of wherever it's lying in up in the forest. After we get it into the open, we'll maneuver to give you the best shot. All right?"

Salmes grunted. His hands were tight on his beautifully finished rifle. He had refused Dieter's offer of the less-bruising camp gun with a scorn that was no less grating for being what all the staff had expected.

Washman dropped them vertically instead of falling in a less wrenching spiral. He flared the blades with a gentle hand, however, feathering the platform's descent into a hover without jarring the gunners. They were less than thirty feet in the air. Pterosaurs, more sensitive to moving air than the earthbound scavengers, squealed and hunched their wings. The ones on the ground could not take off because the downdraft anchored them. The pilot watched carefully the few still circling above them.

"He's—" Vickers began, and with his word the tyrannosaur strode into the sunlight. Its bellow was intended to chase away the shooting platform. The machine trembled as the sound induced sympathetic vibrations in its rotor blades. Coelurosaurs scattered. The cries of the pterosaurs turned to blind panic as the downdraft continued to frustrate their attempts to rise. The huge predator took another step forward. Salmes raised his rifle. The guide cursed under his breath but did not attempt to stop him.

At that, it should have been an easy shot. The tyrannosaur was within thirty feet of the platform and less than ten feet below them. All it required was that Salmes aim past the large head as it swung to counterweight a stride and rake down through the thorax. Perhaps the angle caused him to shoot high, perhaps he flinched. Vickers, watching the carnosaur over his own sights, heard the big rifle crash. The tyrannosaur strode forward untouched, halving the distance between it and the platform.

"Take us up!" the guide shouted. If it had not been a rare trophy, he might have fired himself and announced that he had "put in a bullet to finish the beast." There were three other gunners who wanted a tyrannosaur, though; if Salmes took this one back, it would be after he had shot it or everyone else had an equal prize.

Salmes was livid. He gripped the bolt handle, but he had not extracted the empty case. "Goddamn you!" he screamed. "You made it wobble to throw me off! You son of a bitch, you robbed me!"

"Mr. Salmes—" Vickers said. The tyrannosaur was now astride the body of its prey, cocking its head to see the shooting platform fifty feet above it.

"By God, you want another chance?" Washman demanded in a loud voice. The platform plunged down at a steep angle. The floor grating blurred the sight of the carnosaur's mottled hide. Its upturned eye gleamed like a strobe-lit ruby.

"Jesus *Christ!*" Vickers shouted. "Take us the hell up, Washman!"

The platform steadied, pillow soft, with its floor fifteen feet from the ground and less than twenty from the tyrannosaur. Standing on the sauropod's corpse, the great predator was eye to eye with Vickers and his client. The beast bellowed again as it lunged. The impulse of its clawed left leg rolled the sauropod's torso.

Salmes screamed and threw his rifle to the grating. The guide leveled his Garand. He was no longer cursing Washman. All of his being was focused on what would be his last shot if he missed it. Before he could fire, however, the shooting platform slewed sideways.

Then they were out of the path of the charging dinosaur and beginning to circle with a safe thirty feet of altitude. Below them, the tyrannosaur clawed dirt as it tried to follow.

Salmes was crying uncontrollably.

"Ah, want me to hold it here for a shot?" Washman asked nervously.

"We'll go on back to the camp, Don," the guide said. "We'll talk there, all right?"

"Whatever you say."

Halfway back, Vickers remembered he had not dropped another marker to replace the one that was malfunctioning. God knew, that was the least of his problems.

"You know," Brewer said as he forked torosaur steaks onto the platter, "it tastes more like buffalo than beef, but if we could get some breeding stock back, I'd by God find a market for it!"

Everyone seemed to be concentrating on their meat—good, if pale and lean in comparison with feedlot steer. "Ah," Vickers said, keeping his voice nonchalant. He looked down at the table instead of the people sitting around it. "Ah, Dieter and I were talking . . . We'll bunk outside tonight. The, ah, the rest of that pack of dromaeosaurs chased some duckbills through the camp this morning, Steve thinks. So just for safety's sake, we'll both be out of the tent . . . So, ah, Mrs. Salmes—"

Everyone froze. Jonathan Salmes was turning red. His wife had a forkful of steak poised halfway to her mouth and her eyebrows were rising. The guide swallowed, his eyes still fixed on his plate, and plowed on. "That is, you can have your own tent, ah, to sleep in."

"Thank you," Adrienne Salmes said coolly, "but I'm quite satisfied with the present arrangements."

Dieter had refused to become involved in this, saying that interfering in the domestic affairs of the Salmeses was useless at best. Vickers was sweating now, wishing that there was something to shoot instead of nine pairs of human eyes fixed on him. "Ah," he repeated, "Mrs. Salmes—"

"Mr. Vickers," she overrode him, "who I choose to sleep with—in any sense of the term—is none of your business. Anyone's business," she added with a sharp glance across the table at her husband.

Jonathan Salmes stood up, spilling his coffee cup. His hand closed on his fork; each of the four staff members made unobtrusive preparations. Cursing, Salmes flung the fork down and stalked back to his tent.

The others eased. Vickers muttered, "Christ."

Then, "Sorry, Dieter, I . . ."

The thing that bothered him most about the whole incident was that he was unsure whether he would have said anything at all had it been Miss McPherson in Don's bed instead of someone he himself found attractive. Christ . . .

"Mr. Vickers?" Adrienne Salmes said in a mild voice.

"Umm?" His steak had gotten cold. With Brewer cutting and broiling the meat, the insertion group was eating better than Vickers could ever remember.

"I believe Mr. Brady is scheduled to take me up in the platform tomorrow?"

"Yeah, that's right," Vickers agreed, chewing very slowly.

"I doubt my—husband—will be going out again tomorrow," the blonde woman continued with a nod toward his tent. "Under the circumstances, I think it might be better if Mr. Brady were left behind here at the camp. Instead of Don."

"Steve?" Dieter asked.

Brady shrugged. "Sure, I don't need the flying time. But say—I'm not going to finish ditching around the tents by myself. I've got blisters from today."

"All right," said Dieter. "Henry, you and Don—" no one was looking directly at Washman, who was blushing in embarrassment he had damned well brought on himself—"will take Mrs. Salmes up after the tyrannosaur tomorrow." Vickers and Brady both nodded. "The rest of us will wait here to see if the duckbills come through again as they have become accustomed. Steve, I will help you dig. And if the duckbills have become coy, we will ride down the river margin a little later in the morning and find them. Perhaps Mr. Salmes will feel like going with us by then."

Thank God for Dieter, Vickers thought as he munched another bite of his steak. He could always be counted on to turn an impossible social situation into a smoothly functioning one. There would be no trouble tomorrow after all.

The bulging heads of three torosaurs lay between the gun tower and the fire. There the flames and the guard's presence would keep away the small mammals that foraged in the night. As Miss McPherson followed her brother to their tent, she paused and fingered one of the brow horns of the largest trophy. The tip of the horn was on a level with the dentist's eyes, even though the skull lay on the ground. "They're so huge, so . . . powerful," she said. "And for them to fall when you shoot at them, so many of them falling and running . . . I could never understand men who, well, who shot animals. But with so many of them everywhere—it's as if you were throwing rocks at the windows of an abandoned house, isn't it? It doesn't seem to hurt anything, and it's . . . an attractive feeling."

"Mary!" objected her brother, shadowed by the great heads.

"Oh, I don't mean I'm sorry that I didn't bring a gun," continued Mary McPherson calmly, her fingers continuing to stroke the smooth black horn. "No, I'm glad I didn't. Because if I had had a gun available this morning, I'm quite sure I would have used it. And after we return, I suppose I would regret that. I suppose." She walked off toward the tent. The rhythms of her low-voiced argument with her brother could be heard until the flaps were zipped.

"Dieter tells me they bagged sixteen torosaurs today," Vickers said. "Even though the intrusion vehicle hasn't room for more than one per client." Only Washman, who had the watch, and Adrienne Salmes were still at the campfire with him.

"*I* bagged one," the woman said with an emphatic flick of her cigar. "Jack Brewer shot five and I sincerely hope that idiot Mears hit no more than ten, because that's all Dieter and I managed to finish off for him." She had unpinned her hair as soon as she came in from the field. In the firelight, it rolled across her shoulders like molten amber.

"Dieter said that too," Vickers agreed. He stood, feeling older than usual. "That's why I said 'they.'" He turned and began to walk back to the tent where Dieter was already asleep. There had been no point in going through with the charade of sleeping under the stars—overcast, actually—since the dromaeosaurs were daylight predators. They were as unlikely to appear in the camp after dark as the Pope was to speak at a KKK rally.

To the guide's surprise—and to Don Washman's—Adrienne rustled to her feet and followed. "Mr. Vickers," she said, "might I speak to you for a moment, please?"

Vickers looked at her. As the staff members did, and unlike the other clients, the blonde woman carried her weapon with her at all times. "All right," he said. They walked by instinct to the shooting platform, standing thirty feet away at the end of the arc of tents. The torosaur heads were monstrous silhouettes against the fire's orange glow. "Would it bother you as much if I were a man?" she asked bluntly.

"Anything that makes my job harder bothers me," Vickers said in half-truth. "You and Don are making my job harder. That's all."

Adrienne stubbed out her small cigar on the platform's rail. She scattered the remnants of the tobacco on the rocky soil. "Balls," she said distinctly. "Mr. Vickers—Henry, for Christ's sake—my husband was going to be impossible no matter what. He's here because I was going on a time safari and he was afraid to look less of a man than his wife was. Which he is. But he was going to be terrified of his rifle, he was going to pack his trunk with Scotch, and he was going to be a complete prick because that's the way he is."

"Mrs. Salmes—"

"Adrienne, and let me finish. I didn't marry Jonathan for his money—my family has just as much as his does. I won't claim it was a love match, but we . . . we seemed to make a good pair. A matched set, if you will. He won't divorce me"—her dimly glimpsed index finger forestalled another attempt by the guide to break in—"because he correctly believes I'd tell the judge and the world that he couldn't get it up on our wedding night. Among other things. I haven't divorced him because I've never felt a need to. There are times that it's been marvelously useful to point out that 'I *do* after all have a husband, dearest . . .'"

"This is none of my business, Mrs. Salmes—"

"Adrienne!"

"Adrienne, dammit!" Vickers burst out. "It's none of my business, but I'm going to say it anyway. You don't have anything to prove. That's fine, we all should be that way. But most of my clients have a lot to prove, to themselves and to the world. Or they wouldn't be down here in the Cretaceous. It makes them dangerous, because they're out of normal society and they may not be the men they hoped they were after all. And your husband is very goddamned dangerous, Adrienne. Take my word for it."

"Well, it's not *my* fault," the woman said.

"Fault?" the guide snapped. "Fault? Is it a pusher's fault that kids OD on skag? You're goddamn right it's your fault! It's the fault of everybody involved who doesn't make it better, and you're sure not making it better. Look, you wouldn't treat a gun that way—and your husband is a human being!"

Adrienne frowned in surprise. There was none of the anger Vickers had expected in her voice when she said, "So are you, Henry. You shouldn't try so hard to hide the fact."

Abruptly, the guide strode toward his tent. Adrienne Salmes watched him go. She took out another cigar, paused, and walked carefully back to the fire where Washman waited with the alarm panel. The pilot looked up with concern. Adrienne sat beside him and shook her hair loose. "Here you go, Don sweetest," she said, extending her cigar. "Why don't you light it for me? It's one of the things you do so well."

Washman kissed her. She returned it, tonguing his lips; but when his hand moved to the zipper of her coveralls, she forced it away. "That's enough until you go off guard duty, dearest," she said. She giggled. "Well—almost enough."

Jonathan Salmes hunched in the shadow of the nearest torosaur head. He listened, pressing his fists to his temples. After several more minutes, he moved in a half-crouch to the shooting platform. In his pocket was a six-inch wooden peg, smooth and close-grained. It was whittled from a root he had worried from the ground with his fingers. Stepping carefully so that his boots did not scrunch on the metal rungs, Salmes mounted the ladder to the pilot's seat. He paused there, his khaki coveralls strained, white face reflecting the flames. The couple near the fire did not look up. The pilot was murmuring something, but his voice was pitched too low to hear . . . and the words might have been unintelligible anyway, given the circumstances.

Jonathan Salmes shuddered also. He moved with a slick grace that belied the terror and disgust frozen on his face. He slipped the dense peg from his pocket. Stretching his right arm out full length while he gripped the rotor shaft left-handed, Salmes forced the peg down between two of the angled blades of the stator. When he was finished, he scrambled back down the ladder. He did not look at his wife and the pilot again, but his ears could not escape Adrienne's contented giggle.

"Hank, she just isn't handling right this morning," Don Washman said. "I'm going to have to blow the fuel lines out when we get back. Must've gotten some trash in the fuel transferring from the bladder to the cans to the tank. Wish to hell we could fuel the bird directly, but I'm damned if I'm going to set down on the intrusion vehicle where it's sitting now."

Vickers glanced down at the treetops and scowled. "Do you think we ought to abort?" he asked. He had not noticed any difference in the flight to that point. Now he imagined they were moving slower and nearer the ground than was usual, and both the rush of air and the muted turbine whine took on sinister notes.

"Oh . . ." the pilot said. "Well, she's a lot more likely to clear herself than get worse—the crud sinks to the bottom of the tank and gets sucked up first. It'll be okay. I mean, she's just a little sluggish, is all."

The guide nodded. "M—" he began. After his outburst of the night before, he was as embarrassed around Adrienne Salmes as a boy at his first dance. "Ah, Adrienne, what do you think?"

The blonde woman smiled brightly, both for the question and the way it was framed. "Oh, if Don's willing to go on, there's no question," she said. "You know I'd gladly walk if it were the only way to get a tyrannosaurus, Henry—if you'd let me, I mean. We both know that when we go back in today, I've had my last chance at a big carnosaur until you've rotated through all your clients again. Including my husband."

"We'll get you a tyrannosaur," Vickers said.

Adrienne edged slightly closer to the guide. She said softly, "Henry, I want you to know that when we get back I'm going to give Johnnie a divorce."

Vickers turned away as if slapped. "That's none of my business," he said. "I—I'm sorry for what I said last night."

"Sorry?" the woman repeated in a voice that barely carried over the wind noise. "For making me see that I shouldn't make a doormat of . . . someone who used to be important to me? Don't be sorry." After a pause, she continued, "When I ran for Congress . . . God I was young! I offended it must have been everybody in the world, much less the district. But Johnnie was fantastic. I owe what votes I got to hands he shook for me."

"I had no right to talk," Vickers said. By forcing himself, he managed to look the blonde woman in the eyes.

Adrienne smiled and touched his hand where it lay on the forestock of his rifle. "Henry," she said, "I'm not perfect, and the world's not going to be perfect either. But I can stop trying to make it actively worse."

Vickers looked at the woman's hand. After a moment, he rotated his own to hold it. "You've spent your life being the best man around," he said, as calm as he would be in the instant of shooting. "I think you've got it in you to be the best person around instead. I'm not the one to talk . . . but I think I'd be more comfortable around people if more of them were the way you could be."

With a final squeeze, Vickers released Adrienne's hand. During the remainder of the fifteen-minute flight, he concentrated on the ground below. He almost forgot Washman's concern about the engine.

Dieter Jost flicked a last spade full of gritty soil from the drainage ditch and paused. Steve Brady gave him a thumbs-up signal from the gun tower where he sat. "Another six inches, peon," he called to the guide. "You need to sweat some."

"Fah," said Dieter, laughing. "If it needs to be deeper, the rain will wash it deeper—not so?" He dug the spade into the ground and began walking over to the table. They had found a cache of sauropod eggs the day before. With the aid of torosaur loin and freeze-dried spices from his kit, Brewer had turned one of them into a delicious omelet. Brewer, Mears, and the McPhersons were just finishing. Dieter, who had risen early to finish ditching the tents, had worked up quite an appetite.

"Hey!" Brady called. Then, louder, "Hey! Mr. Salmes, that's not safe! Come back here, please!"

The guide's automatic rifle leaned against the gun tower. He picked it up. Jonathan Salmes was carrying his own rifle and walking at a deliberate pace down the trail to the water. He did not look around when the guard shouted. The other clients were staring in various stages of concern. Cradling his weapon, Dieter trotted after Salmes. Brady, standing on the six-foot tower, began to rotate the heavy machine gun. He stopped when he realized what he was doing.

The guide reached Salmes only fifty yards from the center of the camp, still in sight of the others. He put a hand on the blond man's shoulder and said, "Now, Mr. Salmes—"

Salmes spun like a mousetrap snapping. His face was white. He rang his heavy rifle off Dieter's skull with enough force to tear the stock out of his hands. The guide dropped as if brain-shot. Salmes backed away from the fallen man. Then he turned and shambled out of sight among the trees.

"Goddamn!" Steve Brady said, blinking in surprise. Then he thought of something even more frightening. He unslung his grenade launcher and jumped to the ground without bothering to use the ladder. "If that bastard gets to the intrusion vehicle—" he said aloud, and there was no need for him to finish the statement.

Brady vaulted the guide's body without bothering to look at the injury. The best thing he could do for Dieter now was to keep him from being stranded in the Cretaceous. Brady's hobnails skidded where pine needles overlay rock, but he kept his footing. As the trail twisted around an exceptionally large tree, Brady caught sight of the client again. Salmes was not really running; rather, he was moving like a man who had run almost to the point of death.

"Salmes, goddamn you!" Brady called. He raised the grenade launcher. Two dromaeosaurs burst from opposite sides of the trail where they lay ambushed. Their attention had been on Salmes, but when the guard shouted, they converged on him.

The leftward dromaeosaur launched itself toward its prey in a flat, twenty-foot leap. Only the fact that Brady had his weapon aimed permitted him to disintegrate the beast's head with a point-blank shot. Death did nothing to prevent the beast from disemboweling Brady reflexively. The two mutilated bodies were thrashing in a tangle of blood and intestines as the remaining clients hurtled around the tree. They skidded to a halt. Mr. McPherson, who held Salmes' rifle—his sister had snatched up Dieter's FN a step ahead of him—began to vomit. Neither Salmes nor the other dromaeosaur were visible.

Jonathan Salmes had in fact squelched across the mud and up the ramp of the intrusion vehicle. He had unscrewed the safety cage from the return switch and had his hand poised on the lever. Something clanged on the ramp behind him.

Salmes turned. The dromaeosaur, panicked by the grenade blast that pulped its companion's head, was already in the air. Salmes screamed and threw the switch. The dromaeosaur flung him back against the fuel bladder. As everything around it blurred, the predator picked Salmes up with its forelegs and began methodically to kick him to pieces with its right hind foot. The dinosaur was still in the process of doing so when the submachine guns of the startled guards raked it to death with equal thoroughness.

The broad ribs of the sauropod thrust up from a body cavity that had been cleared of most of its flesh. There was probably another meal on the haunches, even for a beast of the tyrannosaur's voracity. If Adrienne missed the trophy this morning, however, Vickers would have to shoot another herbivore in the vicinity in order to anchor the prize for the next client.

Not that there was much chance that the blonde woman was going to miss.

Adrienne held her rifle with both hands slanted across her chest.

Her hip was braced against the guardrail as she scanned the forest edge. If she had any concern for her balance, it was not evident.

"Okay, down to sixty," Don Washman said, barely enough height to clear the scrub oaks that humped over lower brush in the clearing. The lack of grasses gave the unforested areas of the Cretaceous an open aspect from high altitude. Lower down, the spikes and wooden fingers reached out like a hedge of spears.

The tyrannosaur strode from the pines with a hacking challenge. "Christ, he's looking for us," the pilot said. The carnosaur slammed aside the ribs of its kill like bowling pins. Its nostrils were flared, and the sound it made was strikingly different from the familiar bellow of earlier occasions.

"Yeah, that's its territorial call," Vickers agreed. "It seems to have decided that we're another tyrannosaur. It's not just talking, it wants our blood."

"S'pose Salmes really hit it yesterday?" Washman asked.

Vickers shook his head absently. "No," he said, "but the way you put the platform in its face after it'd warned us off . . . Only a tyrannosaur would challenge another tyrannosaur that way. They don't have much brain, but they've got lots of instinctive responses; and the response we've triggered is, well . . . a good one to give us a shot. You ready, Adrienne?"

"Tell me when," the blonde woman said curtly. Washman was swinging the platform in loose figure eights about 150 yards distant from the carnosaur. They could not circle at their present altitude because they were too low to clear the conifer backdrop. Adrienne aimed the Schultz and Larsen when the beast was on her side of the platform, raising the muzzle again each time the pilot swung onto the rear loop of the figure.

"Don, see if you can draw him out from the woods a little farther," the guide said, squinting past the barrel of his Garand. "I'd like us to have plenty of time to nail him before he can go to ground in the trees."

"Ah, Hank . . ." the pilot began. Then he went on, "Oh, hell, just don't blow your shots. That's all I ask." He put the controls over and wicked up.

There was a noticeable lag before the turbine responded to the demand for increased power. The section of root slapped as it vibrated from the stator and shot into the rotors spinning at near-maximum velocity.

"If you'll stand over here, Mis—Adrienne," Vickers said, stepping to the back rail of the platform. The client followed with brittle quickness. "When I say shoot," Vickers continued, "aim at the middle of the chest."

Washman had put the platform in an arc toward the tyrannosaur. The big carnivore lunged forward with a series of choppy grunts like an automatic cannon. The pilot rotated the platform on its axis, a maneuver he had carried out a thousand times before. This time the vehicle dipped. It was a sickening, falling-elevator feeling to the two gunners and a heart-stopping terror to the man at the controls who realized it was not caused by clumsiness. The platform began to stagger away from the dinosaur, following the planned hyperbola but lower and slower than intended.

"Nail him," Vickers said calmly, sighting his rifle on the green-mottled sternum for the backup shot.

Partial disintegration of the turbine preceded the shot by so little that the two seemed a single event. Both gunners were thrown back from the rail. Something whizzed through the side of the turbine and left a jagged rent in the housing. Adrienne Salmes' bullet struck the tyrannosaur in the lower belly.

"Hang on!" Don Washman shouted needlessly. "I'm going to try—"

He pulled the platform into another arc, clawing for altitude. To get back to camp they had to climb over the pine forest that lay between. No one knew better than the pilot how hopeless that chance was. Several of the turbine blades had separated from the hub. Most of the rest were brushes of boron fiber now, their casing matrices destroyed by the peg or harmonics induced by the imbalance. But Washman had to try, and in any case they were curving around the wounded tyrannosaur while it was still—

The whole drive unit tore itself free of the rest of the shooting platform. Part of it spun for a moment with the rotor shafts before sailing off in a direction of its own. Had it not been for the oak tree in their path, the vehicle might have smashed into the ground from fifty feet and killed everyone aboard. On the other hand, Don Washman just might have been able to get enough lift from the auto-rotating blades to set them down on an even keel. Branches snagged the mesh floor of the platform and the vehicle nosed over into the treetop.

They were all shouting, but the din of bursting metal and branches overwhelmed mere human noise. Vickers held the railing with one hand and the collar of his client's garment with the other. Both of the rifles were gone. The platform continued to tilt until the floor would have been vertical had it not been so crumpled. Adrienne Salmes was supported entirely by the guide. "For God's sake!" she screamed. "Let go or we'll go over *with* it!"

Vickers' face was red with the impossible strain. He forced his eyes down, feeling as if even that minuscule added effort would cause his body to tear. Adrienne was right. They were better off dropping onto a lower branch—or even to the ground forty feet below—than they would be somersaulting down in the midst of jagged metal. The platform was continuing to settle as branches popped. Vickers let go of the blonde woman.

Screaming at the sudden release of half the load, he loosed his other hand from the rail.

The guide's eyes were shut in a pain reflex. His chest hit a branch at an angle that saved his ribs but took off a plate-sized swatch of skin without harming his tunic's tough fabric. He snatched convulsively at the limb. Adrienne, further out on the same branch, seized him by the collar and armpit. Both her feet were locked around the branch. She took the strain until the guide's overstressed muscles allowed him to get a leg up. The branch swayed, but the tough oak held.

Don Washman was strapped into his seat. Now he was staring straight down and struggling with the jammed release catch. Vickers reached for the folding knife he carried in a belt pouch. He could not reach the pilot, though. "Don, cut the strap!" he shouted.

A large branch split. The platform tumbled outward and down, striking on the top of the rotor shafts. The impact smashed the lightly built aircraft into a tangle reeking of kerosene. Don Washman was still caught in the middle of it.

The limb on which Vickers and Adrienne Salmes balanced was swaying in harmony with the whole tree. When the thrashing stopped, the guide sat up and eyed the trunk. He held his arms crossed tightly over his chest, each hand squeezing the opposite shoulder as if to reknit muscles which felt as if they had been pulled apart. Nothing was moving in the wreckage below. Vickers crawled to the crotch. He held on firmly while he stepped to a branch three feet lower down.

"Henry," Adrienne Salmes said.

"Just wait, I've got to get him out," Vickers said. He swung down to a limb directly beneath him, trying not to wince when his shoulders fell below the level of his supporting hands.

"Henry!" the blonde woman repeated more urgently. "The tyrannosaur!"

Vickers jerked his head around. He could see nothing but patterns of light and the leaves that surrounded him. He realized that the woman had been speaking from fear, not because she actually saw anything. There was no likelihood that the carnosaur would wander away from its kill, even to pursue a rival. Adrienne, who did not understand the beast's instincts, in her fear imagined it charging toward them. The guide let himself down from the branch on which he sat, falling the last five feet to the ground.

Adrienne thought Vickers must have struck his head during the crash. From her vantage point, thirty feet in the air and well outboard on the limb that supported her, she had an excellent view of the tyrannosaur. Only low brush separated it from the tree in which they had crashed. The beast had stood for a moment at the point Washman lifted the platform in his effort to escape. Now it was ramping like a creature from heraldry, balanced on one leg with its torso high and the other hind leg kicking out at nothing. At first she did not understand; then she saw that each time the foot drew back, it caressed the wounded belly.

Suddenly the big carnivore stopped rubbing itself. It had been facing away from the tree at a 30-degree angle. Now it turned toward the woman, awesome even at three hundred yards. It began to stalk forward. Its head swung low as usual, but after each few strides the beast paused. The back raised, the neck stretched upward, and now Adrienne could see that the nostrils were spreading. A leaf, dislodged when Vickers scrambled to the ground, was drifting down. The light breeze angled it toward the oncoming dinosaur.

Vickers cut through one of the lower cross-straps holding Washman five feet in the air with his seat above him. The pilot was alive but unconscious. The guide reached up for the remaining strap, his free hand and forearm braced against the pilot's chest to keep him from dropping on his face.

"Henry, for God's sake!" the woman above him shouted. "It's only a hundred yards away!"

Vickers stared at the wall of brush, his lips drawn back in a snarl. "Where are the guns? Can you see the guns?"

"I can't see them! Get back, for God's sake!"

The guide cursed and slashed through the strap. To take Washman's weight, he dropped his knife and bent. Grunting, Vickers manhandled the pilot into position for a fireman's carry.

The tyrannosaur had lowered its head again. Adrienne Salmes stared at the predator, then down at Vickers staggering under the pilot's weight. She fumbled out one of her small cigars, lit it, and dropped the gold-chased lighter back into her pocket. Then she scrambled to the bole and began to descend. The bark tore the skin beneath her coveralls and from the palms of both hands.

From the lowest branch, head-height for the stooping Vickers, Adrienne cried, "Here!" and tried to snatch Washman from the guide's back. The pilot was too heavy. Vickers thrust his shoulders upward. Between them, they slung Washman onto the branch. His arms and legs hung down to either side and his face was pressed cruelly into the bark.

The tyrannosaur crashed through the woody undergrowth twenty feet away. It stank of death, even against the mild breeze. The dead sauropod, of course, rotting between the four-inch teeth and smeared greasily over the killer's head and breast . . . but beyond the carrion odor was a tangible sharpness filling the mouths of guide and client as the brush parted.

Vickers had no chance of getting higher into the oak than the jaws could pick him off. Instead he turned, wishing that he had been able to keep at least his knife for this moment. Adrienne Salmes dragged on her cigar, stood, and flung the glowing cylinder into the wreckage of the platform: "Henry!" she cried, and she bent back down with her hand out to Vickers.

One stride put the tyrannosaur into the midst of the upended platform. As flimsy as the metal was, its edges were sharp and they clung instead of springing back the way splintered branches would. The beast's powerful legs had pistoned it through dense brush without slowing. It could still have dragged the wreckage forward through the one remaining step that would have ended the three humans. Instead, it drew back with a startled snort and tried to nuzzle its feet clear.

The kerosene bloomed into a sluggish red blaze. The tyrannosaur's distended nostrils *whuffed* in a double lungful of the soot-laden smoke that rolled from the peaks of the flames. The beast squealed and kicked in berserk fury, scattering fire-wrapped metal. Its rigid tail slashed the brush, fanning the flames toward the oak. Deeply indented leaves shriveled like hands closing. Vickers forgot about trying to climb. He rolled Don Washman off the branch again, holding him by the armpits. The pilot's feet fell as they would. "While we've got a chance!" the guide cried, knowing that the brush fire would suffocate them in the treetop even if the flames themselves did not climb so high.

Adrienne Salmes jumped down. Each of them wrapped one of the pilot's arms around their shoulders. They began to stumble through the brush, the backs of their necks prickling with the heat of the fire.

The tyrannosaur was snarling in unexampled rage. Fire was familiar to a creature which had lived a century among forests and lightning. Being caught in the midst of a blaze was something else again. The beast would not run while the platform still tangled its feet, and the powerful kicks that shredded the binding metal also scattered the flames. When at last the great killer broke free, it did so from the heart of an amoeba a hundred yards in diameter crackling in the brush. Adrienne and the guide were struggling into the forest when they heard the tyrannosaur give its challenge again. It sounded far away.

"I don't suppose there's any way we could retrieve the rifles," Adrienne said as Vickers put another stick on their fire. It was a human touch in the Cretaceous night. Besides, the guide was chilly. They had used his coveralls to improvise a stretcher for Washman, thrusting a pruned sapling up each leg and out the corresponding sleeve. They had not used the pilot's own garment for fear that being stripped would accelerate the effects of shock. Washman was breathing stertorously and had not regained consciousness since the crash.

"Well, I couldn't tell about yours," Vickers said with a wry smile, "but even with the brush popping I'm pretty sure I heard the magazine of mine go off. I'd feel happier if we had it along, that's for sure."

"I'm going to miss that Schultz and Larsen," the woman said. She took out a cigar, looked at it, and slipped it back into her pocket. "Slickest action they ever put on a rifle. Well, I suppose I can find another when we get back."

They had found the saplings growing in a sauropod burn. Fortunately, Adrienne had retained her sheath knife, a monster with a saw-backed, eight-inch blade that Vickers had thought a joke—until it became their only tool. The knife and the cigarette lighter, he reminded himself. Resiny wood cracked, pitching sparks beyond the circle they had cleared in the fallen needles. The woman immediately stood and kicked the spreading flames back in toward the center.

"You saved my life," Vickers said, looking into the fire. "With that cigar. You were thinking a lot better than I was, and that's the only reason I'm not in a carnosaur's belly."

Adrienne sat down beside the guide. After a moment, he met her eyes. She said, "You could have left Don and gotten back safely yourself."

"I could have been a goddamn politician!" Vickers snapped. "But that wasn't a way I wanted to live my life." He relaxed and shook his head. "Sorry," he said. She laughed and squeezed his bare knee above the abrasion. "Besides," Vickers went on, "I'm not sure it would have worked. The damned tyrannosaur was obviously tracking us by scent. Most of what we know about the big carnivores started a minute or two before they were killed. They . . . I don't mean dinos're smart. But their instincts are a lot more efficient than you'd think if you hadn't watched them."

Adrienne Salmes nodded. "A computer isn't smart either, but that doesn't keep it from solving problems."

"Exactly," Vickers said, "exactly. And if the problem that tyrannosaur was trying to solve was us—well, I'm just as glad the fire wiped out our scent. We've got a long hike tomorrow lugging Don."

"What bothers me," the blonde woman said carefully, "is the fact it could find us easily enough if it tried. Look, we can't be very far from the camp, not at the platform's speed. Why don't we push on now instead of waiting for daylight?"

Vickers glanced down at the responder on his wrist, tuned to the beacon in the center of the camp. "Five or six miles," he said. "Not too bad, even with Don. But I think we're better off here than stumbling into camp in the dark. The smell of the trophies is going to keep packs of the smaller predators around it. They're active in the dark, and they've got damned sharp teeth."

Adrienne chuckled, startling away some of the red eyes ringing their fire. Vickers had whittled a branch into a whippy cudgel with an eye toward bagging a mammal or two for dinner, but both he and his client were too thirsty to feel much hunger as yet. "Well," she said, "we have to find something else to do till daybreak, then—and I'm too keyed up to sleep." She touched Vickers' thigh again.

All the surrounding eyes vanished when a dinosaur grunted.

It could have been a smaller creature, even a herbivore; but that would not have made it harmless. In the event, it was precisely what they feared it was when the savage noise filled the forest: the tyrannosaur hunting them and very close.

The fire was of branches and four-foot lengths of sapling they had broken after notching with the knife. Vickers' face lost all expression.

He grabbed the unburned end of a billet and turned toward the sound. "No!" Adrienne cried. "Spread the fire in a line—it won't follow us through a fire again!"

It was the difference between no good chance and no chance at all. Vickers scuffed a bootload of coals out into the heaped pine needles and ran into the night with his brand. The lowest branches of the pines were dead and dry, light-starved by the foliage nearer the sky. The resin-sizzling torch caught them and they flared up behind the guide. Half-burned twigs that fell to the forest floor flickered among the matted needles. Vickers already was twenty yards from their original campfire when he remembered that Don Washman still lay helpless beside it.

The dozen little fires Vickers had set, and the similar line Adrienne Salmes had ignited on the other side of the campfire, were already beginning to grow and merge. The guide turned and saw the flames nearing Washman's feet, though not—thank God—his head. That was when the tyrannosaur stepped into view. In the firelight it was hard to tell the mottled camouflage natural to its hide from the cracked and blistered areas left by the earlier blaze. Vickers cursed and hurled his torch. It spun end over end, falling short of its intended target.

The tyrannosaur had been advancing with its head hung low. It was still fifteen feet high at the hips. In the flickering light, it bulked even larger than the ten tons it objectively weighed. Adrienne looked absurd and tiny as she leaped forward to meet the creature with a pine torch. Behind her the flames were spreading, but they were unlikely to form a barrier to the beast until they formed a continuous line. That was seconds or a minute away, despite the fact that the fuel was either dry or soaking with pitch.

Adrienne slashed her brand in a figure eight like a child with a sparkler. Confused by the glare and stench of the resinous flames, the carnosaur reared back and took only a half-step forward—onto the torch Vickers had thrown.

The guide grabbed up the poles at Washman's head. He dragged the pilot away from the fire like a pony hauling a travois. When the tyrannosaur screeched, Vickers dropped the stretcher again and turned, certain he would see the beast striding easily through the curtain of fire. Instead it was backing away, its great head slashing out to either side as if expecting to find a tangible opponent there. The blonde woman threw her torch at the dinosaur. Then, with her arms shielding her face, she leaped across the fire. She would have run into the bole of a tree had Vickers not caught her as she blundered past. "It's all right!" he shouted. "It's turned! Get the other end of the stretcher."

Spattering pitch had pocked but not fully ignited Adrienne's garments. The tears furrowing the soot on her cheeks were partly the result of irritants in the flames. "It'll be back," she said. "You know it will."

"I'll have a rifle in my hands the next time I see it," the guide said. "This is one dino that won't be a matter of business to shoot."

The alarm awakened the camp. Then muzzle flashes lit the white faces of the clients when the first dinosaur trotted down the trail. Even the grenade launcher could not divert the monsters. After a long time, the gunfire slackened. Then Miss McPherson returned with additional ammunition.

Somewhat later, the shooting stopped for good.

If he had not been moving in a stupor, the noise of the scavengers would have warned Vickers. As it was, he pushed out of the trees and into a slaughter yard teeming with vermin on a scale with the carcasses they gorged on. Only when Mears cried out did the guide realize they were back in the camp. The four clients were squeezed together on top of the machine gun tower.

Vickers was too shocked to curse. He set down his end of the stretcher abruptly. The other end was already on the ground. "Henry, do you want the knife?" Adrienne asked. He shook his head without turning around.

There were at least a dozen torosaurs sprawled on the northern quadrant of the camp, along the trail. They were more like hills than anything that had been alive, but explosive bullets from the 12.7mm machine gun had opened them up like chainsaws. The clients were shouting and waving rifles in the air from the low tower. Vickers, only fifty feet away, could not hear them because of the clatter of the scavengers. There were well over one hundred tons of carrion in the clearing. Literally thousands of lesser creatures had swarmed out of the skies and the forest to take advantage.

"Lesser" did not mean "little" in the Cretaceous.

Vickers swallowed. "Can you carry Don alone if I lead the way?" he asked. "We've got to get to the others to find out what happened."

"I'll manage," the woman said. Then, "You know, they must have fired off all their ammunition. That's why they're huddled there beside—"

"I know what they goddamn did!" the guide snarled. "I also know that if there's one goddamn round left, we've got a chance to sort things out!" Neither of them voiced the corollary. They had heard the tyrannosaur challenge the dawn an hour earlier. Just before they burst into the clearing, they had heard a second call, and it was much closer.

Adrienne knelt, locking one of the pilot's arms over her shoulders. She straightened at the knees, lifting her burden with her. Washman's muscles were slack. "That's something I owe my husband for," Adrienne gasped. "Practice moving drunks. When I was young and a fool."

Vickers held one of the stretcher poles like a quarterstaff. He knew how he must look in his underwear. That bothered him obscurely almost as much as the coming gauntlet of carrion-eaters did.

A white-furred pterosaur with folded, twenty-foot wings struck at the humans as they maneuvered between two looming carcasses. Vickers slapped away the red, chisel-like beak with his staff. Then he prodded the great carrion-eater again for good measure as Adrienne staggered around it. The guide began to laugh.

"What the hell's so funny?" she demanded.

"If there's an intrusion vehicle back there," Vickers said, "which there probably isn't or these sheep wouldn't be here now, maybe I'll send everybody home without me. That way I don't have to explain to Stern what went wrong."

"That's a hell of a joke!" Adrienne snapped.

"Who's joking?"

Because of the huge quantity of food, the scavengers were feeding without much squabbling. The three humans slipped through the mass, challenged only by the long-necked pterosaur. Fragile despite its size, the great gliding creature defended its personal space with an intensity that was its only road to survival. Met with equal force, it backed away of necessity.

Dieter Jost lay under the gun tower, slightly protected by the legs and crossbraces. He was mumbling in German and his eyes did not focus. Vickers took the pilot's weight to set him by the ladder. Mears hopped down and began shrieking at Adrienne Salmes, "Goddamn you, your crazy husband took the time machine back without us, you bitch!"

Vickers straightened and slapped the contractor with a blow that released all the frustrations that had been building. Mears stumbled against the tower, turned back with his fists bunched, and stopped. The blonde woman's knife was almost touching his ribs.

"Where's Steve?" the guide asked loudly. He was massaging his right palm with his left as if working a piece of clay between them.

Miss McPherson jumped to the ground. In the darkness, the tower had drawn them. Since both boxes of 12.7mm ammunition had been sluiced out into the night, it was obviously irrational to stay on a platform that would not reach a tyrannosaur's knee . . . but human reason is in short supply in a darkened forest. "One of the dinosaurs killed him," the older woman blurted. "We, we tried to keep Mr. Jost safe with us, but we ran out of bullets and, and, the last hour has been—"

Brewer had a cut above his right eyebrow. He looked shell-shocked but not on the edge of hysteria as his three companions were. "When it was light enough to search," he said, "I got your ammo out. I thought it might work in his"—he gestured toward Dieter beneath him—"rifle. Close but no cigar." The meat packer's fingers traced the line which a piece of bursting cartridge case had drawn across his scalp.

"Well, we put the fear of God into 'em," Mears asserted sullenly. "They've been afraid to come close even though we're out of ammo now. But how'd we get *out* of here, I want to know!"

"We don't," Vickers said flatly. "If the intrusion vehicle's gone, we are well and truly screwed. Because there's never yet been an insertion within a hundred years of another insertion. But we've got a closer problem than that, because—"

The tyrannosaur drowned all other sounds with its roar.

Vickers stepped into the nearer of the ponies without changing expression. The engine caught when he pushed the starter. "Adrienne," he said, "get the rest of them down to the slough—Don and Dieter in the pony. Fast. If I don't come back, you're on your own."

Adrienne jumped in front of the vehicle. "We'll both go."

"Goddamn it, *move!*" the guide shouted. "We don't have time!"

"We don't know which of us it's tracking!" the woman shouted back. "I've got to come along!"

Vickers nodded curtly. "Brewer," he called over his shoulder, "get everybody else out of here before a pack of carnosaurs arrives and you're in the middle of it." He engaged the pony's torque converter while the blonde woman was barely over the side. As they spun out southward from the camp, the guide shouted, "Don't leave Don and Dieter behind, or so help me—"

"How fast can it charge?" Adrienne asked as they bounced over a root to avoid a tangle of berry bushes.

"Fast," Vickers said bluntly. "I figure if we can reach the sauropods we killed the other day, we've got a chance, though."

They were jouncing too badly for Adrienne to stay in a seat. She squatted behind Vickers and hung onto the sides. "If you think the meat's going to draw it off, won't it stop in the camp?" she asked.

"Not that," said the guide, slamming over the tiller to skirt a ravine jeweled with flecks of quartz. "I'm betting there'll be gorgosaurs there by now, feeding. That's how we'd have gotten carnosaur heads for the other gunners, you see. The best chance I can see is half a dozen gorgosaurs'll take care of even *our* problem."

"They'll take care of us too, won't they?" the woman objected.

"Got a better idea?"

The smell of the rotting corpses would have guided them the last quarter-mile even without the marker. The tyrannosaur's own kill had been several days riper, but the sheer mass of the five titanosaurs together more than equaled the effect. The nearest of the bodies lay with its spine toward the approaching pony in a shaft of sunlight through the browsed-away top cover. Vickers throttled back with a curse. "If there's nothing here," he said, "then we may as well bend over and kiss our asses goo—"

A carnosaur raised its gory head over the carrion. It had been buried to its withers in the sauropod's chest, bolting bucketloads of lung tissue. Its original color would have been in doubt had not a second killer stalked into sight. The gorgosaurs wore black stripes over fields of dirty sand color, and their tongues were as red as their bloody teeth. Each of the pair was as heavy as a large automobile, and they were as viciously lethal as leopards, pound for pound.

"All right," Vickers said quietly. He steered to the side of the waiting pair, giving the diesel a little more fuel. Three more gorgosaurs strode watchfully out of the forest. They were in an arc facing the pony. The nearest of them was only thirty feet away. Their breath rasped like leather pistons. The guide slowed again, almost to a stop. He swung the tiller away.

One of the gorgosaurs snarled and charged. Both humans shouted, but the killer's target was the tyrannosaur that burst out of the forest behind the pony. Vickers rolled the throttle wide open, sending the vehicle between two of the lesser carnivores. Instead of snapping or bluffing, the tyrannosaur strode through the gorgosaur that had tried to meet it. The striped carnosaur spun to the ground with its legs flailing. Pine straw sprayed as it hit.

"It's still coming!" Adrienne warned. Vickers hunched as if that could coax more speed out of the little engine. The four gorgosaurs still able to run had scattered to either side. The fifth thrashed on the ground, its back broken by an impact the tyrannosaur had scarcely noted. At another time, the pack might have faced down their single opponent. Now, the wounded tyrannosaur was infuriated beyond questions of challenge and territory.

"Henry, the river," the woman said. Vickers did not change direction, running parallel to the unseen bank. "Henry," she said again, trying to steady herself close to his ear because she did not want to shout, not for this, "we've done everything else we could. We have to try this."

A branch lashed Vickers across the face. His tears streamed across the red brand it left on his cheek. He turned as abruptly as the pony's narrow axles allowed. They plunged to the right, over the ridgeline and into the thick-set younger trees that bordered the water. Then they were through that belt, both of them bleeding from the whipping branches. Reeds and mud were roostering up from all four wheels. The pony's aluminum belly began to lift. Their speed dropped as the treads started to act as paddles automatically.

"Oh dear God, he's stopping, he's stopping," Adrienne whimpered. Vickers looked over his shoulder. There was nothing to dodge now that they were afloat, only the mile of haze and water that they would never manage to cross. The tyrannosaur had paused where the pines gave way to reeds, laterite soil to mud. It stood splay-legged, turning first one eye, then the other, to the escaping humans. The bloody Sun jeweled its pupils.

"If he doesn't follow—" Vickers said.

The tyrannosaur stepped forward inexorably. The muddy water slapped as the feet slashed through it. Then the narrow keel of the breastbone cut the water as well. The tyrannosaur's back sank to a line of knobs on the surface, kinking horizontally as the hind legs thrust the beast toward its prey. The carnosaur moved much more quickly in the water than did the vehicle it pursued. The beast was fifty yards away, now, and there was no way to evade it.

They were far enough out into the stream that Vickers could see the other pony winking on the bank a half-mile distant. Brewer had managed to get them out of the charnel house they had made of the camp, at least. "Give me your knife," Vickers said. Twenty feet away, the ruby eye of the carnosaur glazed and cleared as its nicitating membrane wiped away the spray.

"Get your own damned knife!" Adrienne said. She half-rose, estimating that if she jumped straight over the stern she would not overset the pony.

Vickers saw the water beneath them darken, blacken. The pony quivered. There was no wake, but the tons of death slanting up from beneath raised a slick on the surface. They were still above the crocodile's vast haunches when its teeth closed on the tyrannosaur.

The suction of the tyrannosaur going under halted the pony as if it had struck a wall. Then the water rose and slapped them forward. Vickers' hand kept Adrienne from pitching out an instant after she had lost the need to do so. They drew away from the battle in the silt-golden water, fifty yards, one hundred. Vickers cut off the engine. "The current'll take us to the others," he explained. "And without the paddles we won't attract as much attention."

Adrienne was trying to resheathe her knife. Finally, she held the leather with one hand and slipped the knife in with her fingers on the blade as if threading a needle. She looked at Vickers. "I didn't think that would work," she said. "Or it would work a minute after we were . . . gone."

The guide managed to laugh. "Might still happen," he said, nodding at the disturbed water. "Off-hand, though, I'd say the 'largest land predator of all time' just met something bigger." He sobered. "God, I hope we don't meet its mate. I don't want to drown. I really don't."

Water spewed skyward near the other pony. At first Vickers thought one of the clients had managed to detonate a grenade and blow them all to hell. "My God," Adrienne whispered, "you said they couldn't—"

At the distance they were from it, only the gross lines of the intrusion vehicle could be identified. A pair of machine guns had been welded onto the frame, and there appeared to be a considerable party of uniformed men aboard. "I don't understand it either," Vickers said, "but I know where to ask." He reached for the starter.

Adrienne caught his arm. He looked back in surprise. "If it was safer to drift with the current before, it's still safer," she said. She pointed at the subsiding froth from which the tyrannosaur had never re-emerged. "We're halfway already. And besides, it gives us some time—" she put her hand on Vickers' shoulder—"for what I had in mind last night at the campfire."

"They're watching us with binoculars!" the guide sputtered, trying to break away from the kiss.

"They can all sit in a circle and play with themselves," the blonde woman said. "We've earned this."

Vickers held himself rigid for a moment. Then he reached out and began to spread the pony's front awning with one hand.

The secretary wore a uniform and a pistol. When he nodded, Vickers opened the door. Stern sat at the metal desk. Dr. Galil was to his right and the only other occupant of the room. Vickers sat gingerly on one of the two empty chairs.

"I'm not going to debrief you," Stern said. "Others have done that. Rather, I am going to tell you certain things. They are confidential. Utterly confidential. You understand that."

"Yes," Vickers said. Stern's office was not in the Ministry of Culture and Tourism; but then, Vickers had never expected that it would be.

"Dr. Galil," Stern continued, and the cherubic scientist beamed like a Christmas ornament, "located the insertion party by homing on the alpha waves of one of the members of it. You, to be precise. Frankly, we were all amazed at this breakthrough; it is not a technique we would have tested if there had been any alternative available."

Vickers licked his lips. "I thought you were going to fire me," he said flatly.

"Would it bother you if we did?" Stern riposted.

"Yes." The guide paused. The fear was greater now that he had voiced it. He had slept very little during the week since the curtailed safari had returned. "It—the job . . . suits me. Even dealing with the clients, I can do it. For having the rest."

Stern nodded. Galil whispered to him, then looked back at Vickers. "We wish to experiment with this effect," Stern continued aloud. "Future rescues—or resupplies—may depend on it. There are other reasons as well." He cleared his throat.

"There is the danger that we will not be able to consistently repeat the operation," Dr. Galil broke in. "That the person will be marooned, you see. For there must, of course, be a brain so that we will have a brainwave to locate. Thus we need a volunteer."

"You want a baseline," Vickers said in response to what he had not been told. "You want to refine your calibration so that you can drop a man—or men—or tanks—at a precise time. And if your baseline is in the Cretaceous instead of the present, you don't have the problem of closing off another block each time somebody is inserted into the future before you get the technique down pat."

Stern grew very still. "Do you volunteer?" he asked.

Vickers nodded. "Sure. Even if I thought you'd let me leave here alive if I didn't, I'd volunteer—for that. I should have thought of the— the research potential—myself. I'd have blackmailed you into sending me."

The entryway door opened unexpectedly. "I already did that, Henry," said Adrienne Salmes. "Though I wouldn't say their arms had to be twisted very hard." She stepped past Vickers and laid the small receiver on Stern's desk beside the sending unit. "I decided it was time to come in."

"You arranged this for me?" Vickers asked in amazement.

"I arranged it for us," Adrienne replied, seating herself on the empty chair. "I'm not entirely sure that I want to retire to the Cretaceous. But—" she looked sharply at Stern—"I'm quite sure that I don't want to live in the world our friends here will shape if they do gain complete ability to manipulate the past. At least in the Cretaceous, we know what the rules are."

Vickers stood. "Shlomo," he said shaking Dr. Galil's hand, "you haven't failed before, and I don't see you failing now. We won't be marooned. Though it might be better if we were." He turned to the man behind the desk. "Mr. Stern," he said, "you've got your volunteers. I—we—we'll get you a list of the supplies we'll need."

Adrienne touched his arm. "This will work, you know," she said. She took no notice of the others in the room. "Like the crocodile."

"Tell me in a year's time that it *has* worked," Vickers said.

And she did.

BOUNDARY LAYER

The great carnivore's jaws slammed like a tomb door. "Henry," said Adrienne Vickers, "the drug's wearing off. We're going to have a very angry tyrannosaurus in a moment." The blonde woman's voice was slightly louder than was necessary to be heard over the unmuffled blatting of the crawler's diesel. She lowered the muzzle of her rifle, well aware that if she stretched the weapon out at arm's length, it would rap the dinosaur's jagged yellow teeth.

Henry Vickers risked a brief look over his shoulder. Although the crawler moved at little more than a fast walk, it was twelve feet wide and the forest had not been cleared for its passage. The last thing the hunter wanted was to have to back the articulated vehicle, especially if the tyrannosaur shackled to the bed was really awakening. "Umm," he said to his wife, "it's probably just reflex. Anyway, we don't have much farther to go. Give it another jolt from the capture gun if you have to—" he ran a finger down the barrel of the smoothbore clipped to the crawler's splash board—"but we don't want it to overdose and die on us."

"We don't want it to wake up and eat us, either," the blonde woman said tartly. She was standing, facing backward in the open cab of the vehicle. Her buttocks rested on the rim of the splashboard. "Besides, it'll die a few days after they get it back Topside anyway. From the fungus or whatever. You know that."

Thus far, the dinosaur's yawn did seem to have been an isolated incident, Vickers thought. He countersteered to square off his approach to the gap between two huge pine trees. "They may have cured that problem by now," he said, keeping his voice more reasonable than he felt. The tyrannosaur's teeth *were* very close to his back, and he too was far from certain that the shackles would hold if the creature lunged with all its strength. "Anyway, Adrienne, even if it dies, we'll have brought back a live tyrannosaur. That . . . that's worth having done, I think. I don't need to apologize for the things I've brought in dead, but . . . I think this is worth doing." After a pause he added, "Besides—I trust you to handle our friend if he gets rambunctious."

Adrienne snorted, but she smiled as well. The flattery showed affection and, in addition, it was true. Vickers' back was turned toward an eight-ton predator, with nothing but his wife's cool accuracy to save him if the creature broke free. "Well," the tall blonde said, "if it were me, they'd make do Topside with something a lot easier to handle than this boy, at least until I was sure they could keep it alive themselves. But I suppose I can humor you this once."

The crawler bulled into, then mounted, the decaying mass of a fallen tree. Vickers had climbed the obstacle on the way out, racing from camp toward the drug-numbed tyrannosaur. Until he had returned with the crawler, his wife had to guard the creature alone and fend off lesser predators. The vehicle's bed, a twelve-by-fifty-foot trough on six axles, had been empty the first time it encountered the tree bole. Now . . . the crawler had carried heavier loads: adult torosaurs with horns like flint spears, and once an immature sauropod which weighed at least twelve tons. Never before, however, had the cargo been so potentially dangerous if it awakened before being unloaded into the holding cage at the permanent camp.

The diesel bellowed as the tracks of the cab unit bit, spewing fibers of russet, rotting wood over the bed and its burden. Then the log gave way and the multiple wheels lurched over its remains, squealing and creaking like sows at the trough.

There were no other problems before the crawler snorted out of the forest into the large clearing of the base camp. "Home is the hunter," Adrienne murmured ironically as she glanced over her own shoulder. But it *was* home to the pair of them, though it had few enough amenities. They had never even bothered to name it. For safety from the things that rushed to water and the things that preyed on them there, the camp had been built five hundred feet from the river. The current drove rams that lifted water into a settling tank. Purification had proven unnecessary: repeated testing had failed to turn up any microbes which would be harmful to humans who had evolved some seventy million years in the future.

The house itself was on posts three feet high to discourage some of the nastier vermin. For a hundred yards in every direction stretched a belt of broad-leafed ground cover akin to ivy. Adrienne had wanted grass, but the Israeli officials Topside had vetoed the notion. True grasses had appeared in the Eocene, ten or so million years further up the line. It was no secret—to the pair of them in the Cretaceous base camp—that the intentions of the scientists working on time intrusion, and the orders of the government officials above them, were to modify the present by selectively changing the past. The potential for change from the early introduction of grass was considerable and of utterly unguessable direction. It was not a chance that those in charge were willing to risk for aesthetics.

There was a twenty-meter patch of raw earth and sand, well to the west of the house: the impact point for the intrusion vehicles which served as the only communication between the station and Topside. Topside was what had been the present when Vickers and Adrienne had volunteered to run a permanent base in the Cretaceous. When an intrusion vehicle impacted, everything within the sphere of its field was exchanged with an identical sphere at the impact point. On one-shot hunting intrusions, that was of no significance. Here, where repeated transfers would otherwise have dug a deepening pit in the Cretaceous soil, it had been necessary to stack the return point in the hangar Topside with sandbags. Vickers sometimes wondered what effect the synthetic fabric of the bags would have had if it had been discovered in Cretaceous strata during the historical past. But it hadn't, of course; and if the non-degradable plastic *had* been dug up in 1920, say, then that fact would simply have become part of the present in which Dr. Shlomo Galil of Cambridge University developed a technique of time intrusion.

At least, that was one theory.

Vickers declutched the left track to swing the crawler wide around the impact point. The next intrusion was not due for forty hours, but there was no reason to take chances with an effect that could lop you into pieces separated by seventy million years. Adrienne looked from the holding cage they were approaching back to the slack-muscled tyrannosaur. "Well," she said, "you were right, Henry. Though I'd as soon you were as careful with your own safety as you used to be with your clients'."

If Vickers intended a reply, it was lost in the hissing of a corona discharge. An intrusion vehicle was appearing almost two days early.

Vickers halted the crawler in surprise, just short of the gate of the great steel holding cage. Adrienne touched her husband's shoulder. Her eyes were back on their drugged captive. "Run it in, Henry," she said. "They won't be ready to load for a while anyway—" though the sides of the intrusion vehicle were down and the platform looked empty save for six passengers—"and I don't want our friend to lie here with just the chains to hold him. Not any longer than he has to."

The hunter nodded and drove on into the cage. He left the tyrannosaur shackled and the crawler in the cage instead of driving it out the far end empty. The two humans exited through the narrow escape hatch in time to meet their visitors in front of the house.

Five of the newcomers were young men in fatigue uniforms, glancing about nervously at the lowering forest as if they expected a pack of carnosaurs to burst upon them. The sixth man's name was Avraham Stern, and he was head of the Time Intrusion Project. Only in its advertising was that project primarily concerned with safaris of rich civilians entering the past to hunt the biggest of game. Stern was a dumpy, bulky man who looked as uncomfortable in fatigues as he usually did in a business suit. "Mrs. Salmes," he said, "Mr. Vickers, good day. I regret to surprise you this way."

The captive dinosaur was beginning to gurgle with increasing power. Stern and Vickers ignored it, but the five young soldiers edged together instinctively. "Events," Stern continued, "require that we borrow you from the, ah, habitat phase for a time. Since that means closing down this station, I thought it best to inform you in person. I have brought these gentlemen—" he nodded toward the clustered soldiers—"to aid in carrying materials to the intrusion vehicle."

"What do you mean, 'close down the station'?" Vickers asked very softly. Both Stern and the blonde woman showed they recognized the emotions underlying the words. The official ostentatiously moved his hand away from his sagging trousers pocket. Adrienne ran her finger along the noses of the bullets in her cartridge belt, counting the rounds.

"Nothing like that, I assure you," Stern said in careful reassurance. "There will be another station soon, and you two will be manning it. Only . . . for the moment, we have need of the best Cretaceous hunting guide available. And that is you, Mr. Vickers."

The hunter relaxed a trifle, but Adrienne asked sharply, "Getting one particular guide is that important? More important than the project?"

Stern frowned. "Mrs. Salmes—" he began.

"Mrs. Vickers now, as you damned well know," Adrienne snapped.

"Mrs. Vickers," the official continued, nodding again toward the soldiers, "you understand that while these gentlemen are discreet, they are young. And there is no reason for them to be concerned with the research aspects of our program." No reason for them to learn, that was, that the permanent station was a hinge in experiments to calibrate the intrusion vehicles more accurately. When that governmentally desired end was achieved, it would be possible to insert a body of men into the historical past. With the Israeli government choosing the place and purpose of such an intrusion, the world could be expected to change very abruptly.

The blonde woman shook her head with the perfect arrogance of one born to wealth and beauty. "Give me a reason to believe you, Stern," she said. "Sure, Henry's the best"—she squeezed her husband's arm without breaking eye contact with the Israeli official—"but you have other guides. I know how important this . . . habitat phase is to you. I don't believe you're closing it down, even temporarily, just because somebody wants to go hunting for dinos."

Stern sighed. For a moment he looked less like a bear than like a great, sad ape who faced a world too complex to be understood and too dangerous to be ignored. "Mrs. Vickers," he said, "a party of important persons will be hunting the Cretaceous. It is necessary that one of them . . . the US Secretary of State . . . have a good hunt in order that he become—receptive to proposals of the host government. Our government. Otherwise"—Stern tongued his lips but continued—"otherwise, it is believed in some quarters that there will be no time to pursue the habitat experiments to their conclusion. Madame, that is as open as I can possibly be."

"All right," said Vickers, touching his wife's hand to end the discussion. He too had a weary look, that of a workman who had ended his shift and been unexpectedly recalled to deal with an emergency. Behind him, the tyrannosaur grunted savagely. "It'll take two loads," the hunter said. "I'll put another dart in the dino and we'll send him Topside alone. Then they can return the vehicle for the rest of us and the gear."

Stern shook his head impatiently. "I regret, Mr. Vickers," he said, "that I have not made myself clear. Duration in the past is concurrent with duration—Topside, as you know, unless the point of intrusion or of return is changed. There will be no second trip. Time, ah, Topside, is of . . . considerable importance. We cannot now afford the delay of staging a second intrusion into this time horizon. Further, there have been excellent results achieved by homing insertions in on your alpha pattern, Mr. Vickers . . . but it is by no means a certain technique. Even if *I* were willing to risk being stranded in the Cretaceous myself"—he ventured a smile that had as much humor in it as Stern's smiles ever did—"I assure you that my superiors would be quite displeased at the realization that I had risked stranding *you* at this juncture. No, the animal stays."

"Henry," said Adrienne, "go ahead and give him another dart before he tears the crawler apart." She looked at Stern. "The animal goes, I think," she added calmly. "We'll leave everything else except the guns and go back with the tyrannosaur ourselves."

One of the soldiers blurted something in startled Hebrew. All five of the young men looked aghast. Even Stern seemed to have lost some of his aplomb. "Do you live to infuriate me, woman?" he demanded, his hands at his sides and clenched. "Is this your only joy? There are millions, *billions* of every sort of beast to be captured at your leisure. I have said *this* is an emergency. The creature will die within days anyway, surely you know that? Why do you persist in goading me?"

"Because," Adrienne said in a voice as gray and frigid as her eyes, "we've taken a live tyrannosaur, Henry and I, and we're going to bring it back no matter what happens to it then. Because we've come this far with it . . . and because it's worth doing, I think."

Henry Vickers chuckled companionably and turned. The great carnivore had lifted its head off the bed of the crawler and was making metallic noises as it strained against its shackles. The capture gun thumped. Its long, white-feathered hypodermic arched through the bars of the cage to bury itself in the tyrannosaur's throat. Vickers broke the action of the gun and drew another dart cartridge from his pouch.

Stern blinked as if the previous conversation had not taken place. "You have only that with you, Mr. Vickers?" he asked. "Not a real rifle, that is?"

Vickers smiled, no longer weary. "I have Adrienne," he replied. "I don't have anything to worry about with her around, Mr. Stern. You of all people should appreciate that." He began to laugh aloud as the drug took hold and the dinosaur shuddered back into restive somnolence.

Their boots clashed on the concrete floor as they inspected the equipment. The heels sent a babble of echoes whispering from one end of the warehouse to the other. Stern carried a briefcase, Vickers only the stapled flimsies listing the equipment and personnel of the safari. Both men were accustomed by their professions to speak in a voice that carried only to the intended listener; and even that murmur was masked by their ricocheting footsteps.

"The public relations team with its cameras, the cook, and supplies for such supernumeraries will be inserted on the other vehicle," Stern said.

The guide shook his head in disgust. "Christ," he said, "I wish somebody'd talked to me while this was still being planned. It's going to be a mare's nest on site with all these untrained people running around, you know." He ran his finger over the fresh rubber of the track beside him. The half-tracked vehicles themselves were at least forty years old, but Stern assured him that they had been rebuilt and re-engined for the intrusion. "I want Martinus Duisberg for the other guide," Vickers said. "You must have a line on where he is, even though you've retired him."

The official nodded. "Mr. Duisberg is on his farm outside Bloemfontein," he said. "Unfortunately, he is not suitable for guiding safaris—and especially this safari—since his accident."

The guide spun, popping the papers in his hand. "You want them safe?" he demanded. "Fine! I want them safe too. Cooch Duisberg is a crack shot and as steady a hand as you've ever had on your payroll. This accident you're talking about—"

"There is more required, Mr. Vickers, than—"

"—this *accident* occurred when a client panicked and wrapped his arms around Cooch from behind! And he *still* dropped the megalosaur, even though it caught his face in its foreclaws before it died."

Stern nodded in agreement. "Mr. Duisberg was not held responsible for the accident," he said. "As you know, he was retired on full pension. But a guide whose face—shall we say, bears the stigmata of catastrophe?—is not a suitable advertisement for a sports activity. There is more required than skill in hunting. The client in this case *must* return satisfied. The other guide will be Mr. Thomas Warren, whose skill in the . . . client relations aspects is perhaps equaled only by your skills in the hunt itself, Mr. Vickers. You, of course, will be in charge."

Vickers snorted. "Except," he said, "that with the US Secretary of State and the Prime Minister of Israel present, we're none of us in charge, are we? If Secretary Cardway has to be kept happy at all costs, then do I have the authority to say 'no' if he wants the helicopter to set down right in front of a carnosaur?"

"We have considered that point," the official said, looking up at the lighted ceiling instead of meeting Vickers' eyes. "The risk of a shooting platform failing while in the air is unacceptable on this hunt."

"That was sabotage before. You know that."

"Turbines can fail under field conditions in the Cretaceous," Stern continued inexorably. "As you imply, we could not realistically deny the Secretary use of a shooting platform, a helicopter, if one were available. Therefore, the equipment for this safari does not include a shooting platform. These half-tracks"—he patted the steel side—"will carry the hunters. Each has a swivel for a heavy machine gun on the bulkhead behind the cab. That way there will be a pair of machine guns protecting the Secretary at all times. And the Prime Minister, of course."

"Christ," the guide muttered, "Christ." He looked again at the long personnel list in his hand. "All right, this one—Craig, John C. Attendant. What the hell does that mean? And why is he starred as a 'must include' on the first intrusion with the brass?"

"Mr. Craig is a Secret Service employee, as I understand," Stern said. He still would not look at his companion.

"A bodyguard," Vickers said. "Marvelous, absolutely necessary on a safari—a bodyguard." His voice was growing harsh in timbre without becoming louder. "Bloody tanks that'll raise a racket and a dust cloud for miles around, no helicopter to locate game, and now I'm squiring around a bodyguard to keep me from assassinating somebody besides! Is everybody Topside gone crazy?"

Stern looked at him. With his right hand, the official rubbed his forehead and the edge of his gray, short-cropped hair. "Sometimes I wonder, Mr. Vickers," he said at last. "But I soldier on despite that. I think you can appreciate the . . . attitude. As to the reason we did not protest at Mr. Craig's presence . . . Well. Our understanding is that the request comes from the permanent officials—the civil service officials, that is to say—rather than from Secretary Cardway himself, who likes to perceive himself as being able to cope with anything. He is from Texas, I believe. But since the Secretary cleared the request, we thought it—impolite—to object to what others considered to be a necessary precaution. The Americans, you Americans, are understandably concerned about, yes, the possibility of assassination. And since the . . . unexpected can occur, we agreed."

"'We Americans,'" Vickers repeated disgustedly. "I voted for somebody or other when I turned eighteen, and that's as much contact with politics as I needed to have in this life, Stern. I could do without what this hunt's turning into." The guide sighed and looked at the half-track again. The armor had been stripped off and replaced with sheet metal paneling on a tubular steel frame. "All right," Vickers said. "Get a twelve-foot step ladder and weld it, open, to the bed of one of these trucks. No, that won't take the stress when we run cross-country. Weld a series of brackets front and back and clamp the ladder into them. It's got to hold when we're going hell for twenty through the brush."

The official blinked. "If you wish," he said. "But God in heaven, why?"

"Because if we're in brush ten or a dozen feet high," the guide said, "we won't be able to spot game without a shooting platform. With the ladder here, we'll be able at least to see over anything but a proper forest . . . and that'll be open lower down anyway. If your main job is to make Secretary Cardway happy, you're not making it any easier on yourselves by leaving the bird Topside."

"As you wish, of course," Stern said. He looked around. "Are there any other changes besides the ladder you feel necessary?"

"Adrienne's going."

"No."

Guide and official stared at each other, measuring, judging. "Mrs.—your wife," Stern said at last, "is an estimable but self-willed person. This safari will not be a place for a—for another person who is self-willed."

"I want a back-up gun I can trust on this one," Vickers said flatly. "Adrienne's quite attractive, she won't scare anybody away. If you won't send Cooch Duisberg, you'll send her. Or I don't go. I'm sorry, Stern, that's the way it is."

Stern frowned, but in perplexity rather than anger. The furrows cleared slowly. "You know, Mr. Vickers," he said, "I believe you are concerned about your own safety."

Vickers' face was very still. His index finger probed an old boil scar on his left elbow. "That's against the law?" he asked.

Stern shook his head abruptly. "No, on the contrary," he said. "A man must be willing to take what risks are necessary—but I have never felt comfortable around those who would as soon be dead as alive. I sometimes have thought that you were in that category, Mr. Vickers."

The guide did not smile. "Maybe I was. I'm not now. Does Adrienne go, or do I stay?"

"She goes, Mr. Vickers, she goes," the official said with a sigh. "I will assume that you know what you are doing, unlike the remainder of us. Is there anything further?"

Vickers turned and turned back, his pale eyes flicking around the warehouse, empty except for the two of them and the piled stores. "This is very important, isn't it?" he said, his words little more than movements of his lips. "Why, Mr. Stern? What is Israel about to do that absolutely requires the support of the United States?"

Stern's lip quirked. He said, "Do you make that a condition of your cooperation, Mr. Vickers?" he asked with a sneer. "Is that what you are telling me?"

The guide shook his head. "No," he said, "I'm sure I'm not supposed to know that. And God willing, Adrienne and I will be back in the Cretaceous before whatever happens happens. The thing is, it's just possible that if I knew what you were trying to accomplish, I could help. But that's your decision."

"No, you are not to know that," the official agreed. He smiled, an expression without humor but one with which Vickers could readily identify. "I thought you were going to try to force me to tell you. That would not have happened, of course."

Vickers thumbed a track idler. He was not looking at Stern.

"Some three years ago," Stern whispered, "an atomic weapon was shipped from Pakistan's nuclear research facility outside Islamabad. Its intended delivery point was Tripoli, Libya. But there was an accident."

"Israeli aircraft sank the freighter carrying the bomb in the Persian Gulf," Vickers remembered aloud.

"That is correct," Stern said, without expression, almost without sound. Vickers was watching his lips now. "It is our understanding that another Arab-developed weapon is about to be shipped. There will be another incident. But this time the weapon is to be carried by a Russian frigate."

"Jesus Christ," the guide said, and the words were not a curse. "And you think the Russians'll roll over and play dead if the US is willing to back you—back you without reservation. With its collective finger on the button." He paused again. "And I hear it said that Secretary Luther Cardway might as well be President, so far as foreign affairs go."

The Israeli official shrugged minusculy. "The Secretary is known to view matters in a very—masculine—fashion. This hunt appeared to be an ideal way to broach the question to him. Because without American support . . . we cannot fight all Russia alone. And what chance is there for the State of Israel with nuclear weapons in Libyan hands?"

It was Vickers' turn to sigh. "What chance is there for the rest of the world if nobody backs down this time?" he asked, but it wasn't a question that anyone could answer yet. He kicked the track again. "All right," he said, "I'll do my best. But"—he looked down at the floor—"I've learned in my work not to ask questions that are too narrow." Vickers caught the official's eyes again. His voice took on the crisp certainty of a rifle chambering the next round. "You ask, 'How can my client get that particular dino . . . ?' and you wind up taking a chance. If you ask instead, 'How can my client have a good safari and take home trophies that'll knock their eyes out in Dubuque?'—that's a different question. And it's the right question. You're asking, 'How can we get away with sinking a Russian ship?' and—" Vickers broke off abruptly, shaking his head. "But that's your affair."

During the rest of the afternoon, the two men spoke to each other only in monosyllables.

The exhaust boomed and paused, boomed and paused, then grunted in one final burst before the driver cut the engine. He had maneuvered the half-track atop the intrusion vehicle and parked it next to its twin. The ground guide who had directed him lowered his arms. The echoes were lost in the roar of the fans in the hangar ceiling. Intrusion Vehicle Beth and its hangar were both larger and far slicker than the prototypes which Vickers' previous safaris had used. Instead of being completely open like its predecessor, the central area of Vehicle Beth could be closed behind hinged steel walls as a protection against all but the largest life forms that might encounter it. The fifty-caliber machine guns, mounted during the intrusion on all four corners, could handle anything that ever lived on Earth. Vickers felt uncomfortable around the stucco and sleek armor not because it was less functional than what it replaced but because it differed. Vickers knew he would have been happier a block away on cramped, rusty Vehicle Aleph—but of course, he needed to accompany the clients on the primary vehicle.

He wondered where Adrienne was.

A pair of men wearing field gear, one of them carrying a rifle, came through an access door across the hangar from Vickers. The older man was Stern, but Vickers recognized also the tall, sandy-haired fellow to the official's left. The newcomer tilted back his snakeskin-banded bush hat, then waved and called, "Ah, Vickers, there you are! We'd been expecting you in the office, you know."

Now that the two half-tracks were loaded on the intrusion vehicle, lines of workmen with forklifts were running up and down the ramp like columns of driver ants. Vickers kept a careful eye on the equipment as he walked toward Stern and his companion around the edge of the hangar. It would have been easier to stride under the pillarlike legs of the intrusion vehicle—but that was as bad a habit here as it had been in the Cretaceous. "Good morning, Mr. Stern," Vickers said, shaking hands with the official. "And you're Thomas Warren, I believe. I think we met a few years ago. A pleasure to work with you." The guides shook hands. "But I don't know," Vickers continued, "why anyone expected me in the office. I've been here watching the loading, like always."

"We thought perhaps a brief assembly away from the machinery," said Stern over the background noise, "and the, ah, crowd, was desirable. Just yourselves and the main participants."

"Umm, well," Vickers said, agreeing not in words but by the fact he was following the other two men as they drifted back toward the door through which they had entered. "I hope," he added to Warren, "that you've had a chance to check them out with their weapons. I just dropped in the day before yesterday, so to speak." The other guide's rifle was a heavy bolt-action, old but well-cared for. The cartridges in loops in Warren's vest were larger than a man's middle fingers. Judging from them, the rifle was chambered for .416 Rigby, a round no less adequate for being over eighty years old.

"I say, that would be a help, wouldn't it?" Warren was remarking cheerfully. They were out of the hangar now. Most of the racket was absorbed by the door and the acoustic tile of the hallway. At that, they almost collided with a pair of harassed technicians pushing a laden utility cart toward the intrusion vehicle. "No chance of that, though," the British guide continued as the cart squealed away from them around a corner, "what with the schedule fellows like that are on. Stern got me an interview with Cardway, thank goodness, and he told me that he had the very rifle his father had taken a big tusker with in 1927. That's something, at least."

"But can he use it?" Vickers demanded, scowling unconsciously at the floor as he strode along between the two bigger men.

Warren laughed. "Well, I doubt that, old boy," he said with a sudden twang in his voice. "But then, he'll scarcely be the first of my clients who didn't know his arse from a hole in the ground, will he?"

Stern grunted a warning before he opened the door marked "Coordinator" in English and Hebrew. At a desk within sat a female secretary, looking acutely uncomfortable in the midst of the dozen armed men who otherwise filled the room. A firecracker in the hall would set off World War III, Vickers thought. He caught himself before he said the same thing aloud. Uniforms alternated with clothes so plain as to be uniforms themselves. "They're waiting in the inner office," said Stern with a scowl that cleared a path as abruptly as his big shoulders could have. He reached for the doorknob.

"Just a minute," Vickers muttered. To the secretary he said, "Would you have gotten any calls for me to the facility?" He was looking at the typewriter, not the girl's dark face.

"Ah—"

"Yes, she would have done so," said Stern impatiently. "Mr. Henry Vickers, child."

"Ah—" the girl repeated.

"Nothing from my wife?" pressed Vickers. "Adrienne, ah, Vickers?"

"N-no, sir," the girl said, terrified by the situation and the guide's expression. Actually, the expression derived from embarrassment as great as the secretary's own.

Vickers swallowed. He pushed past Stern and entered the inner office before his companions.

There were three men dressed in coveralls in the inner room. The older pair rose with the false smiles as habitual to a politician as dung-eating is to some dogs. The youngest of the three, a clean-shaven man of thirty with black hair and a face as blank as the nose of a bullet, also reacted to the surprise. His hand dropped reflexively within the attaché case open on his lap. It gripped but did not raise the Uzi submachine gun in the case. When he recognized Stern and Warren, his fingers relaxed but his expression did not. "Mr. Secretary, Mr. Prime Minister," Stern said quickly, "this is Henry Vickers, our chief guide for the operation. That is, the hunting expedition."

"Good to meet you, Vickers," rumbled Luther Cardway. He gripped the hunter's hand, firmly enough to feel the muscles beneath the calluses respond. He did not squeeze quite so firmly that even Vickers could have sworn it had been a contest. "They tell me you're an American. That's good. Guess it's you, me, and Craig here against the rest." He nodded down at the bodyguard. Craig was trying with embarrassment to aim his weapon away from the principal who had stepped into his line of fire.

"Ah," said Vickers, looking at Cardway's chin instead of raising his eyes to meet the other's, "it won't be a contest, Mr.—sir. There's enough game in the Cretaceous for anybody. And big enough for anybody."

"Yes, indeed," said Thomas Warren, in a jovial voice as well-modulated as the Secretary's. "At my suggestion, we're making quite a High Cretaceous insertion—just before the extinctions, when the most impressive species were present. We may get you a world's record triceratops, Mr. Secretary."

Cardway gave a quick negative jerk of his head, the amicable mask slipping. "A tyrannosaurus," he said. "Screw the rest. I want to go back with a tyrannosaurus rex that could've eaten my father's elephant for lunch. You'd have thought the old man was the bravest son of a bitch in the world to see him act out the kill back in Brownsville with the stuffed head over the mantle and the gun he got it with. Say"—the good humor returned—"let's see what you think of this, Vickers."

Luther Cardway was big without being soft, as handsome in person as he was on television with his make-up on—and far more forceful. Only the relative thickness of individual hairs betrayed them as the result of a scalp transplant. It was not until Cardway turned to fumble with the walnut gun case beside his chair that Prime Minister Greenbaum came out of the shade. The Israeli was smaller than his American colleague and looked frail. Vickers remembered that Greenbaum was supposed to be a landscape painter of more than hobbyist reputation; that fitted well enough with the man's appearance. Only Greenbaum's eyes belied the general look of benign forgetfulness. The eyes might have suited General Patton. Catching Vickers' glance, the Prime Minister said, "I'm glad to see you turned up, Mr. Vickers. Though Avraham assured us that you must be nearby, that there was no one in the world more dependable than you." His accent was as British as Warren's.

"Ah, crossed wires," Vickers said, certain he was flushing. "I, ah, assumed we'd meet in the hangar."

"Assume makes an ass of 'U' and me," Cardway said, dominating the gathering again. He held a double-barreled rifle, an elephant gun in the classic sense, and was presenting it to Vickers. The guide took the weapon in his right hand and broke the action by habit. He was edgy at being in a room full of people carrying loaded guns. The muzzle of his own cradled M14 pointed at the ceiling, and even that made him uncomfortable.

Though not as uncomfortable as the live cartridges winking from the twin chambers of the rifle he had just been handed. Cardway had indeed been carrying the weapon loaded. Safety or no, it would not have been the first rifle to go off when it was dropped. "Ah," Vickers said. "Might be best to carry it open till we're ready to insert. Ah, not many tyrannosaurs in Tel Aviv."

"Fine weapon, there, fine," Warren put in, watching Cardway's expression carefully out of the corners of his eyes. "A Gibbs, yes. You bloody well can whistle for this sort of quality today."

Actually, as Vickers knew and Warren surely knew, the rifle was by no means an exceptional example of its type. The only engraving was a scroll on either lock plate, and the wood-to-metal fit of the parts was adequate rather than ideal. Whatever the elder Cardway had told his son, he had spent less on his elephant gun than others had been known to do. Still, finish and engraving never killed a game animal, and this .470 Nitro Express was quite capable of smashing through the heart or skull of a dinosaur. "Serviceability" had always been Vickers' watchword. No one was likely to point to the guide's own fiberglass-stocked military rifle as a triumph of the gunmaker's art either. "Looks a very fine gun," Vickers said, handing it back. "Ah, I hope you've had a chance to practice with it to, to get the feel of it?"

"I've shot it, sure," the Secretary said in a hardening voice. He snapped the breech closed. Vickers winced but held back a comment. The bodyguard, Craig, was noticeably disturbed also. "I'm not afraid of the kick, if that's what you mean," Cardway continued. "And I'm not afraid to get close to my work, either. My father shot his elephant when it came out of the bamboo right on top of him. Mordecai told me—" the Prime Minister winced in turn, knowing what was coming and knowing now that he should not have said it—"that the dinos'll let you get about as close as you've got the nerve for. Well, I've got the nerve to poke this right in their guts." He brandished his rifle. "Believe me."

Vickers believed him. So did Stern, judging from the official's stiff expression. The guide remembered Stern's explanation of why there would be no helicopter on this safari. That decision made increasingly good sense.

"Well then, gentlemen," Stern said. "I think it has become time to report to the hangar. The support personnel have—"

Rising voices in the outer office focused Stern's whole attention as well as that of the men around him. Over the deeper rumble of the males, Vickers heard Adrienne saying, ". . . and I'll be god*damn*ed if you do any such thing!"

"Ah, my wife," the guide explained hurriedly. "She spent yesterday on business affairs, the trust she set up when we"—Was Secretary Cardway supposed to know about the Habitat Phase?—"ah, two years ago. She's just arrived." As much as anything to forestall questions, Vickers opened the door.

Adrienne stood in the outer office, looking like a Doberman in the midst of wolves. A burly man wearing the eagles of an American colonel had poised his hand an inch away from the receiver of Adrienne's Schultz and Larsen rifle. The colonel turned when the inner door opened. "Hello, darling," Adrienne said, striding past the colonel to kiss her husband's cheek. "Paunchy here—" the officer's gut sucked in reflexively—"thinks I'm going to trust him with my rifle ten minutes before we insert!"

"Sir," said the colonel stiffly to the Secretary of State, visible through the doorway, "she isn't on my list, and I had no intention of letting somebody with a gun—"

"Colonel Platt," said Stern, overriding the American's voice as he stepped toward the man, "the error is mine entirely. Mrs. Vickers is indeed a part of the expedition, and she should properly have been admitted." He cleared his throat heavily. "Now, as I was saying. I believe the support personnel have gathered at their respective stations. If we proceed to Hangar Beth, our insertion can go forward as scheduled. The pressure of time on our . . . our principals is of course very great." He motioned toward the hall door.

Vickers' tongue touched his lips. He followed Stern's gesture without comment. His wife wore coveralls, faded like his own by months of sun and use. The fabric slid easily over the skin by which it had been worn smooth. Her rifle was the one she had bought after her first time safari, also worn to perfect functioning by two years of service around their Cretaceous base. But Adrienne Vickers herself wore her hair in a coif as rigid and golden as a Cellini casting, and her face was still in tiger-striped make-up, which Vickers presumed had become fashionable while he had been living in the Cretaceous. While Adrienne and he had been isolated in the Cretaceous.

"Alex took me out after we finished with the records," Adrienne was prattling. "I swear I never thought Tel Aviv had a night life, and

I suppose it really doesn't, but my God, I'm not about to complain. But we wound up in Jaffa and I looked at the time, well—I had to *buy* a taxi to get me back to the suite in time to change. Literally buy one! I left Alex trying to decide whether the check should be charged to entertainment or as a business expense. After all, that's the sort of thing I *pay* an accountant for, isn't it?"

They pushed through the swinging doors. The bustle within the hangar had given way to a sullen hush. The exhaust fans were shut down, leaving the air still. Eight men wearing fatigues and holding grenade launchers came to attention along the far wall. On the intrusion vehicle, laden already with the paraphernalia of a time safari, were the technicians making their last-minute adjustments to the machinery.

"Glad you had a good time," Vickers said. "Ah, I've been thinking. You . . . I'm sure you can't have cleared up all your affairs in one day. Why don't you stay for now?" He was examining the receiver of his rifle, his index finger digging into the pock mark left by the old boil. "I'll be back in two weeks, I suppose. Then we'll, we'll . . ."

"My God, Henry, you think I'm going to leave you alone with this rat pack?" the tall blonde said in a clear voice. "Not likely. Not likely at all!"

The chime which replaced the buzzer at the old facility sounded. Aboard the intrusion vehicle was an older man with an air of authority. He waved. He was not Dr. Galil, who was probably superintending the more difficult follow-up insertion in Hangar Aleph. Stern called a command and the uniformed men began to trudge up the ramp onto the vehicle's open veranda. Refinements in technique had permitted the new platform to stand on six-foot pillars instead of the braced twenty-foot I-beams which had supported the original vehicle. There was no longer any possibility that the vehicle would be inserted with its base platform more than a few feet above the terrain of the intrusion site. Still, though Vickers trusted Dr. Galil and his team completely, the change made his subconscious uneasy.

At least it was better than wondering if the Secretary of State was going to stumble and put a 500-grain bullet through your back.

The uniformed men had stationed themselves on the intrusion vehicle. One stood on each of the sides, while the remaining four were manning the heavy machine guns.

"Mr. Vickers," Stern said formally, "you will please take charge."

Like hell, the guide thought, but he glanced over the line of men following him. Craig had discarded his attaché case and carried the submachine gun openly. Prime Minister Greenbaum was armed with a half-stocked Mannlicher, heavy and glisteningly new. So far as Vickers knew, the Israeli was no hunter. He had apparently been given—and accepted—some excellent advice regarding equipment. Thomas Warren was last, cradling his Rigby comfortably. "Who's manning the old vehicle?" Vickers asked Stern abruptly.

The official raised his eyebrows. "The photographic team," he said, "and the cook. The follow-up insertion carries none of the truly necessary supplies and personnel, of course."

"Wait a minute," the guide insisted, trying to pitch his voice low. Adrienne stirred at his side. "You mean there's nobody aboard who's made an insertion before? Good God, man, if the timing's only three seconds out, they'll insert five klicks away from the initial group! They need somebody experienced along."

Stern shrugged impatiently. "They have weapons," he said. "They have been instructed."

"Instructed my ass," Vickers said. "Warren! Ah, Thomas. Get on over to the old hangar ASAP and nursemaid the back-up crew, will you?"

"Mr. Warren!" Stern snapped. In a lower voice he said, "Mr. Vickers, you are both essential to the initial intrusion. The follow-up vehicle is not to be your first concern."

"Henry, I'll go," Adrienne said quietly. Vickers turned, the anger meant for others in his eyes. "No," she said, "it'll be all right. Somebody has to be with the vehicle, but you know Dr. Galil will bring it in on time. You needed someone you could trust along for just this sort of job. Well, that's why I'm along."

"Adrienne—"

"You *do* trust me, don't you?"

Vickers sighed. He checked his watch, a mechanical chronometer because the intrusion field interfered with quartz-synchronized watches. "Right," he said. "We—I'll see you in thirty-seven minutes."

His wife flashed him a smile and strode back out of the hangar. Her hips were as sleekly functional as they had been the day he first noticed them, climbing the steps of an intrusion vehicle ahead of him. Adrienne was pulling a handkerchief from her pocket. As she swung through the doors, she appeared to be rubbing the skin tone from her face.

"Mr. Warren," Vickers said to the other guide, "if you'll lead the Prime Minister to Side 3, we'll begin boarding. Mr. Secretary, you and I will stand on Side 1, that's the one with the ramp. Mr. Stern, Side 4; Mr. Craig—"

"Side 1," the bodyguard said flatly. "With Secretary Cardway."

"I hope you never get a chance to see what a charging carnosaur would think of that toy you carry," Vickers said.

"Look," Craig retorted, "I've got orders, I've got a job to do, and I'm going to do it."

The guide shrugged. "All right," he said, "since you're unarmed, it won't affect the vehicle's safety no matter where you stand. Shall we go?"

It was going to be a great hunt, Vickers thought as he waited for the others to board. But he had known that from the beginning.

The insertion was flawless, a textbook job. The indirect lighting on the sand-finished ceiling of the hangar suddenly flared into a blue-white sky with the sun directly overhead. Simultaneously, a volume of landscape and Cretaceous atmosphere replaced the intrusion vehicle in what had been the present but now was the future 65,000,000 years removed.

Secretary Cardway grunted. Vickers glanced at him after a quick scan indicated there was no danger immediate to the vehicle. The Secretary looked as if his elevator had dropped the last ten feet. Time intrusion always involved sensory scrambling, but that was momentary. Already the big politician had regained his composure and was staring out at his new surroundings with his rifle near his shoulder.

The vehicle had been inserted onto a plain extending across the arc of Vickers' eyesight. It was covered by a brushy mixture of evergreen and spiny succulents. The foliage was made duller and paler by a coating of dust. From the slight vantage of the intrusion vehicle's height, it was possible to see that game trails webbed the brush, meandering as dark shadows against the blurred reflectance of the shrubs they separated. And all across the plain, sunlight flashed on scales as dinosaurs lifted up to see what had caused the sudden noise.

Eighty yards from Secretary Cardway one of the misnamed duckbills, a saurolophus, raised its head. It sniffed the air while its teeth continued grinding what looked like fronds of Spanish Bayonet. The dinosaur's lower jaw was ratcheting back and forth, pulling in more of the fibrous mass at each stroke. The motion was bizarrely alien to men subconsciously expecting the creature to slide its jaw sideways as a cow does when chewing. The saurolophus' beak was bright red, and the beast's head bore a hollow, bony crest faired to the back of its neck by a flap of azure skin. It was an adult male, a large one, and an excellent trophy.

But Vickers did not expect to hear the Secretary say, *"Goddamn, a tyrannosaur!"* the instant before he loosed off his right barrel at the herbivore.

Dust leaped from nearby foliage stricken by the muzzle blast of the rifle, but the windless plain drank all echoes of the shot. The dinosaur lowered its head, untouched by the bullet. Neither the sound nor the human scent caught by its keen nostrils were labeled as threats by the creature's brain. It had simply returned to its meal.

Secretary Cardway broke his rifle open. The automatic ejector spat out the empty case, leaving the live round in the left breech to gleam like Odin's eye. Fumblingly, Cardway reloaded. "Goddamn, first shot and I got a tyrannosaur!" he was saying. "Goddamn, it was easy. Goddamn, I wish the old bastard was alive now to see what I'll have looking down at his goddamn elephant!"

"Of course, they're devilish brutes to kill," said Thomas Warren from nearby. Vickers' breath caught. The other guide had left his station, walking around the platform to attend what was going on. It was only a slight mitigation of his offense—what if a *real* carnivore had sprung onto the side of the platform Warren was supposed to be covering?—to note that he had brought Prime Minister Greenbaum with him. "I think Henry or myself need to go down and crack the blighter again, just to be on the safe side," the Englishman continued, winking at Vickers past the Secretary's turned head.

"It was a saurolophus," Vickers said, his left hand as tight on the forestock of his rifle as he wished it could be on Warren's throat. "And what the—"

"Nobody finishes my kills without me!" Cardway said, snapping closed the breech of his Gibbs. "Come on, then."

"Wait!" cried three voices simultaneously, Vickers joined by Stern and Greenbaum. The Secretary of State had already taken a step forward while Vickers cursed himself mentally for positioning the damned fool on the side with the ramp. "Ah," the guide said, "we'll crank up one of the trucks and go down in it when we get the machine gun remounted. I don't like to enter this brush on foot." Behind Warren, Stern's head was nodding vigorously, like a donkey engine.

"Like hell we will!" Cardway retorted. He gestured with his rifle at the walled center of the intrusion vehicle. "It'll take a goddamn hour to unpack one of them—" and that was, Vickers knew, a conservative estimate. Cardway's heavy rifle slashed back like a saber, tracing a line across the guide's chest with its double muzzles. "Come on, Mordecai. You and I can show 'em what men are like if they're too pussy to walk fifty feet!"

Vickers' mind clicked over possibilities like beads of an abacus. All anger—all emotion—was gone. If there had been carnivores in the immediate vicinity, the plant-eaters would not have returned to feeding so soon after being aroused. The worst danger, therefore, was the chance that one of the herbivores would bolt out of the brush and trample the hunters. That was not a risk the guide cared to take, but the alternative appeared to be clubbing the Secretary of State and carrying him back Topside unconscious. "All right," Vickers said. "Mr. Secretary, you and I will—"

"And Mordecai!"

The Prime Minister nodded without enthusiasm. Vickers

swallowed and continued, "The three of us will go down after that saurolophus. Warren, you'll stay up here where there's enough height to warn us if necessary. And for God's sake, stay where you belong this time!"

"Mr. Vickers," said Stern, "I am under your orders if you desire another gun."

The guide's mouth opened, but he bit off the response frustration had intended when he realized that Stern was armed after all. The official had obviously had his rifle waiting on the intrusion vehicle instead of carrying it around the Tel Aviv facility like the rest of them. It was a Browning FAL, for many years the Israeli service issue. Seeing it reminded Vickers in a rush of Dieter Jost, who had carried a similar weapon . . . and who, had he survived his last safari, might have been present now in the place of Warren.

Stern caught the stare and misinterpreted it. His heavy face darkened in something like a blush. "I am not boasting that I am a crack shot like you and need only the small bullets, Mr. Vickers," the official said. "This I carried in the Sinai—better than a weapon I do not have time to learn, though it was many years ago." He raised his chin. "My nerve will not fail."

Vickers quirked a smile that was half-embarrassment. "Neither would your good judgment, Avraham," he said. "Stay up here with Warren and the troops, and yell if you see trouble coming." To the pair of officials he continued, "We'll follow the trail we've landed in the middle of, cut through the brush if we have to when we get close. You'll have the shot, Mr. Secretary, so you'll lead if it gets tight. I'll be right behind you, and—"

"I'll be right behind him," said the bodyguard, "and look, I don't like the idea of anybody firing past the Secretary. You can—"

"Craig, shut the hell up!" Cardway snarled impatiently before Vickers could form a response. "Come on, let's go!" The bodyguard, blank-faced and clutching his Uzi like a reliquary, brought up the end of the short column.

Secretary Cardway reached the bottom of the ramp, took two steps further along the game trail, and paused. He had realized for the first time what a difference the intrusion vehicle's height had made. The brush on which dinosaurs could be heard browsing was only about eight feet tall. The trails, worn through it by the hips of the great beasts, were broad but often not cleared to the sky. To either side the brush grew gnarled and spiky, as inhospitable as a barbed-wire entanglement. The effect was less that of standing in a grape arbor than it was walking down the center of a subway tunnel, listening to the tracks hum.

Vickers started to move forward. The trail was wide enough for two to walk abreast. The Secretary began to move again, with more determination at each step. "Sir," the guide whispered, "not so fast. We don't want to—we want to have time for a good shot."

Cardway looked puzzled. Vickers had forgotten that their quarry was supposed to be wounded. The Secretary slowed from the near run toward which he had been building, however. The guide glanced back to check Greenbaum and Craig. They were all right, though Craig seemed to be crowding the Prime Minister somewhat. Vickers could no longer see the men on the intrusion vehicle through the dappled tanglings of brush. He should have thought to bring along a wand with a pennon for this sort of situation. Of course, if he had expected the situation, he might have refused to take out the safari after all. The millstone-crunching of a dinosaur's teeth was becoming very loud. Hadrosaurs, like the beast they were after, were not carnivorous, of course, but neither was a threshing machine carnivorous; and threshing machines had killed their share of the unwary over the years.

The bush to their right was a multi-stemmed clump with leaves like green glass teardrops. It shuddered as something pulled a huge mouthful out of the other side. Cardway raised his rifle. Vickers touched the politician's shoulder for attention and shook his head. Then he knelt and used the fore-end of his own weapon to gently press a line of sight between the bush and its neighbor. A male saurolophus, possibly even the one Cardway had fired at, was facing them within spitting distance.

The dinosaur was chewing with its short forelegs lowered but not quite touching the ground. Its neck was raised at right angles to the straight, horizontal line of its back and counterbalancing tail. If it saw

Vickers, it ignored him. The guide leaned his head back out of the way. With his free hand he motioned Cardway forward into the gap he was holding open. Then Vickers tapped himself on the breastbone with index and middle fingers to indicate the proper aiming point. Secretary Cardway knelt with a set expression, advancing his rifle.

Vickers knew the shot would be deafening, but the reality was stunningly worse than he had expected. Cardway spun over on his back like a sacked passer, losing his grip on the rifle. The meat-axe *smack!* of the bullet was lost in the muzzle blast, but the ground shook as the stricken hadrosaur fell.

Vickers backed a step. He leveled his own rifle one-handed toward the brush in case the saurolophus burst through. Then he picked up the Secretary's weapon as well. Vickers' head rang. His first thought had been that the old Gibbs had exploded, either because metal had crystallized or because of trash in the bore. The big weapon was apparently undamaged, however, except for the dirt that now clung to its exterior. Vickers thumbed the locking key. The breeches clicked open and the ejectors kicked out both the cartridges, empty. The rifle had doubled, shock of the first discharge firing the second barrel almost simultaneously.

The Secretary was rising groggily to his knees. Vickers thrust the empty Gibbs at him. His hearing was beginning to return. The wounded hadrosaur was kicking on the ground close by. "Load one barrel," the guide shouted. "It's firing both together."

"Goddamn if I do!" Cardway replied. His mouth was shouting, but his words rang through a long tunnel. "Give me yours!"

Vickers twisted his M14 away from the hands spread to grasp it. "No," he said, "just load one round."

"You worthless sonofabitch!" snarled the white-faced politician. "You give me that gun now or you'll regret the day you were born!"

The guide's knuckles tightened on the Gibbs, held now in bar rather than in offering. The surface of his mind was slick as glass. The instant before Vickers might have acted, Prime Minister Greenbaum stepped between the two men. He held out his Mannlicher, saying, "Here, Luther. I'm sure this will finish the job."

Cardway's rage evaporated. He snatched the bolt-action rifle from his colleague without a word. Instead of kneeling again to fire beneath the spreading foliage, the big Texan began thrusting himself between the bushes. He seemed oblivious of the thorns that ripped at his coveralls.

Vickers paused momentarily, but he could neither restrain his client nor allow him to go alone. Throwing himself on his belly, the guide squirmed on knees and elbows around the other side of the bush past which they had fired. He cleared the obstacle an instant before Cardway could. The hadrosaur lay on its side, its spine toward the hunters. Its tail was flailing sideways, cracking against the earth on every downward stroke. The brush was splashed with bright arterial blood, further evidence that at least one of Cardway's bullets had been a solid hit.

The dinosaur was only six feet away. Vickers aimed at the beast's spine but did not fire. He prayed that if it became necessary to shoot, the grit on the bolt of his M14 would not jam it. The magazine was loaded with modern armor-piercing rounds, penetrators of depleted uranium which could drill through an inch of steel. Anyone can miss a shot, however, no matter how short the range; and the nineteen rounds remaining in the magazine might as well be on the Moon for all the good they would be to a jammed rifle.

Secretary Cardway forced through the brush with thorns hanging from his sleeves and the backs of his hands bleeding. He aimed the Mannlicher and emptied it with five point-blank shots as quickly as he could work the spoon-handle bolt. The recoil of the big rifle—it was chambered for .458 Magnum—did not appear to bother him, despite the bruising his shoulder must have taken when the Gibbs doubled. Vickers watched his client carefully. The look on the Secretary's face as he fired was chilling.

The crashing shots ended when Cardway ran out of ammunition. The struggles of the hadrosaur had disintegrated into a quivering as lifeless as the collapse of a house of cards. Splotches of blood gummed the dust that obscured the patterning of the beast's back-scales.

Vickers stood up slowly, porting his rifle. "Splendid trophy, sir," he said.

The Secretary was lowering the muzzle of the Mannlicher. "Yes," he said in a thick voice. "Goddamn it, yes." Behind him, the brush quaked to pass his wild-eyed bodyguard.

Time safaris always held an element of danger, Vickers thought. Usually, however, the greatest danger was from the local wildlife.

"Right," said Thomas Warren, as if he were an amateur magician demonstrating card tricks. "Here's the culprit."

The lock-work of the Gibbs double was strewn on the linen tablecloth in front of the British guide. Around him sat Vickers and his wife, Stern, Greenbaum, and Cardway. The audience wore expressions of interest and, in the last case, considerable impatience. Craig, the bodyguard, stood stiffly a pace behind the Secretary. He continually moved his head in nervous jerks to check behind him. "The sear, you see," Warren continued, prodding the little piece again with his index finger. "Not worn, really, just polished down a little too closely in the final assembly. These big express chamberings give quite a jolt—as you know, old chap, as you know. In this case, it's enough to jolt the left hammer spang off its sear when the right barrel fires. Sometimes, at any rate. More common a problem than you might think with these old darlings—" the guide rapped the joined barrels with his fingernail. "One reason I've always kept to a magazine rifle."

"Well, fix the goddamn thing, then!" Secretary Cardway snapped. "You're not on the payroll to run your mouth."

Adrienne's hand, resting companionably on her husband's shoulder, tightened. Warren's smile, however, appeared to be quite genuine as he replied, "Well, you see, old boy, that's the problem. Short of fitting another sear, there's not a great deal to be done. Not a bloody thing, really. Use it as a single shot, that is. Or I dare say, there's a spare gun or two about the camp—isn't that so, Vickers?"

Henry Vickers had a good idea of how the Secretary would react if he were offered the camp gun—a functional but very battered Ruger in .375 H&H. Fortunately, Prime Minister Greenbaum forestalled him by saying, "Luther, when I held your gun, I found that it suits me far better than the one I purchased for myself. I would appreciate it no end if you would agree to exchange with me."

Adrienne got up, muttering something under her breath. The support crew was sprawled around the campfire, a discreet ten meters from their betters at the table. A pair of startled soldiers made room for the blonde woman when she tapped them on the shoulders.

"All right, that's settled," the Secretary was saying as if he had just made a concession. "Now," the Texan continued, poking an index finger across the table at Vickers, "I've got another bone to pick. *You* told me that I was going after a tyrannosaurus this morning."

The guide's fist clenched in his lap. "Ah," he temporized, "your hadrosaur is really an exceptional trophy."

"I'm not wasting my time here to bring back a goddamn duckbill!" Cardway said, jabbing with his finger as if it were a pistol. "You lied to me once and you won't do it again, hear? I want a tyrannosaurus rex." He stood abruptly and strode toward his private tent. His back was straight, his carriage in every way that of a leader. Craig followed him at a respectful distance.

Vickers was pale. Stern said softly, "He has a very—selective— memory. I suppose we can hope that if matters in the long run turn out to his liking, his memory will select the positive aspects of the hunt as well."

In an equally low voice, looking at Vickers, the Prime Minister said, "I am not a hunter, you understand. It does not matter what gun I carry or indeed if I carry one. But if I *did* hunt, if I were as keen on the chase as, as you are, as anyone could be—I would still have done the same thing I just did." The little Israeli took a deep breath and continued, his whispered words freighted with genuine concern. "I am here to be the dutiful child, you see, the child who does whatever his papa pleases and is therefore rewarded with a treat. Only this time, the treat is his . . . his right to exist, his life. You see? I regret what I must bear, and what I must ask able gentlemen like yourselves to bear; but there is no choice."

Vickers shook himself. "It's all right," he said, looking at his hands. "Only . . . only, I don't see how anybody that—abrasive— expects to get elected *anything*. But they say he was almost President in the last election and he probably *will* make it the next time."

The Prime Minister's smile was tired. "Oh, you must not think

Mr. Cardway is this way at all times. Only with people who must accept the behavior, underlings, dependents. If the United States needed a concession from Israel, he would be in a very different temper with me, with us, I assure you. Though he would still treat his own aide like dirt." Greenbaum paused, shaking his head ruefully. "I sometimes find myself giving speeches even in the shower," he said. "Well, gentlemen, good night."

Stern watched the smaller man walking to the tent the two of them shared. "Best I go as well," the official said. "Otherwise I will disturb him when I enter. A man of great courage, that one. Great courage." He stood.

"But not great enough courage to refuse to start World War III," Vickers said.

Stern looked down at the guide for a long moment, but in the end he walked off without responding.

The whole compound area was covered with a tent of mosquito netting, suspended from high poles. The covering must have been manufactured for the hunt. Reflected light brightened the inner face of the net to opacity, except where insects clung and fluttered on the exterior. There appeared to be a breed of hawk moth with wings the size of a man's hands. Vickers had seen no flowers impressive enough to justify such a monster, but perhaps they were night-blooming. He hadn't trained himself to observe flowers, anyway. He'd never guided a client who wanted to kill a rose.

There was laughter from the group around the fire, half-stilled at a sergeant's gruff order. Adrienne's liquid trill choked off a moment later. "Quite a lady, your wife," said Thomas Warren. He was fitting a screw into a sideplate. "Must prove quite a—" his eyes flicked sideways, toward Vickers—"handful for you."

"Instead of worrying about that," Vickers said, "you might give some thought to how we'll keep Cardway from running into the brush after his first carnosaur, the same as he did with the duckbill this morning." Then, "I'm going to bed."

Warren whistled between his teeth as he finished reassembling the rifle. His face bore the smile of a death-camp guard.

* * *

The ten-inch lizard racing down the center of the game trail actually gained on the half-track momentarily. Then the little creature's burst of energy gave out. It faltered, an olive shadow against the gray soil. From Vickers' vantage point, clinging to the front rail of the truck box beside the gun, it looked as if the front wheels would inevitably crush the lizard. At the last instant, however, the reptile spurted sideways into the shade and safety of the brush. Vickers found he was unexpectedly pleased at that.

"Hold it up here," he said on his cordless throat mike. There was no point in trying to speak directly to the driver while they were in motion. Even though the cab was open-topped, the treads and the racket of brush clanging constantly on both sides of the vehicle provided a background of deafening white noise.

Obediently, the soldier driving slowed the half-track to a stop. He shared the cab with one of the propaganda staffers who looked a little green. Not only was the ride a rough one for anyone not accustomed to it, quite a few of the higher branches were slapping the wind screen. Its Plexiglas held despite deep scarring, but masses of six-inch thorns at eye height were bound to be disconcerting. The ponies, the little diesel carts which time safaris ordinarily used, would have slipped down the trails with less noise and infinitely greater comfort, but you couldn't mount a fifty-caliber machine gun on one of them.

Well, it had yet to be proven that you could hunt dinos from these monsters.

"Give me those binoculars," Secretary Cardway said. He pushed past Vickers as the guide started to mount the ladder. The cargo area of the half-track was cramped. Besides the gear and the braced ladder, there were six people: Vickers and his wife, Cardway and his bodyguard, the soldier manning the machine gun, and a holograph cameraman like the one in the cab. Only the fact that too many people were in the way kept Adrienne from jerking the Secretary back by his collar.

"Adrienne," the guide cautioned in an undertone, hoping the cold-eyed Craig had not interpreted her brief tension correctly. "Here you are, sir," he continued, handing up his binoculars. With luck, Cardway would not drop them. "There's sign of ceratopsians—ah, that's triceratops and the like, the horns—and, ah, duckbills, hadrosaurs, all around. With the ladder, it should be possible to pick out a number of nice trophies. We'll ring them with the other track, then, and move in."

Secretary Cardway had climbed a few steps and begun to scan their surroundings in a cursory fashion. The air was almost dead still. The plume of dust raised by their passage lay behind them like a still picture. A kilometer to the right hung a frozen ridge of gray, the track of the other vehicle more or less paralleling their own progress on another trail. That half-track stopped as well. Though it was not fitted with a ladder, Vickers could see Warren standing on the hood to eye the plain.

"Look, I'm tired of this dicking around," Cardway said as he dropped to the bed again. He allowed Vickers to retrieve the binoculars and scramble up the ladder, but he did not seem interested in what the guide was doing. "I didn't come to get duckbills and what-have-you," the Secretary continued, "and I didn't come to get my kidneys pounded out on some goddamn antique. If this is the best you Jews can manage, maybe the Arabs ought to get a crack at it."

"Not only will a ceratopsian head make an elephant's look like something the cat caught," Vickers said, glad for their sakes that Stern and the Prime Minister were in the other vehicle, "but the meat is a first-rate way to lure the big carnosaurs—like tyrannosaurus—in. We didn't dare use the hadrosaur carcass that way—I'm not about to toll a tyrannosaur to within fifty yards of where I'm sleeping. But when we drop a triceratops a reasonable distance away, it'll bring meat-eaters from horseflies to as big as they come on land." He waved skyward. "The big ones follow those," he added, waggling his index finger cryptically without taking the glasses from his eyes.

Adrienne stepped onto the side bulkhead, using the ladder to steady her. She caught the look of bafflement on Cardway's face as he stared upward. He was uncertain whether Vickers had been pointing or merely gesturing. "What look like little dots up there," explained the tall woman, "see them? Those're pterodactyls the size of airplanes—heavier than a man is, at least. They have eyesight to shame a condor, and a ten-ton carcass draws them from a hundred miles. The carnosaurs follow, unless they're on a fresh kill of their own." As an afterthought Adrienne said, "That's how we captured a tyrannosaur alive, you know—followed them to a kill. Just Henry and I."

"I don't care what you've—" the Secretary began.

"Hush!" snapped Adrienne, her body suddenly rigid. She leaned into her own binoculars as if bracing against their recoil. "Henry," she said in a tense, quiet voice. "Between us and the others, just ahead. Doesn't that look like . . . ?"

Vickers looked down to be sure of the bearing, then found the target with his naked eyes. Targets, three of them—he raised and refocused the glasses—sure enough, dryptosaurs or a carnivore damned similar, and the leading one had to be ten yards long.

"Mobile One to Two," Vickers said urgently into his lapel mike.

"Go ahead," crackled Warren's voice from both the unit on Vickers' shoulder and the console in the cab. The words were slightly out of phase, echoes of themselves.

"We've got three carnosaurs between us, just three hundred meters ahead and quartering across our front. See them?" The dryptosaurs' heads were flexed back on serpentine necks. From the withers rearward, the beasts' spines were straight and parallel to the ground save for the slight hump over the hip joint. The long bodies flexed from side to side but not vertically as they cut through the brush. The vegetation was sparser here than it was near the camp, but it still should have been more of a hindrance to the beasts' progress than it seemed to be. The dryptosaurs trotted through the brush like cruisers on a calm sea, only their heads and backs visible to the watching hunters. Their hides were dun, splotched with maroon as dark as dried blood.

"Give me those!" Cardway said.

"Go buy your own binoculars," Adrienne retorted. "*I* did."

"Yes, by God," the radio said. "I'd say we were in a bit of luck, wouldn't you? Shall we—"

The rest of Warren's words were lost in the unexpected crash of a rifle. Vickers looked down, open-mouthed. The PR man in the cab had bent over as if clubbed. His hands were covering his ears—too late. Secretary Cardway was still ajar from the recoil of the

Mannlicher. He ejected the spent case and raised the weapon for a second shot.

Three-hundred-yard accuracy with an elephant gun was a task beyond most experts; it was assuredly beyond the Secretary of State, shooting off-hand with a weapon he had not sighted in himself. The carnosaurs paused in their lazy striding, cocking their heads back to seek the source of the noise. The gunshot had not panicked them, for it was unique to their experience.

"Hold up!" Vickers said, staring at the Secretary but keying his lapel mike as well. He was too late in both cases. Cardway's rifle boomed again, and the other half-track lurched toward the dinosaurs in a fresh spray of dust. The three animals jerked their heads forward and leaped with the unanimity of a flock of birds.

"Follow them!" the Secretary was screaming. "We'll run 'em down!"

The driver let out the clutch without waiting for Vickers' orders. The guide had to jump down from his perch. Only Adrienne's hand kept him from smashing painfully into the back bulkhead.

The driver's obedience caught the Secretary himself by surprise, as it turned out. The half-track had ridden rough at part throttle; opened up, there was literally danger that everyone would be thrown out of the box. The trail they were following would have seemed smooth enough at a walking pace, but at 40kph it was like going through the rapids in a canoe—sideways. Vickers was clinging to the sidewall with one hand and trying with the other to keep his slung M14 from pounding him to death. Cardway had dropped the Mannlicher and had both arms around the waist of the soldier at the machine gun. The gunner was holding on for dear life to the spade grips of his weapon. When the half-track yawed, the gun pivoted and made an absurd conga line of the pair.

"Slow down for Chrissake!" Vickers screamed. The vehicle pitched abruptly enough to snap both legs of the ladder just above the topmost braces. Then the half-track broadsided to a stop as brutally abrupt as the previous ride had been.

"Threw the left track," the driver said in the sudden stillness. Vickers and his wife stood up, Adrienne unslinging her rifle.

In their crazy rush, they had gained on the dryptosaurs. Their quarry was forging well ahead now, however. The other vehicle seemed to be on a converging course, but it had fallen considerably behind. Perhaps the carnivores thought they were being pursued by a pair of the biggest ceratopsians they had ever met. In any case, they showed no sign of slacking off.

Adrienne leaped over the cab to the hood of the half-track. "What's she doing?" demanded, in Hebrew, the photographer in the front seat. His fellow in the box had unlimbered a holocamera. With a professionalism Vickers could appreciate, he had mounted the stump of the ladder and was rolling tape.

Adrienne's shot was sharp and clean, coming as it did on the heels of a racket so loud that it had been felt rather than heard. Secretary Cardway rose, holding the .458 by the pistol grip. To fire, he would have had to aim through the blonde woman. Vickers' own free hand closed over the forestock of the Mannlicher. He kept the muzzle slanting upward despite all the pressure the bigger man could bring to it.

"Goddammit, she missed!" Cardway shouted.

Five hundred yards downrange, the leading dryptosaur turned a cartwheel and fell. The remaining pair of carnivores leaped its body and continued to run.

Adrienne clicked the safety on as she turned toward her audience. "Not too bad for iron sights," she said coolly. Reslinging her rifle, she lighted a small cigar.

Secretary Cardway's face was a study in gray savagery while they waited for the other vehicle to reach them. Cardway had said nothing more after the dryptosaur tumbled, but to say he had relaxed was to ignore his eyes. Those eyes were directed toward the oncoming half-track, but their focus was somewhere deep in the politician's imagination. Both Craig and Vickers watched the Secretary sidelong, each for his own reasons uncertain how to react if worse came to worst.

They had taken the Rome Plow blades off the half-tracks as soon as the campsite had been cleared. Warren's vehicle might have found the brush-shearing blade handy now, as it cut across the plain to reach its disabled consort. Vickers' driver had already dismounted and was morosely surveying the track. It had been flung from the left-hand bogeys when it skewed on a root at excessive speed. He and his mate, the gunner, would have to straighten the heavy track and then carefully back the bogeys over it before it could be repinned. Vickers felt sorry for the gunner, facing a dirty job that was none of his making. As for the driver, the guide could imagine without a qualm that fool doing the whole job alone in the sun.

The other half-track struggled through the last of the separating brush like a lifeboat in the surf. It turned and stopped on the trail just ahead of the disabled vehicle, the dust it raised still retaining enough forward motion to drift across the passengers. "A bloody fine shot, Mr. Secretary!" Thomas Warren was shouting from the back. Behind him, Stern and Greenbaum were trying to conceal anxious expressions. "I saw the dust fly from its hide at your second shot," the British guide lied enthusiastically, "right over the brisket. That's why it was lagging behind, you see. In fact, old boy—" Warren leaned over the bulkhead matily—"I shouldn't be a bit surprised to find it was your ball alone that put paid to him. They can run quite a distance when hit hard, you know."

"Yes, that's so," Vickers managed to say. He had noticed the other guide salvaging a pair of .458 bullets from the hadrosaur when they butchered it the previous night. At the time, he had wondered why. Now Vickers realized that one of the big bullets would be "found" in the fresh carcass as proof of the Secretary's marksmanship. Warren really *was* very good—at what he did. Stern had probably made a mistake in wanting Vickers along at all.

Secretary Cardway was blooming like a moonflower at dusk. "Well," he said, "the way it took off, you know, I thought it was just wounded. I'd hate to lose a wounded animal that way."

"Bloody sporting!" Warren agreed. "But say, it still may be thrashing around, you know. Let's hop aboard this one while your crew puts your own lorry ship-shape."

Adrienne had jumped down from the hood and was already stepping to the other vehicle. "Ah, Adrienne," Vickers said in a bright voice.

She turned to her husband with a genuine smile. "Oh, I'll be good," she called. "Mr. Cardway's shot the biggest dryptosaur I've ever seen, is all. I'd just like to look at it up close before it's mounted."

"Levi, Asch," Stern said to the PR men on Vickers' half-track, "you will stay here. Two photographers are enough for our needs."

The vehicle was crowded, but Stern had obviously directed the driver to take it slowly no matter what anyone else might say. Several times Vickers called a halt while he and Warren climbed onto the hood to take bearings. The dryptosaur had disappeared when it fell, and its high-striding companions were already over the horizon. In the end, it was hearing and not sight that guided them to their quarry. While they paused, with the diesel engine only a background whine, Vickers heard the throaty wheeze of the carnivore.

Both guides turned to the right. In the box of the half-track, Adrienne and Stern leveled their rifles toward the noise. A moment later the politicians followed suit. The holographers capered in the background trying to get a vantage of what was about to happen without jostling the line of gunners in front of them. Vickers felt the muzzle of the heavy machine gun stir the air past his hips as its crewman rotated the weapon to bear.

Twenty feet from the vehicle, the dryptosaur crawled through a clump of mimosa. It hissed with murderous fury, but its head was barely raised to the level of the knee-high scrub still separating it from the humans. The great jaws champed and ground, clicking the serrated teeth together as if they had flesh between them to shear.

"Its back is broken," Adrienne said. She lowered the butt of her rifle, sure now that there would be no need of a quick shot at a charging killer. "It's just dragging itself along on its forelegs."

"All right, Mr. Secretary," said Thomas Warren, "now remember, you don't want to damage the skull. Anywhere through the body, that's the ticket."

"Luther?" interjected the Prime Minister. He held the double rifle, its heavy barrels looking much too big for his slight form. "Might I join in—finishing the death of your trophy? I would like to think of this as a bond between us, as statesmen and as men."

"Yeah," said Cardway in a drugged voice, looking down the sights of the Mannlicher. Then, more sharply, "Go ahead, goddammit," and fired himself.

The recoil of the Gibbs pushed Greenbaum backward as if the Israeli had caught an overlarge medicine ball, but he did not need the restraining hand Adrienne had unobtrusively raised between his shoulder blades. Beside him, the American cabinet official rocked as he fired, lowered his weapon to work the bolt, and raised it to fire again. As before, Cardway emptied the magazine on the struggling dinosaur; but the shots died away sooner this time because he had forgotten to reload after the two distant attempts. His rifle empty, the Secretary swung his leg over the side of the half-track.

"Christ, wait!" Warren shouted in sudden concern. "It may not be—"

Vickers fired his M14 once. After the blasts of the elephant guns, the crack of the military rifle was as sharp as a heartbreak. The ejected case sailed in a flat arc, back over the heads of the rest of the party. The dryptosaur had squirmed under the repeated impacts of the heavy bullets. Now all its muscles relaxed with a shudder, their strain transmuted to the purposeless quivering of dropped gelatin. Everyone stared at Vickers.

The guide lowered his rifle. A little defensively he said, "I pithed it. The little hole this makes in the skull"—he tapped the barrel of the M14—"won't be a problem in mounting. And if you've *got* to get close to a dino this fresh, you've got to destroy the brain first. Or it's apt as not to snap."

Without speaking, Secretary Cardway stepped from the tread to the ground. Stern and Craig leaped down instantly, more in a determination to die at their posts than in any realistic hope of saving the Secretary from whatever danger he might get himself into. Warren, Vickers, and the Prime Minister joined them more circumspectly, while Adrienne and the soldiers kept watch from the vehicle. If the PR cameramen were frightened, they submerged their fears in an orgy of concentration on their view finders.

And the dryptosaur was indeed well worth taping. It was a female, lacking the spinal fringe of the males, but it was certainly the thirty feet in length that Vickers had initially estimated. Had it not been in company with two smaller adults, Vickers would have suspected it was of a different species despite the markings. "This is, well, it's unique," the guide said honestly. "I don't believe there's another specimen so fine been taken . . . unless in the past two years?"

"My God, look at the ticks," muttered Craig.

At a distance, the rims of the dryptosaur's eyes and the webbing of its three-clawed forepaws appeared to be red. Close up, the color could be seen to be that of the masses of gorged ticks, each individual the size of the first joint of a man's thumb. The bodyguard looked down and began convulsively to rub at his booted ankles. It was the first time Vickers had seen the man apparently forgetful of the Secretary of State.

"I've never found them to be a problem with human beings," the guide said sympathetically. "As for those particular ones, the stabilization chamber back at the compound should take care of them. The sealant clogs their breathing pores, of course."

"When do you find me a goddamn tyrannosaurus, Mordecai?" Secretary Cardway asked.

"Soon, Luther, I am sure," the Israeli Prime Minister responded calmly. "This—mighty creature here that you have felled, this is a magnificent thing too, of course."

"Not what I came for, not what you promised," said Cardway, staring as if toward the horizon. "And it better be soon, old buddy, because this is the last night I spend here." The big Texan spun suddenly, as if to strike Greenbaum. "One thing I learned early—if somebody's got it, he's got it; and if he doesn't, giving him more time or money's just pissing down a rat hole. I've pissed away about all the time you're going to see." The Secretary of State marched back to the half-track. "All right," he called over his shoulder, "let's get this show on the road, shall we?"

"Right," said Vickers, not looking at anyone. "We're carrying a collapsible sled in the other track. We'll get that and drag the dryptosaur back to camp—"

"Screw that. Let's get moving," Cardway said.

"May as well have the other crew earn their keep, eh Vickers?" Thomas Warren suggested, his smile fluffing the tips of his moustache. "They can take care of this when they get the lorry running again. We'll take a look where all these trails seem to be going. I dare say that line of trees to the west means water, and that should mean sport."

A shadow razored across the straggling group of humans. All looked up. The pterosaur that had been a dot in the far heavens an hour before was now only a hundred feet above the ground, a monster with the wingspan of an F-86. The fur of its lower surfaces was a dirty blue-gray. The upper side of its wings, visible as the creature banked, was a white dazzling with the sun it reflected. Skimming in a silence that belied its size, the great carrion-eater turned and swept back at an even lower altitude. Its beak was a yellow chisel the length of a man's forearm.

"Titanopteryx," Vickers said. "Saw the dryptosaur go down and wants a meal. Always wanted to send back a living one to see—"

Adrienne's Schultz and Larsen slammed. Both the twenty-foot wings collapsed upward and back as the muscles controlling them relaxed. Inertia carried the heavy reptile over the heads of the onlookers. Its limbs and long neck spun as gravity accelerated what was no longer a glider. When it struck the ground a hundred feet beyond the half-track, brush crackled and a pall of dust rose.

"Nice shot!" said one of the holographers.

"Why on Earth did you do that?" Vickers asked, trying to keep the concern out of his voice.

"It'll be an hour before the other track gets here," the blonde woman said. Her voice seemed calm. She was already reloading the rifle with one of the cartridges from her tunic loops. "I didn't want the flying belly over there chopping up the . . . Secretary's trophy before then. That dryptosaur is a trophy"—she slung her rifle and stepped up to remount the vehicle—"to be proud of."

They drove westward toward the trees at the same deliberate pace that had brought them to the fallen carnivore. There was much to discuss, but there was no way to do so while Cardway and his bodyguard were in such enforced propinquity to the staff. As a result, the only speech on route was Vickers' radioed directions to the crew of the other half-track, telling them how to home on the beacon he had left and how to load the carcass when they got there. The Secretary's disinterest was obvious, though he seemed to have accepted without question that he had brought down the dryptosaur himself.

It grew increasingly easy to proceed as they drew nearer to their destination. Additional trails forked into the one they were following. After each confluence, the way grew broader. Clawed feet had worn the way deeper, as well, so that the surrounding brush now loomed above the vehicle. On Earth in a later day, each bush would have stood on a mound protected by its own roots from the sculpturing wind. Now only rain and the feet of passers-by affected the terrain.

One hundred yards from the edge of a meandering stream, the brush had been browsed away and the ground trampled flat. In the shade of the broad-leafed cottonwoods and the magnolias fringing the water rested an incredible profusion of animals. The PR man in the front was muttering what seemed to be a prayer, and Mordecai Greenbaum kept repeating. "Superb! Superb!" in Hebrew. The driver stopped at the edge of the brush without needing orders.

There were hundreds of animals in plain sight. The splotches of shade held groups of up to a score, usually of mixed species. One or more of each assemblage greeted the half-track with a snort or a stiffness and focused eyes; then the sentinel would relax, having determined that the newcomer was not a hunting carnivore. Beyond that, a resting dinosaur had no brain capacity to find interest.

A single bull triceratops paced toward them. Its huge forehead bulged with jaw muscles instead of gray matter. Fifty feet away, the ten-ton beast halted and waggled its horns in sidewise arcs, its beak low. When the half-track did not respond to the challenge, even the triceratops struck it from its short list of significant stimuli. It waddled back toward the shade. Dried mud clinging to the ceratopsian's hide turned it white. Where the mud had flaked off, the scales were as black and shiny as graphite.

"Oh, that I had brought my paints," the Prime Minister murmured. "It is a landscape not of hills and trees but of animate creatures."

In a carefully businesslike tone, Vickers said, "Here's the bait to call down your tyrannosaur, Mr. Secretary. And besides using the carcass for the purpose, there are any number of fine heads. The ceratopsians make trophies that draw attention to themselves in any room they don't absolutely fill. That triceratops that looked us over, or one of those pentaceratops over there"—he pointed—"the spikes are striking and the coloration is quite impressive if the shadow didn't hide it."

"And they'll let you shoot, old boy," Warren put in from behind Secretary Cardway. "No need to content yourself with one, not where the game's never been hunted before." He took his left hand from his gunstock to gesture in a wide arc. Though stretches of mud flats broke the stream into a series of connected pools, the line of cottonwoods and magnolias squirmed unbroken as far as the hunters could see in either direction. There was no reason to doubt that the herds of animal life in midday somnolence extended as far as the watercourse.

"There must be a dozen species of hadrosaurs in sight from here, crests of every shape and size," the British guide gloated. "Just as many ceratopsians—take one of each. If they spook here, we'll simply cruise a little further up the line to where they—"

"Let me see that," the Secretary grunted, elbowing aside the soldier manning the fifty-caliber machine gun. The startled trooper resisted momentarily, his left hand still gripping the weapon. Stern gave him a quick order in Hebrew. Puzzled, the soldier slid aside. The driver, seated directly below the big muzzle, covered his ears with his hands.

"Pull the charging handle once more," Stern said quietly. Cardway frowned. The Israeli official reached past the politician and drew back the lever on the right side of the receiver himself. When he let the handle go, the breech-block clanged like a horseshoe striking an anvil. "Now it is ready," Stern said. "You press the trigger with your thumbs."

Secretary Cardway's face grew intent while those around him watched with varied expressions. The elephant guns had roared. The blast of the cal-fifty was by contrast as sharp as that of Vickers' Ml4, as loud as a stick of bombs going off nearby. The first three rounds were high. One of them touched a cottonwood and exploded, shattering a branch as thick as a man's thigh. Splintered wood and then the branch itself tumbled down on a trio of duckbills leaping upright from their sleep. Cardway corrected, lowering the muzzle and firing again. This time the explosive bullets raked the tree trunk and the bellies of the dinosaurs as they bolted straight at the gun. The duckbills flopped to the ground, squealing like freight trains slowing.

One of the wounded creatures staggered to its feet again. Cardway ignored it, swinging his gun onto a cluster of ceratopsians. Vickers leveled his own rifle. It was hard to sight on the duckbill's head. It bobbed and dipped as the creature tried with its short forelegs to pat away the coils of its own intestines tangling it. A rush of tears blinded the guide. He cradled his weapon again, whispering to himself.

The half-track shuddered with recoil as Cardway hosed a triceratops standing broadside to them, thirty yards away. One of the beast's long brow horns shattered, then a string of white flashes traversed its side. The triceratops plunged forward, bawling, and collapsed with its beak in the furrow it had plowed. The smoky line of tracers continued to snap through the air which its target had vacated. Bullets walked across the surface of the stream, gouting spray at two-foot intervals. Then they crashed into a gaggle of four pentaceratops staring blankly at the ruin of their fallen kinsman. The nitroguanadine-bursting charges slashed the beasts. Two fell, two turned to run. The latter drew with them the panicked creatures to either side. Mud and water sprayed as the line of animals rushed across the stream, stretching away from the gunfire as if it were an arrow drawing a bowstring.

The muzzle blasts ceased abruptly. An instant later the last explosive bullet cracked. The only mechanical noise remaining was that of an ejected case, ringing like a wind chime on the ground among the brass that had preceded it. The stench of propellant, pooling about the half-track in layers, was ripe and cloying. At least it hid the stink of blood and excrement from the dozen wounded and dying dinosaurs nearby. It did not hide their cries. Nothing could have done that, but the crashing gunfire had made even the bellows of pain sound reedy and distant.

Henry Vickers climbed over the side of the vehicle. Behind him,

Secretary Cardway was saying, "I've wanted to do that ever since the Convention when those bastards from New York gave me the shaft so deep it clicked on my molars. Yeah . . ." Without turning around, Vickers could not tell whether the Secretary of State was addressing someone in particular or was just letting his thoughts spray the landscape. Vickers was afraid of what he might do if he turned to look at the man.

The gut-shot hadrosaur was still standing. It eyed Vickers' approach as it might have that of one of the scavengers of its own time. Pain and shock kept the beast shackled into place, hooting at the guide through its tongueless palate. Even crippled, it towered above the man.

"Henry!" Adrienne cried.

Vickers shot the duckbill through the roof of its mouth. Soft tissue spattered him. The two-ton dinosaur arched backwards as if it had touched a high-tension line. Both the hind feet left the ground for the instant before the body thudded down on its side. The muscles were spasming under the russet hide, but there was no brain left to register pain.

Vickers walked to the next hadrosaur, sprawled in a heap on the ground. He socketed the slotted muzzle brake of the M14 in the creature's ear and fired. The carcass did not move. The guide stepped toward the third beast, which had begun squirming in the direction of the stream after the explosive bullets smashed both hip joints.

"Henry!" Adrienne repeated, close at hand. She caught him by the shoulder. "What are you doing?"

"Let go of me," the guide mumbled.

"Then get hold of yourself!" his wife said. Vickers pulled free. The blonde woman stepped in front of him and brain-shot the wounded hadrosaur herself. Vickers paused at the crash of the Schultz and Larsen. When Adrienne turned to face him, he met her eyes.

"All right," Adrienne said angrily, "we'll do what we have to do. But we don't need to stand on top of the goddamned things to put paid to them!"

"No, I'm sorry," the guide said. "I didn't—I won't do something foolish like that again."

The phrase "do what we have to do" echoed through Vickers'

mind while he and his wife finished off the wounded animals. He continued to think about it far on into the night.

In a landscape that had no light source other than the stars, the propane mantle lantern inside turned the whole compound of mosquito netting into a pearly prism. The intrusion vehicles, the half-tracks, and the individual shelters within were blocks of shadow. A man, a shadow himself, stood just inside the zippered gate.

Vickers paused, still in the darkness as far as the person waiting was concerned. Beside him, his wife sighed. It was the only sound or sign of restiveness that she had given during the silent hours outside the compound. The guide smiled invisibly at himself and stepped forward again, fumbling for the zipper. Avraham Stern leaned toward him from the other side and opened a slit with a single motion. "Henry," he said in greeting, "Mrs. Vickers. A pleasant night."

Though the netting could not have made a significant difference, night sounds seemed distanced within the compound. The carnivore snarling at a lesser fellow was suddenly millions of years away. Adrienne lighted one of her small cigars; it belonged to this world, not the other one beyond the nylon gauze.

"Henry, might I speak with you for a moment?" the Israeli official asked. "You are well, I trust?"

Adrienne's face glowed orange beneath the brim of her bush hat as she drew on her cigar. The smoke she exhaled hung in the distant lantern light like the ink of a squid in still water. "Me for a bath," she said. "There's no point hunting in the lap of luxury if you don't— luxuriate now and again." She sauntered toward the trailers that served as kitchen and showers, part of the cargo from the back-up insertion. Her rifle slanted past her left shoulder, safe and ready to use at an instant's notice.

"I'm all right," Vickers said, both men watching Adrienne disappear into the trailer. "I just—thought it might be a good idea to be outside for a time."

"Certainly," the official said. His right hand was toying with the breech of his rifle. When he noticed the fact, he stopped. "A good night to sit and talk, certainly."

The guide laughed and dropped to seat himself cross-legged on the ground. "Avraham, every word anybody says within three hundred meters of the compound gets routed through the alarm system. Straight into the command post. Now, I'm not going wandering around farther than that into the dark; and do you really think I was going to say the things you're afraid I was saying where the guard is going to run straight to you with them? No, I went out to sit and think; and Adrienne came out to sit with me and I suppose think too . . . or not. And then we came in." He looked at Stern, who could see the outlines of his smile and feel the falseness of it. "We've got a problem that needs solving, you know," Vickers continued softly.

"Henry," the official said.

"No, no." The guide brushed away the unspoken fear with his free hand, the hand that did not hold an automatic rifle. "No, I mean the problem you pay me to deal with, making important clients happy. Getting one a tyrannosaur, in this case."

Stern did not attempt to hide his relief. "And you have?" he asked. "That is . . . is very good. Mr. Warren does not feel there is any certainty that a tyrannosaur will visit the, ah, bait, in the time at hand. And the Prime Minister is equally sure, with which I concur, that the time cannot be extended. Secretary Cardway will hunt tomorrow with us. To keep him longer must be against his will; which would, of course, be even worse than the present unfortunate circumstances."

Vickers rose again in the limber motion of a man younger than he was. "All right," he said, "we'll see. Can you get the others together— Warren and the Prime Minister, that is?"

The official chuckled. "They are waiting in the command post," he said. "I gave the guards—the soldiers—leave from listening to the warning microphones when I realized where you were. Not that I needed to have worried, of course."

The command post was another trailer. It housed the radio, the alarm system, and the banks of nicad batteries on which they could operate when the half-track generators were not present to drive them. The lantern, which burned continuously in the center of the compound, hung on a pole nearby; but within the trailer, the only light was that from the instruments. In the blue glow, Thomas Warren disappeared behind his moustache and the Prime Minister looked like a skull. The amplified sounds of the Cretaceous night wove a blanket that smothered the words whispered within.

Vickers followed Stern inside. The guide started to close the door, then frowned. He gestured out into the darkness, toward the distant quadrant where the Secretary of State's tent had been pitched.

Stern's smile was a shift of the planes of his face in the dim light. "He was dictating in his tent," the official said. "Now he is asleep. One of the sensors—" he tapped a separate display panel above a larger area screen—"was set within the compound, you see. It will register footsteps, long before they reach us. And his dog is sleeping at his feet."

Vickers grinned back. Craig had been billeted in the large tent with the soldiers. By his own choice, however, the bodyguard had spread his bedroll on the ground a few yards from the entrance to the Secretary's tent.

"That one concerns me, sometimes," said Mordecai Greenbaum. "He is under too much strain. Either they should have sent three or four guards—or they should have been sensible and not sent any."

Vickers shrugged. It was too late to worry about that now. "All right," he said. "I've got a notion of how to get Cardway what he wants. But it's going to be expensive. It'll take one, maybe two round trips of the big intrusion vehicle to do it and to cover up afterwards what we've done."

"The expense of not being successful," said Greenbaum in measured tones, "is the existence of Israel, I am afraid. Tell us what you need."

"All right," Vickers repeated. "There's probably a tyrannosaur in the area . . . and butcher's work like that on the creek bank may bring in more than that in a week or so. Food in that quantity overrides territory, while it lasts."

"That's fine, old chap," said Thomas Warren. His voice had the sharpness of a man who knows he is considered second rate in the instant discussion. "But we don't have a week or so." In the close confines of the trailer, the British guide had not lighted his pipe. He gestured nervously with the stem, like a child holding a revolver. "And besides, you know as well as I do that there may be nothing bigger around here than the dryptosaur we took this morning. You know, I think that with a little better support, old boy, I could have convinced Cardway that it really was a—"

"Horseshit," said Avraham Stern in heavy, careful English. Warren fell silent.

Vickers brushed his hand back and forth in frustration. "No, no," he said. "Warren's right. About being no tyrannosaur near enough, maybe. There's only one living tyrannosaur we can locate for sure— and that's the one in a cage at the Institute for Zoology. Topside in Tel Aviv. It's also the one I want returned for Cardway."

The other three men began to talk simultaneously, stopping themselves when they realized that Vickers was still poised to continue. "Please go on, sir," the Prime Minister said. His hinted smile showed his awareness that the guide, too, was smiling.

"We'll leave the compound in the morning," Vickers said, "beat up the bait area. Who knows, maybe there'll be something worth going after there. As soon as the Secretary is out of sight, though, Mr. Stern, here, and Warren carry Vehicle Beth—Aleph isn't big enough for the cargo, and anyway, maybe the walls on Beth might help if the dino started to get loose early . . . anyway, they go back Topside. Avraham does what has to be done to rig the beast with a radio beacon and get it loaded." The guide paused, then added, "Ah, you don't think there's going to be any difficulty getting your orders obeyed ASAP, do you? I mean, there's not going to be much time, and I know what bureaucracy can be like."

Stern snorted. "There will be no trouble," he said. "Those who know me will obey. Those who do not know me will obey, or they will have a company of paratroopers in their offices until they *have* obeyed. I—I do not get much excitement anymore."

"Then it's just a matter of getting Dr. Galil to drop you a few klicks out," Vickers continued. "We don't want to turn a tyrannosaur loose in the compound, after all. That'll take some very close figuring, but . . . well, it's required. And Shlomo can do it, he's never failed yet."

"I don't see precisely what I'm supposed to be doing, old boy," said Thomas Warren. He was clutching his pipe against the row of looped cartridges over his heart.

"Well," said Vickers, "ah, Thomas, I think it's going to require more than one man to off-load the dino. And apart from the security angle, I think it has to be someone who's familiar with the beasts."

"I'm familiar enough with bloody tyrannosaurs that I don't share an intrusion vehicle with living ones!" the Englishman exploded. He either did not notice or did not care that the trailer door had begun to open. "*You* can do silly-arse things like that if you want, but Mrs. Warren didn't raise any fools!"

"I'll go," said Adrienne Vickers from the doorway.

"You've been listening?" Stern demanded.

The woman spun her cigar out into the darkness, then exhaled in jets from both nostrils before she squeezed into the trailer. She was in no hurry to speak. Though the nicotine had stripped her visual purple so that she could not see by the instrument lights, she knew that she was the focus of the eyes of the four men. "I don't listen at doors," Adrienne said at last, "though everybody in camp's heard Mr. Warren's little outburst, I'm sure."

"Adrienne," Vickers said, "this isn't a game."

"Look, dammit," the tall blonde said. She leaned forward and gestured, her fingernails glinting. "There's only one tyrannosaur we can promise, that's really *promise*. The one Henry and I captured alive. I don't have to listen to you talk to know that."

"You didn't say anything tonight," her husband commented.

"Neither did you!" Adrienne responded sharply, though not in a loud voice. "And we didn't have to, did we? We both knew what had to be done. Anyway"—she drew a breath—"anyway, I'm the one who needs to nurse the baby back. He'll be sedated, but we don't dare have him knocked on his ass, not if he needs to be upright for Cardway the same morning."

"Well then," the Prime Minister said briskly. "We are agreed?" Stern nodded. Warren shrugged.

"Does it ever bother you," Adrienne Vickers asked, "that a— certifiable madman like Cardway has the sort of power you're encouraging him to use? I mean, it's your world. I've found I could do all right without it . . . though I suppose I'd have to get used to a crossbow and smoke banana leaves or something."

"Banana leaves would be an improvement, I'm sure, Madame," the Prime Minister said, bowing courteously.

"And we joke about it," the woman continued wonderingly. "Well, it's your world. For however long. Henry, I'm for bed."

"We've said our say," the guide remarked, reaching past his wife to the door catch. "We'll see in the morning. We'll all see in the morning."

Either the sun slanting across their backs was hotter than it had been the day before, or the anger in the box of the half-track made it seem that way. The shadow of the dust they raised stretched ahead of the vehicle, bulking across the scrub like chaos made manifest. Secretary Cardway rode grimly at the front bulkhead, to the right of the cal-fifty. The gunner, wedged tightly between the Secretary and Vickers on the other side, looked nervous. He was the same soldier who had manned the gun the day before. What he had seen then had convinced him that both of the men beside him were dangerously insane.

In the distance, flecks spun against the white sky like flakes of cardboard hurled from a giant bonfire. Cardway's face softened minusculy from the stony anger he had maintained since getting up in the morning. Vickers saw the interest and said over the intercom, "Pterosaurs again, sir. For the carrion. What we have to hope is that the bigger carnivores will be there too."

The Secretary of State looked across at Vickers while the soldier between them cringed away. "You goddamn better hope so," the politician said. His voice in Vickers' ears was out of synch with his moving lips, because the sound was being picked up by Cardway's throat mike.

In the back of the box, the Prime Minister frowned. Warren, beside him, appeared to take no notice. The Englishman had been morose all morning. When he looked at Vickers, it was with a degree of animation; but the spirit animating his eyes was one of dull anger. Warren had not been pleased to be subordinated to Vickers. It was now evident to him that his employers considered Adrienne also a far more valuable member of the operation than the junior guide was . . . and that made one more factor for Vickers to consider.

Craig and a holographer rode in the middle of the box. The PR staffer at least could be trusted not to actively endanger anyone else.

As they neared the scene of the previous day's slaughter, the circling flecks resolved into pterosaurs descending. There were never fewer than a dozen in sight at a time, even though the lowest continually disappeared at the bottom of the falling helixes. Newcomers, by now from many kilometers distance, replenished the pattern from above. Their fragile wing membranes enabled the great creatures to lift from the ground in air so still that pollen scarcely drifted. The converse of that delicacy was the fact that severe braking forces like those habitually employed by the feathered scavengers of later ages would have shredded pterosaur wings at the first application. Silent and awesomely large, the creatures spiraled down with the gentle beauty of thistledown.

There was something angelic in the descent of the pterosaurs with their dazzlingly white upper surfaces. Then the half-track rumbled through the last of the masking brush. The ground on which the winged scavengers were landing was a living hell of previous arrivals.

Thirty meters in front of them, a dryptosaur glared up from the carcass of the duckbill it had finished disemboweling. The carnivore was probably one of the pair that had escaped the day before, a smallish male with scar tissue ridging the left side of its head including the eye socket. Not a choice trophy, but closer than Vickers cared to see a carnivore to one of his clients. "Go ahead, sir," he said, aiming at the top of the beast's sternum himself.

"It's smaller than the other one," Cardway muttered correctly. He sighted and fired anyway.

The dryptosaur was facing them astraddle of the herbivore's neck. Its head and body were raised higher than they would normally have been. Like a dog on a morsel, the carnivore was trying to look as threatening as possible to drive away its competition. The half-track was probably equated in the beast's limited mind with an unusually large ceratopsian—not a creature that a dryptosaur or even a tyrannosaur of several times the bulk would normally have charged. Still, the beast lived by killing, and a wound could be expected to bring a response. The guide tensed.

And promptly felt a fool when the Mannlicher blasted and the dryptosaur crumpled like a wet sheet. Cardway had placed his bullet perfectly, shattering the carnosaur's spine after wrecking the complex of blood vessels above the heart. The beast flopped over on its back, the hind legs kicking upward convulsively. A drop of blood slung from a talon spattered coldly on Vickers' wrist, but the danger was over. "Perfect!" the guide said with honest enthusiasm. "Now—"

Secretary Cardway cut off the instructions with another thunderous shot. Beside himself, Vickers started to curse. Then he stepped back. There was no point cursing an avalanche or a waterspout. The Secretary was as ungovernable as those forces of Nature when he once began firing. The muzzle of the .458 jumped three more times, each thrust preceded by a momentary spurt of orange as the last of the powder charge burned outside the barrel. The reports lessened in apparent intensity, though only because they were literally deafening to the listeners. After the fifth shot, the ringing that persisted was loud enough to challenge the myriad squalling of the scavengers remaining on the scattered corpses. There were no herbivores in sight where there had been hundreds the preceding day. Possibly that was a reaction to the carnage itself, the slaughter and the stink of blood. More likely, the plant-eaters would avoid the area only so long as the sharp-toothed throng were bolting the carrion like locusts on Spring wheat.

"Pull up a hundred meters or so to the right," Vickers ordered the driver. "Dead slow." The guide squinted though the Sun was behind him as he surveyed the crop of vermin. Usually the presence of the pair of dryptosaurs—the second was slashing at a pentaceratops which had died on the far bank of the stream—would mean that nothing bigger had found the kill. A tyrannosaur would drive away the one-ton dryptosaurs, though it was likely to ignore anything smaller. Here, however, the volume of flesh was so great that Vickers hoped against hope that the clanking of their treads would lift the dragonlike head of the greatest of the carnosaurs into sight from where it rested behind a fallen triceratops or the like.

Nothing of the sort happened. Even the lesser meat-eaters, which *were* present, ignored the vehicle. That was just as well. There were at least a score of dromaeosaurs visible, half-ton predators with the habits and vicious temperament of hyenas. The slaughter had drawn several packs together, some of them surely out of their range. When the food had been bolted down to the last scraps, the bush would be the scene of fighting which nothing human could equal in savagery. For the nonce, all were fully occupied with stuffing down gobbets of meat. Their mouths expanded like snakes' to accept larger pieces than rigid jaw hinges would have permitted. The number and proximity of the carnivores still made Vickers nervous, even with the heavy machine gun to back him up in an emergency.

Smaller than the toothed dromaeosaurs but still potentially lethal to a man were the ornithominids, beaked omnivores in appearance much like the ostriches for which some were named. Their normal diet was of seeds and insects. But as when the lemmings swarm in Norway, the reindeer feed on them, here a similar abundance of flesh had summoned the swift runners from far across the plains to feast. They pecked and squabbled, darting in to seize a strip of meat and dragging it back to a distance of a few meters. They bolted their food, defending it with glaring eyes and legs whose kick could rip sheet metal.

The least of the scavengers were feathered, though only a few of them were true birds in the sense that they or their ancestors could fly. Many of their descendants would, however. Warm-blooded creatures like dinosaurs needed either bulk or insulation to prevent their high metabolisms from outstripping any possible food source. The smallest of the dinosaurs crawling over the bloating carcasses were no bigger than chickens. Like chickens, they could not have survived without the dead air space provided within their layers of feathers—the feathers being modified scales, as was the fur of mammals and the pterosaurs. Some few had made the insulation do double duty, adding wing beats to the powerful thrust of their hind legs when they wished to climb a carcass or escape to a nearby bush with a chosen morsel. The high skies were still the province of the great pterosaurs now descending, however, their delicacy more efficient until the storms of the coming age swept them into oblivion.

There were no mammals visible save the occupants of the half-track. The night would bring them out again from the holes to which they had been driven tens of millions of years before by the ancestors of the dinosaurs. So long as Earth hosted the dinosaurs, the mammals would grub for insects in the dark and would fall prey to the least of the swift-striding creatures with whom they in no sense competed.

The vehicle halted as Vickers had ordered. Craig, the bodyguard, said, "You did this as an insult, didn't you?" His voice was high, on the edge of control.

The guide turned in surprise. He had become accustomed to thinking of the bodyguard as a tool rather than a human being, an object with a programmed set of responses to stimuli . . . rather like his own Uzi submachine gun. It was disconcerting to hear Craig volunteering statements that had no bearing on his duties. It was more than disconcerting that the statements made no sense. Vickers wondered if the strain had in fact pushed the younger American off the deep end, ready to spray all those around him with bullets too small to be useful except on men.

Perhaps Secretary Cardway had the same thought. "Craig, what the hell do you mean?" he demanded with something less than his normal assurance. Greenbaum edged backward, trying to get behind the bodyguard without being obtrusive about it. Adrienne and Stern had been left in camp with the "vehicle that wasn't running right" according to the story the Americans had been told. They would have been comforting companions at this juncture. Thomas Warren merely watched with a glimmer of a smile.

"He's trying to shame you with this filth, sir," Craig said. He gestured with his left hand at the landscape, the slaughtered dinosaurs lying like hillocks completely covered by the mass of creatures feeding on them. "This, this—disgusting . . . he'll make you out to be a butcher to the world, sir. He's just brought you here to discredit you!"

Vickers was very still. There was an instant's fear within him that perhaps Craig had seen within him a truth that the guide had hidden even from himself. There was nothing unnatural about the scavengers, any more than the sight of maggots festering in a dead rabbit is unnatural. But it was true that this circus of carrion and corruption would affect many voters with the repugnance with which the machine gunning had affected the guide himself.

But Secretary Cardway blinked incredulously. "Oh, for Christ's sake," he said. "I had to bring you but I don't have to listen to crap. Keep your mouth shut if you still want a job when we get back." He turned to Vickers, utterly ignoring the bodyguard whose insight he was unable to credit. "And we're going back right now," he said. "I've wasted enough time." Rotating his head to fix the Prime Minister, he added, "If this is your idea of fun, Greenbaum, you must love campaigning. Heat, dust, rubber food, and idiots."

The responder on Vickers' wrist looked like a watch. It now gave a tiny chime and tickled his skin with just enough current to get his attention. The guide glanced down, certain that God must answer prayers in the Cretaceous. The device was tuned to the radio beacon Stern and Adrienne carried to tag the tyrannosaur. The responder's face had lighted dull orange, meaning that the beast had popped back into the Cretaceous within two—or three, at the outside—kilometers of the responder. That was almost too close, since it would take some minutes to unload the tyrannosaur and ride the intrusion vehicle back Topside. But Vickers could easily kill time en route until Adrienne radioed with the coded message that gave him the all-clear.

"Well, this is a washout, it seems," Vickers said, beaming at the others, "but there's a spot I noticed just a—a few minutes from here where I'll give you my word there's a tyrannosaur."

Even Greenbaum and Warren looked askance at the senior guide. Vickers' enthusiasm had carried him momentarily out of the present setting. The incongruity of his triumphant tone did not strike him until he saw everyone else in the vehicle gaping as if he had lost his mind. "Ah," he continued, in a more reserved fashion, "I'll sit beside the driver there and guide him. Mr. Secretary, if you'll stand ready but not shoot until Mr. Warren or I say, say to shoot, that is, we'll put you in the best place."

As the guide clambered down to exchange places with the

holographer, he surreptitiously set his responder on search mode and swept it in an arc. The lighted face glowed green until the guide's arm pointed within one degree of the beacon. There it flashed red, giving Vickers the bearing. Setting the little device back on ranging, he said to the driver, "We're headed northeast, friend." He gestured. "Take it easy. One of these trails to water should lead us back the way we want. When it branches, I'll give you directions."

The soldier frowned in puzzlement, but Stern had made it clear that morning that Vickers was to be obeyed no matter what he ordered. The vehicle shuddered into gear, then swung wide so that the driver could steer it into what looked like a suitable gap in the brush.

This time, no one had suggested salvaging the dead dryptosaur. Vickers wondered silently whether even bagging a tyrannosaur would affect Secretary Cardway as Greenbaum and Stern hoped it would. Very possibly it would not—which was probably to the world's benefit.

Branches flapped toward Vickers' face and sprang away as the half-track crawled through brush that was growing denser. Occasionally a cluster of stumps would appear where some ceratopsian had sheared off a thicket near the ground and spent the next ten minutes stuffing it all down his gullet. More often, an alcove had been stripped of leaves and bark by some hadrosaur's enormous battery of teeth. The naked white branch cores splayed skeletally toward the beaten trail, then were gone and past and replaced by similar signs.

Twice at a forking, Vickers checked his responder and pointed the driver on. Above and behind him, Secretary Cardway's expression showed an increasing impatience for something to happen. The guide in turn was concerned that he had not yet received clearance from Adrienne. He was planning a delay—taking the next wrong turning should be enough—when Nature accomplished the desired end herself. Brush crashed to the right of the trail and a huge ceratopsian head loomed over the half-track.

"Hold it!" Vickers cried. The driver's foot, poised between brake pedal and accelerator, slammed down on the former. The juddering halt sprayed dust forward, but their speed was low enough to avoid injuries. It was a triceratops, snorting a dozen feet in the air. Its beak was open, displaying rows of knife-edged shearing teeth behind it. "My God, Mr. Secretary!" Vickers cried as he swung his door open, "I think we've got a pair mating! I don't think any clients ever had a look at this before!"

"Nail the blighter right through the throat!" said Thomas Warren in the box above.

Vickers, shocked and furious, spun around. *"Wait, for Chrissake!"* he shouted. Cardway had already leveled the Mannlicher and it was doubtful that he even heard. The guide leaped, trying to get out of the cone of shock when the big rifle fired. He was partly successful. The muzzle blast sledged him but did not knock him down with a nose bleed as would have resulted from slightly closer proximity. Leaves trembled in an arc to either side of the gun. The triceratops lurched upright with both its broad front paws lashing at the sky.

Vickers snapped off two shots at the dinosaur forty feet away. From his angle, all he could see beyond the brush was the creature's weaving skull—but a shot anywhere else would be useless at this point anyway. Then a hawthorn thicket splintered toward the half-track to pass the female, charging with her head down and her black-tipped horns aimed at the cab.

If the two ceratopsians had stayed coupled, they would have been harmless even to spectators approaching close enough to touch them. Violently dismounted by her mate, the female's certain reaction was to run in the direction she was facing. While that was not a charge, technically, the effect was the same on anything that happened to be in the path of the ten-ton missile. It was really the first time the heavy machine gun could have been useful. It was not useful, of course, because the range was too short and the gunner was unprepared for a target appearing twenty feet below the rearing head he had trained on. Vickers, leaning over the hood of the half-track, fired.

The tiny uranium penetrator, moving at 3,500 feet per second and no more affected by skull bones than it was by the air between muzzle and target, took the dinosaur just behind the right eye. Eight feet away, the bullet exited behind the left shoulder. The exit hole gaped momentarily like a hungry mouth, but flesh is plastic at hypersonic velocities: the wound spasmed back to normalcy almost as suddenly as it opened. Within the skull, however, the shock waves of the penetrator's passage were still reverberating. The lump of nerve tissue serving the triceratops as a brain was scrambled as thoroughly as an egg dropped from an airplane.

The female's hind legs continued to drive her, as a headless chicken's will, but the thrust was no longer forward since the forelegs had buckled and the creature's beak was gouging the soil. The right brow horn struck the frame under the vehicle's left fender and pierced it with a crash like an anti-tank gun firing. The tip broke off. The dead triceratops came to rest with its eyes open and its vertical nose spike touching the bumper.

Vickers stepped to one side and smashed the sacral thickening of the spine to end the thrashing of the corpse's hind legs. Then he looked up at the men in the half-track. Everyone else had been too startled to shoot. "Warren," Vickers said, speaking loudly over the tinny ringing in his own ears, "if I ever hear you intend to go on a time safari again, I'll come back from wherever I am and beat you within an inch of your life."

The three faces peering at Vickers over the front bulkhead of the truck were a study in contrasts. Secretary Cardway looked bemused. His rifle was raised. He had recocked it too slowly for a second shot at the male triceratops, and in his focus on the male, the Secretary had not noticed the rush of the female until it was over. The soldier in the middle gazed down at the dead female, well aware that he had been too slow to stop it with his cal-fifty. The gunner knew that he had not prevented disaster himself, and that had disaster occurred . . . shit rolls downhill, and he was on the bottom.

Thomas Warren was smiling, apparently because he did not know what else to do. It dawned on Vickers that the Englishman really was not aware that his advice to Cardway had almost gotten them all killed. Had Vickers been a hair slower or a hair less accurate, the ceratopsian's charge would at best have left them stranded in the bush with no vehicle and no radio. The worst . . . a search team would have been hard put to find human traces after a creature larger than a pair of elephants had trampled them all into the ground. Warren's own rifle had slumped back to high port—but like Cardway, he had been aiming at the male triceratops. It was as if the female of the pair, by being unseen, had become nonexistent.

Mordecai Greenbaum laid a hand on the shoulder of the machine gunner, rotating him out of the way to make room. "I do not think that will be necessary, Mr. Vickers," the small Israeli said. His voice penetrated easily the sounds of the male triceratops dying close off in the brush. "When the beasts were mating, shooting one was sure to provoke the other, was it not? I do not think the Ministry of Tourism needs employees who exhibit such bad judgment. I will speak to Avraham."

"Say, hold hard a minute," said Warren. The fatuous smile dripped away as full realization of what was happening struck him. "We're supposed to be entertaining the client, right? And he's not a bloody photographer, he's a gunner, so I—"

"Are we ready to proceed, Mr. Vickers?" the Prime Minister asked.

"*I* damned well am," said the Secretary of State. He had lost the open-eyed stare he wore over his sights, relapsing into the arrogant impatience which Vickers found only a touch less intolerable.

"Now listen!" Warren shouted. "You sods aren't going to do this to me! If you think I'm going to keep quiet while you—"

"Mr. Warren!" said Greenbaum. Listening to the snap of his voice, Vickers for the first time realized how the man could rule his coalition cabinet as if it were a drill team. "I will remind you that breaches of security can be viewed as treason, and treason trials may be held *in cameru* if the need warrants."

"I'm not a Jew," the guide said, gray-faced and too stunned to edit the words bubbling from his subconscious.

"You need not be Jewish to be tried for treason to the State of Israel," Greenbaum said crisply, "nor even a resident to be tried. Eichman was not a resident either, you may remember . . . Driver, let us go on."

"Mobile Two to Mobile One," the radio said in Adrienne's attenuated voice.

"Thank God," said Vickers aloud before he thumbed his lapel mike. He raised his index finger unnecessarily to quiet the others before saying, "Go ahead, Mobile Two. Is everything all right?"

"More or less," the radio hissed. Then, "Yes, it's all right. We're proceeding to join you. We're on a pony, not the half-track."

The guide blanked his face. Cardway probably did not know that the expedition had brought none of the four-wheeled utility vehicles, so Adrienne's appearance on one would not give the deception away. Still, the initial plan had been for her and Stern to ride the intrusion vehicle back Topside after they had dropped the tyrannosaur in the bush, then to be reinserted at the compound. That way, everything at the camp when Cardway returned would look the same as it had when he departed. Instead, Stern and Adrienne had brought back a pony along with the tagged dinosaur, and they were obviously proceeding from the drop site rather than the camp if they expected to join the hunters before they made the kill. The change in plans concerned Vickers as much as did his wife's initial "more or less" on the radio.

"We could name this one," Warren said in an odd voice. Vickers looked up. The British guide's face was stiff and his gesture toward the triceratops, dead under the wheels, was broadly theatrical. "We could call her Adrienne, do you think? And the other one, maybe we'll name it Stern?"

"Warren," Vickers said. His left hand touched the receiver of his rifle, but the fingers sprang away again as if the metal were afire.

"Or maybe, Washman, I hear he was one," Warren continued. His eyes were unfocused and his voice had no inflection. "Of course, we could scarcely find all the names for—"

Vickers sprang upward, his left hand closing on the Englishman's tunic and his right whistling in a punch that would have smashed his knuckles had it more than grazed the other's head. Warren's snake-skin-banded hat fell off. The barrel of the heavy machine gun was in Vickers' way, blocking him from a closer grapple. His feet were on the seat and he was trying more or less unconsciously to climb through the gun and the bulkhead on which it was mounted. Prime Minister Greenbaum shouted an order as he and the soldier dragged Warren backward. The British guide had thrown an arm across his face. His expression was that of an awakened sleepwalker.

Under the pressure of the two Israelis, Warren surged back and over a chest of camera equipment. Vickers' anger broke when his grip did. He steadied himself against the machine gun, panting. John Craig's Uzi was six inches from Vickers' left eye. The safety was off. "Put that goddamned thing away," said Vickers wearily. "I'm no danger to you and yours." He flexed his right hand. He had skinned the back of it somehow, probably by brushing the cal-fifty when he swung at Warren. "I'm no danger even to that shit, it seems," he said. "Mr. Prime Minister, if you'll keep him where I don't see him for a while, I'd be obliged. We can go on now." Vickers sank back into his seat. "We've had enough dirty laundry."

The driver backed, ignoring the crunch of brush buckling under his treads. He cramped the front wheels sharply, steering toward a wall of thorns and vines to clear the triceratops dead across half the trail. As the soldier engaged forward again, a little utility vehicle with two persons aboard swung around a bend in the trail ahead. The man at the machine gun almost fired by reflex.

Everyone was cursing. The half-track clashed to a stop, more from unexpectedness than real danger of running over the aluminum pony. Stern was at the tiller guiding the vehicle awkwardly. Adrienne was far more experienced with the ponies, but shots had been fired and there was a triceratops making the earth shudder as its muscles continued to die. The blonde woman squatted behind Stern, trying to look in all directions at once and ready to respond instantly with a bullet from her Schultz and Larsen.

Stern jerked the tiller. To the men on the half-track, the smaller vehicle disappeared behind the bulk of the female triceratops. Moments later, Adrienne and the Israeli official scampered around the great carcass. "Came by a trail that put us ahead of you," the woman explained loudly as she opened the door to the cab. "Move over." In a voice that Vickers saw on her lips rather than heard, she heard, "We need to move fast. That dino isn't going to last long."

Stern was being handed into the back by one of the holographers. Secretary Cardway was speaking in a cold rage, though Vickers did not turn to see who the recipient might be. As the half-track moved forward again, he mouthed to Adrienne, "An overdose of dope? We could dick around in the brush and hope it'll wear off."

"Left at the next fork!" Adrienne shouted to the driver. Then, to Vickers under the rising whine of the diesel as they plowed through brush, "We brought it back in shackles, no drugs at all. You know, Avraham may be a desk jockey but he's got enough guts for two."

Vickers smiled, calmed by the scent and touch of his wife in the cramped cab. "I think he's seen his share of fieldwork of one kind and the other," the guide said. "He's . . . a good soldier. Jesus, a good German. I think . . . I'm afraid that's what we all are, good Germans doing our jobs and keeping quiet."

The flash of lights and shadow as the half-track lurched down the trail was a peripheral distraction to Vickers and Adrienne as they faced each other in the close quarters. "Well," she said, "the tyrannosaur's about to become a good dinosaur. In the sense of being dead as one. They've figured out what the problem is when dinos come Topside: parrot fever . . . or bird fever in general, I guess. This one's caught it just like the rest, and its lungs are already hemorrhaging."

"What?" Vickers demanded, certain that he had not understood his wife correctly.

"Bird fever," she repeated. She put a hand on her husband's shoulder to steady her as the wheels bounced on a head-sized rock. "Ornithosis. It's not a serious disease in birds today, ah, Topside. But dinos are close enough genetically to catch it, and they have no natural immunities. It's like smallpox and the Pacific Islanders to them."

Everyone on the half-track ducked involuntarily as the dappling of the vegetation blackened momentarily into solid shadow. The driver steadied on the wheel again. Vickers let out his breath and lowered the rifle he had been trying to clear with too little room to do so. The titanopteryx sailed on, barely faster and barely higher than the half-track. The straggling limbs of the brush hid the pterosaur again.

The responder on the guide's wrist pinged twice, flashing red. They were within one hundred meters of the beacon and—God willing—of the tyrannosaur. Of the end of this charade of a safari.

"Stop, stop!" Vickers ordered, touching the driver on the forearm.

They slowed to a halt with barely a quiver. As the driver thumbed dust from his instrument dials, the guide stood on the seat facing back toward the other men. "We've sighted fresh spoor," he lied. "The trophy is very close. For the, ah, remainder of the stalk, one of the holographers and W-warren will ride in the cab. Mr. Secretary, you'll stay where you are, if you please, and I'll ride in the front on the other side of the machine gun. Adrienne, Mr. Stern, if you will take the back corners and watch your quadrants—"

"No," said Secretary Cardway, bracing a hand on the bulkhead. "I'm not going to shoot it from a tank. I'm getting down."

"Sir!" Vickers blurted, trying to come up with a suitable lie. He had almost said the truth, "That's too dangerous to allow—" and that would have made the big Texan's decision irrevocable.

Adrienne, swinging lithely out of the cab, supplied the right words before her husband or anyone else could use the wrong ones. "It's not a matter of safety, Mr. Car—Mr. Secretary," she stated matter-of-factly. "It's visibility. That extra four feet of height gives you a shot the bush can't block." She began to climb into the back, her right foot on the fender and a hand raised to the one Stern outstretched to meet her. Warren and a PR man were getting out over the rear bulkhead as the Prime Minister watched with steel points in his eyes. "And besides," the blonde woman said with an apparently absent glance at Cardway's bodyguard, "on the ground you'd be between a charging tyrannosaur and all the other guns, that one—" she flicked a thumb at the cal-fifty as she stepped over the bulkhead— "included. Standing in front of one of those when you know somebody's going to fire it isn't the sort of courage that . . . brings back elephants."

Craig leaned forward to whisper to his principal. His knuckles were white on the grip of the submachine gun. Cardway brushed him back with a scowl, still poised to climb down. The bodyguard's face contorted. He shouted, "I won't have it! I swear to God, I'll blast the first man that aims near you! If you step down, *everybody* gets down or else disarms!"

Stern and Adrienne both shifted their stance, a change more mental than physical at the moment. Craig's outburst appeared to bother even Secretary Cardway. The cabinet official opened his mouth for a curt retort, but he swallowed the words unspoken a moment later. He frowned. "All right," he said, "goddammit. Let's get this show on the road."

Vickers used the gun mount as a grip to lift himself over the bulkhead. Not only was it faster, it kept him away from the sullen Warren standing by the cab door. The box of the half-track was still more crowded than Vickers liked when they were facing dangerous game, but he did not feel that he could safely unload the supernumeraries so near to a carnosaur either. "Real slow, now," he said to the driver, settling the fore-end of his M14 in his left palm. "Dead slow."

The squeal of bearings in several of the bogeys was high-pitched and in keeping with the alien atmosphere. Inevitably, the noise would announce them to the tyrannosaur, but Vickers was not concerned that it would frighten him away. It was the tyrannosaur's world, and he was king in it. Perhaps the beast would stalk down the trail to investigate. That would give them the appearance of danger and a simple, no-deflection shot that the Secretary could be expected to make.

The half-track brushed through a slight kink in the trail. They were on the edge of a sharply defined clearing. The guide recognized it as being cut by the boundary of the intrusion field when a vehicle snapped back Topside with its immediate surroundings. Directly across the clearing, twenty meters away, sprawled the tyrannosaur in a field of white-leafed wormwood. The beast had probably not moved since Stern and Adrienne dragged it from the intrusion vehicle with a tractor. It lay on its belly, facing three-quarters of the way away from the hunters. Its hind legs were stretched back along its tail like those of a huge tadpole. Pulmonary blood had painted the beast's jaws and muzzle, drawing a black mist of flies.

"It's asleep," the guide said sharply. "Quick, Mr. Secretary, put one through its chest and be ready for the charge!"

The titanopteryx was skimming toward them so low over the field of wormwood that the tyrannosaur's haunches hid it. It pulled up to brake its flight like a parachute opening. The huge pterosaur seemed to lower its hind legs as it hung in the air, gripping the dinosaur's hide as if its wings rode on something more tangible than air. The maneuver was so effortlessly graceful that Vickers would have gasped in delight—if it had not just made an obvious liar of him.

For a moment, no one said anything more. The diesel clattered. After glaring at the half-track, the pterosaur arched its neck and slammed its chisel beak into the haunch of the sprawling tyrannosaur. The flesh beneath the mottled scales rippled away from the impact, but the dinosaur as an entity did not move.

"You sons of bitches," Secretary Cardway said. Deep-throated venom was thick on his voice. "You shot it yourself and dragged me here to make a fool of myself." Cardway's voice rose. "Did you have pictures of yourselves killing it, is that the idea? Wait till I was all over the national press with 'my' tyrannosaurus and then blackmailing me into supporting you? Was that it?"

No one was answering. Vickers turned toward his furious client, not because he had a response but because the anger had to be faced like any other catastrophe. The soldier between them at the cal-fifty was shrinking away, disassociating himself from a rage as inexplicable to him as an astrobleme was.

Cardway reached across the receiver of the big gun and slapped the guide with his right hand. "Go ahead and laugh, you bastard!" the Secretary shouted. "Laugh at how you played me for a fool."

Vickers could not see for tears and the bloody rage that pulsed behind his eyes. "Look, here's something for you to tape!" the Secretary was shouting. He raised the Mannlicher and fired. The bullet slapped dust from the tyrannosaur's haunch, near the bloody gash the pterosaur had already torn. The winged creature screeched and hopped to the ground. Its beak quested for an adversary.

"You sons of bitches!" Secretary Cardway repeated. He jumped to the ground, stumbling as he hit. He used the butt of his rifle to brace himself and began to stalk toward the fallen dinosaur.

In the cab of the half-track, Thomas Warren was grinning like a madman. The two holographers were rolling tape, though they must have known it would probably have to be wiped. "Sir!" Avraham Stern cried. "You mustn't—"

For an instant, Vickers saw everything with the clarity of inclusions in a crystal lens: the Secretary's hunched shoulders; the incised margins of the wormwood leaves; the flicker of the tyrannosaur's right eyelid. Then the whole world shrank to the front sight of the Ml4, with everything beyond it as blur as it was supposed to be when the guide's fingers squeezed the trigger. He paused.

"I warned you!" Craig shouted.

Adrienne Vickers did not fire. There were too many people in too confined an area, and a 250-grain gilding-metal bullet from her rifle would penetrate everything it hit except perhaps the engine block. Instead, the tall blonde dropped the Schultz and Larsen and leaped a five-gallon thermos of water to tackle Craig as he shot. Adrienne's right hand gripped the bodyguard's throat, her left seized the Uzi at the juncture of barrel and front sight. Together, the pair of them cannoned into Vickers. Craig fired a six-round burst through the bed of the truck before Adrienne's leverage broke his finger against the trigger guard. His screaming stopped a moment later when Avraham Stern leaned forward. With a short axial blow as if he were playing billiards, Stern brought the butt of his rifle down on Craig's skull. The Israeli official kept the muzzle of his FAL vertical, just in case the shock jarred the hammer off its sear.

Vickers was jammed forward against the bulkhead while 9mm bullets blew splinters into his shins. He had not fired. The tyrannosaur's head lifted an inch on its bed of wormwood. Its tail swept in an arc like a scythe, catching first the titanopteryx, then Secretary Cardway. The great pterosaur squawked and spun, hurled toward the carnivore's thorax by the impact. That was accidental, however. The tip of the tail took the Secretary of State across the buttocks as the dinosaur had intended and flung him forward. The four-foot jaws were already open to receive him. When the jaws closed, they thudded like a casket dropping. The Secretary's left arm flew off. His hand and chest disappeared into the carnivore's mouth.

The Israeli driver stood up in the cab, waving a short-barreled grenade launcher. The gunner in the back of the half-track was gripping his weapon, despite the group struggling at his feet. Neither soldier shot. Mordecai Greenbaum leaned over the side of the vehicle and fired the cast-off Gibbs double twice into the chest of the tyrannosaur, still belly-down in the white-dusted foliage. The dinosaur stiffened. A tiny, two-clawed forefoot flicked up, too short even to pick the beast's great teeth. Then the carnivore relaxed, its head falling back sideways to the ground. The jaws lolled open. The Secretary of State, impaled on a score or more of four-inch teeth, did not spill out. His body above the rib cage lay within the dinosaur's mouth. The left arm and the borrowed Mannlicher, dropped when the tail struck, lay on the ground like storm wrack.

Henry Vickers straightened. Stern and Adrienne were dragging away the unconscious bodyguard. The official looked up. "Is there a chance?" he asked.

The guide grimaced. "Not even if it had happened in the operating room of Walter Reed," he said. He turned and fired a single round through the carnosaur's skull, aiming between the jaw hinge and the ear hole. The beast did not move as its brain was destroyed. "But I suppose it's safe to drag out what's left now," he said quietly.

The Prime Minister was in a whispered conversation with the holographer who had been beside in the back. Greenbaum looked at the heavy rifle he still carried and set it down. "We have holographic tape of—what has happened, Mr. Vickers," he said. "You attempting to finish off the animal before it harmed the Secretary, and the American bodyguard preventing you by his attack. The blame is clear." The little Israeli paused, shaking his head. "It will not gain us the—end for which this exercise was planned, of course. That has become impossible. But at least we can apportion blame."

Vickers jumped down from the half-track, holding his rifle at the balance in his left hand. Adrienne glanced at the unconscious bodyguard, now being trussed by Stern with a rifle sling. Seeing Craig was safe, the blonde woman poised to follow her husband. Before she could do so, Vickers looked back. "Adrienne," he said, "there's a net in one of those chests. Would you bring it, please?"

Adrienne blinked. "Why?"

Vickers gestured toward the titanopteryx. The creature mewled as it struggled back toward the shelter of the tyrannosaur's carcass. Its left wing, injured by the sweep of the dinosaur's tail, dragged behind it like the train of a troll queen. "We're taking that back with us," the guide said. "Alive."

"D-darling," said his wife, her mouth more dry with fear than it had been when she saw Craig aiming his Uzi at her husband, "I don't think—"

The guide's face contorted. "I'm through with killing-for-a-business!" he screamed. "Through with it! This is alive and I'm sending it back alive! And if I never see another tourist hunter, it'll by *God* be too soon!"

The two soldiers and the older cameraman—the one who had served in the Golan—retrieved Secretary Cardway's body. Greenbaum watched them grimly, holding the reloaded .470 with its muzzles an inch from Craig's face. The bodyguard remained unconscious, slumped away from the stanchion to which he was bound. The younger PR man thought of taping that too, but the look on the Prime Minister's face deterred him. Thomas Warren remained seated in the cab. Occasionally he would spit out another fragment of the plastic stem of his pipe.

It took Vickers, Adrienne, and Avraham Stern half an hour to capture the injured titanopteryx and load it onto a cargo skid. That was respectable time. The creature was half-again as heavy as any of the three of them, and it was capable of ripping the armored hide of a dinosaur with its beak. They made a good team, the blonde woman thought. All three of them were willing to do whatever was necessary to accomplish the task at hand.

"Ah, there you are, Mr. and Mrs. Vickers," called the pudgy man with the clipboard. He began trotting toward them across the busy traffic of the hangar.

Avraham Stern paused in mid-sentence and turned from the Vickerses, to whom he had been talking. "Professor Wayne," he said loudly, "we will have completed the final briefing in a few moments, if you please." He managed a smile as he looked back at the American couple. "I should not be harsh with him, should I?" Stern said. "He was extremely helpful about releasing the tyrannosaurus to us when we came back for it. For all the good that that did."

The Israeli official's voice was surprisingly mild as he spoke the last words. Adrienne narrowed her eyes and said, "That's over with now? The—the plan isn't being carried out without US support?"

Stern shrugged. "The frigate *Gromky* docked in Tripoli seven hours ago," he said. "Such cargo as she carried—a number of large drums—was immediately escorted by an armored convoy toward El Adem. The air base, you know. Where the containers go from there will be the question, of course."

"They may stay there till the cans rust away," said Vickers. "And . . . and anyway, it's better than World War III, I think."

Stern looked around. He was back in a dark business suit, a dumpy, balding man who might have chased ambulances or sold used cars for a living. "Among the three of us," he said quietly, "I also think it is better. However, I do not think it is good." He stretched out a hand to Vickers, paused, then gave his left hand to Adrienne as well. "God be with you," Stern said. He began to walk away.

"If the Holocene gets too hot, Avraham," Vickers called after the departing official, "you're always welcome in the Cretaceous."

Professor Wayne, head of the Zoology Section, had been waiting tensely a dozen feet away. Now he stooped like a hawk on the couple. He moved so suddenly that he almost collided with a quartet of turbine pumps whining toward the intrusion vehicle on fork lifts. The plump American professor scuttled safely through the equipment, his clipboard tight against his chest as if it were a poker hand he was hiding. "Ah, good, good," he bubbled. "The committee—the Biological Oversight Committee—only now reached a decision. I was very much afraid that I would have missed you with the message."

Adrienne smiled, more tolerantly than she would have been able to do a few years before. "We still have half an hour, Doctor," she said. "Though I hope it won't take that long, since we've got other business to attend to . . ."

"Oh, of course, of course," said the zoologist, sounding shocked. "It shouldn't take anything like that. It should—" he paused. "Well, it will take less time if I say it, of course. Very simply, we want you to hold the size of individual living specimens you send, ah, Topside, to two hundred kilograms apiece. Until we inform you otherwise. It's a matter of space, you see. We hope to expand the facilities shortly, but for the next six months we can no more care for an adult ceratopsian than we could—eat one at a sitting." He grinned brightly to emphasize his joke.

Adrienne responded with a frown as her fingers toyed with the sling of her rifle. "But you have thirty acres, don't you?" she asked. "I mean—I was there just, well, ten days ago to bring back the tyrannosaur."

"Oh, of course, but I mean *secure* space," Wayne said. His tone was that he would have used if he had been accused of faking experimental data. "That is, an area not only free of birds and bird droppings, but sterilized. It's quite amazing how virulent the least trace of ornithosis has proven to the higher Cretaceous life-forms. It seems to be no exaggeration to say that every archosaur you sent back from the previous base was killed by the sparrows in our compound here."

Adrienne laughed. Vickers smiled, though it was through an unwillingness to dampen his wife's good cheer than from any humor he himself saw in the wasted effort. Still, he and Adrienne had accomplished their own tasks. That was the only thing they would have had to be ashamed of . . ."

"How's the pterosaur coming along, then?" the guide said aloud. "It's within your size limit, I suppose?"

"Yes, yes . . ." the zoologist said, frowning. He tapped his clipboard with the hinge of his glasses. "Frankly, I don't understand that at all. To begin with, I would have thought that the Order Pterosauria had diverged from the main stem of the dinosaurs—and birds, of course—so far back that they would not be susceptible to diseases of the latter. Of course, humans can catch ornithosis too, under extreme conditions . . . But still, I'm quite sure we kept the titanopteryx in a sterile environment from the moment you returned with it. And—"

"Wait a minute," Vickers said, waving his free hand palm down. "You mean that it died?"

"Yes, this morning, that's what I've been saying," Wayne responded. "Technically, we'll have to wait for the pathology report to be sure, but there's no real doubt that it was ornithosis again. The surprising thing is that the pterosaur must have been infected before we received it. Infected in the Cretaceous, that is. Which ought to be impossible."

Vickers and his wife stared at each other.

"Christ," whispered the blonde woman, "the tyrannosaur. It had the bug, God knows, and we carried it back—"

"You took the tyrannosaur back to the Cretaceous?" the zoologist exclaimed. "Oh, my goodness—why did you do that?"

The guide shrugged away the question. "What's going to happen?" he demanded. "I mean—back where we left the carcass. In the Cretaceous."

"At the end of the Cretaceous," Adrienne said, her eyes staring out beyond the walls of the hangars and the present time. "As close as Dr. Galil could place us to the boundary between the Cretaceous and the Cenozoic. Where the dinosaurs were the biggest, and just before they all disappeared."

"Well, I don't know, exactly," the zoologist said with a look of increasing concern. "Introduction of the bedsonia-chlamydia organism causing ornithosis could radically reduce a non-resistant population, of course. But even myxomatosis didn't wipe out hares in Europe and Australia, just reduced their numbers to a few percent of what they had been before the, well, plague. And that was only until natural increase built up the—oh, dear!"

"Yeah," Vickers said. "Rabbits breed like rabbits. But some of the bigger dinos aren't sexually mature until they're thirty years old."

"And the small ones, the ones that *do* breed quickly enough to build up an immune population," said Adrienne, the distant expression still in her eyes, "they're the ones that don't have enough body weight to depend on for insulation. The ones that have already grown feathers. The birds are the only . . . dinosaurs to survive Secretary Cardway's safari."

"Oh, dear," Professor Wayne repeated. He started backing away from the conversation, oblivious to the final loading operations still going on. "I really must discuss this—" A workman with a cartload of steel framing shouted an angry warning. Wayne stopped, turned, and walked quickly toward a door. The plump man was almost at a run when he disappeared from sight.

A technician called something unintelligible across the volume of the hangar. He reconsidered and spoke into a microphone. The speakers on Vickers' and Adrienne's lapels rasped, "Insertion Group? We will be ready for final countdown in ten, repeat, one-zero minutes."

Vickers keyed his mike. "Acknowledged," he said. To his wife he added, "I suppose we can board now. It'll be . . . good to get back, I think."

"Cardway brought the end of the dinosaurs," Adrienne said. Even next to her, Vickers could barely hear the words. "If he'd lived, he would have ended . . . human civilization, wouldn't he? Perhaps not over Avraham's little plot—"

"It wasn't his."

"Whosoever. Cardway would have had four, eight years of his own soon with his finger on the button. He—wasn't going to make it that long without stepping into the deep end, was he?"

"Adrienne, I think we'd better board," Vickers said. The hangar was growing quieter as the last of the workmen filed out through the doors to the storage bay.

"Henry, I was watching you," his wife whispered. "I don't think anyone else could tell, not even Craig. But you weren't aiming at the tyrannosaur. You had your sights in the middle of Cardway's back. And you didn't fire."

The guide's face was as calm as a saint's. He took Adrienne's left hand in his own, but he was looking toward the loaded intrusion vehicle. "It wasn't that he slapped me," Vickers said, as softly as his wife had spoken. "I could have taken that. But it made me think . . . I don't want to die, not anymore—" He squeezed the tall blonde's hand, the pressure reassuring to him at a level below consciousness. "I thought for a moment that there were things more important than whether I lived or not, though. And there are. But I couldn't pull the trigger, not on a man. Even a man like Luther Cardway."

"You were wrong about your life not being more important," Adrienne said. She broke into a bright smile and began leading the guide toward the intrusion vehicle. Her left arm crossed her chest to reach him. "The world can take care of itself," she said. She laughed aloud and added, "As it did, you know. As it did."

"It didn't if you were a dinosaur," Vickers replied bleakly. "And I was responsible for that, not the world."

His wife sobered. "Henry, no one is responsible for what happens sixty-five million years before he's born. Not even if he's there. We *can't* change the past—whatever the bloody-minded dreamers in the Ministry of Defense may hope. The Cretaceous *now* Topside is exactly the same way it was when Stern and I left here with the dino to go back."

"Even if I didn't change it," said the hunter, "I made it happen!" In his mind, the tyrannosaurus still lay dying, its lungs destroyed by the disease, and the scene was multiplied millions, billions of times across the face of the Earth in ripples spreading from his action.

"All right then," snapped Adrienne, "but think of *what* you made happen. You made a world that mammals could grow and evolve in. Are you going to be sorry about that? Are you sorry that you're—that *I'm* not two inches long, snapping up bugs that blunder by in the dark? Because sure as hell that's what we'd be if something hadn't wiped out the dinosaurs!"

Vickers looked at his wife. After a moment he squeezed her hand. "No," he said, "I'm not sorry about that." Together, they began to walk slowly toward the intrusion vehicle.

TRAVELLERS

Carl had not seen it coming over the eastern horizon toward the farm.

As the trickle under which he had washed died away, Carl slid the bucket beneath the pump. He worked the handle with three smooth, powerful strokes, the creaking of the cast iron evoking squeals from the piglets in the shed. Over his head the sky was clear enough that stars already flecked it, but the west beyond the farmhouse was a purple backdrop of cloud. Carl stretched, sighed, and picked up the bucket his mother would need for the dinner dishes.

A spotlight threw his long shadow on the ground before him. Carl turned, the bucket splashing some of the muck from his boots. The light was round and for an instant as harsh as the Sun. Prismatic changes flickered across the face of it. The beam spread to either side of Carl in a fan that illuminated but no longer blinded him. The light was hanging above the barn. There was a bulk beyond it, solider than the sky: an airship such as Carl had never dreamed he would see.

"Stand by to take a line, lad," called a male voice. Carl's knees were trembling and the bucket was forgotten in his hand as the airship drifted upwind toward him. Something aboard made a sound like chains rattling, muted where Carl stood but loud enough to have roused the cows. Their bawling would bring his father out at any moment, a part of Carl's mind recognized, but nothing in the world of a moment before was real any longer.

The airship crawled directly over Carl. It was huge, blocking most of the hundred feet of sky separating house from barn. Besides the spotlight, now diffusing its radiance across most of the farmyard, there were rectangles of yellower light from the gondola hanging beneath the main hull of the airship. A hatch opened in the side, silhouetting a gangling figure. "Here it comes," said the figure in the voice that had spoken before. A grapnel on a line thudded to the ground in front of Carl. It began to dig a double furrow in the dust as the airship drifted backwards. "Well, set it, lad—set it!" the voice called. "So that we can land."

Carl came out of his numb surprise. He dropped the water bucket and ran to the line. It was of horsehair, supple and strong. Someone played it out above as Carl carried the grapnelled end to the pump. He hooked it to the underedge of the concrete well-cap.

As soon as Carl had set the grapnel, the line stiffened. There was another rattle from above and a whine like that of an electric pump. The airship began to settle. Four jointed, mantislike legs were extending from the belly of the gondola. Carl backed toward the house a step at a time while the great form sank into the farmyard. The legs touched, first one and then the four of them together. Their apparent delicacy was belied by the great plumes of dust which the contact raised. The whine rose to a high keening, then shut off entirely. The light died to a glowing ember in the night.

Behind Carl the screen door banged. "Carl," called Mrs. Gudeint, "where are—oh, dear Lord have mercy! Fred! *Fred!*"

The gangling man reappeared at the gondola door. He swung three metal steps down with a crash. The stranger wore a brown tweed suit of coarse weave with a gold watch-guard and a fob of some sort hanging across the vest. He smiled at Carl, crinkling the full moustache that looked so incongruous beneath his high forehead. Looking back into the gondola he said, "Oh—if you will snuff the light, my dear?" A girl appeared in the doorway, turning down the wick of an oil lamp. Carl stared at her as he had at the airship itself. There was a bustle behind him as his father and brothers pushed out of the house with eating utensils still in their hands.

The girl was beautiful even in the dim light. Her hair, caught neatly in a bun, was as richly black as the pelt of a sable. She wore a patterned percale wrapper, simple but new and of an attractive cut.

"Carl, what have you brought here?" Mr. Gudeint rumbled from close to his youngest son's shoulder.

"Gentlemen," said the stranger, turning again with the girl beside him and the airship a vast gray backdrop beyond, "I am Professor John K. Erlenwanger, and this is my daughter Molly." The girl curtsied. Erlenwanger caught sight of Carl's mother beyond the wall of broad-shouldered men. He made a little bow of his own. "And madam, of course, my apologies.

"Madam and gentlemen," he continued. "I am, as you see, an aeronaut. My daughter and I are travelling from Boston to California, testing my airship, *The Enterprise*—which, I may say, contains certain advances over all earlier directable designs. We have stopped here for a safe mooring during the night and perhaps some assistance in the morning."

"You're from Boston?" demanded Fred, the eldest of Carl's brothers. "You flew this thing a thousand miles?"

"We have indeed flown a thousand miles," the Professor said with a quick nod, "and I expect to fly twice again that distance before completing my endeavor. But although we have set out from Boston, I am myself a Californian by birth and breeding."

"Well, they'll have dinner with us, surely," said Carl's mother, twisting her hands in the pockets of her apron. She looked up anxiously at Erlenwanger. "You will, won't you? We've a roast and—"

The Professor cut her off with another half-bow. "We would be honored, Mrs. . . . ?"

"Gudeint," Carl's father grunted. He wore a blue work shirt, buttoned at the throat and cuffs as it had been all day despite the heat of the Indian summer Sun. His sons wore sleeveless undershirts or, in Carl's case, only a set of galluses that had blazed a white cross in his otherwise sunburned back. Mr. Gudeint extended his hand, broad and as hard as the head of a maul from fifty years of farming. "I'm Fred Gudeint and that's my wife Maxine there—"

"Fred, I'll take the stoneware off and put out the china and the silver since—"

Carl's father turned on her, his red forehead furrowed like a field in springtime. "Maxine, you'll pretend you've got the sense God gave a goose and do no such thing. We've already started eating from the stoneware!"

Mrs. Gudeint bobbed her head and scurried back into the house with a worried look on her face. Carl's father shook his head and said, "Your pardon, Professor, but we're not used to guests dropping out of the sky on us. It upsets the routine." He grinned perfunctorily, as if that would make his statement less true. "That's Fred there, my oldest"—Fred, his father's surrogate in form as well as name, shook hands in turn—"George, Danny, and that's Carl, the last by six years. Boy, be sure to fill that bucket before you come in."

"Yes, Father," Carl said. Professor Erlenwanger's hand was cool and firm and smooth as a farmer's hands can never be. As Carl's father and brothers led the guests into the house, the Professor's daughter tilted her eyes at Carl and gave him a timid smile. *Why, she looks as nervous as I am,* Carl thought as he pumped the bucket full again beneath the airship.

Carl entered the house through the side door to leave the bucket beside the sink. His mother had already slipped a third leaf into the table and replaced the checkered oilcloth with her best Irish linen table cover. As Mr. Gudeint had insisted, the stoneware plates still remained with the mashed potatoes and slices of beef with which they had been heaped before the excitement. The two new place settings, to right and left of the head of the table where Carl's father sat, were of the Sunday china. The delicate cups and saucers looked particularly incongruous beside the heavy mugs at the other places. From the front room came the creak of Grandpa Roseliep's rocker; nowadays, he always ate before the rest of them.

Carl sat quickly between his mother at the foot of the table and his brother George. He began serving himself. Danny was saying, "I'd read a story about your balloon in the *Register* last week in the barbershop, Professor, but I recall it gave the name as Cox. Sure, Cox."

Professor Erlenwanger ladled gravy onto his mashed potatoes with a liberal hand. "I can't say who Mr. Cox may be, sir, but I assure you that he and I are not the same. I have eschewed all publicity for the Erlenwanger Directable Airship—not balloon, I must protest, any more than your Guernsey milkers are steers—eschewed all publicity, as I say, until I have proven the capacity of my invention in a fashion none can doubt. Unless I am fully satisfied, no one will hear a word from my lips about it. Except, of course, for the good people like yourselves who have acted as hosts to my daughter and myself. Madam," he added, nodding to Mrs. Gudeint, "these fresh peas are magnificent."

Erlenwanger ate like a man who appreciated his food. His bites were gentlemanly and were chewed with the thoroughness demanded by a roast from a superannuated dairy cow, but he cleaned his plate handily despite the constant stream of questions directed at him by the Gudeints. Carl noticed that Molly spoke rarely and then with a distinct Irish brogue at variance with the Professor's cultured accents.

Carl said little himself. The Professor's descriptions—sunlight flaring from cloud tops, tailwinds pressing the airship along faster than a railway magnate's special—were in themselves so fascinating that Carl was unwilling to interject a question. It might break the spell.

At last Fred, speaking through a mouthful of roast and gesturing with his fork, said, "Look here, Professor. You're an educated man. What do you think about all this business about Cuba? Isn't it about time those Dagoes're taught what they can and can't do on Uncle Sam's doorstep?"

Erlenwanger paused, staring across the table. The light reflected from his high forehead. He looked half the bulk of the big farmer, but at that moment, the stranger's dominance was no less certain than that of a diamond over the metal of its setting. "I think," he said with neither conciliation nor overt hostility in his firm tones, "that misguided men will fight a foolish war over Cuba very soon. The world as a whole will be none the better for such a war, and many individuals will be very much the worse." He stared around the table as if daring anyone to disagree with him.

In a sudden rush of bitterness, Carl said, "The Army might be better'n the back end of a plow horse, day in and day out."

"There are roads to adventure that are not built on the bodies of your fellow men, lad," Erlenwanger said. He turned back to Fred and added more harshly, "And there are ways of honoring the flag that do not call for 'civilizing' native races with a Krag-Jorgensen rifle. It will take men a long time as a race to learn that; but until we have done so, we have done nothing."

Mr. Gudeint sopped the last of his gravy in a slice of bread, swallowed it, and pushed his chair back from the table. Professor Erlenwanger cleared his throat and said, "You have been so generous to my daughter and myself that I wonder if I might impose on your time for one further moment? You will have noted the cases I brought in with me." Erlenwanger nodded toward the leather grips now standing against the wall next to the curio cabinet. "They contain my camera equipment. I would be most appreciative if you would permit me to photograph your whole family together."

"You mean in the daylight, don't you?" said George, who had his own Kodak. "You can't take one now?"

"On the contrary, the process I am using is so sensitive that what the eye can see, my lens can record," the Professor replied. He turned to Mr. Gudeint. "With your leave, sir?"

Carl's father frowned. "Strikes me that you're wasting your plates, but then, I never saw a fellow fly before, neither. Sure, we'll sit for you. How do you want us?"

"In your front room, I believe," said the Professor, his hands already busy with the contents of one of his cases. "In whatever grouping seems good to you; though with seven subjects to fit into the plate, I trust you'll group yourselves rather tightly."

"Seven?" repeated Fred. "There's only—oh, sure," he broke off, looking at Grandpa Roseliep in his stuffed rocker.

"You will join us, will you not, sir?" Professor Erlenwanger said, looking up at the old man as he fitted his camera onto its collapsible wooden tripod. Beside him, Molly had removed a plate from the other grip and was carefully polishing dust from its surfaces with a soft cloth.

Roseliep was reading *Der Kanarienzüchter,* one of the three bi-weekly issues that had arrived from Leipzig in yesterday's mail. From the shelter of the paper he grunted, "What do you want with me? I know nothing about cows, so I am useless—nein? And with these hands, I am surely no cabinetmaker anymore." The paper shook, perhaps in frustration rather than from a deliberate attempt to emphasize the arthritis-twisted fingers which gripped its edges. "Go on, leave me alone."

Professor Erlenwanger stood, the brass and cherry-wood of his camera glinting under the light of the dining room lamp. He spoke in German, briefly and fiercely.

Grandpa Roseliep set down his canary-breeders journal. His full, white beard blazed like a flag. The old man fingered the stem of his pipe on the end table, but he left that sitting as well. In deliberate English he said, "An old man is a man still? Wait till you become old, Professor." The two men stared at one another. Abruptly, Grandpa Roseliep said, "But I will be in your picture, since you ask."

The old man levered himself out of his chair, stiff-armed. Carl moved to him quickly, holding out an arm for his grandfather to grip. The old man's shoulder brushed the covered canary cage beside his chair. One of the birds within peeped nervously. Absently, Roseliep soothed it with a murmur from deep in his throat.

Carl's parents and brothers were standing by the fireplace, looking a little uncomfortable. The Professor had set up his tripod in front of the staircase across the room. Molly stood beside him, holding out the photographic plate. Carl led his grandfather into the center of the group between his father and Fred. He knelt down in front of them, facing the camera as the Professor loaded it.

Granda Roseliep turned slowly. His foot caught on the edge of the fireplace fender. He stumbled, gripping Mr. Gudeint's arm to keep from falling. The farmer jerked back. He looked down at the knotted fingers with instinctual distaste.

Roseliep followed his son-in-law's glance. "Yes," he said, "but once they were strong, were they not? Strong enough to build this house for my daughter on her marriage." With his left hand he rapped the carven oak mantelpiece. "And the house gives shelter yet."

Mr. Gudeint bit his lip. He put his arm around his father-in-law, gripping him under the arm and absorbing enough of the weight that the old man's body could stretch back to its full six feet of height. "We're ready for your picture now, Professor," he said. Across the room the camera lens winked, and the Professor's bright eyes winked above it.

Carl and his father returned from the barn together for breakfast. The three older sons were already at their pancakes, along with Professor Erlenwanger and Molly. Mr. Gudeint called into the front room, "George? Come on in and sit with us, will you? Your birds can take care of themselves for a while. I want to rig a pole and winch to load bales into the barn, and I figure you can help."

Grandpa Roseliep walked slowly into the kitchen on his crutch-headed cane. "You know, Frederick," he said, "I am no longer a woodworker."

Carl's father grunted. "I know you can figure how to make a piece of wood do everything but talk," he said. "We'll do the muscle work, me'n'the boys, if you'll tell us what to do. For that matter, we're not talking about fancy work—and I don't know but what swinging a hammer'd loosen your joints up some. But that's up to you."

The big farmer took his usual place at the head of the table and noticed for the first time that all the place settings were china. He poured milk into the wine goblet beside his coffee cup and said with half-humor, "Professor John K. Erlenwanger, hey? From the way Maxine's acting, I'd judge the 'K' must stand for 'king.'"

Erlenwanger touched his napkin to his lips. "Kennedy, sir. To my parents, a greater man than any king could ever be." Mr. Gudeint looked puzzled, but before he could speak the Professor added, "Last night you thought it would be possible to take my daughter and me into town to purchase supplies. Is that still the case?"

Carl's father nodded with his mouth full of pancake and molasses. "Sure, the boy can haul you along when he carries the milk into the dairy after breakfast. But I'd have thought you'd just fly?"

"I prefer to avoid built-up areas," Erlenwanger explained. "The appearance of my airship would arouse more interest than I desire at this time, and maneuvering a construct as large as *The Enterprise* becomes a . . . difficult proposition in close quarters." The shadow of the great, gray cylinder darkened the dining room, lending weight to the stranger's shrug.

"Look," said George abruptly, "I'll carry the milk in today instead of the kid."

Carl jumped to his feet, flushing, and cried, "Look, I'm going to take them in. And get off this 'kid' business—I'm eighteen and I'm as much a—"

"Carl, sit down!" Mr. Gudeint snapped. "And George, you be quiet, too. I'll decide who's going to do what around here."

"Though I was rather hoping that Carl would drive us to town, as you'd said," Molly interjected unexpectedly. She gave a nervous smile to Mr. Gudeint, who blinked at her. She was wearing a bengaline cotton dress with vertical stripes of green and olive this morning. The silk threads gave it a sheen like that of her black hair.

"The boy'll do it," Carl's father said. "It's his chore." He turned to Carl. "About time you got started, isn't it? The Sun's high enough, though you don't see it with that great metal thing out in the yard."

"Yes, sir!" said Carl, bolting the last of his breakfast and washing it down with his milk. To the visitors he added, "I'll have the wagon loaded in two flips of a lamb's tail. I'll holler when it's ready."

It was killing work to hand the heavy, tin-plated milk cans up to Danny on the wagon bed. Carl finished the job in record time, however, and without any spillage past the pressure-fitted lids. Erlenwanger and Molly came out of the house just as Danny ran the safety rope across the box of the wagon to keep the cans from oversetting on the bumpy ride. "Just in time," Carl called to them. "I'll get the horses and we're off."

Molly sat between Carl and Erlenwanger as the pair of bays plodded along the familiar trail with only voice commands. A light breeze from the south kept the worst of the road dust from the travellers, but a plume rose behind the wagon like smoke from a grass fire. "It'll be all over us coming back," Carl said.

"And you have to drive this every day?" Molly asked. "There's so much work on a farm."

"Not enough for four sons," Carl said gloomily. He caught

himself and added, before anyone could follow up his earlier comment, "I guess you need food, hey?"

"Not at this point, I think," Erlenwanger replied. "What we particularly need is lamp oil."

"Lamp oil?" repeated Carl. "Good Christ, Professor—sorry, miss—we'd have given you lamp oil if you'd spoken. We're not electrified out where we are!"

The older man smiled past Molly's bonnet. "Not a hundred gallons, I think."

"Good Christ—oh hell, I'm sorry again," Carl blurted. "What on earth do you want with that much lamp oil?"

"It's for our motor," Professor Erlenwanger explained. "Other researchers into directed airship flight are concentrating on petrol-burning motors of the Benz type. This is a serious error, I believe. Compression-ignited kerosene engines built to the design of Herr Rudolph Diesel are far more efficient. In addition, lamp oil is available at even the most out-of-the-way farmstead in a pinch, no small recommendation on a journey which crosses the very continent."

The city limits were marked by a metaled road. It was bright with the rich yellow limestone gravel crushed out of the bluffs on which the city was built. A bicyclist passed the wagon, free-wheeling with the momentum he had picked up coming down a side street. "Darn fool," Carl grunted, noting Molly's attention to the speedster. "In town, a gadget like that's good for nothing but running you under a wagon. Now I've rode 'em, but it was at Starways Rink where they belong."

Carl turned onto Central Avenue, letting the horses ease along despite his desire to oblige the Professor. The brick avenue was slippery, and it would be easy to throw a shoe if haste brought nothing worse. Carl pulled around the yellow-brick building of the dairy and backed expertly to the loading dock, clucking to his team. "Won't be a moment," he said to his passengers. He poised on the wagon seat, then vaulted over the milk cans to land on the pine bed with a crash. "Charlie!

"Jess," he shouted into the dairy. "Lend me a goddamn hand! I'm in a hurry."

Erlenwanger and his daughter watched with silent interest. Carl rolled the heavy cans on their rims up the loading gate to the dock where the two dairymen manhandled them into the building. His muscles rippled, but the familiar effort did not even raise sweat-stains on his shirt. "Christ, you guys're slow," Carl grumbled as he rolled the last can onto the dock. "I'll hook out the empties myself." It took him two trips, carrying a pair of the heavy cans in either hand each time. They would be hauled back and refilled the next day. Life was an endless cycle of milk cans and horse butts, Carl thought savagely to himself.

As he settled back onto the wagon seat, Carl noticed for the first time that the Professor's two camera cases were on the shelf beneath. "Frummelt's is just down Central," he said. "Say, you carry that camera most everywhere, don't you?"

"I do indeed," Erlenwanger agreed. "No amount of trouble in carrying the apparatus along is too great to be justified by the capturing of one scene that cannot be duplicated. And compared to the effort of bringing the apparatus . . . to the vicinity . . . any trouble to be endured on the ground, so to speak, is nothing."

Carl pulled in through the gate in the green-painted hoardings, into the yard of Frummelt's Coal and Ice. It was crowded with delivery wagons. Carl locked wheels with one and traded curses with the Irish driver as he angled into a place at the dock.

"We need twenty cans of coal oil," Carl shouted to the squat loading master.

The Frummelt employee cocked an eyebrow at them, lifting the brim of his bowler. "Christ, boy," he said, "I see why you came here steada' the front. If it's charge, you'll have to go up to the front anyhow, though."

"It's cash," said the Professor, balancing his weight carefully as he stepped onto the dock with his camera. He reached into his coat and brought out a purse from which he poured silver dollars into his left palm. One of the coins slipped and rang on the concrete. Carl knelt and handed it back to the older man. It bore an 1890 date stamp, but the finish was as bright and clean as if the coin had just been issued. Carl's eyes narrowed, but the loading master took the payment without comment. He counted a quarter and two dimes from the change-maker on his belt and shouted an order to a pair of dock hands.

"I wonder if I might photograph you and your men at work?" Erlenwanger asked as he watched the load of lacquered rectangular cans being rolled out on a hand truck.

"Good God, why?" demanded the loading master, ignoring the driver of an ice wagon waiting for orders.

"Today, this is the petroleum business," the Professor explained obliquely. "If a time comes during which all carts and wagons are replaced by self-powered vehicles, the whole shape of the world will change. You and your men here will be important in the way the first lungfish to scramble onto dry land to snap at an insect was important. Your feelings, your sense of place in the world—this will never come again."

The loading master touched the right curl of his handlebar moustache. "You can't get all that in a picture," he said.

"What I call my photographs capture more than one might think," Erlenwanger responded.

"Then go ahead and waste your time," grunted the squat man as he turned away. "So long as you stay clear of the wheels and don't waste my time too."

As the bays plodded back along Bluff Road, Carl said, "I've thought about what you were saying back at Frummelt's, Professor."

"And?" the older man prompted.

Carl turned and saw Molly's intent smile instead of the Professor. He lost his train of thought for a moment. At last he said, "Well, it won't happen. The wagons with motors, I mean. Not in Iowa, at least." He gestured toward the road in front of them. "When it rains, this's mud. Two, sometimes three feet deep, up to the bed of a wagon. I've seen traction engines get stuck in fields in a wet year and us have to hitch the plow horses, three teams all told, just to get the milk to town. They'll never make an engine that'll handle mud like a good team will."

Professor Erlenwanger nodded seriously. "There's reason in what you say, Carl. Many men much older and better educated would say the same thing. But one of the most important lessons that people must learn if they are to deal with the coming age is that nothing, whether good or bad, cannot happen. If there is something to do with the way humans interact with their world, it probably will happen. It is only when we all recognize that as a fact that we have a chance to guide some of the change that will occur anyway."

The Professor waved as Carl had at the track of rich, black earth pulverized by horse hooves and the iron wheels of wagons. "No one today—or a century hence—will find it conceivable that sane human beings would build roads of concrete a hundred feet wide in place of this. Such roads would be to the benefit of self-moving vehicles and the detriment of everything else, humans in particular. Yet, if it shall have happened, the humans of the twenty-first century will have to accept it as true; and the humans of the nineteenth and twentieth centuries will bear the burden of failing to have guided and controlled a development which they thought was impossible—until it became inevitable."

Carl looked at the horses ahead of him. He licked his lips, ignoring from long familiarity the gritty taste of the dust on them. "Professor," he said without turning around, "I want to come with you. On your airship."

"Molly and I can use another hand on *The Enterprise*," Erlenwanger said mildly, "and there is ample room and lifting capacity, to be sure. But have you considered just what leaving home will mean to you?"

Carl risked a glance. Molly was looking straight ahead, twisting her ungloved hands in her lap. The Professor was leaning forward with a bland expression. Carl nodded, his throat tight. "I'm leaving, that's decided," he explained. "I thought it was going to be the Navy, is all. You see, it's not that I don't love my folks . . . or them love me, for that matter. But I'm the little kid. I'm eighteen and I'm the little kid. So long as I live and even one of my brothers lives, I'll be the little kid—if I don't get out now. Maybe after I've made my own way for a time, I can come back. Maybe I could even work the farm again, though I don't guess I'd want to. But for now, I've got to cut the traces."

"Very well, Carl," said the Professor. "I won't insult you by questioning your decision. If I did not think you were capable of soundly assessing a situation, I would not have considered making you the offer. You no doubt realize that we will leave as soon as *The Enterprise* has been refueled?"

"Oh, that's best," breathed Carl in double relief. "I'll bundle my clothes and . . . say what needs to be said. Then it'll be best all 'round if I leave." His eyes sought the Professor's, caught Molly's instead. They both looked away.

Carl's mother came into the room her two youngest sons shared. Carl was rolling the extra set of dungarees around the rest of his meager belongings. He tied the bindle off with twine. Mrs. Gudeint said nothing. Carl glanced at her, saw her tears, and looked away again very quickly. She was in the doorway and Carl was finished packing. Looking out the window, he said, "Mom, I brushed down the horses before I came in. I'm not going to stay here, I never was— you know that. So just kiss me and don't . . . all the rest."

Turning very quickly, the boy pecked his mother on the cheek and tried to swing around her in the same motion. She clung to him, her face pressed against his blue cotton work shirt. At last she said, "You've told your father?"

"I'll be back one day soon and I'll tell him," Carl said. He squeezed his mother closer and, in the instant that she relaxed, disengaged himself from her. "Mom, I love you," he said. He reached the staircase in one stride and was down its ten steps in three great jumps. He did not look back after the screen door banged behind him.

While Carl finished his business with the farm, Professor Erlenwanger had poured the twenty cans of kerosene into the funnel-mouthed nozzle he had extended from the rear of the gondola. Molly was stacking the empty cans up against the wall of the barn for the Gudeints to use or return for credit. She nodded to Carl as she entered the gondola and sat primly at a bank of sixteen levers, each with a gauge above it. The Professor himself stood at a helm like that of a ship. The spokes appeared to have additional control switches built into them. To the right front of the helm, along the glazed forward bulkhead, was a double bank of waist-high levers. The control room was no more spacious than the garret bedrooms Fred and George each had to themselves, but it was only the front third of the gondola.

"Carl, if you'll take a seat at the other console," Erlenwanger said, gesturing to the chair just aft of the gondola's door. "Soon I'll teach you how to operate the motor controls yourself, but now, in the interests of a prompt departure . . ."

Carl nodded and sat as directed, eyeing the north field where his father and eldest brother were haying. The Professor leaned over him and threw a switch. "Since we ride on hydrogen," he said cryptically, "it's no difficulty to bleed some into the injectors in place of ether for starting . . ." He flipped a second switch. Something whined briefly and the motor grunted to life. It sank quickly into a hum that was felt but not really heard in the forward compartment. Erlenwanger listened for a moment, then said, "Very good." He pointed to a knob with a milled rim. "When I direct you to, Carl, please turn this knob a quarter turn clockwise. It engages the airscrew, which we don't want to do until we have a little altitude, do we?" He smiled brightly at both his crew members. "Not pointed at the house as we are, that is."

Erlenwanger returned to the helm. "There doesn't seem to be enough wind today to require us to make an immediate jump for altitude. I'm always concerned about that, for fear that a line stoppage will lift us asymmetrically; so Molly, if you will fill tanks five and eight."

The girl quickly threw two levers. The gauges above them began to rise as the metal fabric trembled to a mild hissing. The older man said, "Each of the sixteen tanks is split in two by a movable partition. The partition acts as a piston when the pressure on one side of it becomes higher than that on the other side. One and sixteen, Molly; then two and fifteen," the Professor continued.

Molly worked the requested pairs of switches, pausing after the first to make sure the operation was smooth. She glanced at Carl over her shoulder and said, "What he means is, the gas pushes air out of the tanks when we want to go up, and the air pushes the gas out when we want to go down."

Erlenwanger turned and blinked. "That's very good, Molly. I'm afraid I often talk more than I communicate. Though air is a gas as well as hydrogen, of course . . . still. If you will fill the next three pairs in order, please."

The hiss of gas was a living sound now. The gondola was rocking like a rubber ball on the surface of a lake, not lifting off the ground but responsive to every ripple in the air. "I think we're about ready," said Erlenwanger. "Carl, I'll give you the word in a moment. Molly, fill the central tanks."

The gondola shuddered. The pattern of light through the side windows shifted as they swung beneath the lifting hull. The ship was rising at a walking pace, drifting toward the barn and rotating about thirty degrees in the grip of the mild breeze. "Carl, engage the screw," said the Professor. The boy obeyed, his hand so tight on the knurled brass that it did not slip despite its sweatiness. Erlenwanger rocked his helm forward on its post as he felt the propeller bite. The side-slipping continued but was lost in the greater surge of the airship's forward motion. They were still rising. Looking through the windows beyond Molly, Carl could see the hay-cutting rig at the point of the bright swathe cut from the darker green of the north field. The horses were the size of Chihuahuas. The two men in the field shaded their eyes with their hands as they stared at the shimmering oval in their sky. They were too far away for Carl to have recognized them by sight alone. They did not wave. After a moment, as the field and his former life slipped behind at locomotive speed, Carl did.

Professor Erlenwanger released the helm and stepped over to where Molly sat. The airship continued moving smoothly at better than twenty miles an hour. The rolling land was now almost three thousand feet below. "We're a little higher than I care to be without a reason," Erlenwanger said. "Probably because the Sun is so bright. Molly, would you care to balance all the tanks at seventy-five percent? That should bring us down about a thousand feet. Besides, I prefer to have some pressure in all tanks rather than flying with some voided and others full."

Using the bar that fitted the full length of her panel, Molly slid the fourteen open switches down to three-quarters. Simultaneously, she slid the other pair up to the bar with her free hand. The airship lurched, steadied, and continued to skim through the air. It was dropping noticeably, a sensation less like diving into a pond than it was like a toboggan ride down Indian Mound Hill. Erlenwanger studied the line of silver in the etched glass column above his helm. His lips pursed and he touched another display to the side of the column. "We aren't getting the lift we should out of the forward tanks," he said to no one in particular, "though we seem to have leveled off satisfactorily. Moisture in the tanks, I suppose. We'll have to empty them in the near future."

"Where do you buy your hydrogen, Professor?" Carl asked, staring down through the transparent quarter-panels of the gondola. He had seen fields from atop the sharp bluffs which wrinkled eastern Iowa, but there was something marvelous in watching solid ground flow by below like a river choked with debris.

"I manufacture it from water," the older man said. "Our motor powers an electrical generator. When it is necessary to fill a hydrogen tank, I simply run a current through a container of water and collect the separated hydrogen atoms above the cathode."

Warming to his subject—though little of what he had already stated made sense to Carl—Erlenwanger continued, "You see, that is where some theorists go wrong in asserting that helium is safer than hydrogen because it cannot be ignited. What they ignore is the *cost* of helium. The only way to keep an airship safe over a long period is to clear it of the condensate that otherwise—and inevitably—loads it down to the point that a storm smashes it. And the only sure way to clear the condensate is to vent your tanks and dry them periodically. Helium is rare and far too expensive to be 'wasted' in that fashion— so lives will be wasted instead. Hydrogen is cheap and can be manufactured anywhere, either from acid and iron filings or—much more practically—by electrolysis, as I do."

The Professor shook his head. "It will be a long time, if ever, that men will stop sending other men to their deaths by ignoring the practical realities which make their theories specious. We should not enshrine human realities, my young friends, whether economic or otherwise; but neither should we expect them to disappear because we ignore them."

Erlenwanger caught himself. He smiled wryly at both his companions. Their eyes were focused at about the level of his stick-pin in determined efforts not to look bored. "Well," he said, "I think it's far more important to teach Carl the rudiments of *The Enterprise* than it is for me to go on about things that only time will change. Molly, would you care to show our new recruit how your panel functions? I can listen and make suggestions if it seems useful."

The older man sat in Carl's chair, watching as Carl moved over beside Molly. The airship flew on at a steady pace, over farms and wooded hilltops, water courses in which cattle stood to their bellies, and occasionally a small town in a web of dry, gray roads. Throughout the afternoon, Carl learned the workings of the machine which was less wonderful to him than was the girl at whose side he sat. The levers of the starboard panel controlled the flow of hydrogen between the buoyancy tanks and the storage reservoir in the keel. "It's held in a liquid state," the Professor interjected, "and the insulation of the reservoir is an improvement—a very great improvement—over previous applications of Dewar's principles."

Understanding the technique of raising or lowering the airship was easy, but executing the technique was another matter again. Carl made several attempts to modify the craft's buoyancy at Erlenwanger's direction. Each experiment sent *The Enterprise* staggering through the air at an unexpected angle or altitude. At the end of the session, the boy had a fair grasp of what the duties entailed—and he had enormous respect for the girl who performed them.

"How long have you been practicing this?" asked Carl as Molly brought them back to level flight at two thousand feet following his own series of unintentional aerobatics.

"Well, about four days, now," said the girl, glancing over at the Professor for confirmation. "I've been doing it ever since the Professor—oh dear." She broke off in indecipherable confusion, blushing and looking away from both men. "I'm sorry, I didn't mean to—"

"Nor did you, my dear," Professor Erlenwanger said calmly. "And in any case, I intended to explain the situation to Carl at once anyway.

You see," he continued, turning to the boy, "Molly is no more my daughter than you are my son—which is how I intend to describe you to those whom we meet on our travels. I assure you, there is no improper conduct involved in Molly's accompanying me, any more than there would be had she been a blood relation. However, so as not to offend those persons whom we meet, I determined to tell an untruth—a lie, if you will. I dislike lying, and I will not lie to another's harm, but the truth is less important than the fellowship of many humans meeting without enmity."

Carl licked his lips. "What did your real parents say?" he asked.

Molly looked down. "I haven't real parents," she said softly.

"Molly was a foundling," Erlenwanger said. "She was in service at a house in Boston until she refused a—an improper demand by the master of the house. She was turned out of her place the day before I met her."

"I never told you that!" the girl blurted.

"Nor do I mention it to embarrass you, my dear," Erlenwanger said. "We will be together for some days and in close proximity, however, and I think it necessary that Carl understand your situation as clearly as you do his."

They proceeded through the airship's two other stations. The motor-starting drill appeared to be ridiculously simple: depress the hydrogen feed for three or four seconds, release it, and flip the starter switch. Shut-down was even more basic, a third switch that "shut off the injectors," which meant nothing at all to Carl but obviously seemed an adequate explanation to the Professor.

There were a dozen circular gauges above the switch panel. "While the motor is running," Erlenwanger said with a gesture, "the pointers should all be in the green zone. If one of the pointers falls into the red or rises to the white, tell me. Nothing very dreadful is going to happen without our hearing it, though, so don't feel you have to stare at the dials."

"It isn't really very simple, is it?" Carl said thoughtfully.

"Umm?" said Erlenwanger, pausing in mid-step as he moved to the helm.

"You make it look easier than running a feed mill," Carl went on.

"Maybe it is, too. But it's not simple, it's just simple to run. Being able to milk a cow don't mean you could build a cow yourself."

"That's true, of course," the older man agreed with a pleased expression. "I'm really delighted to have met you, Carl. One has an emotional tendency to equate ignorance with stupidity, which meeting you—meeting you both"—and his hand spread toward Molly—"has dispelled.

"But to answer your implied question, Carl, *The Enterprise* is unique in the world. However, if she were examined at length by today's finest scientists and engineers, they would find only her workmanship to be exceptional. Others—many others today—have all the 'secrets' I have embodied in the Erlenwanger Directable Airship. I have refined metals to great purity and machined them to—great—tolerances; but all this can be duplicated." The Professor paused and smiled again. "So while I will agree that the construct is not simple, my friend, it is simple enough."

The helm station was another example of the horribly complex overlaid by barnyard basic. Rotating the spokes did not change the direction of travel, as Carl had assumed from analogy to a steamship; rather, it controlled the amount of power the motor developed. "The diesel runs at constant revolutions," Erlenwanger said, "with the output delivered through a torque converter."

"I don't understand."

"Oh." The Professor blinked. "Well, you know how a block and tackle work," he began. At the end of half an hour's discussion, Carl *did* understand a torque converter, because he had seen the one in the engine compartment. The diesel squatted there, hot and oily but as silent as heat lightning. The humming of the prop drew up and down the scale as the Professor adjusted its pitch to demonstrate. They went forward again, through the central compartment with its three fold-down bunks and a tiny but marvelously equipped lavatory. Carl was conscious (as he had not been before) of the *machineness* of what they were riding. Flying had been like drifting in a cloud or—better—floating on his back in the stock pond with water-wings at his ankles and neck. Now . . . the diesel made no sound, but the gondola trembled to its power; and the linkage of control to power to

motion had become part of Carl's universe. Amazed by the concept
rather than any single object, Carl and Molly watched Erlenwanger
change their direction by turning the helm on the axis of its vertical
support.

"What do these do?" Carl asked, reaching out a hand toward the
levers in front of the helm.

"Oh, careful—" Molly cried, her own hand catching Carl's. "These
spill the gas out through the top. As low as we are now, we could—
well, it wouldn't be a pleasant drop."

"I wasn't going to move it," Carl explained, but the incident
reinforced the dangerous reality of what had initially seemed to be a
fairy tale.

They were heading west by southwest—255 degrees on the
compass which somehow flashed onto the forward window when the
Professor thumbed a button on the helm. The sky darkened with
awesome suddenness. Because *The Enterprise* was headed into a
horizon as rich with color as any Carl had seen since the aftermath of
Krakatoa, even that darkening was not an immediate warning. "I
think we had best find a place for the night," Erlenwanger was saying.
"The land beneath is a good deal more broken than that in the
glaciated portion of the state, isn't—"

The first gust of the storm racing down from the north caught *The
Enterprise*. The gondola rotated twenty degrees around the axis of the
buoyancy chamber.

Carl had youthful reflexes and a farmer's familiarity with shifting
footing. His left hand caught the edge of the diesel control panel,
firmly enough to twist the light metal. His right hand caught Molly
as she rebounded from the starboard bulkhead when the gondola
swung back. Professor Erlenwanger was slower and in a worse
position to act. A leather strap hung from the roof above him, but
instead of snatching for it the older man froze on the helm. The helm
simultaneously turned and pivoted, and the airship nosed into the
squall with its prop idled and unable to keep a way on. *The Enterprise*
tumbled in a horizontal plane, swapping ends twice and shuddering
as updrafts sucked it toward the thunderheads invisible above.

Erlenwanger got his footing and thumbed a button. Lime-colored lights brightened the cabin. They were dim, but in contrast to the storm's sudden blackness, they felt as warm as the kitchen stove in winter. The craft steadied, the motor giving them enough headway for control despite the buffeting of the wind. Rain slashed *The Enterprise* with a sound like tearing canvas, and the interior lights reflected in surreal nightmares from water-rippled windows.

Then the lightning bolt hit them.

Carl had heard the boiler blow at the Star Brewery in 1893. Perhaps that was louder than the thunderclap—but Carl had been half a mile from the brewery, not inside the boiler at the time. Now the thunder was only a stunning physical counterpart to the blinding dazzle of the lightning. Carl's flesh tingled. Molly's hair was standing out straight from her head like the fuzz on a dandelion, crackling with tiny blue discharges from the tip of each tendril. Rubber was smoldering everywhere. It did not occur to Carl to marvel that the direct voltage of the lightning had been insulated from the occupants of the gondola.

"I have to land," Erlenwanger cried, his voice tinny in the aftermath of the thunderclap. "Molly, can you—?"

The girl nodded. The emergency lights were gone but St. Elmo's Fire frosted all the external metal surfaces and illuminated the cabin through the glass. Molly's mouth was open as she struggled to her feet, but the muscles of her cheeks were set in a rictus, not a scream. A fat blue spark popped to her fingertip. Her gasp was a soft echo of the spark, but she grasped her controls without hesitation and slid two of the levers down to their bottom positions.

They were presumably dropping, but with the darkness and the wind's hammering it was impossible to tell. The altimeter column was invisible; it would have been uselessly erratic even if Erlenwanger had had enough light to read it. The Professor was leaning over the helm, peering helplessly at the black countryside. Carl wondered why the older man did not use the spotlight. Then he noticed that Erlenwanger was ceaselessly flipping a switch in the center of the helm, back and forth, back and forth, though he must have realized minutes ago that the lightning bolt had put the spot out of commission until repairs could be made.

Erlenwanger slid the gondola door open. Droplets slung from the doorframe eddied and spattered within the compartment. The tendrils of St. Elmo's Fire were growing longer and brighter. They blunted the night vision of those in the gondola without helping to illuminate the ground beneath. Carl hung from the door jamb, his head and shoulders out in the onrushing night. Big, wind-flung raindrops bit his cheeks like horseflies. Molly sat at her controls, feet locked on the bench against the hammering gusts. Her face was pale but prepared.

"There's a level field beneath us!" the Professor cried over a roll of thunder from half a mile away. "I'm going to void a tank to set us down quickly." He reached for one of the levers beside the helm. A landing leg extended across Carl's field of vision like the arm of a mantis. The boy peered forward, blinded by a lightning flash and trying to superimpose what its instant had showed him over the yellow after-image on his retinas.

"Trees a hundred yards ahead," Carl shouted.

The Enterprise lurched. In the same moment there was light, a great blue flare reflecting from the cloud ceiling as static ignited the hydrogen released from tank nine. Carl screamed, "Jesus Christ, we're over water! Get up, *get up!*"

Even as Carl spoke, Molly was thrusting her levers to the top, a help but too slow a help. The silent fire still blazed above them, mirrored by clouds and the storm-tossed Missouri River beneath. It was a huge sheet of illumination a mile in diameter. The Professor slammed his throttle forward, to and through the gate that blocked it with an inch of potential travel. The diesel roared, racketing even against the storm as yard-long flames spurted rearward from exhaust cut-outs. *The Enterprise* wallowed like a bogged wagon. A landing leg touched a wave top and dragged a line of spray to tilt the gondola. They were over mudflats, the wind swinging them as they struggled to rise above the line of willows that fringed the Kansas shore. The storm whipped a willow-frond up at them, the tendril snaking in through the open door and stripping off its leaves on the trailing corner as they pulled past. But that was the last touch of the storm and itself more a love-pat than a threat.

They were skimming a pasture, the six-foot heads of bull thistles throwing sharp silhouettes against the cropped grass as lightning flared again. Erlenwanger throttled back and swung the airship into the wind. Molly's fingers played on the controls. They sank, brushing the ground as they drifted back toward the dark bulk of the far hedgerow. The Professor edged his throttle a half-point open and the ship steadied, bumped, and settled solidly onto the field. The pumps whined to empty the tanks into the hydrogen reservoir. Lightning skipped across the sky to the south of them, but the thunder was half a minute coming.

The Professor looked at his companions, like him exhausted. He beamed. "I think we all owe ourselves a vote of thanks for able action under difficult circumstances. Now, who would care to join me in a supper of ham, fresh corn, and . . . cider, I think, from New Hampshire?"

Carl looked away from the sparse vegetation below them. "Are you trying to set a record time crossing the country?" he asked Professor Erlenwanger.

"Goodness no," said the older man, squinting a little in surprise. "That's for the railway barons, cleared track and fifty miles an hour. I will reach San Francisco in—a matter of time. But for me, the . . . well, the journey is itself the destination."

Carl nodded. "I just wondered," he said, "from the way we spent a day there at the river."

"Oh, well," Erlenwanger said, gesturing down at the alkaline landscape. "We needed to replenish our hydrogen, and I thought it best to do so before we got much farther west. As we have. Besides, the peddler we met was a fascinating person."

"He was just a peddler, wasn't he?" Molly asked. "I wouldn't've thought you would want a picture of him in particular."

The Professor bobbed his head, animated by the discussion though he disagreed with the implications of the statement. "Yes," he said, "an ordinary peddler. But have you ever considered for how brief a time a peddler may be normal?" He spread his hands, palms upward. "With growing centralization, with the better communications that metaled roads will bring, there will no longer be a need for goods to be trucked from door to door, from farm to farm. That man with his mule and his wagon and his . . . little bit of everything civilized—he is on the end of a chain stretching back ten millennia. And he really is the end of it."

Erlenwanger smiled at Molly to show there was no hostility in his disagreement. "He is very much worth—photographing—you see. Very much worth preserving for another age."

From the air, western Kansas was a waste of chalk gullies and buffalo grass. *The Enterprise* had sailed over cattle too scattered to be called herds; there had been no other signs of human habitation for forty miles.

"That's a campfire," Carl said, pointing out the forward window.

"Why yes, I believe it is," agreed the Professor. He tilted the helm a point, centering the tendril of gray on the pale evening sky. Molly sat quickly at her bench, waiting for instructions.

In the fading sunlight, the airship must have been a drop of blood to the slouch-hatted man who saw it as he tossed another buffalo chip on the fire. He yelped. The younger man across from him, turning the antelope haunch, spun around. He jumped to the rifle leaning against the wagon box and levered a cartridge into the chamber. The gondola door was already open. Neither the Professor nor Molly could leave their stations. Carl leaned far out into the air, clinging to the jamb as he had two nights before in the storm. He shouted, "Hey, what's the matter with you? We don't mean you no harm!"

"Great God, there's men in it!" the rifleman blurted.

Behind him, the tent flap quivered to pass a third man wearing dungarees over a set of combinations. He was older than either of the others, balding and burly with a gray moustache drooping to either side of his bearded mouth. "Of course there's men in it, Jimmy," he thundered. "Did you think it was alive?" He glanced down at the meat and added to the slouch-hatted man, "Watch the roast, Corley, or it's back to rice and beans."

The airship had drifted very close to the campsite. The landing legs creaked out. Carl picked up the grapnel and a handful of its coiled line. He had learned that the hooks were not a necessity but that they made a landing easier by keeping the vessel headed into the wind. "Can you set this solid?" he shouted and hurled the grapnel to the ground. The burly man took the idea at once. He nodded and wedged the hooks just downwind of the camp between a pair of the boulders that dotted the surface of more friable rock. A moment later they were down, the airship wheezing to itself as it resettled its hydrogen.

Carl stepped to the ground and shook the great, calloused hand which the eldest of the campers thrust at him. "Carl Gudeint," he muttered.

"Claudius Bjornholm," the other said. "And these are my assistants, Mr. James Beadle and Mr. Corley, whom I hired to drive and to cook for us."

Carl found himself spokesman from his location. "Ah," he said, "Professor Erlenwanger and Molly, ah, Molly Erlenwanger. The Professor built this bal—airship."

There was mutual murmuring and shaking of hands, though Carl noticed that Corley was hanging back. Apparently he was afraid to step beneath the looming buoyancy chamber of *The Enterprise*.

Most of the light now came from the campfire. Carl eyed the array of digging implements stacked near the wagon and asked, "You, you're . . . prospecting?"

"You mean, 'You're crazy?'" Bjornholm replied good-naturedly. "No gold in this chalk, of course. But it could be that I'm madder still, you know. I'm here—we're here—hunting for bones. It's been my life now for thirty-seven years, and I expect to carry on so long as the Lord gives me the strength to do so."

Carl and Molly exchanged blank glances. The youngest of the campers, Jimmy—he must have been Carl's age though he was much more lightly built—knuckled his jaw in some embarrassment. Professor Erlenwanger, however, said, "Yes, of course. Searching for the fossils of the Great Nebraska Sea. Have you had much success?"

"Very little this far," Bjornholm admitted, "though Jimmy believes he spotted something in a gully wall while bringing back our supper here—" he nodded at the antelope haunch. "We'll see to it as soon as there's enough light to work without chancing damage to the finds." The big man looked at Erlenwanger appraisingly. "You're a learned man, sir," he said, "as one would have expected from your"—he nodded—"creation. It seems far too huge to be so silent."

The Professor smiled. "People accuse machinery of being a curse when their real problems are with the side effects rather than the machines themselves. Noise is one of the most unpleasant side effects, I have found; but it can be cured." Waving at the fire from which Corley had just removed the meat, Erlenwanger added, "Perhaps you'd be willing to share your fire? We can of course provide our share of the supplies. And—if possible—I would greatly appreciate it if we might accompany you in the morning on your search."

Bjornholm straightened. With the glow of the fire behind him and the power of his stance and broad shoulders, he was no longer a part-dressed figure of fun. "Sir," he said, "we would be honored by your presence—tonight and whenever else."

Fresh vegetables from the airship were well-received by the bone hunters, but the greatest delicacy Erlenwanger provided was fresh water. Bjornholm savored his first sip, tonguing it around within his mouth until he finally swallowed. "You don't know what it's like," he said slowly, looking at each of the visitors in turn, "to have nothing to drink for months at a time but water so alkaline that even a handful of coffee beans can't kill the taste. Every mug is a dose of salts—literally, I'm sorry to say." He nodded solemnly at Carl, who was farthest around the circle from Molly. "You waste away during a dig, and the good lord help the poor fools who try to live here and farm."

"But why do you stay?" asked Molly, handling her plate ably on her knees as she squatted on the ground with the men.

"You see, it's not really like this," said Jimmy unexpectedly, lowering the dainty antelope femur at which he had been gnawing. He waved out at the endless, gullied night. "This was a great bay, ten times the Gulf of Mexico and more. Still water, hiding monsters the like of none on Earth today; still air with gliding reptiles greater than any birds. It's—" He stopped, his lips still working as he decided what words to frame. More than the fire lighted his narrow face. He continued, "I'm at Haverford. Last year I heard Professor Cope lecture and . . . it wasn't a new world opening, it was a thousand new worlds, as many new worlds as there had been past ages of our Earth. Can you imagine that? Can you—see tarpons sixteen feet long, flashing just under the surface as the mackerel they chase make the sea foam? Or the tylosaur, the *real* sea serpent, lifting itself long enough to take a sighting before it slides through the depths toward the disturbance? Can you see it?"

Bjornholm was nodding. "I've worked for Professor Cope—God rest his soul—on several occasions in the past. He sent Mr. Beadle to me with a letter of introduction; and Mr. Beadle has proven a splendid and trustworthy companion in my search of the world of two million years ago."

"Two million?" Erlenwanger repeated. "Oh, yes, of course. Lord Kelvin proved from the temperature of the Earth that it could be no more than—twenty to forty million years old, wasn't that the figure? I am sometimes amazed at the conclusions a great scientist can draw from data which a man of more—common—understanding would have found hopelessly inadequate for the purpose." He smiled.

"Yes indeed," agreed Bjornholm heavily. "I have always envied men like Professor Cope the understanding which I can only draw on second hand. I grew up in Cincinnati, where every building stone is marked by a crinoid or a clam preserved eternally from a past age. When I was fifteen, I determined that I would have some part in bringing that past to light, whatever it might cost me personally."

He looked around the circuit of firelight, the tent and wagon, both of them worn; the tools and the brutal labor they implied; the faces of his companions, like his unshaven for the waste of water shaving would entail. "It has a cost. But though I've done things besides digging for fossils, nothing else will really matter after I'm dead except the part of the past I leave to the future."

Corley spit into the fire. "Bones," he said without looking up. "Bones and stones and durned fools."

"And yet you're here too, Jake," Beadle said sharply. "A dollar a day, all found, and corn for your horses. Well, maybe those're better reasons than ours, but—you're here too."

The fire popped back in emphasis, and the dark moved a little closer.

* * *

Leaving the tent and the great, hollow bulk of the airship behind, Professor Erlenwanger's party climbed into the wagon with Corley and the equipment. There was barely light enough to see by. Carl was not surprised to notice that Professor Erlenwanger carried his camera cases. Bjornholm and his assistant rode their own horses, the burly man displaying a quiet mastery of his beast that belied his apparent clumsiness.

"Too much for the team to draw," Corley grumbled as he harnessed the horses.

"With three months of my feed in their bellies, they'll draw this load better than they did the empty wagon when I hired you," retorted Bjornholm.

Jimmy Beadle directed them, scowling under his hat brim as he searched for landmarks in a country of ruts and scrub grass. He looked older by daylight than he had seemed around the fire. Far on the horizon they could see a pair of prong-horns. Beadle laid a hand on his saddle-scabbard, but Bjornholm noted curtly, "We've better ways to spend our time today."

They skirted one gully and crossed a second, the wagon passengers dismounting as the iron-bound wheels crumbled the rock of the far rim. The Sun rose higher and the wind picked up with a burden of dust so finely divided that it looked like yellow fog. At last, as they approached a gully that almost deserved the name of canyon, Jimmy pointed and said, "There—on the far wall. See where the speck of white is?"

They halted at the rim, squinting across the hundred feet or so at a brighter splash against the yellowish chalk. "We can't get across that," Corley said suddenly. "It's sixty feet down and durned near straight up and down on t'other side."

"Be easier to hang down from the rim, wouldn't it?" Beadle suggested. "It's about halfway up the wall, and I'd sure rather swing down than climb up."

"We'd have to climb that wall to be able to hang over," Bjornholm said. "Unless you've found a way around this arroyo that I haven't. We can get down this side easy enough—"

"Not the wagon!" Corley interjected.

"Not the wagon," Bjornholm agreed, "but on foot. We'll figure a way then to get up the other side."

They used their hands to descend the draw, and Carl made the last ten feet in an uncontrolled rush besides; but they all made it. Molly had less evident trouble than Carl did, picking her footing and getting to the gully floor with no more than a smear of chalk dust on her linen wrapper. But the wall that loomed above them was nearly as straight as a building's, though there was enough batter from the middle upwards to hide the fleck of bone from their eyes.

Bjornholm absently worried a twig from one of the mesquite bushes that pocked the arroyo. "We'll have to cut steps," he said. He set the blade of the shovel he carried against the wall and twisted with his weight on it. Flecks of chalk spat and the steel rang. "Have to use the hatchet, I guess," he said disgustedly.

"I can get to it if you give me a boost," Jimmy said, eyeing the stone.

Bjornholm frowned. He laid down his shovel, leaned on the arroyo wall, and looked upward. "It's still too high," he observed.

Corley said, "Bjornholm, if you can take the weight, I'll stand on your shoulders and tug the kid up."

The burly man turned his head to stare. Corley seemed to shrink inward, but he did not lower his eyes. "Climb up, then," Bjornholm rumbled. He braced himself against the chalk. Corley gripped Bjornholm's shoulder and raised a cracked boot to the bigger man's jutting right hip.

"Here!" Carl said, springing to Bjornholm's side and gripping a handful of Corley's dungarees to haul him upward. The gangling teamster balanced bent over for a moment, then straightened with a boot on the shoulder of each of the bigger men beneath him. "All right," Corley grunted, reaching one hand back and down for Jimmy while his other hand clamped a knob of rock. "Come if you're coming, boy."

Jimmy caught Corley's hand, his boot a brief agony on Carl's outthrust hip as the student pushed off. Then there was only the doubled weight being transmitted through Corley. Carl locked hands with Bjornholm, less for mutual support than for commiseration of the sharp leather soles cutting to their collar bones. Then Jimmy cried, "Okay, okay, I'm getting there," and half the weight was gone. In relief as if he were wholly unburdened, Carl flexed his shoulders.

"Hold on, I'm coming down," said Corley. He jumped, falling to hands and knees on the hard soil. Carl backed away, rubbing his muscles and staring up at Jimmy. The student was using minute projections and the slight tilt of the rock to climb steadily toward the exposed bone. From beneath, the watchers tensed as the student's increasingly greater deliberation showed that he was nearing the prize.

"I've got it," Jimmy said, the chalk muffling his voice. Then, "Oh . . . Oh."

"What is it, Jimmy?" Bjornholm demanded hoarsely.

The younger man half-turned, no longer particularly interested in keeping his position. "It's a buffalo thigh, Mr. Bjornholm," he said flatly. "It must have rolled over the lip of the draw and caught here in a little crevice. I doubt it's as old as I am."

Bjornholm nodded silently, his great shoulders suddenly stooped. "Another time, then," he said. "I've searched longer and found less at other times." But the last words were spoken so softly as to be almost inaudible.

"Look out," Beadle said. He dropped the buffalo femur. It clattered twice on the gully wall before raising a puff of dust on the ground. Bjornholm's assistant eased one foot onto a lower projection, then the other. His boot soles slipped. Jimmy skidded down the side of the arroyo, boots and hips grinding away a shower of pebbles as they slowed him. Carl took a half-step to catch the sliding man, realized that the student was in control of everything but his speed, and got out of the way lest interference cripple both of them. Beadle hit the ground with his legs bent at the knees. His feet flew out from under him at the shock and he sprawled. Bjornholm and Carl both reached out to help the slender man up. "Well, that's it for this pair," Jimmy said glumly, sticking his hand through the hole the rock had abraded in his trousers. "The others haven't been washed in six weeks, neither."

Claudius Bjornholm was not listening to him. The burly man had knelt, his mouth open and his tongue absently exploring his cracked lips. He brushed his left hand over the surface of the ground where Beadle's boots had scarred it. After a moment he slipped a reground oyster knife from his hip pocket and began scraping. Jimmy looked down and his own jaw dropped. "Oh, oh . . ." he whispered, kneeling as if joining the older man in prayer.

Corley thrust his narrow shoulders between his two companions. "Goddamn," he said, "that sure's hell *is* a skull!"

"It's more than a skull," Bjornholm said, his big index finger pointing along the gully floor. Regular projections were visible against the chalk, now that they had been pointed out. They were bony knobs running for twenty feet in a straight line. It was as if the tips of a huge saw blade were sticking up above the gully floor. "I think we have—everything here. Just below the surface. Those are the upper processes of the vertebrae of a mosasaur, unless I mistake what I can see of this skull. If none of it has been lost by weathering, it will be as perfect . . . more perfect than anything I've—I've—" The big man paused, blinking back tears. "As anything I've found in thirty-seven years of searching."

"Gentlemen," Professor Erlenwanger said, "would you object to my taking a photograph?"

Carl looked around in surprise and saw that Erlenwanger really had set up his camera. How he had brought the cases down the slope without disaster was more than the boy could imagine.

"Of the find in place?" said Bjornholm, edging back so as not to block the field of view. "Of course, of course."

"No," said the Professor sharply. He gestured the three bone hunters closer together with both hands. "These bones have been in the ground a hundred million years. Others like them will still be there to be found in another hundred million years. But you're like, with the whole of the past fresh under your fingertips—that will pass with your generation."

"But you don't want *us*, then," Jimmy Beadle said with a puzzled frown. He was still kneeling. "You want a picture of the real greats . . . Well, Dr. Cope is gone now, but Dr. Osborne or Milius of Tubingen."

Erlenwanger flicked his eyebrows back a millimeter in utter denial. "Did you shoot that antelope yesterday in the chest?" he asked.

"Huh?" said Jimmy. "No, it wasn't but fifty yards away, so I shot it through the head."

"That ruined the trophy, didn't it?"

"Trophy?" repeated the student. "I don't understand. I didn't want a trophy, I wanted meat."

The Professor's smile was beatific. "So do I," he said, and he bent back over the camera. The rim of the arroyo still hid the morning Sun. The three oddly assorted bone hunters linked arms and stared back at Erlenwanger, the triumph bright in their faces.

"I don't know why anybody'd want to live like those cowboys in the line camp yesterday," Carl said, staring through the side windows at the increasingly rugged terrain below.

Molly was at the helm while Professor Erlenwanger sent what he said was a "wireless message" back to his associates in Boston. She said, "It's not that they want to, I think . . . any more than I wanted to be in service with the O'Neills. But I was willing—for a while. And those fellows were willing to live their lives in a little hut, ride fences while the weather lets them and spend three months of the winter reading the catalog pages pasted to the walls. Someday they won't do that. They'll get a few cows of their own and marry, or they'll move in town and work at a feed store. But for now, they're willing."

Carl looked over at the Professor. His eyes were open but unfocused. His thumb and index finger made a muted tapping on the brass key he had set on the ledge in front of the buoyancy controls. "Did he take a picture of you too?" Carl asked quietly, still looking at the older man.

"Oh, yes—right there on the street before he bought me a meal," the girl replied. "He—oh! Carl! Look at this!"

Both the men jumped to their feet, their eyes following Molly's pointing finger down to the gullied foothills below. The scale was deceptive. The beast could have been a dun-colored hog rooting through mesquite until Carl took his thousand feet of altitude into account. "My goodness!" gasped Professor Erlenwanger, his wireless gear forgotten. "It's a grizzly bear. I *must* get it!"

The Professor threw open the dunnage locker in the rear bulkhead. Carl expected him to draw out an express rifle, but instead it was the pair of camera cases again. "Carl," he said as he unlatched the equipment, "will you take the helm and bring us up to the bear dead slow? And Molly, since you're more experienced with altitude correction, can you drop us to twenty feet and hold us there?"

Molly throttled back and handed the wheel to Carl. "You're going to take a picture from the doorway, Professor?" she asked in some concern. Her fingers began playing with the gas chamber controls.

"Well, from this instead, I think," Erlenwanger said. He lifted a ladder of ropes and wooden battens from the locker and fastened the ends to staples set in the floor for that purpose. Then he slid the door open and tossed the ladder out to twist and dangle, blown sternward despite their present slow speed. "I think I will need the greater field of view, since the bear may have its own notions about being photographed. And—well, this keeps *The Enterprise* herself a little further from the ground in case something . . . untoward happens." His tongue touched his lips. Molly, keeping a close watch on the terrain which they now had approached so closely, blinked but said nothing.

The Professor fitted the strap of the bulky camera over his left shoulder. He looked down at the dangling ladder. "Well . . ." he said, and paused. He turned and opened a drawer beneath the engine control panel which Carl had not noticed before. From it he took an angular handgun. He stuck the weapon into his hip pocket where the tails of his tweed coat hid it. "Well," he repeated, and he began to climb carefully down the ladder.

They were barely moving forward now. The bear was a hundred feet ahead, ambling between dwarf cedars with an odd, sidelong gait. It looked very large. Molly bit her lip and made an infinitesimal adjustment to a pair of her controls. The airship dipped. Carl thought the girl had overcorrected, but they recovered and stabilized with the ground just twenty feet below them as the Professor had directed. Carl eased on a little more throttle and started his final approach.

The only sound *The Enterprise* made was the minute whistle of the air curling around it, and that was lost in the rustle of the trees. When their sharp-edged shadow fell across the grizzly, however, the brute paused and turned with its snout raised. Erlenwanger was steadying himself with his arms through the loop of the ladder as if it were the sling of a rifle. His camera was ready. The bear coughed and charged without hesitation.

Carl's heart leaped as he saw through the port in the gondola floor that the grizzly was rearing onto its hind legs. The beast slashed the air with its claws, black and worn by use to chisel edges instead of points. The gondola lurched as the Professor jerked his knees up to his chest, supporting his whole weight on his arms. Then they were safely past. Carl turned to call something to Erlenwanger, and five thousand feet above them a cloud passed before the Sun. The hydrogen cooled and shrank. The airship lost buoyancy almost as suddenly as if Carl had dumped a tank. *The Enterprise* dropped ten feet to a new equilibrium. The end of the rope ladder clattered on the ground. The gondola itself was well within the range of claws that could rip open trees to get at the honey within.

The grizzly coughed again and charged, as quickly as a cat sighting prey. Professor Erlenwanger had pulled his torso into the gondola. Carl leaped from the controls to drag him the rest of the way to safety. The older man, gripping the jamb with his left hand, drew his pistol. The shots rattled like a dozen lathes cracking, sharp but overwhelmed by the blasts of the bullets themselves bursting on the ground beneath. Shards of rock sang off the underside of the gondola. One bit hummed through the doorway to sting Carl's outstretched hand. The snarl deep in the bear's throat *whuffed!* out instead as a startled bleat. The Professor laid his pistol on the gondola floor. "Now, Carl," he gasped. "If you would."

Carl grasped the older man under both armpits and hefted him aboard. Molly had slammed all her levers upward when she realized what was happening. The airship was soaring and already near its normal cruising altitude. Beneath them the grizzly sat back on its haunches, washing its face with both paws.

Professor Erlenwanger unstrapped his camera and slid the door shut. He was breathing heavily. Carl had returned to the helm but kept only steerage way, uncertain of what the Professor would want to do. Molly had leveled them off at a thousand feet again. She was beginning to regain some of her normal color. "I think we can resume course," Erlenwanger said at last. He picked up the little handgun and extracted the magazine from its grip.

"You shot the bear?" Carl asked, watching the older man. He was thumbing brass cartridges into the magazine from a box that had shared the drawer with the pistol.

Professor Erlenwanger looked up sharply. "I fired into the ground in front of the bear," he said. "That was sufficient." He slid the reloaded magazine back into the butt of the pistol, his lips silently working as he considered whether or not to continue. "I dare say it is sometimes necessary to kill," he said finally. "In order to stay alive, or sometimes for better reasons. But it isn't a decision to be taken lightly or as anything but a last resort."

Erlenwanger shook his head as if to clear it of his present mood. He set the weapon and the box of ammunition back into the drawer and closed it. Smiling he added, "It's an automatic pocket pistol of European manufacture. And I suppose you're familiar with the use of explosive bullets in hunting dangerous game?"

Carl nodded. "I've heard of that."

"Well," the Professor said, "I had a—Belgian gunsmith of great ability make up some explosive rounds for the pistol. On stony soil they produced quite a startling effect, don't you think?"

Molly took a deep, thankful breath. "More to the point," she said, "the bear thought it was startling."

"Goodness," said the Professor, noticing that his wireless apparatus still sat out on the ledge, "I'd best complete my report, hadn't I? Especially now that I've had a real adventure!" Chuckling, he sat down at the key again as the airship swept steadily westward through the calm air.

Professor Erlenwanger looked at the altimeter, frowned, and glanced over at Molly's bank of controls. They were all uncomfortably close to the top. Despite that, *The Enterprise* was within five hundred feet of the ground. The dry snow blew like fog around the trunks of the conifers marching up the slopes. "Between the thin air at this altitude and the film of ice we're gathering," the Professor said, "we need maximum lift. And I'm afraid that there's enough condensate in several of the chambers that we aren't getting the lift we should be."

Carl frowned back. "Are we in danger?" he asked, carefully controlling his voice. He did not want to sound as though he were on the edge of panic—but five hundred feet was a long way to fall, and the ground beneath looked as hard as a millstone.

"Oh, goodness," the Professor said, blinking in concern at the impression he had given. "Oh, not at all. I just propose to land in a suitable location—I'm sure there must be one." He squinted through the forward windows. The cabin heat kept the center of each pane clear. The edges, where the aluminum frames conveyed the warmth to the outside more swiftly, were blind with frost. "I'll vent and dry tanks three and seven—they seem to be the wettest—and recharge them. It may not be the most attractive country on which to set down, but I think I can promise you that we will do so gently."

"There's a clear hill over there," Molly said, pointing so that her finger left a smudge on the glass. "But you'll need water to refill the tanks, won't you?"

"Oh, that's quite all right," Erlenwanger explained, already swinging the helm. "We can melt the snow for electrolysis, and goodness knows there's enough snow. See if you can bring us down just a little above the tallest trees, my dear."

Despite the gusty winds and the lack of anyone on the ground to set their grapnel for them, Professor Erlenwanger brought them to the smooth landing he had promised. Twigs, poking through the crust of snow which had come early even for the mountains, snapped beneath the weight of *The Enterprise*. "Well," said the Professor, "I think the first order of business is to clear the chambers, don't you?" He gripped one of the vent levers and tried to slide it to the side. It did not move. All three people looked momentarily blank. "Of course," Erlenwanger said, "the ice! The valve mechanism must be frozen shut."

"Something we can fix?" asked Carl, frowning again but without the immediate concern that the prospect of crashing into the ground had raised in him.

"Well, yes," agreed the older man, "but it means climbing up to chip the valve loose, and I'm afraid it's really too near dusk to do that now. I had hoped to have the chambers refilling overnight."

Carl shrugged. "No problem," he said. "I'll take a lantern up with me and do it now."

Erlenwanger frowned. Then he, too, shrugged and said, "Well, that's all right, I suppose. But don't even think of getting above any other airship with an open flame. Blocking the percolation of hydrogen through the very atoms of the skin was perhaps the greatest of the advances incorporated into *The Enterprise*"—his grin flashed— "though it isn't one I would expect an investigator of the present time to note."

Carl drew on the sheepskin jacket and cowhide work gloves the Professor had bought him at a rail siding the night before. Molly handed him the kerosene lamp she had just lighted. It whispered deep in its throat, and the yellow glow it cast was friendlier and more human than that of the chilly electrical elements. Carl stepped outside, bracing himself against the expected eddy of wind-blown snow. The lantern rocked in his hand but did not go out. He slammed the door and began to climb the open ladder just astern of it, up the side of the gas compartment. There was a slick of ice crackling on the rungs, and the lamp in his left hand made climbing harder; but Carl had carried shingles to the roof of the barn in a drizzle, and this was nothing beyond his capacity.

The snow and the twilight made the evening seem bright, but the vents were deep in a shadowed recess. A catwalk ran along the airship's spine. Without the lantern the trip would have been vain, though the yellow light paled everywhere but where it was needed. Carl set the lamp down on the walk and rapped the valve with the bolster of his clasp knife. He took the glove off his left hand and opened the blade to scrape the joints in the brass.

Movement at the wood line caught the corner of Carl's eye. A pair of steers bolted into the open. One had horns which had been cropped to stumps shorter than its ears. Carl stared, squinting into the failing light. "Professor!" he called, just as the light on the gondola's prow spread its broad fan down the hillside. The floodlight glared red from the eyes of the cattle and the three horses following them. The nearest of the three riders was wrapped in a dark-colored blanket. Even his hands, gripping a long-barreled rifle across the saddlebow, were hidden. Trotting his pinto just behind the first rider was a second whose straight black hair fell to his shoulders. A youthful whoop died in his throat at the blaze of light. His left arm, upraised with an unstrung bow, jerked down as his right hand sawed the pinto's reins back.

The third Indian was far the oldest, though his twin braids were still so black as to give the lie to a face wrinkled like walnut burl. He wore a buffalo robe—as old, perhaps, as he was—pinned at the shoulder but open down the front to display a buckskin shirt. The old cap-and-ball revolver thrust through his waistband was nickeled. It sparkled like a faceted mirror in the instant before the rider slid it out and down into the shadow of his horse's neck.

The gondola door rumbled open, thumping against its stop. Carl peered over the side. The curve of the buoyancy chamber hid the Professor until the older man stepped out in front of his floodlight. His shadow flashed suddenly toward the Indians. Its outline was misshapen with the angles of camera and tripod.

"Professor!" Carl called. "Those aren't reservation cows!" If the older man heard Carl, he did not understand. He continued to walk downhill toward the Indians, calling to them in a language unfamiliar to Carl. Carl swung down the ladder, leaving skin from the palm of his left hand frozen to the top rung. He was muttering an unconscious prayer.

The steers had shied from the light, disappearing again into the trees. The eldest of the riders spoke. The rifleman swung his weapon clear of the blanket. The knob of its bolt handle, polished by decades of wear, winked. As Carl jumped into the gondola, a trick of the breeze brought Erlenwanger's words up the hill: "Why, my goodness, a Dreyse needle gun here!"

"Where's the lantern!" Molly cried.

"Jesus Christ, I left it!" Carl shouted, slamming open the pistol drawer. The cartridge box flew out, spilling the deadly brass to roll in a shifting pattern on the floor. Carl leaned out the doorway, leveling the unfamiliar pistol.

Molly vented tank three. The hydrogen bathed the lantern and ignited in a blue glare spraying a hundred feet in the air. The pinto reared, spilling its young rider. The rifle muzzle wavered from Erlenwanger to the airship, then back into the woods as the leading rider wheeled his mount. Molly opened tank seven. The eldest Indian fought his horse for an instant, the reflection from his revolver no harsher than that of his eyes. Then he gave the beast its head to gallop into the forest, followed by the pinto and the third of the cattle thieves. That last Indian was holding the pinto's reins with both hands and running along beside it. A steer bawled from a distance. Then the night was silent again, leaving the Professor poised awkwardly in the light of his own airship.

Erlenwanger turned and began trudging up the hill. Molly cut the floodlight. Carl lowered the pistol which he had not fired. It apparently had a safety catch somewhere, like a hammerless shotgun. His left palm was burning and he noticed the blood for the first time.

Professor Erlenwanger slid the door shut behind him and set down his camera carefully. "One can get carried away and make mistakes," he said softly. "They were doing something illegal; and of course we frightened them." He looked from Carl to Molly and back again. "When one does something foolish, as I just did, it's important that one have friends with better sense and quick minds. Thank you both, for my life and for much more." Carl set the pistol down to take and squeeze one of the hands the older man stretched to both of them.

"Less than fifty years old," the Professor said, apparently to himself, "and look at it even now."

Molly leaned forward for a better look. She had stared down on Boston, however, and the skeletal mass of lights in the pre-dawn did not impress her. Carl had never seen anything like San Francisco in his life. "Oh, if Dad could only be here," he said. "He wouldn't brag on his trip to Kansas City ever again."

"You can follow the veins of the city out beyond the lighted heart," Professor Erlenwanger said. "Every one of those blue sparks is the collector arm of a trolley, bringing the late shifts home, carrying the earliest workers in to their jobs. Sometimes I think that cities live too, and that one day they will send travellers back in time to record their own births."

The airship had met a mass of cool air over the bay and dropped to about five hundred feet. Molly started to nudge a pair of levers up, but the Professor's hand stayed her. "No," he said. "I'm going to land here."

"Are we staying in San Francisco?" asked Carl, a little surprised because of the Professor's previous avoidance of populous areas. But after all, they were on the West Coast, now; there was nowhere further to go.

The Professor cocked the helm slightly, searching the terrain below so that he did not have to look at his companions. The sky beyond the hills was metallically lighter. "I'm going to land you here and go on," he said. "I've enjoyed your company more than I can tell you, but it is time for me to leave. I am not"—he swallowed—"simply abandoning you; I will leave you with five hundred dollars in gold pieces—"

"Professor, *no!*" Molly cried, her hand shooting out to touch but not grip his elbow. "We didn't come with you for the money—but don't leave us!

Erlenwanger's fingers squeezed the girl's hand to his tweed sleeve briefly, then detached it. "You didn't come with me to save my life, either; but you saved it," he said firmly. "The money is something for which I have no further use anyway." he touched his lips with his tongue. "Please believe me when I say that you cannot accompany me further. It is not something I say lightly. We will meet again, I promise; though that lies still in the future."

Very quietly, Carl said, "I'm not going back to the farm. Not now."

"Bring us down to one hundred feet, please, Molly," Professor Erlenwanger said. He half-turned from the view forward. "You needn't go back, you know," he said. "Kummel and Son, the meat canners on Market Street, will have openings for a stock clerk and a receptionist this morning."

Carl frowned. "I'm not a stock clerk," he said.

The Professor shook his head abruptly. "You're a strong young man who has worked with cattle all his life. You're bright and you're honest—and you will remind Mr. Kummel of his only son, who died last week of influenza." Erlenwanger tongued his lips again. "Kummel's is a very small firm now—only a few years ago it was a butcher shop. But if gold should be discovered on the coasts of Alaska and Canada, the inevitable rush will be supplied from San Francisco. A firm with a solid reputation will be able to expand greatly; and employees who have been trustworthy in small things . . . will be entrusted with great ones. You may live to endow your grandson's education at . . . the California Institute of Technology, for instance."

Erlenwanger trimmed his prop pitch fine. "Set us down gently, now," he said as the landing legs squealed and extended. Molly was blinking back tears, but her fingers worked the controls with practiced delicacy. The spotlight of *The Enterprise* stabbed narrowly, then flooded a barren area at a touch of the Professor's wrist. Gas standards reached up forlornly, installed but unlighted along a three-block line of vacant lots. The older man coarsened the prop to give him a touch more helm and bring the airship's nose around. Carl swallowed and slid the door open. "I don't think we will need the grapnel," Erlenwanger said. They were barely moving forward, sinking as slowly as bodies in a still, cold lake. A moment before they touched, Molly eased back on a lever. The nose tilted up minusculy and the rear landing leg cut the rank grass before the front did. They were down with less jolt than a man got stepping out of bed.

The Professor opened the sleeping compartment and handed out the two small suitcases that were all Carl's and Molly's possessions. They took them silently, Molly holding the grip with both hands and her lower lip with her teeth. Even the cases had been the Professor's gift. Erlenwanger slipped a heavy purse into the side pocket of the girl's coat. He kissed her very gently on the cheek, just forward of her ear. "There'll be a trolley in two minutes," he said without pulling his watch from his vest pocket. "One thing," he added. "There is both good and bad in every life, every age. But always remember what—relatives of mine told me when I was very young: you must never give up on Mankind. Because Mankind never quite gives up on itself." He shook Carl's hand and turned him to the open door.

Carl stepped down. Molly followed, her head bent over. Neither of them spoke. From the gondola behind them they heard the Professor call, "Goodby, Pops. Goodby, Mama Gudeint. I'm proud to have known you."

Air billowed sluggishly as *The Enterprise* rose. Carl and Molly raised their faces to watch the airship. The great cylinder was climbing very swiftly on an even keel. A few hundred feet up it caught the sunrise over the hills and blazed like a plowshare in God's forge. The suitcases were forgotten on the ground. Molly's fingers squeezed Carl's in fear. "What's happening to it?" she demanded.

The blur of light was higher, now, and farther west, but it was growing fainter more quickly than it rose. It seemed to merge with the sky or something beyond the sky. Carl licked his lips. "Goodby," he whispered. He squeezed Molly's hand in return. Still staring at the empty sky, he said, "It's all right. Wherever he's going, he'll get there. And so will we . . . and it'll be all right."